Marita Conlon-McKenna is one of Ireland's favourite authors and a regular number one bestseller. She is the winner of the prestigious International Reading Association award and is a regular contributor on Radio and TV. A romantic by nature, Marita was swept off her own feet and got married aged twenty to her tall dark handsome husband. They live with their family in Dublin.

www.rbooks.co.uk
www.transworldireland.ie

Also by Marita Conlon-McKenna

THE MAGDALEN

PROMISED LAND

MIRACLE WOMAN

THE STONE HOUSE

THE HAT SHOP ON THE CORNER

THE MATCHMAKER

MOTHER OF THE BRIDE

Marita Conlon-McKenna

TRANSWORLD IRELAND

TRANSWORLD IRELAND
an imprint of The Random House Group Limited
20 Vauxhall Bridge Road, London SW1V 2SA
www.rbooks.co.uk

MOTHER OF THE BRIDE
A TRANSWORLD IRELAND BOOK: 9781848270381

First published in 2010 by Transworld Ireland,
a division of Transworld Publishers
Transworld Ireland paperback edition published 2011

Addresses for Random House Group Ltd companies outside the UK
can be found at: www.randomhouse.co.uk

Penguin Random House is committed to a sustainable future for
our business, our readers and our planet. This book is made from
Forest Stewardship Council® certified paper.

Printed and bound in Great Britain by Clays Ltd, Elcograf S.p.A.

Typeset in 11/15pt Sabon by
Kestrel Data, Exeter, Devon.
2 4 6 8 10 9 7 5 3 1

For James with love

Chapter One

Helen O'Connor listened to the deep rumbling snores coming from the other side of the bed. Looking at Paddy's contented face, as he snored on oblivious, she resisted the urge to thump him or turn him over. Instead she snuggled down under the cosy quilt, trying to lull herself into her usual deep sleep.

The house was quiet, the sound from the big grand-father clock in the hall strangely comforting as Helen turned over. She was tired, and could feel herself relax as the familiar comfort of their big bed worked its magic. She was almost asleep when the phone beside the bed began to ring. A quick glance at the bedside clock showed her that the time was after midnight. Concerned, she began to sit up as she answered it; beside her, Paddy was already beginning to rouse himself and wake.

'Hello!' she answered, barely able to disguise the trepidation in her voice. Calls in the middle of the night usually signalled trouble of some sort. She held her breath, anxious.

'Mum, it's all right. It's Amy. I'm just phoning to tell you that Daniel and I have got engaged.' Their elder daughter, Amy, was breathless with excitement on the phone. 'We're in Venice, and it's so romantic. Dan proposed on this lovely little bridge over the canal as the sun went down, and then we went for dinner to this amazing restaurant called La Rondine. We're so happy. Can you believe it, Dan and I are going to get married?'

'Amy and Dan have just got engaged!' Helen shouted, shaking Paddy awake. 'Oh, Amy, that's wonderful news.' Helen was so happy for them both. Amy and her boyfriend Daniel were touring around Italy for a week, and were flying back from Florence at the weekend. Although they had only been together for about two and a half years, Helen and Paddy had secretly hoped that this relationship would work out. They both really liked Daniel, and felt he would make a great son-in-law; everything that the parents of a daughter would wish for. 'Congratulations to you and Dan, we're so pleased for you.'

'Mum, Dan and I don't want a long engagement,' Amy continued. 'We want to get married next summer!'

'Next summer!' Helen was a little surprised. From what she could gather, weddings took a lot of organizing. Still, if that's what Amy and Dan wanted. 'That sounds perfect. Here, I'll put you on to your dad. He's dying to congratulate you, too.'

Paddy at this stage was propped against the pillows, gesticulating madly that he wanted to talk to Amy. Helen passed him the phone, and craned to listen to the conversation.

'Amy, pet, congratulations. We're delighted. Dan's a lovely fellow, and I know that you'll be happy together,' Paddy said, trying to control his emotion. 'From the minute I met him I knew that he would always take good care of you. And now he's going to marry *my little girl*!'

'Oh, Dad,' Amy wailed. 'I'm glad that you and Mum are so pleased for us. It's just so exciting.'

'Put Daniel on the phone a minute,' prompted Paddy. 'We want to tell him just how happy we are with the good news.'

They both pulled the phone off each other telling Daniel Quinn just how happy they were at the prospect of his joining the O'Connor clan. And they were both reassured by his promises to take care of their elder daughter.

'Mammy, is Ciara there? I want to tell her too!'

Paddy yelled for their younger daughter, Ciara. Her dark hair standing on end, she arrived like a zombie in black pyjama bottoms and an ancient T-shirt, and grabbed the phone off them.

'Hey, Amy, I can't believe it. You and Dan getting engaged . . . it's so grown up!'

She curled up on top of their bed as she chatted with Amy, eventually passing back the phone. Helen listened as Amy excitedly went through every detail of the proposal and told them she was sending them a photo of her engagement ring from her cell phone. Ciara went and grabbed her phone as the image appeared on the screen, and passed it to them, Helen being struck by the technology that could enable her to see the ring on her daughter's finger, even though she was in Italy and they were back home here in Dublin. All of them admired Amy's beautiful diamond ring.

'It's absolutely gorgeous.'

'Mum, listen, we've got to go! We have to phone Dan's parents and Ronan and Jess, but we're dying to see you all next week, when we can celebrate properly together.'

'Good night, love,' Helen said as the call ended, Ciara, Paddy and herself all agreeing that the engagement was great news.

'She asked me to be a bridesmaid,' yawned Ciara. 'Does that mean I have to wear some disgusting frilly dress or something?'

'That's great,' said Helen, wondering how in heaven's name Amy was going to get her normally Goth-styled sister into anything resembling a bridesmaid dress. 'I'm sure you'll be a wonderful bridesmaid and a great help to Amy.'

'Mmmm!' said Ciara, before giving them a quick hug and sloping off to her own bedroom.

'That will be something to see!' Paddy joked as he clambered back into bed beside Helen.

'Can you believe it, Amy getting engaged and married?' Helen fixed her pillows as she sat up in bed. Why, it only seemed like yesterday that Amy had been born and they'd brought home a wriggling, squealing baby from Holles Street Maternity Hospital, and had looked at each other with hardly a clue as to what to do with her. Somehow Paddy and herself had muddled through that first year of parenthood and survived it. The years had flown by as their young family had grown.

'She's thirty years old, Helen.'

'Oh, Paddy, you know what I mean. She's our first baby, and now she's going to have a husband, and then a family of her own.'

'I know, love,' said Paddy. 'I know.'

'Can you believe it, Paddy, Dan and Amy engaged!'

'Of course I can. They both love each other, and Dan is a gentleman, and I told him that I'd be delighted to have him as a son-in-law.'

'You told him that . . . when?'

'When he asked me for Amy's hand; he wanted to be sure that I approved of them getting married, and would give my permission.'

'He asked you!' Helen gasped, incredulous. 'When?'

'We had lunch in town together about five weeks ago, and he told me what he was planning.'

'Paddy O'Connor! Do you mean to tell me that you

knew all about this engagement weeks ago, and you never said a word to me!'

'Not a word! I was under strict instructions to keep it a secret. Dan wanted it to be a total surprise for Amy.'

'Paddy!' She couldn't credit it, her husband of thirty-two years keeping a big secret like that from her. 'Why didn't you tell me?'

'I promised Dan, and you know you would never have been able to keep it in, Helen. You know you wouldn't.'

'I could have,' she protested, indignantly.

'Really?' he said, wrapping his arms around her.

She had to laugh. Paddy knew her better than she knew herself. She had to admit that he was right. It would have been very hard to have not said something, or even not smiled every time she was around her daughter. Thank heaven for Paddy's good sense.

Wrapped in her husband's arms, she hoped that her daughter's marriage would bring the same fulfilment and happiness that she and Paddy shared. Like all couples, they had endured the ups and downs that life brings, the good times and bad times, but theirs was a happy marriage, and she knew in her heart that fate had smiled down at her the night she had met Paddy O'Connor.

'Honestly I'll . . .'

'What will you do?' he teased.

A while later she listened as Paddy began to snore again. A bull elephant, a train hurtling down a track, or a juggernaut. The sounds varied but were for the most part consistent. She resisted the usual urge to nudge him, thinking instead of the wedding. There was nothing like it: a big family wedding, with aunts and uncles, cousins and relations and friends, all gathering together to celebrate Amy and Dan getting married.

A summer wedding! Could anything be more perfect?

Chapter Two

Amy looked at the sparkling ring on her finger again. She loved it! Loved the way the beautiful single diamond caught the light. Daniel had chosen the most perfect ring for her, one that fitted her finger exactly. He knew her so well, he knew just what she liked. She still couldn't believe that they were engaged, and were going to get married and live together happily ever after. It was like a dream come true. She smiled, thinking of Dan getting down on one knee on the bridge overlooking the canal and asking her to marry him!

From the minute they had met Amy had realized that Dan was 'the one', the man she wanted to spend the rest of her life with. He wasn't just her best friend and soulmate but the love of her life. She loved Daniel Quinn with all her heart, and now he was going to be her husband. Husband! She liked the sound of it . . . the very word . . . husband.

Her parents had been delighted, and she was sure that secretly it was a huge relief to them that at thirty years and five months she had found a husband. And not just a husband, but Daniel, who she knew they both totally approved of and liked.

'They are over the moon. I knew they'd be!' She laughed as Daniel began to phone his parents and friends. Just imagine! In less than a year she would be Mrs Amy Quinn!

The proposal had been so romantic. They'd been walking through the streets of Venice as night fell. During the day Venice bustled with tourists and their cameras; groups of Japanese visitors following guides around St Mark's Square as they tried to see all the sights; and queues for vaporetti and expensive gondola rides. But as the sun went down on the lagoon and the island emptied, the tour bus crowds left and it became a different place. *La Serenissima*: a place of lovers and trysts and secret history, filled with centuries of romance and intrigue. Where lovers walked hand in hand through narrow streets, and disappeared behind the shuttered doors and hidden balconies of palazzos and villas and old houses, and pledged to love each other for eternity.

No wonder Dan had insisted that they go for a pre-dinner walk far from the Grand Canal, and crossed one of the smaller bridges to a place that was quiet and beautiful, where they could watch the red sun slip from the sky and disappear into the water.

'I wanted to be sure that we were alone.' He had grinned, touching her shoulder.

They certainly had been alone: most people had already crammed into the *bacari* for drinks and to sample the tapas-like *cicchetti*; or were dining in the busy restaurants.

'It's just so beautiful here!' she had said, leaning against him as she'd taken in the breathtaking views all around them. Amy could not believe this City of Bridges on the Adriatic, with its myriad canals, huge lagoon, and waterbuses that ferried people from place to place.

'You know, legend has it that Italian lords and nobles of old would bring their lady loves here, to this Santo Cristo bridge, to look at the city and the water at twilight, so they could pledge their love,' Daniel had said slowly.

Amy had held her breath, barely daring to speak, as he'd got down on one knee and taken her hand in his.

'I love you, Amy,' he had said, his eyes fixed on hers. 'Will you marry me? Marry me!'

She hadn't even had to think or hesitate for a second: marrying Daniel was all she'd ever wanted. 'YES . . . YES . . . YES! A hundred times "yes"!' Amy had shouted, like some crazy mad Irish woman, as Daniel had stood up and taken a small jewel box from the pocket of his trousers. Dumbfounded and delirious with happiness, Amy had looked at the perfect diamond on its slim band of gold which he'd slipped on to her finger. Dan's long face had been intense and serious as he'd held her hand in his.

Lightheaded and giddy for a second, Amy's heart had

flipped over! She had felt it pounding crazily against her ribs as she'd looked at Daniel, overwhelmed, while he'd enveloped her in his arms, kissing her and holding her like he never wanted to let her go.

'I'm so happy,' she'd told him, trying not to cry.

'I wanted it to be somewhere special. Somewhere we'd always remember and think about. Italian legend says that the couples who pledge their love to each other here will love each other till the end of time.'

'I love you now and for ever,' she said aloud, overcome with emotion.

Dan was the best boyfriend in the world, and she was the luckiest girl to have found him. They had been going out for two and half years, but both of them had known almost immediately that they were meant for each other. Now she couldn't believe it: they were engaged and going to get married!

'Come here, you!' she'd said, pulling him closer and kissing him.

A long time afterwards, as they'd watched the last rays of the sun disappear and lights flicker, lighting up the city and sparkling on the dark water, they'd begun to walk back slowly towards the restaurant he had booked for dinner. Hand in hand, they'd laughed and chatted.

'I booked us a table at La Rondine.'

'Oh, Dan, you've everything planned.' Amy had laughed. La Rondine was one of the best restaurants in Venice, and there was a waiting list for a table.

He'd told her that they were going somewhere fairly

fancy for dinner, so luckily she'd decided to dress up a bit and put on her cream linen shoestring dress, instead of her normal jeans and T-shirt and flip-flops. She had flicked her light brown hair softly around her face and pinned a piece of it back with an antique comb he'd bought her in a little shop near the Rialto.

The restaurant was on a small side street and overlooked the water. It had candles on the tables, and fairy lights decorating the beautiful wrought ironwork on the balconies and windows and doors. The former summer residence of an Italian prince, it still had most of its original stonework and carvings, and there was a fresco on one wall.

They had the best table in the house; and Dan, wanting to celebrate, had ordered a bottle of champagne before they'd even had time to study the menu.

'You look so beautiful,' he'd said, kissing her hand.

'And you look so handsome,' she'd said, returning the compliment as she'd gazed at his blue eyes fringed with dark lashes, and his unruly dark hair – which he hadn't combed when he'd got out of the shower earlier. He'd been wearing a light blue shirt and beige chinos which emphasized his lean body.

Knowing this night was going to be unforgettable, Amy had ordered gnocchi to start and the house special of butter fish for her main course. The setting was so perfect, and Dan had squeezed her hand as they listened to the band singing 'L'amore' over in the corner.

Amy hadn't been able to resist every now and then

watching her ring sparkle in the flickering candlelight as they shared the most romantic night ever.

'Wait till the family and everyone hears!' She'd laughed. 'They won't believe it.'

'The lads will be surprised!' Dan had said.

Talk about understatement: most of Dan's friends had been going out with girls for years – some since college and two or three since school – and yet none of them had gotten around to making the relationships permanent. Dan's best friend Liam was an utter player, and went from girlfriend to girlfriend, all of them beautiful and blonde – and none good enough for him to commit to!

'Will we phone them?'

'Let's enjoy the rest of the night here,' Dan had teased. 'You know if you start calling people you'll be doing it for hours.'

She'd laughed. He was so right. 'We'll phone them when we get back to the hotel.'

A long time after midnight they had taken a water taxi back to the hotel. Wrapped in each other's arms, both deliriously happy and a little drunk, they'd been ready to tell everyone the good news about their engagement.

Chapter Three

'Engaged?' Jessica Kilroy screamed. 'You and Dan got engaged!'

She couldn't believe it. Her best friend Amy had woken her in the middle of the night, phoning from Venice to tell her that she had just got engaged to her boyfriend.

'The wedding's going to be next summer, Jess, and I really want you to be my chief bridesmaid. Say yes, please!' insisted Amy, all excited.

'What about Ciara?'

'Of course Ciara's going to be a bridesmaid, too, she's my sister. But I want you to be chief bridesmaid, Jess. Will you do it?'

'Of course I will,' Jess agreed immediately, knowing that no one in their right mind would have a flaky weirdo like Ciara O'Connor as their chief bridesmaid, sister or not.

'Then that's settled,' said Amy, happily. 'Jess, I'm so glad that you'll be there when I'm walking up the aisle.'

Jess smiled. She had always been right beside Amy,

ever since their first day at St Teresa's School. Both terrified and missing their mammies, they'd struck up an immediate friendship, clinging on to each other as they braved the class of twenty-five boys and girls. All through school they had been there for each other: like two little angels dressed in white frilly dresses on their First Communion day; or trying to control their giggles during numerous school plays, which involved dressing up as everything from shepherds to pirates and dancing fish. They'd shared years of birthday parties, and school outings, and tours! They'd both got lost on their transition-year trip in Paris. They'd been seasick together on the car-ferry to Holyhead, en route to Stratford-on-Avon, and both frozen to the marrow up in Mayo on a class outdoor-pursuits weekend which involved bogs and mountains and abseiling – and far too much cold water for their liking. They'd cheered each other on, playing hockey and basketball, both relegated to their school's worst teams. One year they'd worked on a joint science project which got them a place in the Young Scientist of the Year exhibition – much to the surprise of their science teacher, Miss Heaney.

They'd both got drunk for the first time together, followed by a night spent secretly puking in Amy's house, and deep, deep regret – with vows to become teetotallers, which they had promptly both broken at the following weekend's disco in the rugby club. They'd fallen in love in the same week at Irish college, and had bawled like two red-faced babies the whole way home on the bus from Donegal with their young hearts broken. They'd gone to the same university and backpacked around Europe together, got burnt to a crisp in various holiday resorts from Marbella to Crete in their skimpy bikinis, and bailed each other out more times than they cared to remember. Their friendship had spanned almost their whole lives, and Jess knew that she wouldn't have missed being part of Amy's wedding for the world.

'Listen, Jess, Dan says I've to get off the phone or we'll be rabbiting on for the night and it'll cost a fortune.'

'Tell him to shut up.' Jess laughed. 'It's not every day my best friend gets engaged.'

'No, I'd better go.' Amy sighed happily. 'Anyway, I'll see you the minute we get home. There's so much to talk about.'

Jess sat on the side of her bed in her pyjamas. She really was happy for Amy, delighted for her. Daniel Quinn was drop-dead lovely, the ideal boyfriend, and would make a perfect husband. Amy was so lucky to have met him. They were a perfect pair and were meant for each other. Being Amy's bridesmaid was an honour, and one that she would take seriously. She'd have to organize Amy's hen weekend! Help with the wedding! She wanted everything to go smoothly for her best friend.

Looking out at the dark street Jess thought just how differently their lives were running now, both going in different directions: Amy getting married and settling down with Daniel, while she was resolutely single. She could hardly remember the last time she had gone on a decent date, let alone had a romance with someone. She met guys all right, in bars and discos, and they seemed interested in her, but usually she never heard from them again. In teacher training college she'd dated a guy called Brian Carson for a year, trying to convince herself that he was special, but she hadn't been surprised when he'd told her that he had met someone else, a girl from Cork, and had got a job in a school down there. There had been a been a few guys that she had seen briefly since then, but nobody special, and her heart ached to meet someone and love them just the way Amy loved Daniel.

She glanced at herself in the bedroom mirror, seeing a broad face with brown eyes, framed by wavy fair hair. She was wearing an old Mr Men T-shirt and red and black doggy print bottoms. Hardly attractive! Who'd love someone who looked like she did? Guys only wanted to date girls who were anorexic and thin! This wedding was a wake-up call . . . time for her to be not only a bridesmaid but to get herself in order, get focused on finding her own Mr Right. She would lose weight, at least a stone! There was no way she was walking up any aisle the size she was now. She had no intention of looking like an elephant dressed in a bridesmaid dress beside skinny Ciara O'Connor, who hadn't a pick on her. She would get fit. Go for long walks every weekend. Let her nails and hair grow. Set up a file on her laptop immediately called 'Amy's Wedding'. This would be her bible, with lists and plans of all kind. She was a good organizer, all her friends knew that, and first thing in the morning she would text them all and tell them the good news.

Chapter Four

Helen slipped out of bed, pulling on her dressing gown and slippers quietly, so as not to disturb Paddy. How could he sleep with all the excitement of Amy's engagement! Her mind was racing, filled with plans and lists and ideas! Trying not to wake him, she went downstairs to the kitchen and plugged on the kettle. She liked it when the house was still and quiet, sleeping. It gave her time to think, the only noise the sound of a thrush singing somewhere out in the trees.

As the pale sun began to rise she curled up on the window seat with the warm mug of tea in her hand. She still couldn't believe that Amy was all grown-up now and was engaged! It only seemed like yesterday that the kitchen had been littered with a high chair and a playpen and baby toys; then there had been Lego sets and Barbies, My Little Ponies and Sylvanian Families, Nintendos and Amy's rollerblades! Where had those years gone? Soon Amy would be married and creating a family of her own!

All the birds were leaving the nest: Ronan, their twenty-six-year-old, was living with his Polish girlfriend, Krista, in a house in Ranelagh with a few friends. And Ciara, their youngest, who was still in college, had made it quite clear that as soon as she was able to leave home she'd be gone, too. Soon there would be just Paddy and herself and Barney the dog left rattling around the house. Helen suddenly felt old, as if a big chapter of her life was beginning to close while another one opened.

She glanced at the clock. It was only 6.55 a.m. She made another cup of tea and some toast for herself. She was dying to phone Fran Brennan with the news. She'd give her best friend another hour. When Paddy was up and dressed they'd phone Dan's parents. She had met Eddie and Carmel Quinn only once, briefly, when they had bumped into each other at a charity fund-raising concert with Amy, but they had seemed nice. Hopefully they were equally pleased about the engagement, and the fact that they were all going to be in-laws. She was dying to tell everyone the good news. Her eighty-four-year-old mother Sheila would be thrilled with the romance of the proposal in Italy and news of her first grandchild's wedding. It would give Sheila something to look forward to: at her age, births, marriages and deaths became huge milestones.

From her friends, Helen knew that a daughter's wedding was fun but also a lot of work. It was going to be such a happy time, and she couldn't wait till Amy got home to sit down and talk about their wonderful wedding plans! It was so exciting!

Helen put Barney on the lead as she crossed over to Fran's house. Fran, in her navy tracksuit, congratulated Helen with a big hug as the two of them set off for their regular morning walk through Linden Crescent and down through the big public park close by.

'Go on, tell me all about it. I love news of engagements and weddings!' Fran encouraged. Katie, her eldest daughter, had got married only three years ago. She had enjoyed every minute of organizing the wedding – and now was the proud granny of two-year-old Saoirse.

'Well, it was very romantic,' Helen began, retelling the whole story about the proposal overlooking the canal in Venice.

'Lucky Amy,' said Fran enviously. 'When Tom and I got engaged it wasn't very romantic! I was twelve weeks pregnant with Greg. Poor Tom nearly had a fit. We were terrified telling our families. I think Gladys Brennan thought that I was a brazen hussy and had trapped her son and forced him into marrying me. Funny, because when Greg was born she was mad about him. He was her favourite out of all her sixteen grandchildren.'

'I remember when Paddy asked me to marry him it was coming up to Christmas and my family was upstairs in bed. You could hear my dad snoring!'

'Talk about romance.' Fran laughed.

'We were sitting at the fire with the Christmas tree lights on and Paddy took me totally by surprise when he proposed. We bought the ring the next day in town, and came home and told my parents. It's so different to now. Couples fly off somewhere exotic, like New York or Paris or Venice, to pop the question!'

'Engagements are great! But they're nothing compared to the wedding, as that's what it's all about!' insisted Fran. 'You know me, I love weddings.'

'You are such an old romantic,' Helen teased. Fran couldn't see a wedding car pass or watch a bride going into a church without getting emotional.

'But when it's your own daughter's wedding it's so much fun, Helen, I promise. I know there's a lot of work and stress organizing things, but it's great. I loved it! It's just such a special time. I really enjoyed helping Katie organize her wedding, and I'm sure that Amy's wedding is going to be wonderful. You're going to have such fun!'

'I hope so.'

'Have you met Dan's parents yet?' quizzed Fran.

'Only very briefly, but I think we should have a family get-together dinner when Amy and Dan get home. The dad, Eddie, seems grand, but Carmel . . . I'm not that sure about her. She's tall and very elegant and rather full of herself. A bit intimidating!'

'Do you remember I had the mother-in-law from hell?'

Helen laughed, remembering Fran's mother-in-law,

Gladys, who had visited every Sunday and always complained about the dinner Fran had made.

'She was a right rip! She had me scalded. Nothing I could ever say or do was good enough for her. She criticized my cooking, my cleaning, my childrearing, my weight.'

'At least she spoke to you.' Helen laughed. 'Bridey O'Connor didn't speak to me for years. She thought I wasn't good enough for Paddy. She rarely visited, and made me feel so unwelcome when we used to go down to Cork that eventually I stopped going.'

'But you were good to her in the end, Helen.'

'She was Paddy's mother. I wouldn't have it on my conscience not to be good to her.'

'God, I hope we don't end up like that with our daughters-in-law,' worried Fran.

'You and Sandra get on like a house on fire – although of course she isn't actually married to Greg,' teased Helen. 'Anyhow, I don't think Carmel's that bad. It's just she's rather distant and caught up in her own life.'

They walked along the leaf-strewn paths, turning down by the lake, where Barney barked at the ducks dabbling in the muddy water. Then they passed by the new playground, where a few mothers watched toddlers playing on the swings and slides.

'Pity they didn't have that here when ours were young,' said Helen aloud.

'Are you mad? We'd never have got them out of it! I brought little Saoirse here when I was minding her one day last week, and I had to bodily lift her, hysterical, from the swings, and she screamed the park down. A woman came over to check that I wasn't kidnapping her.'

'Things have changed so much.' Helen laughed. 'We used to let our kids run around this place on their own. The only worry was that they'd fall in the water with the ducks. We'd be called unfit mothers these days for letting them loose in the park without an adult.'

'Do you remember the time my Lisa walked to the shopping centre? She can't have been more than three years old and the security guard brought her home.'

'You hadn't even missed her,' said Helen. 'God, it was so easy and uncomplicated then.'

After doing another circuit of the park they turned for home and a celebratory cup of coffee back in Helen's place, with Fran promising to give her an idea of how to start planning a wedding.

Chapter Five

Amy and Dan decided to hold a party to celebrate their engagement a few days after they got back from Italy, but when Amy looked around their two-bedroom apartment in Milltown, she wondered how in heaven they were going to squeeze so many friends and family into such a small space!

As they were one of the first of their group to get engaged there was great excitement, and having a party seemed the perfect way to announce it. Both sets of parents were coming to the party, Dan saying it was a chance for them to meet in a relaxed, informal way. Amy worried that they wouldn't hit it off.

All week everyone had been congratulating them. Norah Fortune and the crew in Solutions, the marketing company where Amy worked, had made a great fuss and bought a big chocolate cake.

'You came home with more than a tan from Italy,' Jilly had joked, admiring her ring.

*   *   *

'Do you think there are enough candles?' Amy asked.

'Enough? The place looks like a church!'

'Candlelight is romantic!' she teased, slipping into his arms.

'I'm feeling romantic, then.' Daniel mussed Amy's freshly blow-dried hair as she tried to stop him. Undeterred, he ran his hand sensually over her hips in the silky blue and grey wrap dress she had bought especially for the occasion.

'Dan,' she teased, kissing him slowly. 'We don't have time! People will be here any minute.'

'Later, then!' he promised, reluctantly letting her go.

She mentally did a run-through: the champagne and white wine were chilling in the fridge, the crates of beer were out on their narrow balcony, and a case of Bordeaux was sitting at room temperature in the corner of the spare room. Both of them had been to scabby engagement parties which hadn't even provided one drink for the guests, an early harbinger of wedding guests having to shell out a fortune to see friends marry in some out-of-the-way location. Neither of them wanted anything like that!

Amy had made some canapés and finger food for the party, and her mum was bringing some quiches.

'People are not coming for the food!' murmured Daniel, wandering into the kitchen and grabbing two cheese and mushroom vol-au-vents. He stuffed them into his mouth.

'They're for later,' she warned, smacking him on the

fingers as he tried to pinch a few more. Then the bell rang downstairs and she pressed to open the door.

'Take these, Amy love.' Her mum and Ciara arrived laden down with four massive home-made quiches – which they would serve later – and a basket of crusty sliced French bread. Meanwhile, her dad and brother lugged another big crate of beer into the apartment.

'Thanks, Mum, here's some wine. You deserve it.'

Helen O'Connor grabbed the reviving glass and glanced around the apartment approvingly. Amy and Daniel had done a great job on the place, and it was a true reflection of both their styles, with two big red comfy couches and a mixture of family photos and quirky art prints decorating the walls.

'Do you have any vodka?' asked Ciara, rooting through the kitchen cupboards.

'No!' said Amy, glad that their bottles of vodka and rum and gin had been secretly stashed away. She had no intention of having her younger sister get plastered drunk tonight in front of her friends. 'There's plenty of wine and beer, though, so help yourself.'

Looking disgruntled, Ciara contented herself with a can of chilled Heineken, then she joined Ronan and his girlfriend Krista, and Dan's friend Jeremy, who were smoking out on the balcony.

Amy watched, amused, as her mum automatically began to serve drinks and introduce people, dragging her dad over to meet Dan's brother Rob and his girlfriend Hannah. Rob was a taller, bigger, fatter version of Dan, and had been going out with Hannah for years. Hannah stared enviously at Amy's ring, and Amy wondered why they hadn't got around to getting married.

'We should all try to get to know each other before the wedding,' she coaxed, as her dad did his best to be polite and friendly.

As her girlfriends arrived they demanded not only to look at her beautiful engagement ring, but to try it on and make a wish.

'Please, Amy, for luck! We just want to make a wish!' begged Lisa and Tara in unison.

Reluctantly, Amy slipped the ring off her finger and on to the fingers of two of her closest friends. She knew exactly what each of them was wishing. Lisa was wishing that Simon O'Keefe, the lazy sod she was living with, would do the decent thing and after six years of being together propose before she was an old lady; whilst Tara was wishing that her boyfriend Johnny would stop cheating on her.

'Amy, the ring is gorgeous,' Tara said, twisting it around her finger.

'If Simon ever gets me jewellery it's usually totally wrong!' sighed Lisa. 'Do you remember that awful watch with the brown leather strap he got me last Christmas? I had to bring it straight back and exchange it and he was in a huff for days as a result. And what about that vile pearl choker!'

Tonight of all nights, Amy wasn't in the mood for a

litany of complaints about Simon. Excusing herself, she moved off to open a few more bottles of wine as the crowd swelled and the music began to get louder and louder. There was no sign of Carmel and Eddie Quinn yet. She glanced across the room to see Dan surrounded by Colm and Kev and a load of his mates, who were downing cans at a fierce rate. Dan raised his can to her, and she silently mouthed I LOVE YOU before grabbing the fancy silver corkscrew.

'Do you want a hand with that?' Jess slipped in beside her and grasped another opener and a bottle of Sauvignon Blanc.

'You look great,' Amy said, noticing that Jess had made an extra special effort to straighten her normally wayward hair and was wearing a short, V-necked dress with tights and a pair of sexy new peep-toe black shoes.

'Do you think so?'

'Yes I do,' Amy said, giving her friend a hug. 'And if Dan's friends don't notice you then they need to go and get laser surgery on their eyes.'

'Is Liam coming?'

Amy groaned inwardly. What Jess saw in Liam Flynn was beyond her. He and Dan might be best friends but she wouldn't wish him on her worst friend, let alone her best one. Liam went through girls like nobody else she knew, charming and winning over each poor sucker before a few months later getting bored and breaking it off, and moving on to some new conquest

35

that he swore to Dan was just the woman he was looking for . . .

'I think Dan said he was bringing that new girl, Hazel, that he has just started seeing,' she said softly.

'Oh.' Jess couldn't keep the disappointment from her voice, and Amy secretly cursed Liam and his ability to manipulate women so well. Dan had already asked him to be his best man, and she'd kill Dan if Liam went and upset Jess in any way between now and their wedding. Being best man and chief bridesmaid they were bound to be thrown together, and she was determined to let nothing spoil their wedding – nothing!

'Amy, when is the big day?' interrupted her friend Nikki Kelly. 'What date is the wedding?'

'Give us a chance!' Amy pleaded. 'Dan and I have had barely a minute since we got back from Italy, with all the excitement. We are hoping some time in June, but the venue is totally undecided.'

'What? You haven't got somewhere yet?' Nikki gasped. 'My sister found it impossible to get a good venue, and she had to book almost two years ahead to get a Saturday in September in Mayfield Manor.'

Amy remembered that for almost a year Nikki had had all of them demented with almost every tiny detail of her sister Georgina's extravagant wedding to her much older American boyfriend, Taylor. The wedding had cost a fortune, and had ended with guests being entertained with a performance by some of the River-dance Irish dance troupe and a magnificent firework display. She'd seen the photos and knew that her parents would collapse with the cost of such a spectacle.

'Well, Dan and I are going to check out a few places next weekend.'

'I'll email you Georgina's list,' offered Nikki. 'She had a massive folder of info which might be useful.'

'Thanks,' Amy said, slipping away to check on the food heating in the oven.

'How's my beautiful future daughter-in-law?' asked Eddie Quinn, who had just arrived with Carmel and Dylan, Dan's eighteen-year-old brother. Dylan was tall and thin like his mum with straggly fair hair and a trace of teenage acne. He was a nice kid and he gave her a big sloppy kiss.

'I'm fine, Eddie. I'm dying for you to see my mum and dad again and meet my brother and sister.' Amy smiled. 'But let me get you all a drink, first.'

'Two beers, please,' said Eddie. He picked up a can of Heineken and passed it to Dylan. Eddie was a smaller, shorter version of Dan. Father and son had the same eyes and nose and easy manner, but Eddie was almost completely bald.

'And I'll have a white wine,' said Carmel, looking around. 'It is good and chilled, I hope.'

Instead of using the wine on the table Amy took a fresh bottle of Sauvignon Blanc from the fridge and opened it. Carmel Quinn was a bit of a wine snob, and Amy had seen her study the label on bottles before drinking. Dan had made sure to get the wine his mother liked.

Amy's mum and dad were over talking to a few of her friends in the living room and she brought Carmel and Eddie over to them.

'Mum and Dad, you remember Eddie and Carmel?' Amy introduced them, hoping that they would get on, as they all stood there awkwardly for a few seconds.

'Nice to meet you again, Carmel.' Helen smiled. 'Isn't it wonderful news about Dan and Amy?'

'It was a surprise,' said Carmel, sipping her wine. 'Daniel getting engaged in Italy was a bit out of the blue, but Eddie and I are delighted to see him settling down at last.'

'Once they're happy and love each other. That's what matters!' Paddy O'Connor added firmly.

'Exactly,' agreed Eddie. 'They make a lovely couple.'

'It's very exciting about the wedding,' continued Helen. 'Paddy and I still can't believe that Amy's getting married.'

'Amy, when are you and Dan thinking of having the wedding?'

Amy sighed. Carmel had already asked them about setting a date when they had called up to her house last Sunday.

'It'll hopefully be early next summer, June maybe, but we have to decide what we both want, and it's been such a rush since we got home we haven't even had time to think yet!' She smiled. 'But neither of us wants a long engagement.'

'But that's only a little over eight months away!' remarked Carmel. 'Not very long to organize a big wedding.'

'Amy's a great organizer,' added Helen.

'And so is Mum!' Amy laughed, excusing herself to check on the party food heating in the oven. All their friends were here and the party was in full swing.

Daniel grabbed her by the hand when she went back into the living room, and got everyone to give a bit of hush as Ronan lowered the music and their friends stopped talking.

'I just want to say that Amy and I are delighted that so many of you are here tonight to celebrate our engagement. Most of you are old school and college friends and have known Amy and me for the best part of our lives. From the minute I met Amy I knew that she was the girl I wanted to marry. Call me old-fashioned or romantic or mad, I don't care – but I just knew that I wanted this beautiful girl to be my wife and to spend the rest of my life with her.'

Everyone cheered wildly, Amy blushing.

'We have no definite date yet, and we still have to decide where we are getting married, but all I will say is that there is definitely going to be a wedding, hopefully in the summer, so that I can make this lady my beautiful bride. Enjoy the night, please, everyone.'

Amy could feel happiness bubbling up inside her.

Daniel was just Daniel: saying what he felt, open and honest and kind. Everyone began to clap and cheer, and Amy felt the comforting grasp of Daniel's fingers in hers.

Her mum was getting all emotional, and even Carmel was moved by her son's words. Amy signalled to Ronan to turn up the music, and everyone began to chat again. The food would be well heated by now, and needed to be served immediately.

Ciara and Jess and Helen and Tara all gave a hand passing everything around. It was a bit of a tight squeeze in their long narrow galley kitchen getting everything on to the plates, but the food was going down a bomb. Ever hungry, Ronan was laying into the vol-au-vents, and Eddie was paying great compliments to Helen about the quiches.

'You should give Carmel the recipe,' he said.

Once the food was out of the way, Amy was able to relax and enjoy herself. The noise level was rising and everyone was having a great time chatting and laughing and drinking. They had warned their neighbours about the party so hopefully there'd be no complaints.

Dan's dad was enjoying himself talking to Dan's old school and college friends.

'That son of mine is a lucky fellow to land himself such a beautiful fiancée,' he chuckled, and Amy thanked heaven that he was such a sweetheart. Dan's mum was sitting on the couch, talking to her mum, and she could tell by the tilt of Carmel's head that they were still discussing the wedding plans. Oh no, she thought. She'd better go over and rescue her mum.

'Amy, you look beautiful in that dress.' Carmel smiled, hugging her. 'It's good to see you dressed up.'

Amy flashed a warning glance at her mum, hoping that she would not rise to the bait of responding to one of Carmel's digs. Dan didn't even notice what she was doing, but poor Eddie spent a huge amount of time covering up Carmel's antics.

'Thanks, Carmel. I'm usually a jeans person, but a little bit of Karen Millen does no harm, especially on a night like this.' Amy laughed, giving a twirl.

'You look beautiful, darling,' said her mum loyally. 'And your party is going really well.'

'Yeah, everyone's enjoying themselves,' Amy agreed.

'I've invited Carmel and Eddie and the boys to come to dinner at our place next weekend,' Helen said, pleased with herself. 'Your dad and I would like the two families to be friends and get to know each other better.'

'We're looking forward to it,' nodded Carmel.

'That's great!' Amy couldn't believe her mum was inviting the Quinns over to their house. Carmel would probably turn her nose up at their four-bed semi-detached on an estate in Blackrock.

'I was just telling Helen that if you want to book a good venue like Slane or Ashford Castle or Dromoland or Mount Juliet for the wedding you would need to be putting a deposit down the minute you go to see it.'

Had Carmel Quinn gone off her trolley? The last time Amy had been at Slane was for a rock concert, with about twenty thousand mud-soaked fans going crazy to U2. She had no intention of having their wedding somewhere like that.

'Dan and I aren't sure about a venue,' she said firmly. 'Nothing is decided yet, nothing!'

'Oh,' said Carmel, disappointed. 'I just thought that, with a big wedding, a venue like a castle or a large country house makes sense.'

'I'm sure Amy and Dan will give lots of consideration to a number of places before they make up their minds,' added Helen O'Connor diplomatically. 'Young people nowadays have their own ideas about what they want. They're not like us old fogeys!'

Amy felt like cheering her mum, who, to her surprise, was well up to handling Carmel.

The wine was flowing and Dan, Liam, Dan's surfing buddy Bren and a huge gang were out on the balcony, smoking.

Ciara, who looked like she had stepped off the set of *Twilight* – with her white skin, and her dark eyes emphasized by a huge amount of eyeliner – was being chatted up by one of Daniel's friends in the hall, while Jess was in a huddle with the girls on a couch near the door to the balcony. Amy grabbed a fresh glass of wine and went to join Jess.

'Great party!' said Amy's friend Kerrie, whose

husband Billy had stayed home minding their two kids.

'Dan's so romantic!' added another, Orla.

'You are so lucky!' said Jess.

Sarah made space for Amy as she curled up on the couch beside Tara and Mel, everyone full of chat about the wedding.

'You have got to put us girls at a good table,' warned Aisling. 'I read in a magazine that weddings are one of the best places to meet someone.'

Amy groaned inwardly. She thought she might have enough to do on her wedding day without worrying about matchmaking her single friends!

'You won't forget?' Aisling pleaded.

'No!' Amy promised.

At 2 a.m. Dan and herself looked around at tables and chairs and shelves littered with empty glasses and plates and cans. Everyone was finally gone, the party was over, the wooden floor was sticky, the place was a mess. Liam and his date Hazel, who had been snogging the face off each other for the past hour, had been the very last to leave. Dan and Amy had practically had to throw them out.

'We could do a big clean-up now or . . .' she suggested.

'Definitely OR,' said Dan, as he pulled her into his arms. Stepping over two beer cans and a few glasses, they made their way to their bedroom and fell into bed . . .

Chapter Six

Helen walked quickly through the park to Frascati, the small café off Carysfort Avenue. Maeve and Ger and Ruth were already there. Fran had gone to the dentist and would be along later. Helen waved to them all as she arrived, ordering an Americano and a nice flaky almond croissant.

'How's the Mother of the Bride?' asked Maeve.

'Great,' Helen said, sitting in beside her women friends.

'How did Amy and Dan's engagement party go?'

'Paddy and I had a lovely time. It was mostly the young crowd. I don't know how they managed to fit so many people into their apartment. We had a long talk with Dan's parents, Carmel and Eddie. They seem nice people, and his two brothers were there, too. I've invited them all to dinner in our place next Sunday.'

Ever since she had told them about Amy's engagement her friends had become a fountain of advice on all aspects of planning a wedding.

'You have such a time ahead of you!' laughed Maeve, sipping her cappuccino. 'It seems so far away when your daughter gets engaged, and there is so much to do. Next thing the wedding is on top of you, then before you know it, it's all over. I loved it when my girls were getting married. We had the best fun. It cost a fortune, and Andy still complains about it, but it was money well spent. We have such great memories and photos of the day.'

'Costing a fortune, that's an understatement!' jeered Ruth. 'When Rachel got married we took out a huge loan from the bank. The costs are enormous, and you really need to watch your budget and stick to it.'

'They haven't even decided the date yet.' Helen laughed. 'So give them a chance.'

As she drank her coffee Ger gave her the rundown on a wedding she'd been to in Connemara. 'The hotel is lovely, just on the water, and the church was so quaint. My niece looked so pretty, and it was such a special day.'

'God, there's so much to bloody do,' moaned Ruth. 'I don't envy you trying to find a venue when every place you like has been booked about two years ahead by other brides, and they can only give you a Saturday in January. Then there's dealing with a bride who has no idea what kind of a dress she wants, and then swans into Vera Wang and orders something as if her parents are millionaires. Making a guest list is bad, too. We argued for weeks about it, and two lots of our friends have never spoken to us since because we didn't invite them. Then there was the table plan! Gordon and I and Rachel and Ian were days doing the bloody thing, and a fight still broke out at one of the tables. And his aunt complained afterwards that we had put her sitting near some cousin she couldn't stand.

'It was the most stressful time in our whole lives, and no wonder Gordon couldn't even put a foot out of bed the next day, he was so bunched.'

'He was drunk and hungover.' Maeve laughed. 'We all were. We had a great time at Rachel's wedding, and that Vera Wang dress was worth every red cent!'

Helen laughed. Maeve was a person whose glass was always half-full; while poor Ruth – who lived in a fine terraced house overlooking the park – was certainly the half-empty type. People were so different.

'Well, I'm looking forward to it. I suppose when you have a daughter you always think that some day they'll be getting married. Paddy and I have always planned for it. Did I tell you that Bibi Kennedy has already phoned to offer to make Amy's wedding cake? She's so good.' Helen smiled. 'Dan is lovely, and I hope that organizing the wedding will be a bit of fun.'

'Sure,' said Ruth, rolling her eyes to heaven. 'All I'll say is thank God we have only one daughter – and the three boys will have to paddle their own canoe.'

'Well, we had great fun with Sally's and Niamh's weddings,' insisted Maeve. 'Bibi is such a friend. She made Sally's cake and it was just gorgeous to look at and to eat. Having Sally's in the marquee in the garden was a lot of work, what with organizing caterers and generators and the band and trying to get the garden prepared, but in the end we had such a lovely day. Niamh's was bit easier, as the staff in the yacht club did a lot of the work.'

'They were two of the nicest weddings I've been at,' insisted Ger. 'So relaxed and fun.'

Helen had to agree. Maeve had a knack for entertaining and making people feel welcome, whether it was in her rather run-down house on Green Road or in the ancient mobile home she and her husband had down in Wexford.

'The only thing I did find difficult,' Maeve admitted, 'was getting the bridesmaids' dresses. I suppose with four daughters you get used to the girls fighting at home, but when it is out in the shops it's a nightmare. Sisters never want to wear the same thing, and unfortunately bridesmaids have to. I don't know what silly person started it, but it's tradition.'

'My two girls nearly murdered each other in Pronuptia,' mumbled Fran, who had arrived back from the dentist. 'I thought we'd be thrown out of the shop. After that I'd hide and pretend I wasn't with them until they called me to see something.'

Helen laughed, imagining the scene, glad of her friends and their support. They'd all be lost without each other, and had gone through so much together over the years. Their lunches and coffees and girls' nights in each other's houses, and dinners and annual weekends away, had kept her going over the years. Women friends were important, and at Amy's party she'd been glad to see her daughter was supported by a great bunch of friends, too.

'Will someone get me a straw for my coffee?' asked Fran, pouring a load of cold milk into her mug. 'My mouth is still numb. I had to get a massive filling, and I'm getting two more next week.'

'Christ, we're falling apart.' Maeve laughed. 'I have to get major dental work done next month: gum surgery and two crowns.'

'I've got a bald patch at the back of my head,' moaned Ruth. 'The doctor says it's from stress.'

Helen and Fran couldn't help themselves and burst out laughing.

'I shouldn't be laughing,' mumbled Fran. 'My mouth is numb. I could bite myself!'

The rest of them had hysterics at Fran and the middle-aged state they were all in.

'Helen, best of luck with your family get-together dinner,' said Ger as they all got ready to leave the café. The other girls added their good wishes. Helen hoped things would go smoothly, as she walked home with Fran, debating what she should cook to impress the Quinns.

Chapter Seven

Amy wasn't at all sure that getting both sets of parents and the two families together over dinner in her parents' house was a good idea. She had suggested changing the venue to a restaurant like Roly's, where everyone could relax, but her mother had taken umbrage and asked was she ashamed of her home?

Amy loved her home, loved the house on Linden Crescent where she had grown up, and the small estate where she had played with her friends – but she was just conscious that it couldn't stack up to the Quinns' big Edwardian house in Rathgar. Carmel was usually very critical and would be biting in her comments, and Amy was worried that she'd look down on the O'Connors and their smaller house in Blackrock. One thing, however, that she had no worries about was her mum's cooking as Helen O'Connor was a great cook.

Paddy had set the big table in the dining room and lit the fire, and the polished mahogany table and sideboard looked warm and inviting. The best dinner service and linen was out, and their crystal glasses were on the table.

'Welcome, welcome,' he called, taking all the coats. 'Helen will be here in a minute. She's just checking on something in the oven.'

Dan's mother was wearing the most expensive black designer suit ever, her make-up immaculate, a smile fixed on her face as her glance flicked around the living room. Her grey-blonde hair was so straight it was almost stiff, and her long legs were made to seem even longer with the addition of a pair of beautiful high heels.

Amy went in to the kitchen to get drinks for everyone.

'Everything OK?' Helen asked.

'Yes, Mum, it all looks lovely, and the food smells great.' Amy smiled, giving Helen a quick kiss as she realized that her mother was nervous, her face flushed. Helen was wearing a black skirt and a wrap-over cream blouse that she had got last Christmas, along with a pair of comfortable 'mumsy' Clarks' black heels. Talk about a contrast to Dan's mum!

Ronan and Krista had collected Amy's gran, and with two sherries inside her, Sheila Hennessy became like the Inquisition, trying to find out all about Dan's family. She even had Carmel rattled when she asked her if Eddie's family were anything to do with the Quinn boys who had served in the old IRA.

Barney, their Labrador-collie cross, was wandering

in and out, investigating everyone, sniffing their shoes and snuffling his black nose into their clothes. Carmel pushed him away, declaring that she wasn't keen on dogs, which was the worst thing you could say to a doggy-mad family like Amy's. Her father called Barney over immediately to sit beside him. Ciara, who was supposed to be helping, had skulked off to text on her phone instead, and Amy could tell something was up when Dan's brother Rob arrived without Hannah. After a few beers he announced that their five-year relationship was over.

'Things between us hadn't been good for the past few months. I guess seeing the two of you made me realize that Hannah and I were not meant for each other. We had just got into a rut and had become used to being together. Marriage would have been a big mistake.'

'God, I'm sorry,' said Dan, consoling his big brother.

They all sat in the living room with its French doors to the garden. It had three big comfortable couches. If you looked close it was obvious they were worn and had seen better days, and Amy was conscious that the place needed a lick of paint. But it was a warm, cosy room all the same, with the fire blazing in the grate, her parents' collection of paintings and books on one wall, and a big sideboard covered in framed family photos on the other. Luckily Amy had spotted Barney's hair all over the cushions on the big armchair, and got it off just before Carmel sat down on it and destroyed her good suit with dog hair.

'You have a lovely home,' remarked Eddie.

Helen was delighted. Ronan got up and poured more wine for everyone before they all moved into the other room to eat. There was home-made fish pâté with brown bread to start with, followed by Helen's speciality of roast pork fillet with an apricot and almond stuffing and roast potatoes and carrots and peas.

Amy's dad stood up as he opened another bottle of wine. Then he looked around the table at everyone, and raised his wine glass.

'A toast to the happy couple,' he said. 'A toast to Amy and Daniel, and a warm welcome to the Quinn family!'

Everyone joined in, and Amy relaxed a little as the heavy atmosphere was broken.

'And a toast to our two families, the Quinns and the O'Connors,' proposed Edward Quinn from the other end of the table.

Good old Eddie! Amy had a soft spot for Dan's dad, who was a retired ear, nose and throat consultant, and would readily admit that he had earned his big house in Rathgar and summer house in Kerry by simply removing the tonsils and unblocking the ears of a huge number of Dublin's children.

'A family wedding,' nodded Sheila, her grey hair freshly permed for the occasion. 'I can't believe my eldest granddaughter Amy is getting married. When is it?'

'Gran, we haven't decided anything yet,' Amy said.

'We haven't even begun looking for a church or a place to have our reception.'

'You must have some idea, surely,' Carmel said.

'It's probably going to be in Ireland, but we're not sure where,' said Dan.

'Well, thank heaven for that, Eddie. I've been invited to far too many big weddings overseas. The guests end up paying out a fortune on flights and accommodation so the bride and groom can save a fortune on their food costs! Of late we just say no to our friends the minute there is a mention of it! Honestly, it is becoming rather passé, especially when you've been to a load of weddings in Spain and Italy and France in some big hotel or chateau, or whatever they call it.' She continued: 'I've nothing against foreign weddings for, say, a smaller, more intimate family occasion in some quaint little place, but you and Amy will surely be having a big wedding!'

'Mum, Amy and I haven't even begun to think of numbers yet,' explained Dan patiently. 'Naturally we want all the people we care about to be there, and our friends.'

'And a few family friends of your father's and mine – and of course Paddy and Helen's,' Carmel added.

'For heaven's sake, woman, it's Dan and Amy's wedding. Let them decide where and when they want to hold it,' admonished Eddie as he poured another glass of wine. 'If the young people want to get married in Provence or Tuscany or Donegal or Kerry, let them. After all, it's their day!'

'We haven't decided anything yet,' sighed Amy. 'Honestly, we haven't a clue what we want, but probably there would be a fairly big crowd there between the two families and all our friends.'

'When your dad and I got married we had a slap-up meal in the Gresham Hotel after the marriage ceremony in White Friar Street Church,' Helen interjected, trying to take the pressure off Amy. 'I had a lovely long white lace dress, and daisies made from lace in my hair, too. Your dad had a velvet suit.'

'It was the fashion,' laughed Paddy. 'Then we all danced to Joe Dolan and his band in the ballroom afterwards, and Sheila was in her element up near the stage dancing with your dad. Lord, be good to him.'

'Carmel and I got married in London, in Brompton Oratory,' added Eddie. 'I was working in Great Ormond Street at the time, and she was a ward sister in Kings College Hospital. Both our families came over, and obviously a few of our medical colleagues attended. It was a small affair as I was due back on duty on the Tuesday, so we had only four days in Paris for our honeymoon. Young Robbie was born almost nine months to the day afterwards. We should have done a David Beckham and named him Paris.'

'Dad!' groaned Rob, who was sitting down near Ciara and was well used to the story of his procreation.

'Well, hopefully Amy and Daniel are planning something a bit more lavish than we had,' said Carmel pointedly. 'People expect more nowadays.'

'Helen and I want Amy and Daniel to have whatever kind of wedding they want,' interrupted Paddy. 'It isn't every day your elder daughter gets married, so we want the best for her.'

'Oh, Daddy,' said Amy tearfully, giving him a big hug.

'Maybe we should start looking at hotels, love,' ventured her mum.

'Places like the Four Seasons and the Shelbourne and the K Club get booked out very quickly,' warned Carmel. 'My best friend Valerie's daughter Sophie had a sumptuous wedding in Mount Juliet, but if you want some place like that you'd need to be on the ball booking now. Most of the good venues are probably already booked out for next year already.'

Amy saw the look that passed between her parents, who were already beginning to feel out of their depth.

'The county is overrun with hotels and castles,' reminded Eddie. 'I'm sure that Daniel and Amy will find just the place they want, Carmel, without our interference.'

Amy was relieved, as she passed the vegetables around, that things had calmed down. Ronan seemed to be getting on fine with Dan's two brothers, and they were all arguing hotly the merits and demerits of vegetarianism with Ciara as they tucked into the pork and she had an aubergine roast with apricot stuffing.

'Meat-eaters are destroying the planet,' insisted Ciara,

about to launch into her usual diatribe about how cows were contributing to the greenhouse gas effect – until Helen shot a warning across her bows.

'Ciara,' she said sternly, fixing her gaze on her younger daughter.

'I hope there won't be beef at this wedding of yours, Amy,' Ciara said. 'There'd better not be.'

Amy cast her eyes to heaven. Her wedding plans had hardly started, and already the rows were beginning.

Four bottles of wine and a mouth-watering sticky toffee pudding later, things at the table had definitely mellowed. There were compliments to the cook, and the consensus was that Dan and Amy were going to have a big family wedding firmly on Irish soil, with the venue to be confirmed. Father Tom Doorly, a family friend and the local priest, would be asked to perform the ceremony. Jess and Ciara were to be her bridesmaids, Dan's best friend Liam would be the best man, and Rob would be a groom's man.

'Can't I be a groom's man too?' asked Rob's younger brother, Dylan.

Amy cast Dan a warning look. If he agreed to that, she'd have to have a third bridesmaid. And there would be utter war among her remaining girlfriends if she had to single one of them out to become part of the wedding party.

'Thanks for the offer, Dylan, but two's enough,' said Daniel diplomatically. 'But I'm sure that there will be plenty that you can help out with when the time comes.'

Dylan grinned, tucking into a second helping of pudding.

Looking around the table Amy realized that now they were all going to be related, and part of each other's lives whether they wanted to be or not. Carmel was very different from her own mother, and it was just a question of accepting her the way she was, and biting her tongue when she disagreed with her future mother-in-law. Eddie was a pet, and she could see that her dad was getting on like a house on fire with him, despite the fact that they had so little in common. Her eyes met Dan's. It was going to be all right . . . everything was going to be all right.

Chapter Eight

'Do we have to go looking again today?' Dan protested as they grabbed a hurried breakfast. Saturday's sacrosanct sausages and bacon and fried eggs and bread had given way to a bowl of scummy end-of-the-packet muesli, two slices of toast, dodgy-looking orange juice, and two cups of strong coffee.

'Amy, why can't we take a Saturday off and just stay in bed or chill? Every weekend it's the same: driving all over the bloody country looking for somewhere to have our wedding. Why can't we just pick a nice hotel with good food and a bar and say that's it!'

'Because we're not having it some place like that,' Amy retorted vehemently. 'Our wedding is special. I'm not having it in some crappy hotel just so you can stay in bed for an extra few hours watching TV. This is our day, and I want it to be somewhere that we will remember for the rest of our lives.'

'We will remember it,' he promised. 'This is about us, not some fancy venue.'

Amy knew that he was right. They were both fed up with looking at places for their wedding, and after almost four weekends of it were still nowhere near picking the one they wanted. And she was spending hours on the internet every night trawling through hotel and bridal websites trying to find somewhere.

Today's schedule was packed: they were visiting four possible venues and – if they liked a place – scouting to see what the local churches were like. She would have far preferred relaxing on the sofa on a Saturday morning instead of haring all over Ireland. Finding a place to have their wedding was taking a lot more time than either of them had anticipated.

'I just want it to be special,' she said stubbornly.

Sometimes she thought Dan just didn't get it. In the beginning he had wanted them to consider having their wedding in one of Dublin's fancy hotels. Having your wedding in the same hotel you went to for parties or where you drank in the bar every Friday night after work was hardly original! No, she wanted something a bit different! Finding it was the problem, and Amy hoped today they'd manage it.

Last week they had driven all down around Meath and viewed an amazing Georgian manor which seemed lovely. The only problem was that the summer dates were already booked out. There seemed to be thousands of couples getting married, and everyone was frantic trying to grab a venue and fix a date. It was a nightmare!

'Have you got the map?' asked Dan as they headed towards the M50.

'Everything,' she said, patting her lap. She had her pink leather Filofax that Jess had given her as an engagement present. It was her wedding office, and contained every bit of information relating to their plans: phone numbers, address book, calendar, contact details, clippings, photographs, samples. She wouldn't be without it.

'Good,' he smiled, in better form as he slipped his hand on her knee. They headed out of the city and down towards Kildare.

The first hotel today was the Cuilinn. It was modern and edgy with great decor and overlooked the Curragh, but after a few minutes talking with the banqueting manager they realized that it held only about one hundred guests, which was too small for them.

'Sorry,' said Amy ruefully, as they returned to the car. 'Their website said they catered for large groups.'

'Another bloody wild-goose chase!' fumed Dan, joining the heavy traffic careering along the busy main road.

'Turn here!' Amy shouted forty minutes later and Dan slammed his foot on the brake. 'Yes,' she insisted, glancing quickly at the map. 'I think Mount Mellick's up here.'

Dan made a kind of grimace as he swung the black Golf up the road and bumped it along over mud and gravel. She had to admit that the roadway leading up to the luxury hotel was less than impressive. After the past few weeks' rain it looked more like a muddy dirt track than the road leading to a hotel that might host their wedding.

'Yes, look! There's the sign.'

The brochure on her lap certainly made the place look far more grandiose than this. They came to a halt in front of a big square building with castellated parapets on the top of it, an Irish flag and an American one blowing limply in the breeze. An enormous bay window looked out over the massive lawn, which resembled a muddy hockey pitch at the moment, rather than the stylish garden area she had imagined for hosting a drinks reception. Granite steps led through the glass doors and up to the dreary, large reception area which had a coat of arms embroidered in the carpet and a long mahogany desk. It looked old-world but slightly run-down, and was cluttered with antique chairs and couches.

'Gina, our banqueting manager, will talk to you in a few minutes,' smiled the receptionist.

Amy got out her Filofax and began to jot down things as Daniel rambled around, peering into the bar and the residents' lounge.

A few minutes later a girl a bit older than Amy appeared in a fitted black suit and took them on a tour of the place.

The function room was at the back of the hotel and was large and square with long windows and a

French door that led out to a tiny walled courtyard for smokers.

'Can't you get out into the garden from here?' asked Amy.

'No,' explained Gina. 'Our residents' lounge and dining room at the front overlook the lawn. We usually set up a few tables and chairs outside and some parasols there for the welcome drinks reception before moving people inside for the wedding meal.'

'What happens if it rains or is too cold?' asked Dan.

'Then we use our residents' lounge. I'll show you that in a minute.'

Amy walked all around the big function room trying to imagine it set up with tables and chairs and crisp linen and flowers and candles. It was pretty soulless, and she hated the colour of the navy and beige patterned damask curtains.

'How many guests were you planning to invite?'

'There will probably be somewhere between a hundred and sixty and two hundred,' Dan said.

'Ideal, then, as we can sit up to two hundred and fifty guests here.'

Amy tried to picture this room filled with family and friends. They were almost two hours out of the city, and yet they could be anywhere, in any big hotel in the country.

'Here, let me show you our bar and the lounge,' offered Gina, walking ahead of them.

The bar was dull and dreary, with racing on the

widescreen TV at the back being watched by a few middle-aged men, while in the large sitting room with its massive bay windows overlooking the grounds, with a collection of shabby navy and yellow couches, two or three friends demolished plates of sausages and chips as their two toddlers raced around. The whole place looked like it needed refurbishment!

Gina opened a folder and took their details.

'Let me check your dates first.'

Amy couldn't believe it; there wasn't a single Friday or Saturday in the summer left.

'How can that be?' gasped Amy, incredulous.

'People book the day they get engaged, or even sometimes a bride might make a provisional booking for a date long before she gets engaged so that they have options.'

'They must be raving mad!' said Dan. 'Amy and I are literally only just engaged, and you're telling us most of the dates are gone. It's absolutely bonkers!'

'That's just the way things work with weddings,' Gina explained. 'Like most hotels, we are booked long in advance: a year or two years. Today, for example, we have a wedding on in the main suite and an anniversary party in the smaller Mellick suite. Looking at my calendar here, I only have two dates free this month, and in December we have all Christmas functions booked in. Otherwise we are talking about the summer after next, and I have two Saturdays in May or a Friday or Saturday in June left.'

Amy couldn't believe it! She didn't want to have to wait nearly two years!

'We'll think about it,' said Dan diplomatically.

Back out in the car Amy angrily fastened her safety belt. 'How could a place like that be booked out so far ahead?'

'Well, it's better than lots of the places we've seen,' Dan said as he started the engine. 'The entrance looks pretty cool, and the function room was massive.'

'It was awful, Dan. How can so many people want to have their wedding there!'

She pulled out her pink wedding folder as Dan drove, checking to see where was next on their list.

'Castle Gregory's next,' she said, getting out the information on it.

Chapter Nine

The only good thing about the search for a wedding venue was seeing the rich green fields and the ever-changing colours of the countryside, thought Amy. They drove through the pretty towns on the River Leighlinbridge, Bagenalstown and Graiguenamanagh, with their bridges and old mills and waterways. She gasped when she first caught sight of the magnificent old castle perched overlooking the River Barrow, near St Mullins, which had been originally built in 1605 and restored over the last century.

'Wow!' she said, taking in Castle Gregory's magnificent backdrop of fields and river and lush countryside.

As the two of them walked under its medieval stone portico and into the great hall, Amy knew immediately that this was it! This was the place where she wanted to celebrate their wedding.

A disdainful young woman in skinny jeans and plaited hair opened the door and disappeared off to get someone, and a few minutes later a tall thin man in shabby cords and a bottle-green jacket appeared and introduced himself as the owner.

'My daughter Tamsin is in the middle of studying for exams, so please let me show you around the place,' offered Hugo Roberts, leading them along a fantastic oak-lined corridor towards the main hall.

'This is where we usually host weddings, conferences or big family parties,' he said, proudly showing them the magnificent long oak tables set with heavy white linen and sparkling crystal. 'Tonight we have a dinner here for sixty guests. They've gone fishing today and tomorrow they'll play golf.'

The walls of the big hall were hung with rich tapestries, and on one side of it there was a massive fireplace. Tall windows with stained glass looked down over the parapet towards the river and valley below. There was a minstrels' gallery, and a sumptuous drawing room, and loads of nooks and crannies where guests could sit and relax. A group of Italians were chatting and consulting their guide books.

'We can serve champagne and drinks or cocktails out here on the terrace when you arrive,' he suggested. 'And of course your guests are free to wander around the rest of the castle and its environs. I always actively encourage our guests to explore. We also have the library and music room, which will take smaller numbers for a sit-down meal, and we use them for pre-dinner drinks if the weather is inclement and lets us down.'

Dan liked the place. She could tell. He was asking

Hugo all kinds of questions about the castle's history. This place was so romantic, and so quirky and different. OK, so it wasn't one of the big famous castles that people raved about and hordes of tourists visited, but it was pretty special. Just imagine getting married in a castle!

'There is a small church near the castle grounds,' Hugo told them. 'Guests often get married in it. Also some of our guests have fireworks at midnight to celebrate their nuptials,' he added. 'We don't disturb anyone, as the castle grounds are quite extensive. Our lands cover about eighty acres of countryside.'

'Fireworks!' Amy definitely wanted fireworks!

'Would you two like some coffee?' asked Hugo. 'I was about to have one myself. I'll get Noeleen to bring us up something.'

Ten minutes later they were sitting in the large front drawing room, helping themselves to sliced home-made gingerbread as they drank fresh-roasted coffee and perused a brochure on the castle and the range of facilities it offered. Another showed the menu options provided by the recommended caterers that the castle normally used. Hugo explained the price breakdown to them.

Amy tried not to blink when he told them it cost ten thousand euros to rent the castle for a wedding, but this included the use of its twenty bedrooms for two nights, providing accommodation for forty people. It was so expensive! Catering and the bar costs were extra; and even tables, chairs, glasses, crockery and linens had to

67

be hired. However, even at a quick glance the prices that the castle's caterers charged seemed far more competitive than those of any of the hotels they had been considering. As Amy looked at the menus she tried to do a quick mental calculation to see if any savings could be made there.

'When were you hoping to have your wedding?' Hugo asked, stirring his coffee.

'We were hoping for some time in the summer,' said Amy, holding her breath.

'I suspect our calendar is very full,' he apologized. 'My wife usually organizes these things, but if you want I'll go to the office and check. I'm not sure if we have any dates left for next summer. Let me have a look in my own diary.'

Amy held her breath as he pulled a small leather diary from inside his jacket pocket and looked through the date planner.

'The only date we seem to have left is a Friday, the twenty-third of October. Then we close after Halloween and don't reopen until Easter.'

Amy loved the place but really didn't want to get married in late October.

'Hold on, I've something crossed out here for the sixth of June. We were holding it for a local opera company's open-air performance but I have a feeling there is a problem with it. I need to check in the office with Tamsin, but I have a feeling that Saturday the sixth of June might actually be available.'

Amy couldn't believe it. A Saturday in June available! She was almost bouncing up and down in the chair with excitement. Renting the castle was exorbitant, but it was so perfect.

'Listen, I'll go and check with my daughter,' excused Hugo. 'You two have a wander around the place and come back to the office afterwards.'

'Dan, I love it!' Amy declared, excited, as they strolled around the garden. 'Please say you love it too. It's perfect. You know it is!'

'It's a great place but it's so expensive to hire,' he said reluctantly. 'And you don't get as much as a chair or a serviette for that!'

'When we went to Sarah's wedding in the marquee in her parents' garden they had to hire everything, too, even three Portaloos!'

'I doubt the marquee cost as much as this place! Listen, Amy, we need to get a calculator and crunch some numbers. Do a few comparisons on price.'

'But, Dan, this is where I want us to have our wedding,' she pleaded. 'It's so perfect.'

'I know it's perfect.' He grinned. 'But what about your parents? I know your dad wants to pay for the wedding, but it's going to cost a fortune, and then there are all the other extra costs you have to take into account. I think we should pay some of those, Amy, it's only fair . . .'

Amy totally agreed with him. Her mum and dad were so good and generous, but they had probably no idea how much a big wedding could cost! She and Dan both had good jobs and savings accounts, and sharing some of the wedding expenses would make it easier on everyone.

'This is exactly what we are looking for,' she insisted. 'We've looked everywhere and this is by far the best that we have seen. It's absolutely gorgeous. My mum and dad and your mum and dad will love it. I know they will. Just wait till they see it.'

'Are you sure, Amy?'

'Of course,' she said, trying to dispel any qualms she had about the price of the castle rental.

'It seems crazy spending so much on a wedding,' he reasoned. 'I think we should talk to Paddy and Helen about it, see what they think before we decide. I know it's by far the best we've seen, but I just don't know if we can afford it.'

'Let's go talk to Hugo,' urged Amy, giving him a big hug.

Hugo's office was in the west wing of the castle, with a huge window overlooking the grounds. A computer and screen were on the massive mahogany desk, and the shelves around the small room were packed with books and maps and photographs.

'I talked to Tamsin and she checked our calendar of bookings,' he said, tapping quickly on the keyboard. 'The summer, as I said, is already totally booked, but you're in luck as that opera date on Saturday the sixth of June is definitely now available. There was meant to be a wonderful open-air production of *Carmen* coming in, but due to the current economic climate the company has decided not to go ahead with staging it this year. It's most unfortunate, and very disappointing for local opera-lovers, but that Saturday in June is available if you are interested. Otherwise we go into October, like I mentioned.'

'You have a Saturday in June, just the day we are looking for,' said Amy, unable to contain her excitement. 'Please can you book us in for the sixth?'

'The procedure is that I will put you in our books and up on the computer so this date will become yours,' smiled the castle owner. 'I will need a small deposit of three hundred euros to hold the booking, and the rest of the deposit will be due in eight weeks, with the full payment due six weeks before your wedding.'

'I want my parents to see it, if that's all right,' explained Amy. Her mum and dad had been looking at a few venues, too. 'Maybe they could come to see it next weekend if they are free?'

'They will be most welcome,' Hugo agreed as he took Dan's credit card details and printed them out a receipt.

Walking back towards the car half an hour later, Amy was elated. It was the most perfect place ever. She and Dan had actually found somewhere they both agreed on. They had their wedding date set and they had Castle Gregory. Amy couldn't believe it!

About half a mile down the road they found the small grey-stone church which Hugo had mentioned. It was locked, but from the outside it looked perfect. It was surrounded by oak and beech trees and there was a little graveyard and a path that led back up towards the castle.

'It's so beautiful,' she whispered.

Dan took her hands in his.

'I love you, Amy,' he said, touching her face. 'If there was a priest here I'd marry you right now and forget all the palaver and fuss. It would be just the two of us here in this little church under the trees.'

'I love you, too,' she said. 'And it will always be the two of us for ever and ever. But having our wedding here with all the people we love around us will be wonderful, Dan. I know it will.'

'OK.' He sighed, kissing her. 'On the sixth of June, in this little church, we will become husband and wife, if that's what you want.'

'I do,' she said, kissing him back. 'I do.'

Chapter Ten

Helen and Paddy were just getting ready to sit down to eat when Dan and Amy arrived. Amy had phoned them, all excited, the night before, saying they had found the perfect wedding venue and that they would call around to talk to them about it.

'Come for Sunday dinner, then,' Helen had insisted. 'You can tell us all about it then.'

She'd a leg of lamb roasting in the oven, alongside a vegetable roast she had copied from a recipe book for Ciara.

Amy's eyes were shining, and she was almost jumping around the living room with excitement as she told them about Castle Gregory.

'Mum, wait till you see the place,' she enthused. 'It's just stunning. Imagine getting married in a castle! It's so gorgeous and romantic, and we can have fireworks if we want!'

'All the footballers and pop stars get married in castles,' nodded Sheila, who came to Helen and Paddy's almost every Sunday. 'I see the photos in *Hello* and *VIP* magazine when I'm in the hairdresser's.'

'Exactly,' murmured Paddy under his breath, 'because it's so bloody expensive.'

'Gran, it's not that type of wedding or that type of castle,' Amy tried to explain patiently. 'It's a much smaller castle, but it has such spectacular views, and it's the most perfect place for a wedding ever!'

'What do you think, Dan?' asked Paddy, leaning forward to look at the brochure and price list.

'The castle isn't as big as Dromoland or Ashford, but it's still amazing, Paddy, and something a bit different from a run-of-the-mill hotel, I guess,' said Dan enthusiastically. 'We can hire the place for the night, and have it all to ourselves, which would be great. There's a church only a few minutes away, which if we get permission to use would make everything so easy.'

'I think it looks fabulous!' Helen enthused, equally excited at the thought of having a big summer wedding in a castle. 'It's really lovely.'

'But wouldn't hiring a place like that be outrageously expensive?' said Paddy, frowning as he began to study the price list.

'It is expensive,' admitted Dan, 'but the total cost also includes the use of twenty bedrooms, which if you factor it in is quite a lot. Also their menu comes in at quite a few euros less than most of the big places that we have looked at.'

'Well, I'm glad to hear that,' said Paddy, somewhat

sarcastically, reading the figures. 'This bloody castle costs a small fortune to rent.'

'Amy and I want to pay some of the costs, Paddy,' offered Dan. 'We couldn't possibly expect you and Helen to take it all on.'

Paddy reddened and buried himself in the brochures.

'Please, Dad, will you and Mammy just go and look at it?' begged Amy, refusing to listen to her father's negative comments. 'We could all go down again next Saturday, and maybe we could see if the little church was open so we could have a look at it, too.'

'That sounds grand, pet,' smiled Helen, wishing that Paddy wouldn't always be such a wet blanket. He was the one who had said he would always pay for his daughter's wedding, and already he was beginning to gripe about it. Honestly, *men*!

Slipping away into the kitchen, she could see the roast was ready, and called everyone to the table. Ronan, with his usual good timing where mealtimes were concerned, had arrived unexpectedly with Krista, the two of them sitting down to eat at the kitchen table, too.

'There's enough for everyone.' Helen laughed as Paddy carved.

Ciara's dish was a mush of brown vegetables, and Helen hoped that it tasted better than it looked. She heaped an extra roast potato on to Ciara's plate.

'Delicious!' praised Paddy. 'That's a fine piece of lamb.'

Helen watched as her mother and Ronan, Paddy, Dan,

Krista and Amy all tucked into the meat with gusto. Poor Ciara squished her vegetables around the plate.

'Is it all right, Ciara?'

'It'll do,' Ciara said grimly, reaching for a helping of carrots and some more golden roast potatoes.

'Your mother has enough to be doing cooking a big meal for everyone, without having to do a separate one for you,' remarked Paddy, looking at her.

'Eating lamb is barbaric,' insisted Ciara.

'We are not discussing it at the table,' insisted Helen. 'Anyway, I don't mind trying out some vegetarian dishes. I just need to find a better cookbook.'

Paddy, a confirmed meat-eater, harrumphed, but nobody else said anything.

'Why don't you two tell us more about this castle,' Helen encouraged. She and Paddy had promised to go and see it the following weekend.

Chapter Eleven

Ciara O'Connor watched from behind the counter of Danger Dan's, the vintage comic shop in Temple Bar where she worked part-time, for Jay to appear. She finished work in half an hour and he had said he'd meet her here.

'Have you got a *Vampire Brides of Transylvania*?' a nerdy guy with silver glasses asked. He was a regular, and Ciara pointed him towards the case over on the right, and the bottom shelf where the rare 1960s editions could be found.

Business had been good, and she'd been on her feet all day. She'd restocked some of the shelves with the latest *X-Men* issues and had taken incessant orders for customers.

'Do you have issue number six of *The Generation*?' asked Alan Swan, another regular. He worked as an editor round the corner in Film Base and Ciara knew that he was writing his own horror film script with the hope of getting the Film Board interested in funding it.

A good percentage of their customers were either writing scripts, writing books or trying to develop games based on obscure comic-book heroes. They were dreamers! But, hey, some dreams do come true!

That was how Ciara had met Jay McEnroe. He was eight years older than she, with a shaved head, black goatee beard and a penchant for dressing like he had stepped out of a Mad Max movie. They'd met at a gig in Curzon's, where her best friend Dara Brennan's band was playing. Jay told her he was writing a big Gothic novel and that she looked just like its main character, Lisette.

A few weeks later, as she lay on the couch in Jay's flat in Rathmines reading a few chapters, Ciara had to admit that Lisette bore more than a passing resemblance to her, and was very flattered.

Jay, she suspected, saw himself as the next Bram Stoker.

She was helping her boss Henry Dunne to cash up, and lock away some of their most expensive editions in the safe, when Jay appeared. Henry nodded to him and told her that she could finish up.

'Thanks, Henry,' she called, grabbing her black leather coat as Jay took her hand.

'Let's eat,' he suggested, and they found a table in a small Vietnamese restaurant over a jeans shop. Ciara ordered a traditional vegetable and rice dish.

Two of Jay's friends were putting on a two-man show in the Project at eight o'clock and he wanted to see it.

'Fergal says that they have only sold a few seats, so we'd better go along.'

Ciara's feet were killing her, and she wasn't really in the mood to watch some crap play, but she went along with what Jay wanted to do on a Saturday night. The theatre was half-empty and the Beckett-inspired monologues of the two main characters were a shambles. What a waste of a Saturday! she thought, as they left and went for a drink in Porterhouse.

'Let's go back to my place,' he suggested half an hour later, bored by the noisy pub.

Back in Rathmines, in the second-floor apartment, they both watched a pirate copy of the latest Quentin Tarantino film. Jay loved it, and kept stopping it and replaying it over and over again, as they smoked and laughed and made love and eventually fell asleep together.

At 10 a.m. Ciara woke with Jay asleep beside her. She studied the tattoos on his back and arms, noticing that he had got a new one of an owl near his shoulder blade. She kissed it and he stirred.

'Love the owl,' she whispered.

'I got it a few days ago,' he explained, leaning over. 'Just came to me that I needed an owl, and I went down to Pete and got him to do it.'

Pete Freedman lived on the landing below, and ran a small tattoo parlour off Essex Street.

Ciara ran her fingers over Jay's skin, tracing the owl's outline.

'Lisette gets a tattoo,' he said nonchalantly.

'What kind of one?'

'A dragonfly.'

She rolled over on her side. She had considered on and off over the past five months getting a tattoo to prove her individuality and her love for Jay, but she knew if her parents or family saw it there would be war. Also, she wasn't into needles and pain!

'Pete's the best in the business,' Jay said, kissing her shoulder. 'You tell him what you want and that's what he'll do. He's a true artist.'

'I'm just not sure.' She sighed.

'You're beautiful,' he soothed. 'My beautiful dragon-fly.'

She liked Jay calling her that, and the thought of a dragonfly tattoo perched on her pale skin was appealing.

'Do you think Pete would do it?' she asked.

'Pete can do anything once I ask.'

'I've to go in a few hours,' she explained. 'I've an assignment due on Tuesday, and I've got to work on it. Plus I've an essay to write.'

'You do what you've got to do, Ciara,' he said, rolling over on his side. 'I just want to chill today.'

Ciara knew that Jay hated being tied down to any form of routine. She saw him twice a week maybe, and that seemed enough for him. He worked in a big computer call centre during the week, telling her that it was only a stopgap till he got some kind of recognition for his writing. She had asked him a few times since they had met to come to her house, even when her parents were away, but he always had some excuse not to. Even on the night of her sister Amy's engagement party he hadn't bothered to show. Jay was like that, immersed in his own life. He was mature, and so different from all the other guys she had dated, who were students and spent their time hanging around the UCD and Whale, the unofficial college hangout, trying to impress everyone with their drinking and stupid talk and stupid music. Jay cared about all kinds of things, and had big plans for the future. He talked about getting out of Dublin and moving overseas.

'New York or San Francisco, that's where it's at,' he explained. 'There's plenty of opportunity and none of the bloody begrudgery and putting you down you get here. People outside Ireland want new voices, experimentation.'

Ciara knew that one day Jay would make it big in whatever field he chose: his writing, his poetry, his scripts. He said she was his muse, and she loved watching him work, and the intensity that surrounded him. He made her feel grown-up. She loved to listen to him read out loud to her or to pore over his laptop screen, trying to make sense of his words and imagination. Jay was confident that it was only a matter of time before he was discovered. He wanted to immortalize her. Immortalize his characters. Being with Jay was so surreal and removed from college life and everything else around her.

'Chilling is good.' She laughed, slipping back into the warmth of his arms, reluctant to leave him.

Chapter Twelve

Helen brushed the chocolate-covered crumbs off the kitchen chair before she sat down. Fran's kitchen was always a mess, no matter what time of the day or night you called. Her best friend certainly wasn't house-proud, and believed that houses should be lived in to their full capacity. Underwear lay drying on the clothes horse over near the radiator, while umpteen baby toys were scattered under the coffee table, and the kitchen table was covered with a mess of the newspapers and gardening magazines which Fran was always reading.

'Katie and baby Saoirse were here earlier.' Fran smiled. 'That baby is a wild child! She has every press and drawer in the place pulled out the minute she crosses the door, and this morning she made a beeline for poor old Suki's bowl, and I caught her eating a fistful of cat food! I don't know how Katie keeps up with her.'

Helen wondered how she would cope when her time came to be a grandmother. She wasn't sure that she would be as easy-going and relaxed as Fran, who seemed to relish the role, seamlessly moving from being the mother of five to a grandmother.

'Do you want sugar in your coffee?'

'No, thanks, I've cut back. I have to lose at least a stone before the wedding, now that Amy and Dan have finally set the date and picked a venue.'

'Oh, that's great news!' exclaimed Fran, sitting down. 'When's the wedding?'

'It's on Saturday the sixth of June in Castle Gregory.'

'A castle!'

'Yes. It's about twenty minutes' drive from Kilkenny. Paddy and I went down with them last weekend, and it's ideal. Wait till you see it, Fran! It's perfect for a wedding, and it even has a small church close by. Here, I brought you over a copy of the brochure to have a look at.'

'God, Helen, it looks fabulous!' Fran said, as she studied the photographs. 'It must be costing you a fortune.'

'Well, it *is* very pricey. Paddy is going on and on about the cost of it. But when you see the place it's worth it, and it is really what Amy and Dan want. They are getting married on the first Saturday in June, so mark it up on your calendar.'

'I hope Amy realizes how lucky she is!' said Fran, looking at the glossy brochure.

'She's a great kid, Fran. Paddy and I have always planned to pay for the girls' weddings. Though God knows what kind of wedding Ciara will have, that's if she ever gets married. She told me the other day she doesn't believe in marriage and thinks that monogamy is a waste of time!'

'God, maybe she's right, and marriage isn't for everyone. Greg and Sandra seem to be happy enough living together with their two kids without any pieces of legal paper or church blessings. It's all changed since our day.'

'Well, maybe Amy's will be the only wedding! And we want to do it properly. You know how it is.'

'Of course, it's a big day in everyone's life! We shared the wedding costs with Katie and Brian when they got married. Everything adds up, you know, and we tried not to cut corners as Katie had her heart set on what she wanted, but we did have a strict budget and we stuck to it.'

'Fran, it was a great wedding, with that little blue wooden church, and then the lovely old-fashioned hotel in Enniskerry. We all had such a good time, and it was great to be able to get taxis home at the end of the night instead of forking out for B & Bs. The only bad thing is that everyone coming to Amy and Dan's will have to stay the night!'

'Don't worry, the young crowd are always up for a night away! And it'll be good for me to get Tom away from the office and work for a night.'

'It's funny,' laughed Helen, 'but now that the castle and church are booked, I'm finally beginning to realize that Amy is actually getting married! She's grown-up and gone from us.'

'It's the beginning,' advised Fran sagely, 'not the end.

It is a change when your daughter or son marries, and suddenly you have a son-in-law or daughter-in-law about the place, and then grandchildren. Life changes, and the family pattern shifts and alters as new people become part of it.'

'What happens if it changes too much, and we rarely see her except for the odd dinner invite?'

'That's not going to happen,' assured her friend. 'Look around you. Katie's here with the baby every day practically, and I mind Greg's boys two days a week after school. Honestly, some days it feels like I'm running a crèche. Married daughters need their mothers.'

Helen remembered how much she'd needed her own mother to give a hand with Amy, who was a colicky baby. Her mother's arms had always welcomed them, and she'd insisted on babysitting regularly to let Helen and Paddy get a few hours off. Sometimes when she'd dropped the kids to her mum's, Paddy and herself used to just go back home to a quiet house and get into bed and sleep.

'Yeah, you're right, Fran.'

'Anyway, Helen, the first thing you need to get through is the wedding. It breaks down into two lists. The big wedding stuff: the dress, the bridesmaids, the flowers, the cake, the invitations, the music, the menus, the guest list, the table settings . . . And then there is the Mother of the Bride stuff. Your dress, your hair, your shoes, your bag, the house, the garden. Believe me, it's just as well that Amy isn't getting married until June, as there is so much to do.'

Helen secretly thanked heaven she had a friend like Fran to help her.

'Now, tell me, what kind of wedding style is Amy going for?'

'I'm not sure,' Helen hesitated. 'We haven't really discussed it yet.'

'Well, you need to, because it determines the whole wedding plan. Is it going to be a very formal wedding with big bouquets and flowers and tuxedos, or is it going to be more standard, with cocktail wear and suits and posies and ribbons? Or will Amy and Dan go eclectic and quirky?'

'I don't think they have decided yet,' Helen said, making herself a second coffee.

'Get the wedding magazines,' advised Fran.

'Magazines!'

'Wedding magazines will be your bible for the next few months. You'll never read any magazine as much as you will read them,' confided her best friend. 'You know something, I really miss them. I used to spend hours reading them. Katie would buy loads and we used to love browsing through their pages. I think Katie found them a great help. Now she spends all her time reading baby catalogues and parents' magazines. There's always something. Here, do you want some shortbread?'

'Fran, I've got to cut back. No biscuits, chocolate, cakes or sugar. Carmel Quinn is sleek like a greyhound, wait till you see her.'

'I suppose it'd do no harm to trim down a bit,' agreed Fran honestly.

'Fran! I thought you'd be on my side.' Helen laughed.

'I am, but being Mother of the Bride is something you've got to put your best foot forward doing, Helen. God, do you remember? I starved myself to lose a measly ten pounds for Katie's wedding.'

'You looked stunning,' said Helen loyally.

'That was honestly the most expensive outfit I have ever bought in my life,' Fran admitted, slipping into the chair across the table from her. 'I loved the colour and fit of it, and it just made me feel good. It made me confident, so I guess it was worth it.'

'You looked a million dollars!' Helen laughed. 'And do you remember how Brian's mother wore that fitted black dress?'

'I know she was trying to look classy and slim, but it drained her and put years on her. Katie told me she almost cried when she saw the wedding photos.'

'Now that we are starting to organize things, it's exciting,' confessed Helen. 'It's all so different from our wedding, which was a small affair with about thirty relations and friends along . . .'

'The girls do things differently than our day. Sure, I was only twenty when Tom and I got married. We hadn't a clue!'

'Paddy and I were the same. Everybody thought we were mad getting married when I was barely twenty-three. His parents were dead set against it, and kept telling us that we were too young and poor. By the time I was Amy's age we had the three kids.'

'Bet you wouldn't change it!' teased Fran.

'Not a day of it,' insisted Helen. 'Not a day.'

'Well, anything you need a hand with, I'm here ready and willing,' Fran offered. 'I love weddings. I just love them.'

'Fran, I'll take you up on it,' Helen promised, grabbing her keys and wallet. 'Listen, I'd better go. I'm collecting Mum and taking her to Poppies for lunch.'

'How is Sheila?'

'Great, getting deafer and a bit more demanding, but she's still living at home. We've home help coming in twice a week, and then I'm around.'

'You're so good, Helen!' praised Fran. 'My mother nearly drove me cracked!'

Helen smiled, remembering the hours Fran spent in her kitchen ranting about her mother, who'd had the family all demented with her demands – up until she'd died ten years ago.

'Do you want to have lunch in my place on Friday?' Helen asked.

'Great. I'll see you then, MOB.'

'MOB?' What was Fran on about?

'Mother of the Bride!' Fran waved. 'Enjoy it.'

Helen smiled. She was really going to enjoy it. It wasn't every day a daughter got married, and she was going to revel in the whole experience.

Chapter Thirteen

Helen parked her car outside the old house, bracing
herself to go inside. Three times a week she visited her
mother, conscious that it must be lonely for her still
living here in the old house, with so many of her old
neighbours and friends gone or living in retirement
or nursing homes. As Sheila grew older the demands
were greater, and she relied on Helen more and more
for everything. Helen did her best, and brought her out
shopping and for drives and walks, and often had her to
stay at the weekends. Getting old was no fun, but Sheila
Hennessy was still full of spirit and determined to be
independent and live in her own home.

The family home where Helen had grown up looked
run-down and unkempt, the grass long and covered
with fallen leaves. The front windows and front door
were both in need of repainting. She remembered a time
when this house had been one of the finest on the street.
Her mother had always insisted on having a border of
colourful seasonal bedding plants running to the front

door, the lawn immaculately clipped and the hedge trimmed.

This house on Willow Grove had been home for so long to Helen and her three brothers. They'd had a great childhood, and she must have swung on the rusting gate thousands of times. Along with her brothers, Tim and David and Brendan, she'd raced and chased up and down the road here, and played rounders and football with the rest of the kids, and endless games of elastics and hopscotch with her best friends, Marianne and Claire. It had always seemed safe, and she could never have imagined a better place to live. Her bedroom was the one up over the garage, with the Virginia creeper rambling beneath the window sill. Number thirty-two looked shabby and neglected now, a complete contrast to the neighbours' houses, many of which had been sold to be gutted and transformed by their new owners.

Billy Maguire's one next door was being extended now. The builders were giving it expensive wooden windows and ceiling-height glass doors that ran the length of the back of the house and opened on to an immaculate paved garden with box hedging, borders of French lavender, and outside silver lighting.

Helen locked the car and went to the front door. She rang the bell two or three times, waiting for her mother's footsteps to sound in the hall. Her mother's hearing was bad; she could see through the patterned glass that

Sheila wasn't coming and opened the hall door with her own key.

'Mum, it's me!' she called loudly, not wanting to scare her as she walked around downstairs. There were newspapers all over the living room, and the curtains were only half-pulled. Passing through the dining room, she noted the table was covered in books and magazines and odds and ends of things. Her mother had become a hoarder of late, unwilling to throw anything out, and even at a quick glance Helen could see some of the papers were months old. The kitchen was worse, with pots and pans atop the cooker and the draining board covered with dirty plates and saucers and cups. Nothing looked clean, and the bin in the corner was overflowing. What was Sylvie, the home help they had hired, doing to have the place in this state? She was meant to help Sheila twice a week with simple household cleaning and washing.

'Mum!' Helen yelled again, hearing movement from upstairs.

Her mother was sitting in front of the dressing table in the bedroom in her dressing gown, trying to dry her damp hair. Helen stifled her annoyance, as her mother was supposed to have been ready to be collected and brought out to lunch and to the shops.

'Mum, what are you up to? You told me that you were ready when I phoned you earlier this morning.'

'I didn't realize the time, love,' Sheila apologized, as she tried to manoeuvre the hairdryer.

'Here, let me do that,' offered Helen, taking the brush from her mother's hands.

Sheila Hennessy might have grey hair but it was still thick and full, with a slight curl to it. She was eighty-four, but was still a very attractive woman. She had great skin and a good figure, with only a touch of arthritis in her hands and trouble with her knee.

'What happened to Sylvie?' Helen asked, as she dried the hair.

Her mother didn't answer, and Helen made a mental note to phone the home help later and find out what was going on. Her mother had already gone through three other home helps, but with Sylvie – the gentle, calm Filipina who had come to work in Ireland – Helen had thought they had found someone who would stay.

'She stole my ring,' her mother whispered.

'Which ring?'

'The sapphire one that your father gave me,' her mother insisted. 'She was a thief.'

'Mum, I don't think Sylvie was a thief,' Helen protested, searching for her mother's gold-coloured jewel box. Four rings sat snug on the top layer in their velvet slits, the sapphire among them.

'Mum!' She pointed it out. 'You are wrong. Sylvie's a lovely girl!'

'I never liked her.'

There was no point arguing and Helen concentrated on drying her mother's hair. 'You get dressed, while I go down and tidy the place a bit before we leave,' she bossed.

In the kitchen she put on the kettle and filled the sink with hot soapy water, lowering the filthy plates and cups into it. Why her mother had refused to get a dishwasher was beyond her, and she vowed to club together with her brothers and buy her one for Christmas, whether she liked it or not.

'I'm ready.' Her mother appeared, smiling, wearing a soft pink pastel twinset and a grey check skirt.

'You look lovely,' said Helen, giving her a kiss. 'The hair looks great.'

'Where are we going?' asked her mother. 'Is Lar coming, too?'

Helen nearly dropped the cup she was drying with a tea towel. Her dad, Larry Hennessy, had died ten years ago.

'Mammy, you know Daddy's not coming,' she said gently. 'We are going to lunch in Poppies, and then we'll do a bit of shopping. We'll get a few groceries, and see if there are a few things you want for Christmas.'

Her mother gave a little smile as Helen helped her to put on her blue wool jacket. Helen tried to hide her concern as she buckled her mother into the front seat of her car.

Poppies restaurant was busy, but the waitress managed to find them a table for two near the back. It was a regular haunt, and there were lots of women friends and mothers and daughters having lunch there. Helen and Sheila ordered Poppies' chicken special and a pot of tea.

'How are you?' asked Sheila, patting Helen's hand. 'You look a bit tired.'

'I am tired,' Helen admitted. 'There's a lot to be done with the wedding. I always seem to be rushing around checking things and phoning people and getting prices. I mean, it's lovely, but there is a lot of work, and I'm trying to give Amy a hand with it all.'

'Will I be going to the wedding?' her mother asked hesitantly.

'Mum, of course you're coming to Amy and Dan's wedding! You're her granny.'

'I love weddings,' smiled her mother, as the waitress put the plates of creamy chicken with crunchy topping and salad down in front of them. 'I'll get my hair done and wear something nice.'

'Of course you will,' laughed Helen, wondering what the hell had got into her mother. She normally demanded a blow-by-blow account of her grandchildren's doings and love lives, and here she was, acting as if she didn't remember about Amy's wedding. She knew old people could be forgetful, but usually her mum was as sharp as they came. She hoped Sheila wasn't coming down with something.

'Mum, are you feeling OK?'

'I'm fine, Helen. My knee is acting up a bit, but I

have those tablets Doctor Shaw gave me. Still, I can't complain at my age about a bit of stiffness when I get up in the morning.'

'I get stiff myself,' confessed Helen, wondering what she was going to be like when she was her mother's age.

'Are we having a dessert?'

'You have one, Mum. I'm cutting back for the wedding.'

'I'll have a meringue, then.'

Watching her mother tuck into the huge meringue shell filled with cream, Helen dismissed the nagging sense of worry she had about the old woman.

Sheila Hennessy was entitled to dislike a home help, and to have a messy kitchen and sitting room. Look at Fran! Some of her other friends had homes like tips, too, and they weren't near her mother's age. Old people let things slide. Anyone who ever went to see a house that was up for sale where elderly people lived was usually appalled by the state of it. She and Paddy would probably be the same when they were eighty. No! She was worrying needlessly. There was her mother sitting across the table from her looking pretty in pink and enjoying her favourite dessert. She'd talk to Sylvie. Find out what had happened, and if she couldn't reconcile the two of them, she'd see if the agency could find Sheila a new home help. Meanwhile, she'd talk to her brothers about getting home help for an extra day a week. Sheila had always treasured her independence and refused to consider moving to a retirement home the way many of her elderly neighbours had done. Helen hoped that her mother would still be able to live alone.

Chapter Fourteen

Jess studied herself in the mirror. Despite heroic efforts, and using all her willpower to stick to her diet, she had only shifted a disappointing three kilos in weight. Her big tummy and plump thighs still stared at her as she tried to camouflage them with long floaty tops and cardigans and leggings. She had taken to walking to school some days, if the weather was in any way dry or good, but usually – faced with winter's torrential rains and cold – opted for the safety and comfort of her own car. In the New Year she swore that she would join a gym, take up exercise and commit to a healthy eating plan, as thoughts of Amy's wedding in June in Castle Gregory haunted her.

Second class was putting on a nativity play, and she was busy rehearsing with them day after day. The melodies of 'Little Donkey', 'Silent Night' and 'We Three Kings' were on a constant loop in her brain as she watched the children run through the play as Christmas grew closer.

For Dan's birthday Amy had organized for a crowd to meet up for drinks in Taylor's on Dame Street after work, and she'd insisted Jess come along, too.

'You'll never meet anyone sitting at home, Jess, or hanging out with seven- and eight-year-olds,' Amy reasoned. 'Dan has loads of nice friends, and a lot of them are single, too.'

Despite her better judgement, and the fact that she was exhausted from trying to construct a mini-Bethlehem for the play, Jess decided to give in to Amy's inducements and go along. Looking at herself in the black trousers and black top with little buttons on the front she was glad that she had managed to limit herself to a Cup a Soup for lunch and only a bowl of tomato soup and three rye crackers for dinner.

Town was thronged with late-night Christmas shoppers and people making their way to work parties. The festive cheer got to Jess as she walked down Grafton Street and listened to a group of buskers belting out 'White Christmas'. The shop fronts were decorated to entice cash-strapped shoppers inside their doors, offering Christmas bargains for all.

Taylor's was busy, and Jess pushed her way through to find that Dan and Colm, Liam, Kev and a gang of his friends were right at the back, drinking. Despite the December cold, Dan was wearing a Musto T-shirt and faded denims, and he gave her a huge hug and a kiss the minute he saw her.

'Hey, Jess, you look beautiful.' He slurred his words,

already a bit drunk. Jess knew that Amy had bought him some new surfing gear for his birthday – an amazing surf camera, new surfing boots and a thermal rash vest – which was to go with the new surfboard she was going to give him for Christmas. Amy was organized like that. All her Christmas presents were probably bought and sorted and wrapped already, while Jess still had no idea what to get most of her family, and would panic at the last minute.

'Happy birthday, Dan,' Jess said, giving him a big kiss. Amy was off in the corner talking to Dan's friend Jeremy. Spotting Tara and Aisling, Jess went over to join them.

'Hey, lady!' they shouted, passing her a glass of Prosecco. Jess suddenly realized that she could kill a drink, and she toasted Dan.

A whole bunch of Dan's friends had turned up, and when Amy joined them the girls got her to do a run-through on all their names. Jess spotted Liam Flynn, who looked even more handsome than ever in a body-hugging black shirt and jeans, his six-foot frame tanned after a trip to Morocco. He seemed unencumbered, and Amy confirmed that he was girl-friendless at present. A flicker of hope lit up Jess's heart as she studied his deep brown eyes and thick dark hair and watched the way he kept up a running banter with a crowd of the lads. She couldn't help herself: she really liked him.

As the night went on she realized that she not only

liked him, but really fancied him, too. Downing another Prosecco she smiled at him as she passed on her way to the bathroom.

An hour later the crowd were moving to the Exchange, a nightclub just off Andrews Street. Jess fell into step with Liam as they walked up towards the entrance. He held the door open for her, and then when they got inside, and she was buying Amy and Tara and Dan a drink, he surprised her by asking her if he could get her something.

'A white wine, please.' She smiled, reckoning that she was all Proseccoed out.

Dan and Amy had snuggled into the corner of one of the long leather seats and were engrossed in each other. Tara had got up to dance with Jamie, one of Dan's friends.

'Jess, do you want to dance?' she heard Liam ask.

Jess looked around for a second, wondering if she had imagined it, but as she felt his hand take hers she jumped up to join him.

He was a good dancer, with a great sense of rhythm, and she found she enjoyed dancing with him as they moved together to the soul set the DJ was playing. Tara gave her a wink, and Jess blushed as she felt Liam's arms pull her even closer. The music slowed. This was heaven. An hour later they had sought refuge on a long brown leather couch, Jess dizzy as Liam caressed and kissed her. Amy and Dan seemed to have disappeared, and Jeremy confirmed that they had got a taxi home about fifteen minutes earlier.

'I'll bring you home,' offered Liam, as his lips reached for hers again.

Twenty minutes later, they too were in a taxi, and Jess found herself inviting him into her little cottage near the canal.

'Hey, nice place,' he said, pulling her on to the couch after they'd opened some chilled Coronas she had in the fridge and she had flicked on the gas fire.

In a haze Jess felt Liam's hand run up under her top. His fingers lifted her bra and cupped her breasts, and she moaned as he began to touch her nipples. She didn't want this to stop, and eagerly helped to tug off his shirt. She kissed him, starting at the top and working her way down to where he wanted. The two of them laughed and touched and kissed as they made love frantically in front of the fire. The next time was slower and was in Jess's bed, with her purring with satisfaction as Liam pulled her on top of him.

She woke at 4 a.m., confused, and thought that she was dreaming or hallucinating. Seeing Liam's long, unshaven, handsome face asleep on the pillow beside her, his body against hers, she didn't know whether to pray for this male apparition to go away or for it to stay.

At eight o'clock she realized that she had definitely not been dreaming, as Liam Flynn lay stretched out beside her, snoring heavily. She felt rough, and longed to hide under the duvet and stay there for the day. To wake her bedmate up and get him to repeat last night's performance, this time with the sun streaming in the bedroom window and the gentle sound of the canal outside and the two of them cold sober.

But she had fecking work! Twenty-seven kids were waiting for her. Bernadette Carroll, the school principal, would have her guts for garters if she pulled a sickie and didn't show up. A temporary teacher would have to be assigned to her class, and the department informed. It was all so complicated compared to people who worked in offices and could pull sickies all over the place. She'd never be in on time with the traffic and everything. She'd phone Bernadette to say she wasn't feeling her best but would struggle in anyway – it was near enough to the truth, and she got out of bed and searched for her phone.

'Get up! Get up!' she yelled at Liam, as she pulled on her clothes after a scalding hot shower, and clipped her hair up. 'I have to go to work.'

Liam worked as an accountant in the same big firm on Harcourt Street as Dan. They were in different departments, and Liam had told her that he specialized in funds, whatever that involved.

'Hey, Jess.' He yawned, patting the bed beside him.

'Liam, I have to go to work,' she shouted. 'You have to get up!'

'Nah.' He groaned. 'Come on, Jess. You're lovely. It was lovely.'

'Are you listening, Liam? I have to go,' she said, grabbing her handbag and her jacket and car keys.

He sat up, all rumpled and unshaven; his eyes were bleary and dazed as he looked at her. 'You're going?'

'Sorry, but I have to,' she said, wishing that she was an uncaring self-centred wagon like Cathy Ryan, the fourth-class teacher, who was rumoured to have been so badly hungover last Friday in school that she had fallen asleep at her desk.

'I have a class and I have to be there.'

He scratched his chin. God, he looked rough! Handsome still, but certainly rough! She gave him the opportunity to say something, anything, about the situation they were in. Instead he grabbed the quilt and rolled over on his side as she stood watching him.

'Liam, let yourself out, and when you leave just pull the front door behind you,' she said, as if she was talking to Oisin O'Brien, one of the troublesome kids in her class.

Out on the doorstep tears pricked her eyes. She hadn't been with a guy for years, and then it had to go and be Liam Flynn. He'd said she was lovely. That it had been lovely. What did it mean?

At lunchtime she texted him, saying: *'Thanks. Jess.'*

She checked and rechecked her messages but there was nothing in reply. At home that evening she searched the bedroom and the kitchen and the sitting room to see if he had left a note.

Nothing. She sat down and, pretending to watch the TV, tried to make sense of what had happened. OK, she had drunk far too much and ended up with a man she fancied. He had drunk far too much and ended up with her!

Amy phoned her, all excited, thanking her for coming along. 'It was a great night!' She laughed. 'Dan got pretty bombed, so I took him home and put him to bed.'

'I went home a while after you,' Jess said, trying to downplay what had happened.

'I believe Liam was pretty bad, and ended up in some girl's bed. He's such a scuzz bag,' confided Amy. 'Imagine: he'd only broken up with Hazel a few days before, you know, but that didn't stop him!'

Jess, mortified, took a sharp intake of breath.

Feck Liam Flynn! Feck him! she thought. He might be Dan's best friend but Amy was right: he was an utter scuzz bag.

Chapter Fifteen

Amy watched drowsily from the bed as Dan in his Santa boxers surfed on their bedroom carpet, testing out his Christmas present. She'd known that he'd love the Dakota surfboard, and felt the warm glow of satisfaction that comes from buying the perfect present. Dan, in turn, had bought her the most divine pair of black leather boots, a new Synan O'Mahoney dress and an iPod loaded with some of her favourite songs. Her old one had fallen down the loo in Café en Seine about two weeks ago when she was out having drinks with her office crew. Listening to the familiar tone of Glen Hansard singing 'Revelate' put a smile on her face as she looked at Dan's tall lean body and happy face and knew that he was perfect. They were perfect together, and this time next year they would be married and Christmas would be even better.

'Amy, surf's up!' yelled Dan, flinging himself on to the bed and on top of her as they collapsed together, laughing.

'Amy, do you want to shower first?' he offered. 'I'm going to watch *The Snowman.*'

'Sure,' she smiled, 'but we'd better get a move on or we'll be late.'

It was such a temptation on Christmas Day to stay snuggled in bed or on a couch together, watching TV all day long, but she was due at her parents' in less than an hour. Dan would drop her off and come in and have a quick drink and say hello to her immediate family and her gran and her uncle and aunt and cousins before disappearing to his folks. Tomorrow she would call over to see his parents and have dinner there. It was a pain having to be in separate houses, but they were both trying to keep their families happy; which meant, bizarrely, they couldn't be together. Next Christmas, when they were married, Dan would come to the O'Connors and then the following one she would go to the Quinns. It was already sorted.

Splashing on some of the new Jo Malone scent that Norah had given her for Christmas, Amy pulled on her beautiful new boots. She finished dressing and checked her make-up as Dan sang 'Walking in the Air' in the bathroom. Amy loved the red fitted dress that she had found in a small boutique in Belfast a few weeks ago, when she had gone north to do a bit of Christmas shopping. She pulled a soft black cashmere shrug over it. Then, after checking that she had all the presents for everyone, she grabbed her weekend bag, and she and Dan left the apartment.

'Happy Christmas!' greeted her mum when they arrived. She hugged them. 'You both look wonderful!'

The house was like a furnace, with a huge fire blazing, and Amy slipped her presents under the Christmas tree. It was massive as usual, taking up about a quarter of the space in their living room. The air was filled with the delicious smell of roasting turkey, and she realized that she was actually starving. Her dad pressed a drink into Dan's hands despite his protests, as Amy, boiling, slipped off her woollen shrug. Gran was already on the sherry, and Fran and Tom were enjoying a glass of Buck's Fizz.

'I'll have one of those, too, please, Dad,' smiled Amy.

'I'm not cooking.' Fran laughed. 'Katie and Brian want to show off their new house and kitchen, and have invited us all there. So no bloody stuffing the turkey or washing a ton of spuds this year! It's my first Christmas off in twenty-five years and I plan to enjoy it.'

Ronan was sitting at his laptop Skyping Krista, who had returned to Krakow to see her family. He was going over to join her for New Year.

'He's got it bad,' whispered Ciara, who looked amazing in a figure-hugging black leather skirt and a black top, her green eyes sparkling as she showed Amy the incredible silver and emerald-colour earrings that Santa had left for her.

Amy's Uncle Tim and Aunt Linda and their four

children had arrived only a few minutes ahead of herself and Dan, and Linda wanted to know all about their wedding plans.

'Hey, I'd better go,' apologized Dan. 'We eat a bit earlier at our place, and you know what Mum's like.'

Amy knew well that Carmel Quinn would freak out if Dan delayed them sitting down. Taking another glass of champagne, she suspected it would be hours before the O'Connors sat down, as her mum was leaving the turkey to its own devices in a slow oven. She was deep in conversation with Fran. Meanwhile, Amy's dad and Tom Brennan were debating the merits of wind power versus sea power with Uncle Tim.

'Say goodbye to my gran before you leave,' Amy whispered to Dan.

Sheila Hennessy, wearing a bright red Christmas cardigan and new white blouse, began to tell Dan all about when she was a child on the farm in Longford where she grew up, and how they got ready for Christmas.

'We started fattening the pig in March . . .'

'Sheila, I have to go,' Dan pleaded, as Amy stepped in to rescue him.

'She tells us all the details about fattening the pig and the turkey and the goose every Christmas.' Amy laughed as they said their goodbyes at the front door. 'Is it any wonder that Ciara has turned vegetarian!'

'Next year it will be different,' he promised, giving her a kiss. 'We'll be married.'

Chapter Sixteen

Jess Kilroy's New Year's resolution was to get fit and healthy and be happy. She had exactly twenty-two weeks to go before she was a bridesmaid at Amy's wedding, and she had set herself a realistic weight-loss goal and was determined to reach her target.

Amy had asked her to come looking for her wedding dress, and Jess knew that once Amy found her own outfit her attention would immediately turn to getting the bridesmaids' dresses, something she was dreading.

Christmas had been lovely, but a calorie disaster! Why her family had each given her a large chocolate selection box was beyond her! Grainne Kilroy, her mother, was far too good a cook, and got insulted if you refused second helpings of anything at her table. She had slaved for weeks making Christmas puddings, pies and a cake, and Jess found it hard to resist the traditional treats. Then there was the constant round of drinks parties and family meals, and there was only so much Ballygowan water a person could drink without spending much of the night in the bathroom.

Her sister Deirdre had announced she was pregnant again, which had thrown her other sister, Ava, into hysterics on Christmas Day as she and her husband Finn had been trying to have a baby for years and were going to have another round of IVF. Jess's dad had sloped over to the neighbours to get away from it all.

She had bumped into Liam Flynn with a crowd out in Kehoe's pub on South Anne Street on Christmas Eve. He'd been drinking in the pub since lunchtime and had been polite, kissing her and wishing her Merry Christmas, chatting to her for a few minutes before rejoining his friends. He made no mention of seeing her again or asking her out. She hadn't meant to spy on him, but later on could see him engrossed in chatting up a small blonde who was all over him.

Feck him! she thought angrily.

Amy and Dan and the crowd were going away for the New Year to Donegal.

'Go on, Jess, come away, too,' begged Amy. 'It's all organized and we've booked three cottages in Bundoran, and there's plenty of space. It'll be fun, a great laugh, and you know nearly everyone going.'

Liam Flynn was going, and although Jess was sorely tempted to take Amy up on her offer the thought of the sheer hell and embarrassment of spending a few days around him was too much. Anyhow, New Year was usually totally overrated, and she decided to forsake driving to Donegal, and opted to ring in the New Year babysitting for her sister Deirdre instead.

At midnight, sitting alone in her sister's house in Castleknock watching TV with a glass of wine, a single packet of Tayto, and two-year-old Adam asleep on her lap, she hoped that this year would be a very good one!

Chapter Seventeen

Amy stood on the beach watching Dan and Liam and Bren and Dan's best surfing buddy, Conor, out on their boards. Dan was testing out his new surfboard with a triumphant hundred-and-fifty-metre ride on the reef break. The winds were gusting, and the waves high, and running so fast that the excitement was electric. Amy fought to catch her breath as she jumped up and down in her wetsuit cheering and filming Dan with her mini-cam. She had been out in the surf a few times herself, letting the waves catch her as she fought to keep her balance and not panic. She'd had a few spills but had got back up again. Now she was tired and ready to chill out in front of the big fire they had lit in the cottage overlooking the beach.

The weather was bloody freezing, and they must have been mad to have decided to come to Bundoran for New Year, where the chill winds of winter blew in from the Atlantic and gusted along the coast.

Tara and Aisling were messing about with a board,

neither of them managing to stay up for more than a few seconds. The rest of the crowd had already legged it to McDaniel's, the local pub, and were nursing pints and hot ports there. Feeling her teeth start to chatter, Amy began to walk back to the car, Tara and Aisling running to join her.

'We're fffrrreeezzzinng!' they both said, wrapping themselves in towels before stripping out of their suits and tugging on fleeces and jeans and big woollen socks.

'Attractive!' Aisling laughed, pulling on a wool hat, too.

'Let's go back to the house and warm up,' suggested Amy. 'We can heat up some soup in the microwave and there's soda bread there, too. The lads will give us a shout when they are ready for home.'

The small holiday cottage was warm, and they sat down in front of the fire. From the window they could just about see where the guys were, and Amy put on the soup for them and threw a few more logs on the fire.

'God, I'm so glad I came,' Tara said. 'It beats me sitting at home while Johnny goes to Edinburgh with his friends. I'd probably just have gone out tonight to some club and had a crap time.'

'I wish that Jess had come,' said Aisling. 'I thought that she was all up for it, and then she just goes and stays at home.'

'I don't know what's happening with her,' worried

Amy. 'She's been acting funny since before Christmas. I'll phone her later.'

Amy, to her surprise, was really enjoying the break from Dublin. They had driven up to Donegal yesterday, a massive drive, but Dan and the guys had still insisted on getting out on their boards when they arrived, even though it was late and the light was fading. They had cooked a huge pot of chicken curry afterwards, and sat in, drinking and chatting and playing music all night. It had been great, and everyone had got up mid-morning to go to the beach or up by the cliffs.

Amy took a second bowl of the warming vegetable soup, all the time keeping an eye on the water and waves.

Tonight they had booked a big table for fourteen in Farraige, the restaurant at the edge of the town. Drinks in McDaniel's first, then New Year's Eve dinner in the restaurant, which had got a great write-up in the *Good Food Guide*. She couldn't wait.

The meal had been superb and Farraige had certainly proved that it deserved its reputation.

'If this place was in Dublin we'd be there every weekend,' said Jeremy, heartbroken that his new favourite restaurant was so far away. The table was littered with wine glasses and beer bottles as they began the big countdown to midnight, Amy clutching Dan's hand in hers.

At twelve o'clock the place went crazy, with everyone

shouting and singing and wishing each other: 'Happy New Year! Happy New Year.'

'This is going to be our year,' Dan promised, kissing Amy. 'We've the wedding, and then I think we should think about buying a house.'

Amy, a little bit tipsy, threw her arms around him. The wedding! A house! It was going be a great year.

Jamie grabbed her to hug her, and Liam kissed her, and Aisling hugged her tight, all tearful at the thought that Amy wouldn't be single much longer.

It was 3 a.m. before they finally left the restaurant, Amy and Dan excited at all that the future held for them.

The next day they straggled to the beach. It was wet, but that didn't deter the diehards, and Amy watched snug in her rain gear as Dan and Liam and most of the lads enjoyed themselves. Kim White, Conor's girlfriend, fearlessly took in a huge run on her board despite the conditions, to cheers from everyone. The rest of the time was spent in McDaniel's, where they stayed eating and drinking for the rest of the night.

As they packed up the next morning and prepared to leave the cottage, Amy realized that she hadn't once opened the laptop she had brought with her. She had been full of good intentions to go through some wedding things, but just hadn't bothered. She had so much to do. The wedding was only five months away, and her first priority was to get her wedding dress.

She'd looked in a few places, but now it was time to make a decision.

'It's beautiful here,' said Dan, wistfully taking a last glance around at the magnificent scenery as he packed their boards on the roof rack. 'I'm going to miss this.'

'Me too,' said Amy, giving him a hug and realizing that she genuinely meant it, and had enjoyed the break far more than she had expected.

The two of them were silent as they started the car and headed for home.

Chapter Eighteen

Ever since she was a little girl Amy O'Connor had had a vision in her head of the kind of dress she wanted to wear on her wedding day as she floated up the aisle on her dad's arm and glided back down on her husband's. She wanted a dress that would make her feel very special, and that was classic and pretty and feminine. A wedding dress that she would be proud to be photographed in and to be reminded of every day of her life, as she looked at the photo in a silver frame and her wedding album.

As a teenager she had covered reams of notebooks and drawing pads with silly sketches and doodles of 'the dress', but now that the time had actually come to buy it she was nervous and in a quandary. What if she got it wrong! Picked the wrong one!

'That's not going to happen,' reassured Jess. 'My sister Ava said she knew the minute she pulled on her dress in the fitting room that it was the right one. She said it was like magic, and that she didn't even want to take it off or give it to the lady in the shop to have it altered and taken up, because she loved it so much.'

Amy had spent the past few weeks browsing the internet, looking at magazines, and scanning rails of dresses as she refined the search for the perfect wedding dress to a handful of bridal shops.

Her mum, and Jess, and a reluctant Ciara, had been roped in to join the search for the perfect wedding dress, and Amy had made appointments in four places.

'You have to make an appointment to go and spend a fortune on a dress! It's mad,' said Ciara. 'Bloody mad!'

Amy had to agree. She had always stupidly imagined that you could just walk into a bridal shop, try on a dress, fall in love with it and buy it there and then. She had never imagined that viewing dresses at these shops was by appointment only, and that even if you were having an early summer wedding many of them put you on a waiting list for a few weeks before they'd even see you. Anyhow, she had finally managed to get appointments that Saturday with four bridal specialists.

'We're going to four shops!' protested Ciara. 'What a waste of a Saturday!'

'Ciara!' warned their mother. 'Choosing her wedding dress is very important for your sister. Honestly, you and Amy will always remember this day in the future.'

'I'm sure I will.' Ciara grimaced. 'I could be asleep in bed or studying for my exams.'

'The exams can wait this once,' Helen O'Connor said. 'They're not for another few months, and if you are that concerned you can study tonight, instead of going out.'

'Thanks, sis!'

'Well, I wouldn't miss it for the world.' Jess laughed.

They started off in the inner sanctum of the most expensive store in Dublin, Brown Thomas, looking at the American designer Vera Wang's selection of wedding gowns. They cost a fortune, but certainly had the 'wow' factor – and of course the 'wow' price. Amy picked out three she really liked and, at the insistence of the ultra-chic 'wedding advisor', two more designs.

'Everything will be made to your exact measurements, so don't worry if a dress is too small or large or too long,' the sales lady soothed.

Amy loved the traditional full Vera Wang design, and felt like she was stepping out of a film set as she spun around to show the others outside the fitting room.

'Oh, Amy pet, you look so lovely.' Helen O'Connor's eyes filled with tears as she groped for a hankie in her bag, and tried to control her emotions. 'Doesn't she?'

'Beautiful,' agreed Jess.

'Nice but a bit old-fashioned,' said Ciara. 'Bit too Disney-princess-looking!'

'Ciara!' warned Helen.

'You asked me for my opinion, and I'm giving it,' Amy's sister retorted candidly.

Amy knew the one thing she could always depend on from Ciara was the truth, even if it was painful.

'It's a beautiful dress, and it really suits you, but

I'm sure you want to try a few more,' encouraged the sales lady as she helped Amy to change from one dress to another, lifting them over her head and carefully fastening the delicate buttons and bows.

Amy gasped when she saw the pale-cream fitted corset with its sparkle of crystals, and the soft flowing skirt that fell to the ground, showing off her figure and skin tone perfectly. She loved it!

So did all the others, and Amy was excited, thinking this could be it.

The next dress had a tiered skirt and a ruffle around a scoop neckline. The material was beautiful and it felt so comfortable as she looked at herself in the long mirrors from every angle. It was floaty and feminine, the kind of thing Dan would like.

'No,' Jess said. 'It's just not you, Amy!'

Then there was a satin sheath dress with a fishtail, that made her feel like a Hollywood star.

'Great for a ball, but not for your wedding,' said Helen.

'This dress I have here is a very special one,' said the sales assistant, producing the most amazing dress ever, which had a row of tie bows at the back of a fitted corset, and a beautiful classic swing skirt. 'I think you should try it on.'

Amy stared at herself. What a dress! It was the kind of dress she had dreamed of. The line of the corset showed off her bust and shoulders perfectly, and the creamy white colour made her skin glow, and suited her light brown hair. She tried a simple veil with it, and felt like she could straight away walk out of the shop and down the aisle. It was exquisite.

Holding her breath, she stepped out of the fitting room, dying to see what the others thought about it.

'Oh, Amy, I wish that your dad was here to see you in that dress.' Her mum sniffed. 'You look so beautiful.'

'Oh, Amy, it's gorgeous,' Jess added, equally entranced.

'Perfect,' said Ciara.

It was perfect, the most perfect of all the dresses in the whole shop, but when Amy saw the price tag her face fell. No wonder the sales lady had brought it out with a flourish . . . it cost an absolute fortune, far more than she had planned to spend.

'My God, this dress costs more than my car,' spluttered Helen O'Connor, who drove around in an ancient green Volvo.

'The dress is lovely.' Jess sighed. 'But it's so pricey for just one day!'

'That's more than my student allowance for the whole year!' Ciara gasped, stunned.

Reluctantly Amy slipped back into the fitting room and let the lady help her take it off.

'If you are interested in this number, it takes over four months for us to have it made and sent here in time for your wedding,' informed the assistant. 'It is a beautiful dress, and on her wedding day a bride should wear the dress she wants!'

'I do love it,' Amy admitted. 'But I need to think about it.'

'Of course.' The assistant smiled. 'The dress is exquisite on you.'

Amy took the assistant's card as she redressed, and left the fitting room with a final goodbye glance at her dream dress.

In the Bridal Design Centre at the top of Powerscourt House, the old Georgian Mansion, just off Grafton Street, Amy spent half an hour picking out dresses to try on. The one she liked the most was slightly similar to her dream dress, though the fit was not quite as good and it was in a different material, which had a slight sheen to it.

'Oh, it's lovely on you!' they all chorused, admiring her. 'Really lovely!'

Amy considered herself in the gilt-edged mirror. She wanted more than lovely, she wanted stunning! Beautiful! And this was not it!

There was a very fitted Empire-line dress with long sleeves and incredible beading; it was beautiful but not really her style. There was a backless pure white silk, but she couldn't imagine walking up the aisle of the church in it.

Bored, Ciara was rooting around, looking at the collection of bridesmaid dresses that hung on one side of the shop.

'Do I really have to wear something like this?' she

complained, holding up a wine-coloured floor-length dress with a big bow.

'Definitely,' teased Amy. 'I love wine!'

Taking a break for coffee on Dawson Street, the four of them talked over what they had seen, Amy hoping that she would find a perfect dress that wouldn't break her bank account.

Their next port of call was Alexis, the busy bridal studio overlooking Stephen's Green, which was up about a mile of stairs and left them all panting as Amy disappeared to another fitting room to try on their selection.

Appearing in a swirl of lace, she gave a twirl.

'Beautiful.' Her mum beamed. 'Amy, you look beautiful in that one.'

'The problem is that you look lovely in every dress,' declared Jess. 'You are tall and slim and have a great figure and great skin so everything looks good on you. It makes it a lot harder to choose a perfect dress. The other girls trying dresses on look awful in some of them, but everything works on you. So we need to find something that is pretty amazing!'

The dresses were lovely, beautifully made, and were more realistic in price terms but there was nothing Amy fell in love with. She was beginning to get worried. No wonder brides went to London or Madrid or New York to get their dress. She had only one place left to go today.

Judith Deveraux, a new young bridal designer, was their final appointment. Her studio was in a basement in Merrion Square, and as they climbed down the stairs to her shop Amy noticed two other brides already busy trying clothes on.

The studio was small and there were only three fitting rooms. Judith, a small, petite redhead wearing a sage-green satin skirt and a black shirt, introduced herself and sat down with them for a few minutes to chat, passing them a portfolio of her designs.

'These are from my latest collection, but often a bride will like a detail from one dress or the skirt from another. My job is to create what she wants.' She smiled. 'We have a range of samples of the designs here for clients to try on, and then when you find one that you like I can make it up to your exact requirements in whatever material, trim or length you decide.'

Amy was impressed, and, looking at a girl trying on a ballet-length champagne-coloured wedding dress on the far side of the studio, itched to try on something herself.

Judith helped her pick out a few designs, each one totally different from the other.

Even as Amy put on the first dress she felt a quiver of excitement. As Judith guided it over her head and shoulders the soft satin material clung to her frame smoothly. The top was beautifully fitted and slightly boned, with a classic round neck, while the skirt fell softly from her waist with a tiny bow detail. It was absolutely stunning. Different from anything she had seen, it seemed to emphasize her dark eyes.

'Audrey Hepburn was the inspiration for this.' Judith grinned, as she slipped a crystal bow of pure white, with a small section of veil, on to Amy's head.

Amy's brown hair looked wonderful against the almost perfect white of the dress. Taking a deep breath, she stepped out from behind the lush purple and cream curtains.

'Oh!' said her mum, her eyes welling up again.

'Wow!' said Ciara, suddenly paying attention. 'You look amazing in that dress.'

'Oh, Amy, you look so beautiful. It's just you!' Jess gasped.

Amy could see she was getting envious glances from the two other girls trying on.

'Do you really like it?' she begged, staring at herself in the mirror.

'It's just fabulous.'

'You look like a film star.'

'Dan will fall in love with you all over again when he sees you in that dress,' insisted Jess.

Amy tried on three or more of Judith's designs. A ballet-style one in a soft cream colour with a frill was stunning, and different, too, but it was the bow dress she kept thinking of, and longing to put back on again.

She had stolen a look at the price tag. It was expensive – but only half the price of the Vera Wang one!

'Try it on again!' urged Ciara.

Amy didn't need much urging, and she slipped into the dress as if it was made for her. Silently, in the fitting room, she stared at herself, knowing that this was it. This was the dress she wanted more than anything.

'Amy, you have to buy this one,' her mum said as she stepped out. 'It's just made for you.'

'It is truly perfect on you.' Judith smiled, checking the dress and running her hands down over the fit of it. 'I'd suggest maybe increasing the size of this bow a little and perhaps narrowing the shoulders, as they are a bit too wide. Also, if we lower this drop at the back a fraction it will have slightly more impact. The waist is perfect, and the dress itself looks so good on you.'

Ciara was biting her lip like she did when she was excited and going to cry, and Jess had a dreamy expression on her face.

'It's the one!'

'Definitely.'

'Amy, do you want this dress?' asked her mum, suddenly serious.

Amy knew that there was no other dress in the world that she could get married in. 'Yes,' she nodded, 'this is "the dress".'

'Then we're buying it,' said Helen O'Connor decisively.

The dress cost far more than Amy had planned to spend, and Judith refused to budge on the price, explaining that it was an original design, and that a huge amount of work would now go into making it. She couldn't reduce the price of the dress, but agreed that she would throw in the headpiece as the two had been designed to go together.

Amy felt like hugging Judith, as she had budgeted separately for a veil and headpiece. She watched as Helen took out her credit card and insisted on paying,

'Mum, are you sure about this? It's so much money. I can pay for it myself.'

'Your dad and I are paying for the wedding, and there would be no wedding without a dress!' Helen laughed.

'Thanks, Mum, you and Dad are the best!' said Amy, hugging her.

'Mum, do you think we could get Judith to make our bridesmaid dresses, too?' Ciara asked. 'I'm sure she could design something not too conventional for us.'

'Do you want me to go bankrupt?'

'I just thought it might save a bit of hassle and be kind of different.'

'We are not discussing bridesmaid dresses today,' said Helen O'Connor firmly. She had heard so many horror stories about the awful search to find bridesmaid dresses that she was dreading it.

'Let's have a bite of lunch to celebrate!' suggested Amy, leading them up to The Unicorn on Merrion Row. She couldn't believe it! She'd ordered her wedding dress. Amy had imagined it taking weeks or months to find the perfect one and couldn't believe how simple it had been. Jill in work had gone to New York to get her dress, and Sarah had taken five months to find hers and been up and down the country like a yo-yo! Yet Amy's had been hanging in Judith Deveraux's just waiting for her. It was fate! It certainly deserved a celebration so they ordered some wine and the pasta house special.

'To the beautiful bride!' toasted her mum.

'To the most stunning wedding dress ever!' Jess grinned, clinking glasses with her.

Chapter Nineteen

Ciara O'Connor had finally worked up the courage to go to Pete's tattoo parlour. She was terrified, and didn't want to tell Jay in case at the last minute she backed out and didn't go through with it. Dead nervous going on her own, she asked Dara Brennan, her best friend, to come along for moral support. They'd grown up a few doors away from each other, and with his mum, Fran, and her mum being best friends they were constantly thrown together as kids. Dara was studying computer science at UCD and was one mega computer-geek. Some people thought that he was weird, but to Ciara he was the funniest, craziest guy she knew. He still texted and Facebooked her every night before she went to sleep.

'Are you sure you want to do this?' Dara asked, concerned.

'Yes, a hundred per cent, but I just don't want to go in there on my own, in case I faint or something.'

They had arranged to meet in The Gutter Bookshop

on Cow's Lane – Dara was engrossed in some computer expert's new book on chaos and global warming.

She wore her worst baggy jeans and a dark T-shirt, and six-foot Dara, with his kind face, held her hand. She closed her eyes as Pete set to work, tattooing a small blue-green dragonfly with pink-tinged wings on her hip. It was like being at the dentist, and she was terrified and couldn't wait for it to be over. Pete, when he finished, proudly showed her the tattoo in a mirror. It did look kind of cool, and Ciara was glad that she had had it done. Dara bought her a reviving pizza and beer in The Bad Ass Café as a reward for being so brave.

Jay kissed and stroked the dragonfly, watching the undulation of her skin as she moved and the tattoo seemed to come to life.

'It's perfect,' he said. Ciara knew that the dragonfly was a sign of just how much he meant to her.

She had worked her ass off all over Christmas and New Year in Danger Dan's, because she was saving to go to Thailand in the summer and also to buy Amy and Dan a wedding present. Henry had let two of the temporary staff go, and it was hectic dealing with customers and making constant trips up and down to their tiny stockroom for boxes of comics. A new X-Men movie had opened, and everyone wanted to get superhero comics; the stuff was literally flying out the door. In January Henry had ordered more stock from the US, and was constantly phoning to see when it would arrive. Writing comic books was definitely the way to go, and Ciara planned to start one of her own. She told Jay, expecting him to be excited and encouraging, as he was such a great writer himself. She was gutted by his response, which was crushing.

'Ciara, don't tell me you think you are going to be the new Stan Lee!'

'I'm just going to have a try.' She laughed. 'For fun!'

She told him about going to Thailand, too, imagining the two of them travelling in Asia together.

'You go with your college friends; it's what girls your age do!'

She hated it when Jay treated her like a kid and acted so superior.

At night they went out less and less, watching DVD after DVD. Jay told her that his hours in the call centre had been reduced and there was talk of redundancies.

'What will you do?' she asked.

'I'll get by.' He shushed her, saying things would work out as he was involved in some new experimental drama project with Feargal. 'We're rehearsing and going to put it on in the theatre in Tallaght, and then we are hoping to take it to the Edinburgh Festival.'

One afternoon, when a lecture had been cancelled, Ciara decided to surprise him, getting the bus to Rathmines in the afternoon and racing up the stairs of the tall red-bricked house to his second-floor apartment. Jay was strangely reluctant to let her in, telling her that he was busy and that he'd phone her later. Why she did it she didn't know, but she sat on the stairs of the first-floor landing, waiting. Waiting for him, perhaps, but instead seeing the petite girl with long dark hair and ribbed purple leggings who emerged from his room hours later. She heard them kiss and say goodbye, and sat rigid like a statue on the stair as the girl passed her by.

She wanted to go and knock at his door and shout at him, scream at him. Call him names and curse him. But instead she stayed silent, looking out of the tall window on the landing until darkness fell.

At home she stayed in bed for nearly five days, telling her mum and dad that she was sick. Helen had fussed and worried about her having the flu. She plied Ciara with hot lemon drinks and tea and toast and tissues, asking her constantly if she was feeling OK, when she clearly wasn't. Ciara felt wretched and weak and sick to her soul, angry with herself for being so stupid. She felt like she had been under a spell, and suddenly it had been broken. Dara told her on Facebook that she was going to be OK, and called Jay every bad name he could think of.

Jay phoned her twice but she lied that she was too busy with college work to see him.

She saw him in the street a few times later. Once, he was with Fergal, and a couple of times with the girl. The girl with the purple leggings was holding his hand, entranced the way Ciara had been, and Ciara wondered if she had got a tattoo, too.

Chapter Twenty

Amy checked her lipstick and hair quickly in the car mirror as Dan pulled up outside his parents' house in the road of sturdy red-bricked Edwardian homes. The Quinns had done well buying the house in Rathgar with its five bedrooms and large garden over twenty-five years ago. It must have been a great place for Dan and his two brothers to grow up.

'Don't forget the wine!' she warned Dan, as she lifted the box of expensive hand-made chocolates she had brought for his mother from the back seat.

Walking up the driveway, she noticed the immaculate lawn skirted by a border of neatly pruned bushes and shrubs. There was a pretty display of snowdrops and spring crocuses pushing through the soil.

'Dan, do I look OK?' she asked nervously as they waited at the front door.

'You look gorgeous,' he said approvingly, taking in the short cream skirt and jacket and the black tights and leather boots she was wearing.

Amy knew it was stupid to be worrying about her future-in-laws but she couldn't help herself. Carmel Quinn was the type of person to notice everything and make a comment on it afterwards. She didn't want to give her mother-in-law-to-be any opportunity to criticize her.

'Dan, my boy, and Amy, welcome!' Eddie Quinn enthused, opening the door for them. 'Carmel's in the kitchen, cooking, and I've just opened a very nice Merlot.'

'Good timing, then.' Dan grinned, hugging his dad.

Amy liked seeing how affectionate Dan and his father were with each other. Though Dan might be taller and broader on the shoulders than Eddie they both got on well with people and were slow to let anything or anyone aggravate or annoy them.

Amy hung up her jacket and trooped down through the hall to the large kitchen-cum-dining-area. The huge oak table was set for lunch for seven and Dan's brother Dylan was sitting in a chair in the window, engrossed in the sports section of the Sunday paper.

'Hey, Amy!' he mumbled, barely lifting his head from the page to acknowledge her. His brother Rob gave her a kiss.

'Amy, dear, you look lovely!' greeted Carmel, rushing over to hug her.

A waft of Carmel's strong perfume filled the air as Amy took in Carmel's immaculately fitted beige trousers, crisp white blouse and pale-pink cashmere cardigan.

Her nails and hair and make-up were flawless. Even when cooking she was always perfectly groomed! She often made Amy feel hopelessly untidy.

'Carmel, the table looks great and the food smells delish.'

'It's just Sunday lunch!' The older woman smiled, as if she was simply used to a certain level of perfection. 'I've done a traditional baked ham with mustard and honey, and a rhubarb crumble for dessert. It's one of the boys' favourites.'

'Amy, here's a glass of wine!' insisted Eddie, passing her a glass of red. 'It's from a lovely little vineyard Carmel and I visited last year. Liz, will you have another one, too?' Carmel's older sister Liz was joining them for lunch. She was about sixty-five and had never married. She had just retired from a job in the Department of Finance and had great plans to travel and see the world. A regular visitor to the house in Orwell Road, she had been a stalwart help to Carmel and Eddie as the boys had grown up. Amy knew that Dan adored his Aunt Liz, and considered her great fun and one of the few people able to manage his mother.

'Well, I won't say no to such a lovely vintage.' Liz laughed as she rinsed spinach leaves at the sink.

'Thanks.' Amy smiled, taking a gulp of red wine to fortify her for the next few hours ahead.

The meal had been delicious, Carmel as usual excelling herself. The men's plates were clear: they had wolfed down every bit of food put in front of them. Amy wished that she had a fraction of Carmel's talent in the kitchen, and vowed once she was married to sign on for a cookery course.

Liz entertained them with stories of her farewell dinner from the department the week before. 'Retirement is to be recommended when you are still compos mentis and young enough to enjoy spending your hard-earned pension,' she joked. 'I've great plans to travel through South America and Cuba, visit a friend of mine in Sydney who has a lovely apartment near the beach, and get my own little place in Dun Laoghaire done up. It's high time it had an overhaul.'

Amy laughed. Liz was lovely: smaller than her sister, with short blonde hair and a sturdier build. She dressed in denim jeans and jumpers, and wore only a slick of lip gloss and mascara. How could she be so different from Carmel?

'Mmmm,' yelled the men appreciatively, as Carmel took the piping-hot dessert from the oven and served it with a big bowl of cream. Amy liked rhubarb crumble, but couldn't fathom why men adored it so much.

'Amy, how are the wedding plans coming?' asked Carmel, finally getting a chance to sit down and relax now the meal was served.

'Fine, Carmel.' Amy grinned. 'I've ordered my wedding dress and things are beginning to fall into place.'

'That's wonderful.' Carmel smiled, impressed, when Amy told her that Judith Deveraux had designed her wedding dress. 'I read about her in *Image* magazine and she's considered one of our new talents.'

'Well, the dress is lovely,' Amy said, not giving anything away.

'Tell me, have you and Dan sorted the numbers for the guest list yet?'

Amy threw a glance at Dan, who was busy arguing over the tactics at the last Leinster rugby match with his dad and two brothers. 'We're getting there,' she confided. 'But trying to decide who to invite and who not to is really hard, so names are coming on and going off the list.'

'How many are Eddie and I allowed to invite, Amy dear?' Carmel asked, leaning forward, eager. 'It's just that with Eddie's work and my large social circle, and of course family, the numbers creep up. We have been to a rake of weddings over the past two or three years and would obviously have to repay the invitations. I suppose about ninety or a hundred would do it!'

'A hundred!' Amy nearly choked on her crumble. Was Carmel gone stark staring mad! There was no way she was going to be able to let the Quinns invite a hundred people to the wedding. Dan and she had a load of friends and people from work to invite first, and her mum and dad were entitled to have their friends and relations, too. 'The numbers haven't been firmed up yet, Carmel, but it certainly won't be as high as you and Mum being able to have a hundred guests each,' she said firmly, wishing that Dan would shut up talking about rugby and back

138

her up. 'We are hoping to keep our numbers at under two hundred guests in total,' she insisted.

'But what are we to do?' demanded Carmel. 'What are we to tell our friends?'

'I'm sorry, Carmel, but we can't invite everyone,' said Amy, trying to maintain control and not waver under the pressure from Dan's mother.

'For heaven's sake, woman,' interjected Eddie suddenly. 'We don't have to invite the crowd from the golf club, and boring old farts like Peter Andrews and Tadhg Flaherty! Amy and Dan are entitled to have who they want to the wedding, and I'm sure Helen and Paddy have plenty of friends of their own they need to invite.'

'I'm just saying, Eddie, that there is a certain level we absolutely need.'

'It's a wedding!' he said slowly. 'Not a fixture on some bloody charity calendar.'

Amy looked at the table. They all knew that Carmel spent a huge amount of her time going to expensive charity lunches and balls. It was her social life.

'Sorry, Mum, I've got to go out and meet a friend,' excused Dylan, making a quick exit from the table.

Carmel glared at him, annoyed.

'I've to go, too,' said Rob. 'I've some work to do for tomorrow. Anyway, I'll leave you to your wedding talk!'

Carmel looked even more displeased as yet another of her offspring disappeared.

'Coffee, anybody?' volunteered Eddie, as he and Dan cleared the dessert bowls from the table.

Amy wished that Dan would suddenly invent some reason for them to retreat, too, but he was oblivious to the atmosphere and was busy packing the dishwasher with his dad.

'You must be so excited, Amy! It must be fun organizing a wedding.' Liz smiled at her. 'I suppose it's like having a big party with everyone you love coming.'

'Yes.' Amy grinned. 'We hope it's going to be a great party!'

'Honestly, Liz,' interrupted Carmel crossly. 'A wedding is far more important than some silly party, far more formal. It's a huge event that needs proper organization to coordinate everything perfectly, so that the day goes smoothly for the bride and groom. It's probably the biggest event in a family's life! Don't you agree, Amy?'

'I suppose,' Amy said. Why did Carmel have to make such a big fuss of everything! Already she was beginning to feel overwhelmed by Carmel's expectations. This was their day, not hers!

'Carmel, can you imagine the palaver there would be if you were organizing a wedding!' teased her sister.

Carmel flushed as she took her coffee. 'Well, I naturally care just as much about my son's wedding,' she said stiffly.

'Mum, give over!' teased Dan. 'All I need is a suit and a tie and a good haircut . . . I think once I look presentable Amy will have me!'

Amy laughed aloud, glad that he had broken the tense atmosphere.

'Just as long as you don't get another crew cut like you did last summer,' she teased, remembering how weird Dan had looked: almost bald after a very close shave with a number one blade.

'Well, I'm looking forward to the big day,' smiled Liz. 'It's lovely to see the two of you so happy together.'

They stayed for another hour. Carmel, like a dog with a bone, kept on and on, trying to find out exactly how many people she and Eddie could invite.

'Mum, we haven't even made our own list yet!' Dan replied, exasperated.

'Honestly, Carmel, we haven't,' added Amy. 'But Dan and I are hoping that we will personally know everyone who is coming to the wedding. I couldn't imagine anything worse than having a load of people we don't know there!'

Carmel gave a harrumph of indignation as she realized that most of her golf-club cronies might not be invited.

'Very sensible,' added Eddie. 'You want to be among friends on a day like that!'

Amy stared into the cold coffee in her cup.

'Look at the time!' Dan said suddenly. 'I'm sorry, but Amy and I have to go. We promised to meet up with Liam later on.'

'Why you went and picked that fellow Liam as your

best man instead of one of your brothers is beyond me!' interjected Carmel.

'Liam's my best friend,' Dan defended stoutly. 'We've done everything together! Of course I want to have him there with me as my best man! Rob and Dylan are OK about it.'

'I'm just saying . . .' Carmel began. 'He's a self centred . . .'

Dan grabbed Amy by the hand, and a few minutes later they managed to leave after saying thanks for the lovely lunch. Liz gave Amy a secret thumbs-up sign as they left the house.

'Wow, that was a bit of an ordeal!' admitted Amy as she fastened her safety belt.

'Honest, Mum has overstepped the mark again, giving out about my choice of best man,' complained Dan as he started the car. 'She's always had a thing against Liam! I don't know why she is always giving out about him.'

Amy disguised a smile; Carmel and herself actually agreed on something!

'What time are you meeting Liam?'

'Not till eight o'clock in McDaid's,' he confessed.

'I'll give it a miss.' She smiled; she had no intention of ruining her Sunday night by spending it listening to Liam boasting about his state of drunkenness the night before and how many girls he had scored. No, she was happy to curl up alone on the couch and watch an episode of *Brides of Franc* on the TV with a mug of hot chocolate. 'But I'd love a bit of a walk to exercise off the crumble before we head home, and maybe your mum is right, we should try and make a start on who we want to invite.'

Dan groaned. They were both dreading the arguments and bargaining that making a list would entail, and consequently had avoided even starting one.

As they were only a few minutes from Bushy Park, they both agreed that fresh air and a walk was definitely needed before they began the momentous task of sorting out the guest list!

Chapter Twenty-one

Helen O'Connor studied the rough list she had worked out for Amy and Dan's wedding. It was a marathon task trying to keep the numbers down. Paddy and she could hardly be described as socialites, yet they both seemed to have accumulated lots of lovely friends over the years. It made her feel good just looking at their names, but guilty as she began to strike them off the list.

'I hadn't realized just how many people we know and are friends with!' She frowned, trying to decide who they should invite.

'Start with the family,' Paddy advised, scanning down the list of names. 'Then we can see how many other places are left. We have to invite family.'

Helen had three brothers, all married, and obviously they were on the list – but should she include their kids? Her brother Tim and Linda had four, David and Anna had four and Brendan and Claire had two younger ones of eleven and nine. Did they all expect to be invited? Then Paddy had his two sisters, Sinead and

Mary, both married with grown-up families. Mary's two eldest were married, and Helen and Paddy had been at both weddings. Sinead's daughter Hilary had always been friendly with Amy as they were the same age, and she was living with her German partner in Kilkenny. They would have to be on the list. Paddy's older brother Eamon lived in Toronto and was married to Margaret, a lovely Canadian, and had five kids. When he had heard of the engagement he had announced the Canadian O'Connors would make a trip back home for a few weeks during the summer to attend the wedding.

'God, that's a huge crowd!' said Helen, thinking of Eamon's four hulking sons and their wives and girl-friends, and his daughter Kerry and her boyfriend, all descending on them in June.

'He's insisting on coming.' Paddy sighed. 'So what can I do? He's my only brother.'

Then her mother Sheila was one of five. Two were deceased, but Aunt Bonnie – who was deaf as a post and almost seventy-nine and living in a retirement home – would have to come, and of course old Uncle Harry and Delia. Then what about all her cousins? It was certainly a conundrum.

'One couple from each family,' suggested Paddy firmly.

Amy had been furious when Carmel Quinn had emailed her a massive guest list, but at this rate the O'Connors were also going to have big numbers.

'Then we have Fran and Tom and Maeve and Andy and all that gang.'

'I'd like to invite Bill and his wife. After all, I work with him every day.'

Paddy got out his calculator to work out the exact cost per head of food and drink for each guest.

'For God's sake, Helen, we have to get this down or we'll be bankrupted!'

Helen was totally flummoxed as to what they should do as she studied the long list of names. They both realized they just had to cut them.

'I tell you what,' said Paddy. 'Copy the list out and we'll both have a go taking twenty people off it. We won't see each other doing it, and then we'll look at the two lists and see who we have both picked out to go. If the name is on both lists, they are gone!' he said triumphantly.

'But these are our friends and relations!' Helen interjected, not sure Paddy's plan would work.

'They'll understand,' he insisted, grabbing a pen and paper and disappearing off to the sitting room.

Helen laughed at the madness of it all as she went over her list one more time. Maybe they could take some of the much younger cousins off the list. The family would understand. Looking at all the names on the page, Helen smiled. It was going to be such a happy occasion having all those that they loved and cared for joining them on Amy and Dan's wedding day.

Chapter Twenty-two

Amy snuggled up in bed with a big bowl of cornflakes. She was starving, and Dan had generously served breakfast in bed, carrying in a tray laden with two big glasses of orange juice, cereal and toast and two mugs of coffee. Lovemaking at 11 a.m. followed by a feed! If this is what marriage is going to be like, she thought . . . bring it on. Dan clambered in beside her as she frantically tried to balance everything. Mm . . . mm, yummy. Dan was playing with her toes as she ate.

'Dan!' she teased. 'If you keep this up we'll have food all over the place!'

'Eat up!' he cajoled, the weight of his foot and leg on hers making quite clear his intentions as he finished his coffee.

'Dan, we should be getting up, look at the time.'

Dan turned their alarm clock over with a flick of his fingers.

'We've all the time in the world,' he said, pulling

the quilt up around them, his lips brushing her bare shoulders.

'No, Dan! We don't. We've so much to do. We've got to look at invitations and our wedding rings and musicians and . . .'

'Ssshh.'

'It's Saturday!' she continued. 'It's our only chance to go and see things together.'

'I do love Saturdays,' he said huskily, his hand against her stomach, rubbing in a circular motion. It was impossible to resist him. She bent over the side of the bed to put her empty bowl and cup on the floor. Then she moved across, letting her fingers caress him, her finger playfully touching his belly button.

Dan. She loved him more than she had ever thought it was possible to love another human being. She loved his body and his mind and his heart and his soul. It was as if he was the missing piece of her that she had been lacking until she'd met him. Laughing, she slid on top of him and kissed and tickled him till he was begging for mercy. The two of them reached for each other at the same time, as need overwhelmed them.

Hours later she woke curled up against him, rain spattering against the window and balcony. She reached for her phone. Shit! It was two o'clock already. She couldn't believe it. They had slept for ages.

'Dan!' she shook him awake.

He moaned against her, his arm snaking lazily around her waist.

'Dan! Wake up!' She raised her voice, trying to get his attention. 'Get up! We've so much to do. If we're lucky we'll make it to the stationers to look at the invitations, and I want to show you the wedding rings I saw in Weirs on Grafton Street.'

'Can't we leave it today?' he protested. 'I'm fed up looking at wedding stuff!'

'No, we've got to get going!' she insisted, trying to push and shove him out of bed. 'This wedding is about what we both want.'

'Look, Amy, you just go and choose what you want. I'm sure it'll be fine with me,' he said, trying to appease her.

'Dan, this is *our* wedding. You have to be involved!'

'I am, I promise.' He laughed. 'We've got a date booked, a church booked and a venue booked! What more do you want?'

'Dan, there is more, a lot more!' she countered, thinking of all the things that had to be done to get them up that aisle and married. 'A whole lot more.'

'Why can't we just keep things simple? It's all getting to be such a fecking hassle!'

'Daniel Quinn! Don't you dare call our wedding a hassle! I've been dreaming of my wedding since I was a little girl.'

Dan closed his eyes, wishing that somehow he could make it all go away. 'I didn't mean it like that.' He tried to explain, realizing that no matter what he said he was on a losing streak. Disgruntled, he gave in and sat up and swung his long legs out from his side of the bed.

'Hurry up,' shouted Amy, racing for the bathroom. 'I want you to see the cream linen invitation. Then there is the classic white, and some lovely embossed ones, and a really unusual stencilled design. We have to work out the wording and how many we need to order so we must confirm our numbers.'

Dan groaned. The guest list was proving to be an absolute nightmare as they both tried to decide what friends to invite or not and how many relations they were having along.

'If we rush we should make it to the jewellers, too, just to get an idea about our rings,' bossed Amy. 'And tonight there is a great band playing in that bar down in the IFSC. They played at Tara's cousin's wedding and she said that they were brilliant. We should really go and watch them.'

'I've arranged for us to meet up with Liam and the lads for a few drinks later,' Dan protested.

'We'll do that later, but we'll go and have a drink or two on our own and listen to the band first.' She smiled, closing the bathroom door behind her.

Daniel stared at the floor. He normally loved Saturdays and Sundays, but ever since they had got engaged his favourite days had been swallowed up with organizing things for the wedding. Was it any wonder so many people were happy to stay the way they were, and refused to make it official?

As Amy let the hot water flow over her skin and face, and rubbed shampoo into her hair and scalp, she mentally ran through her to-do list. It would be great if Dan and she got a few more things done this weekend. She would get some sample invitations to show her family. They had made a rough guest list. They tried not to add names to it, but the list was literally growing by the day! God only knows how many people they'd end up with. Carmel Quinn had been in a bit of a huff when they'd told her last week that she could only bring sixty people to the wedding at most. It was up to her to choose who she and Eddie wanted to invite!

She had seen some photos of bridesmaid dresses in one of the Irish bridal magazines and was itching to go shopping with Ciara and Jess. Then she had all the bouquets to sort out and of course she had to order the cake.

She had intended cooking a nice dinner for Dan later this evening, but instead they could grab a pizza in town before they went to listen to the band.

The water coursed over her, and Amy let the bubbles run down her shoulders and back. She shrugged, trying to ease the knot of tension in her neck, and wished that her thoughts weren't quite so crowded with things to do and lists and plans for the wedding.

Chapter Twenty-three

'Where are you off to?' Paddy asked, as he pored over Saturday's *Irish Times*, which he had spread out on the kitchen table.

'I'm going looking for bridesmaid dresses with the girls,' explained Helen, who was already dressed and ready for today's big shopping expedition. Amy, organized as ever, had worked out quite an itinerary of places to go and emailed them to her, Jess and Ciara. 'Amy's meeting us in town.'

'It's a nightmare!' Fran had warned her. 'There'll be blood and tears before the day is out! Katie and Lisa and the two other bridesmaids we had, Tina and Mary, were like lunatics . . . it was so embarrassing in the shops. I kept trying to pretend that I wasn't with them. Most of the stuff is awful – you wouldn't put it on a cat – so you can't blame them for not wanting to try it on.'

Helen hoped Fran was exaggerating. She thought it would be fun to go shopping for the bridesmaid dresses with her two daughters and Jess, who was generally very affable and easy-going. For the past few months she had pored over bridal magazines like *Wedding Day*, *Bride*, *Beautiful Brides*, *Your Wedding* and *The Irish Bride*. She loved reading them and studying various styles of weddings. It had become almost an obsession, and she enjoyed looking at the photos and menus and reading about the different bridal dramas and problems.

She had showed photos of some dresses to Ciara, who had pretended not to look at them, and she had even caught Paddy glancing at the magazines, and been glad that he was showing some interest, despite his constant grousing about the wedding costs being way over budget.

'Ciara, get up!' she shouted up to her younger daughter. 'I told Amy and Jess we'd meet them in town in about half an hour.'

She immersed herself in the weekend magazine supplement as Ciara appeared in a long grey T-shirt and a pair of Simpsons' socks. Her black hair was in a tangle, her eyes still sleepy as she filled a bowl with yogurt and muesli.

'I'm meant to be studying,' complained Ciara.

'You can study tomorrow,' suggested Helen, worried as her younger daughter had been off-form over the past few weeks, and still looked washed-out.

'I wish that I didn't have to go!' Ciara sighed heavily. 'I don't want to be a crappy bridesmaid and wear a stupid dress.'

They had been over this umpteen times. 'That is

why Amy wants you and Jess to choose exactly what you'd like,' Helen said firmly, putting her mug in the dishwasher. 'She's keen you'll both be happy with your dresses.'

Ciara yawned.

'Ciara, I want you showered and ready to go in a few minutes,' Helen bossed, not brooking any more objections. 'The wedding is only four months away and you need to get a dress.'

When they got into town, Amy and Jess were already in the Powerscourt Centre, busy looking at the huge range of bridesmaid dresses on display.

Helen took a deep breath; there were literally hundreds of styles. Where should they begin?

'I think we should start with a style first, and then see about a colour,' suggested Amy, who was brimming over with enthusiasm.

'I'm not wearing pink,' Ciara said stubbornly.

'We'll see,' said Amy, ignoring her younger sister's objections.

'We can go long, mid-length or shorter and just above the knee,' Helen said.

'I haven't got great legs,' admitted Jess. 'I'm not really a dress type of person.'

'OK, then let's start with these.' Amy and a shop assistant picked out four floor-length dresses in various styles and colours, asking the two girls what size they were. Ciara was a standard size ten but Helen pitied poor Jess, who said she needed a sixteen, but ended up having to try on an eighteen. Amy sent the girls into the dressing rooms with the dresses.

'I'm not coming out in this,' shouted Ciara. 'It's awful.'

Peering in between the curtains, Amy and Helen had to agree the long mauve silk dress did nothing for her. It looked like a nightdress, swamping her skinny frame.

Jess looked marginally better, although the full length and material added pounds, and made her look even plumper.

'Try this gold empire style,' suggested Amy, passing them each another dress.

Emerging from the dressing rooms, Ciara and Jess burst out laughing in unison: they both looked pregnant.

'I don't think a long length does anything for the girls,' suggested Helen. 'Maybe they should try on something a bit simpler and less fussy.'

'I love the colour of this dress,' said Jess, appearing in an oyster-coloured silk knee-length with a lovely swing to the skirt. 'But the bust is far too small for me.'

Helen laughed, as Jess was literally bursting out of it.

The dress fitted Ciara perfectly but made her look as if she needed to go to the doctor for severe anaemia.

'The colour is barf!' she said, sticking her tongue out.

An hour later they had exhausted every possibility in

the shop and hadn't found a single dress that either girl liked or fitted into properly.

'Let's try Coast!' suggested Amy. 'They do great cocktail, dinner and party wear.'

Coast, up on Stephen's Green, was busy, but they bagged a sales assistant and a dressing room. Helen found a comfortable seat from which to survey the proceedings. There were racks of pretty dresses, she thought. They were bound to find something here.

Ciara liked a grey fitted cocktail dress with a tight skirt.

'I'd never fit into that,' pleaded Jess.

'Anyway, the two of you are not wearing grey, black or brown to my wedding,' insisted Amy, as she trawled through the displays.

'This pale pink with the floral hem is very popular for weddings this year,' said the assistant, 'and also lots of people are going for this red with the white tie bow for their bridesmaids.'

Amy didn't really want her bridesmaids dressed like everyone else, but agreed to the girls trying them on.

Ciara looked fabulous in the red, with her long mane of dark hair and pale skin. Even though you wouldn't have expected it to, it suited her Goth style.

Jess emerged from the dressing room puce with effort. 'I can't even get the zip up,' she explained. 'There's no give or stretch. There's no way I'll fit into the bloody thing.'

'That's the largest we have,' said the assistant loudly, embarrassing Jess even more.

'But I like the red,' said Ciara, getting stroppy.

'Well, you're not having it,' snapped Amy, putting the red dresses back.

'Why don't we take a break and all go for a coffee?' Helen said diplomatically, sensing the heated atmosphere and leading them over to the café upstairs overlooking the Green.

'Well, at least we know now,' she ventured, sipping her frothy cappuccino, 'that the girls don't suit floor-length and that we need a material with a bit of softness and give in it for Jess, nothing too tailored. There're bound to be loads of places that have lovely dresses.'

'One of the teachers in my school got married last August, and got her bridesmaid dresses in Monsoon. They looked lovely in the photos,' Jess ventured. 'It's only down the street, so maybe we could have a look there.'

The Monsoon dresses were beautiful – full of colour and detail and sparkling beadwork – but were a little bit too ethnic-looking to Amy's mind.

They tried the other high-street stores like Laura Ashley and Next and found nothing suitable. One sample dress in one of the big stores was so dirty-looking that Ciara refused to put it on. 'I'd get a disease from that!' she said, pointing out the grease and make-up and sweat-stains that spoiled the plum-coloured satin shift.

Footsore and weary, they soldiered on, crossing the

Liffey to Arnotts and Clerys, at both shops drawing a blank.

'Some of the dresses are so fussy,' complained Amy. 'Why can't someone design a simple bridesmaid-style dress that comes in two lengths and a huge range of colours that everyone would wear? It's not rocket science, surely!'

'This is torture,' complained Ciara, downing tools and sitting on a stool. Helen could see that Jess was about to join in the protest, too, so she suggested feeding the troops at the nearest fast-food outlet.

'We can go to the Food Emporium,' coaxed Amy. 'We can get everything we want there, and eat quickly, and get back out shopping.'

Thirty minutes later, revived, they set off again, this time deciding to hit three bridal boutiques in the city centre.

Pink, pink, and more pink and plum was all they seemed to offer.

'I'm not wearing any of them,' swore Ciara, as she pulled on a blossom-pink off-the-shoulder ballet-style dress.

'You used to have something like that when you were younger,' Helen remembered.

'We had matching ones,' Amy joked. 'I was about eleven or twelve and Ciara was four or five! We were like two ballerina girls!'

'I think the colour drains me,' said Jess, pirouetting in the mirror.

God give me patience, thought Helen. Her feet were killing her. She suspected she was getting a blister and she didn't know how much more of this trying on she could take. Anything that suited one bridesmaid seemed to look awful on the other, and the things the girls liked Amy didn't! They were never going to find dresses.

By late afternoon they were back up on Grafton Street searching in Brown Thomas to see if they could find something suitable. The dresses were certainly different, and Amy insisted on picking out a rich heavy satin emerald-green dress with a wide full skirt from the expensive Italian designer collection.

'Try these on,' she barked, ordering the girls to the dressing rooms.

Helen couldn't believe it when the dresses actually suited the girls, and fitted them both. The colour wasn't what they had been looking for, but with Ciara's black hair and pale skin it looked really well and it made Jess's fair hair and skin glow, and her brown eyes look sparkling and enormous.

'I like this,' Jess said, twirling around confidently. 'It's a real party dress.'

'I don't. I feel like I should be doing Irish dancing in it,' complained Ciara, doing a bit of a jig.

Helen tried not to laugh at her antics as Jess copied her.

'I'm too tired to try on any more!' Ciara said defiantly, pulling her jeans and boots back on. 'I'm going home, and I don't care what you say, Amy, I'm not putting on one more thing.'

'Please, Ciara!' begged Amy. 'The shops don't shut for another twenty minutes.'

'I told you, I'm going!'

'It is getting late,' Helen reminded Amy. 'We can always try somewhere else another day. Lots of people go out of Dublin, or you can order online. Anna's girls got their dresses for Sheena's wedding from some website in America, and they looked lovely.'

'But we don't even know what suits them or fits them or what colour to get!' said Amy, exasperated. 'So how could we possibly order something online?'

'It was only an idea!'

'Listen, Amy, I'm going to the cinema at seven thirty so I need to go now, too,' Jess said, grabbing her bag. 'Your mum is right. There are lots of other places to try. I think that there is a big wedding place in Swords and Malahide, and there are some great shops in Kildare. When Deirdre got married we got a dressmaker to make the bridesmaids' dresses.'

Amy couldn't hide her disappointment.

'Your dad will be wondering where I am.' Helen laughed, trying to defuse the awkward atmosphere. 'I promised I'd make a curry as Ronan and Krista are coming over.'

'We'll have to go looking for the dresses after work on Thursday, and then maybe again next Saturday,' Amy insisted doggedly.

'Sorry, but I've a teachers' meeting on Thursday night,' Jess apologized.

'And I'm working on Saturday,' said Ciara.

'Well then, we'll go the following week and I'll book the appointments.'

Ciara gave a groan of protest at the thought of even more shopping.

Jess threw her a look of sympathy as she said goodbye.

'Why don't you and Dan come to dinner, too?' Helen asked her elder daughter, noticing how tired and stressed she looked. 'There's lots and I have poppadums and chutney and the works. It would be nice, all of us together.'

'Mum, I've too much to do,' Amy replied fiercely. 'Dan and I are sorting out the guest list, which is a fecking nightmare, and going through the menus from the caterers.'

'Maybe you could do that afterwards or tomorrow?'

'Mum, do you realize how many things there are to do for a wedding? Dan is out three nights a week, and I work late one or two nights. I need to catch him at the weekends if we are ever going to get things planned properly.'

'Amy, love, it will all sort itself out. Honestly, weddings just come together,' she advised. 'You want to enjoy it. It's such a happy time for you both.'

'It won't happen without a lot of work and effort, Mum!' said Amy grimly.

Chapter Twenty-four

Jess yawned as she answered her mobile. She'd had an awful day at school, as two of her second class had puked in the classroom and had to be sent home. She prayed that it wasn't some kind of twenty-four-hour virus that would hit the rest of the class tomorrow, or she'd be dealing with bowls of vomit all day.

She'd done yard duty with Nell Casey. She'd spent the half-hour lunch break racing around after four ten-year-olds who were playing some kind of dare game. Nell, who was due to retire in the summer, pretended not to see the action when Jenny Fagan fell and almost split her skull jumping from the school wall. Jess had had to clean the gash and Steri-Strip it, and write an accident report for the headmistress.

Tonight all she wanted to do was to go home, have a bite of dinner, go for her hour-long walk and then settle down to watch *EastEnders* and that new *Catwalk Queen* programme, but instead Amy was dragging her all the way over to Swords, to some well-known bridal shop to look for a bridesmaid dress.

'I'll meet you there,' Jess said reluctantly.

Amy had poor Ciara in the fitting room trying on a hideous corset and skirt in a peach colour.

'It's vile,' shouted Ciara, flinging it back out over the door.

'They can get it in other colours,' Amy shouted back.

Helen O'Connor was sensibly keeping out of it, looking at a glossy wedding magazine that belonged to the shop.

Jess braced herself as Maggie, the lady assigned to help them, appeared with an armful of dresses for her to try on. Surprised by the huge range of styles, she slipped off her jeans and top.

The first would barely go down over her chest, and had sleeves so tight they cut under her arms. Why the hell hadn't Amy asked Aisling or Tara or one of her other skinny friends to be a bridesmaid? It would have made things a hell of a lot less complicated. Jess huffed and puffed her way out of the dress and dragged on the next one. This actually fitted. Hallelujah! It was a plum chiffon, with a soft round neckline and a great layered skirt that hid a multitude of sins. It was gorgeous and she loved it.

'Look, Amy,' she called out, delighted, spinning around.

The assistant went and got Ciara the same dress in a size ten and she dragged it on.

'Yuk,' she said, stepping out in front of the mirrors. 'I feel like a birthday cake or a lampshade in this, and the colour is disgusting.'

'But I really like it,' admitted Jess, catching herself at all angles in the mirror.

'What other colours does it come in?' pressed Amy.

'All the shades we have are on the rail here, but we can order different sizes in if they are out of stock,' said Maggie, the helpful assistant, passing Ciara another pretty chiffon dress with shoestring straps, a cinched-in waist, and a lovely full above-the-knee skirt in navy.

'She's not wearing that colour,' said Amy.

'Forget the colour, we are looking for a style of dress first,' Maggie explained patiently.

Ciara and Jess must have tried on at least fifteen dresses. Jess still liked the layered one, and tried it in another colour: a cool sage-green which looked totally different.

'Oh, Jess, that looks really well on you, too,' remarked Helen.

Amy frowned, looking doubtful.

'What a lot of brides do now,' Maggie suggested, 'if they have a problem getting a style to suit all their bridesmaids, is to buy different style dresses in the range but in the same colour and material. Here's a chart with the full colour range.'

Jess understood what she was getting at straight away. She grabbed a dress with a lovely short skirt and straight bodice in the same sage green colour she had on for Ciara to try.

The two of them laughed as they studied each other in the green, not sure it really worked.

'I think if you had three or four bridesmaids or more it would be a great idea,' said Amy. 'But with two it just highlights the differences between them.'

Little and bloody large! thought Jess.

The shop was beginning to fill up, and Maggie excused herself as she went to see to another bride and her mother.

'I just don't know what to do!' screamed Amy, panicking.

'Why don't you take the catalogue and all of you study it at home?' suggested Helen. 'The girls have tried on most of the styles, even if they are not in the colours that you like. We've less than an hour if you want to get over to that other place you had on your list before it closes.'

The massive Wedding Warehouse, with its proclaimed range of bridal dresses and accessories for every type of wedding, proved a massive disappointment. The bridesmaid dresses were mostly full-length with sequins and beads, in shiny materials and colours like baby pink and turquoise and red. 'Yuk', they all agreed, high-tailing it out of there.

As Jess drove home at 9.30, promising herself a lovely long hot soak in the bath, she couldn't believe that she had agreed to give up another precious Saturday to go and search for dresses again with Amy. She had to be mad!

Chapter Twenty-five

Helen was cooking a simple pasta dinner with tomatoes, basil and baby courgettes when Ciara walked in. Her long dark hair looked dirty, its heavy black dye giving it a sooty appearance. Her pale face was accentuated by black kohl eyeliner, and despite the warm weather she was wearing black leggings tucked into chunky black biker boots. Her fingernails were painted black, and every finger was covered in silver jewellery.

Helen bit her tongue and said nothing.

Ciara was a good kid and had gone straight to work from college. She was doing extra shifts trying to raise money for an eight-week trip to Thailand in the summer before she started her final year.

'I wish Amy would get off my case!' Ciara complained angrily, grabbing a glass of water and sitting down to pick at the bowl of salad on the table. 'She's turned into a Bridezilla! I don't see why I have to go and look at stupid dresses again this Saturday. I'm meant to be working, and Henry says that if I can't do my normal shift, then I have to do the Sunday plus a late night on Thursday. It's so unfair. I'm going to miss a big music session in Whale. I've helped set it up and I won't even get to see the band. Why does Amy have to ruin my life?'

'Why do you two fight so much?' asked Helen, weary with it all.

'Because Amy wants me to look like a nerd for her wedding, that's why. I told her I didn't want to be a bridesmaid!' Ciara said. 'She says that I have to, because I'm her sister. You saw the dresses, Mum. They're awful. If Amy thinks I'm going to wear a vile pink dress for her wedding she can think again!'

'Ciara, she's just trying to find a bridesmaid dress that both of you like. Most brides just choose a dress and tell all their bridesmaids that's what they have to wear. When your dad and I were at your Cousin Shay's wedding last July in Cork, the bridesmaids had hideous brown dresses. No way was Joanne, the bride, having other girls upstage her. So you don't realize how good Amy is to let you and Jess have your pick.'

'I'm not wearing any of them. They're not my style.'

'Is it too much for Amy to ask her only sister to support her on her wedding day?' Helen said angrily. 'To tidy herself up and wear a pretty dress for a few hours instead of jeans or leggings and biker boots?'

Ciara refused to answer. Instead she fiddled with her phone, pretending to read a text. Eventually she met her mother's gaze. 'Mum, you know how much I hate dressing up and putting on fake tan like all the other girls, and wearing high heels and pretending to be someone that I'm not. Why should I do it just because my sister is getting married?'

'It is only one day,' reminded Helen sadly. 'One special family day! But if it is going against your principles to be nice and kind and supportive of your sister for a single day – then maybe you are right and it is better if you withdraw from being a bridesmaid. Jess is a good friend, and Amy will have her as her bridesmaid, and maybe one of the other girls will step in for you. Amy will be disappointed and very hurt, so you need to think about it, Ciara. You can be a bridesmaid or you can just be a guest like lots of other people at your sister's wedding. But I am telling you, you will not go to the wedding dressed like you are attending some grunge festival! Do you hear me?'

Ciara stormed out of the kitchen and off upstairs. Her door banged shut and the noise of some God-awful music filled the house.

Helen wondered how two sisters could be so different. The same parents, the same upbringing and education, and yet Amy and Ciara were absolute opposites. No one would think they were related, let alone sisters! They'd sparked off each other ever since they were little, Ronan acting as an easy-going buffer between the two of them. Sometimes she thought that Ciara, instead of trying to copy her big sibling, like most little sisters did, had decided just to be totally different! Helen had grown up with three brothers, and although they were great fun and had always been there for her, she had longed for a sister, dreamed of having one. She envied her women friends who were so connected with theirs. And here were her girls, despite being sisters, totally at odds with each other – over, of all things, a dress!

Poor Barney had been skulking under the kitchen table during the row. He looked up at her, ever hopeful of a walk. She turned off the cooker. She wasn't hungry now, she'd eat later. She had to get away from the noise upstairs. Helen clipped on the dog's lead, slipped on her walking shoes and grabbed her keys. An hour's walk in the fresh air would calm her down and hopefully do them both good.

'Come on, fellah, let's get out of here!' she said.

Chapter Twenty-six

Amy was exhausted and had to drag herself out of bed on Saturday morning. She had been to the launch of a new vodka and cranberry drink they were promoting last night, and everyone had stayed on in Krystle afterwards. She had fallen into a taxi at two thirty and crept into the apartment.

Dan was in a bit of a mood with her and had got up early and gone for a jog, as he was in training for a charity marathon he was undertaking in three weeks' time. Sweaty in his tracksuit, he sat in the kitchen, making breakfast.

'Do you want some?' he asked as he started to put some bacon on to cook.

'No, I'm meeting Ciara and Jess and Mum in half an hour,' Amy explained. 'I've no time for a big breakfast this morning.'

Grabbing a slice of toast and some juice, she raced to get ready.

'Why won't you have a proper Saturday breakfast

with me?' he complained. 'Text them and tell them you'll meet them later.'

Amy stopped for a second, torn, but thinking of the task ahead made her resolute.

'Dan, I've got to go. You've no idea what it's like trying to get bridesmaid dresses to suit two very different people. Mum phoned last night and said Ciara was in a right strop about it. God, I don't know how girls that have five or six bridesmaids manage! You guys are lucky: you just go into Blacktie and rent a suit for the day and pick out the colour tie you want!'

'Sure!' Dan said, gulping down a huge glass of fresh orange juice.

Amy searched around the room for her pink Filofax, and shoved it into her leather shoulder bag. She didn't know what she'd do if she lost it.

'See you later!' she called, grabbing her keys.

'Don't forget Liam and that new girl he's dating, Jade, and Jeremy and Grace are coming here for supper tonight,' Dan reminded her. 'I told them to be here around eight.'

'Shit! I totally forgot,' Amy said, suddenly remembering the long-arranged meal. With so much else on her mind, tonight's dinner had slipped from her radar.

'Dan, would you mind giving the place a hoover?' she pleaded. 'And do you think you could organize the food?'

'I'm watching a rugby match down in the club this afternoon with the lads,' he said. 'Why can't you do it?'

'I told you, I'm meeting the others again to look for dresses. You know what a nightmare that is. Can you not just go down to the supermarket before you go to the match and get some chicken and a few bottles of wine and some beer? You could make that green Thai chicken dish with noodles. I'll make a nice salad and pick up some kind of tart thing in town for dessert.'

'OK, OK,' he reluctantly agreed, burying his head in the Saturday sports section of the paper.

Amy knew it wasn't fair, and that he was annoyed she hadn't remembered and organized things. But Dan was a good cook, and often surprised her with new dishes. He was much more adventurous in his cuisine than she was.

'Thanks,' she said, rushing over to kiss him good-bye.

'Where's Mum?' asked Amy when she spotted Ciara walking across from the bus stop on Dawson Street on her own.

'I don't know, I was at a party last night so I stayed at a friend's house. But I'm sure Mum will be along soon.' Ciara yawned, not mentioning the row Helen had told Amy about.

Ciara was hungover, looked like the wreck of the *Hesperus*, and admitted she had been out till nearly four in the morning. She made it quite clear that she thought she should be back in bed instead of parading around bridal boutiques.

'We'd all like to be back in bed,' muttered Amy, feeling decidedly rough herself.

Jess arrived a few minutes late and was yawning, too.

'Sorry, but I stayed up late watching *Sleepless in Seattle*. I love that movie, but why they have to show it at one o'clock in the morning is beyond me!'

'OK, girls, let's get some dresses!' yelled Amy, trying to be positive. 'There're two wedding shops close by. I had a look at them at lunchtime yesterday.'

They started off in Trousseau, a beautiful French wedding shop off Wicklow Street; it carried a small range of dresses for bridesmaids and flower girls that coordinated with its pretty bridal dresses and accessories.

'The sizes are all French, too, and really tiny,' worried Jess as Amy passed her an apple-green dress with a white bow. Ciara disappeared behind the strawberry-printed curtain and pulled on her one.

'This isn't too bad,' she said, standing in front of the dressing room in her bare feet. 'I suppose it's kind of funky.'

Amy actually liked it, too, and held her breath as Jess appeared in her one.

'It's tiny, Amy,' protested Jess, all hot and flustered, the dress stretched to its limit on her curvy figure. 'I know it's lovely but I feel I'm going to explode in it.'

Amy, looking at her friend, who resembled a big green apple with a white ribbon tied around her middle, had to reluctantly agree. They went to try on another dress . . .

Helen texted to find out where they were and appeared a few minutes later.

'Sorry I'm late,' she apologized, 'but there was fierce traffic in Donnybrook on the way in. Ciara OK?'

'She's a bit hungover but at least she turned up,' said Amy.

Helen and Amy watched as the girls stepped out in another dress Amy liked: a loose-fitting rose top with a tiered, flouncy skirt.

'Boring,' said Ciara loudly. It looked anaemic on Ciara and not much better on Jess.

God, is this torture never to end? thought Amy. We'll never find anything that suits them both. She'd been at plenty of weddings over the past three years where the bridesmaids had certainly not looked their best, and had always put it down to a deliberate ploy by the bride not to be outshone. But now, seeing the sheer impossibility of finding something that looked good on both her sister and her best friend, and beginning to reach desperation point, Amy could totally understand the dilemma. Juliet's, the more traditional bridal shop down the street, had only very formal bridal wear, with stiff, shiny taffeta dresses and long jewel-coloured silk ones with halter necks or corset tops.

'There must be somewhere else we can try,' begged Jess, desperation in her voice.

'I feel awful,' Ciara said, running into the newsagent's to buy a litre bottle of water.

Disaster, thought Amy, having visions of dragging the girls to London or Belfast if they didn't find something soon.

They were walking back up South William Street when Amy suddenly remembered Belle. It wasn't a wedding shop, but it did a great line in party and cocktail wear, and last year she had got an amazing black dress there to wear at a big charity ball that Dan's firm was sponsoring.

'What about trying here?' she suggested.

Ciara and Jess's faces suddenly brightened up as they pushed in the door of the shop.

'You two see if there is anything you like,' Amy said, collapsing on the sofa beside her mother.

Ciara strode off in one direction while Jess looked at the designer wear.

Amy resisted the urge to interfere, and couldn't believe it when the two of them started to go around the rails together looking at stuff.

'I'm going to try these on, Jess,' called her sister.

'Are they together?' asked the model-like blonde assistant.

'Yes, we're trying to find dresses for a wedding.'

'Well, I have just got a new range of evening wear in from Milan, and some fresh stock from two young designers I carry only came in yesterday. It's literally just gone out on the floor.'

'You own the place?'

'Yes.' Mia Anderson smiled and introduced herself. 'I tend to stock the kind of things I like to buy, and hope the customers will like them, too.'

Amy held her breath as Ciara and Jess flitted in and out of the small fitting room with piles of dresses. Dear God, she thought, please let them find something that suits both of them!

Mia Anderson was endlessly patient, and Amy couldn't believe it when she disappeared to the stockroom and reappeared with even more dresses over her arm for Jess and Ciara. Jess came out wearing a vivid fuchsia-coloured cocktail dress. With a corset-style top cinching in to a narrow waist and a classic knee-length skirt in a satin material it showed off her curves while skimming her figure. The shape was perfect on her.

'Ciara, will you try on that style too?' pleaded Amy, not believing it when Ciara appeared in the same dress looking equally good.

'Oh, that dress is gorgeous on you both.' Helen O'Connor beamed.

'I love it!' Jess enthused. 'When I saw it on the hanger I didn't think it was something I would even put on me but it makes me feel pretty and sexy and feminine.'

Ciara was less enthusiastic. 'OK, it's a great shape and style and I like the material but I hate this colour,' she said stubbornly. 'I told you that I'm not wearing pink.'

'But I love the dresses,' Amy said. 'They are the first

ones I've seen that look good on both of you. Honestly, Ciara, you know they do!'

Ciara stood there, pouting.

'Would you like to try them in another colour?' asked Mia quietly. 'They come in a purple shade. Do you want to see what it looks like?'

Amy held her breath as Jess disappeared back into the fitting room. Reappearing a few minutes later wearing the same dress in purple, Jess looked absolutely gorgeous. The bright crocus colour made her eyes sparkle and showed off her skin tones and hair. The dress was so stylish and elegant, and hit her legs and waist and figure in exactly the right spot.

'Is there one for Ciara?' Amy asked, worried.

'There's none on the rails in her size but I'll check the stockroom again,' offered Mia, disappearing.

Amy tried not to get her hopes up.

'I found one,' Mia called out a few minutes later. Laughing, she passed the dress in to Ciara.

Ciara emerged from behind the curtain and stood in the centre of the shop. With her long dark hair and slim figure the dress looked amazing. The colour was such a contrast from the pink. It looked edgy and different on Ciara, and emphasized her long legs and tiny waist.

'Wow!' said Amy. 'You look great.'

'Walk up and down!' ordered Helen O'Connor. 'I want to see what you will both look like going up the aisle in those dresses.'

Amy watched in disbelief as her two bridesmaids

walked in perfect unison in the matching dresses. They looked gorgeous and slightly edgy. It wasn't the usual boring bridesmaid look.

'Those dresses are perfect.' Amy watched as they paraded towards the mirror, seeing the impact the two dresses were making. 'The whole thing works! You both look stunning.'

'Beautiful,' added Helen O'Connor.

'I feel great in this dress.' Jess beamed. 'I love it.'

'I told you I wasn't wearing pink,' said Ciara smugly.

'Shut up!' said Amy and Helen and Jess in unison. 'We're getting these dresses!'

'I can't believe we've finally found "the dresses",' Amy laughed as they left the shop. 'I thought we'd have to go to the moon to get them!'

Jess, to her surprise, had insisted on paying for her own bridesmaid dress, saying that she loved it so much that she would have gone and bought it anyway.

'I'd love a toasted sandwich,' said Ciara. 'I'm starving after all that bloody trying on.'

'Me, too,' agreed Amy, conscious suddenly of her stomach rumbling.

The four of them turned into Duke Street, and headed straight for Davy Byrnes pub. Amy was relieved that she could mentally cross another thing off her wedding list as they sat down and ordered soup and sandwiches. She'd swing by the Avoca Shop on her way home and buy a tart or cake for dessert, and some of Dan's favourite chocolate brownies.

'Mum, you will be the next one getting an outfit,' joked Amy. 'Are you going to wear a hat or not for the wedding?'

Helen O'Connor threw her eyes up to heaven, hoping that finding a Mother of the Bride outfit would prove a little bit easier and a whole lot less stressful . . .

Chapter Twenty-seven

Paddy O'Connor cooked up a load of sausages and potato bread for himself, lardering on the butter since Helen wasn't around to admonish him . . .

The women of the house were gone mad, and seemed to spend their whole time shopping for some sort of wedding thing or another. Helen had the place full of bridal magazines, and the notice board in the kitchen was full of clippings about flower arrangements and photographers and musicians. He was demented with it. Now here she was, gone off shopping again!

Every time they went out Helen prattled on about the wedding as if she had lost her ability to talk about anything else. Money was being splashed around left, right and centre, and he had already had to go to Mick Dunne, his bank manager, to get him to agree to an overdraft just in case the wedding bills ate up all the money they had allotted. When they had started saving for the girls' weddings they had never envisaged the cost being so enormous. Dan Quinn was a generous type of young man, and had offered to pay his fair share towards it, but Paddy knew that Amy and he were saving to buy a house. A home for the young couple was more important than a big day out, but he would accept the groom paying for a few things like the car and the church flowers and some other expenses, and maybe putting money towards the drinks bill.

It only seemed like yesterday since Helen and he had got married with barely the arse in their trousers, as his father would say. They had both worked long and hard to build a home and a good life for their family, and he had no regrets. There had been no fancy cars or holidays or luxuries for years, but they had, with hard work, managed to move from a small three-bed semi-detached in Dundrum to a new house in a small estate in Blackrock long before the prices had gone through the roof and property madness had taken hold of the nation. Their three kids had gone to good local schools and done well going to college and getting good jobs. They weren't out of the woods yet with young Ciara, but she was a good student and he knew that she would make them as proud as Amy and Ronan had.

The past two years had been tough, with work harder to come by. Still, O'Connor's were holding their heads above water when lots of businesses were closing down, and letting staff go. He had planned to retire in another few years, improve his golf game, and take off with Helen to see the world, going to the sun for a few weeks in the winter, but now he would likely have to keep working for longer than he'd planned to boost his pension.

'Paddy, I'm home.'

'She's back,' he said to Barney, who was sitting at his feet.

'We got the dresses.' Helen was all excited as she opened the bag and showed him the dress she had bought for Ciara. 'Isn't the colour lovely?'

It was, but it had cost a small fortune. Still, he could see Helen was relieved that another piece of the wedding plan had finally fallen into place.

'Do you fancy a cup of tea?' he offered, sticking on the kettle.

'That would be great.' She smiled. 'I'm jaded from walking around the shops, but at least it was all worth it. Paddy, everything is just coming together, and it's going to be such a lovely day.'

'Of course it will,' he said, getting some more milk from the fridge. 'Where are the girls?'

'Amy and Dan are having friends in for dinner to-night, so she's gone home to help organize things, and Ciara disappeared off to see some friend of hers. She said not to expect her home.'

'Then what about the two of us get a bite to eat down in Flanagan's later, save you cooking?' he suggested. 'Tom and Fran might join us.'

'I'll phone Fran and ask her,' Helen said, picking up the phone and settling down in a chair for a chat with her best friend.

Paddy sighed. Helen would give Fran a blow-by-blow account of the day's shopping and then, when they went out, spend most of the night talking about it, too. Roll on the end of June when the wedding and all the wedding talk would be finished with.

Chapter Twenty-eight

Amy and Dan had been arguing half the night over the stupid guest list, Amy insisting that she wanted to invite about a dozen of her closest school friends to her wedding.

'That means twenty-four people,' said Dan ominously. 'If we are having one hundred people between us you have used up almost a quarter of the quota on your school friends, some of whom you haven't seen for years. You have to cut them back.'

'They are the girls who shared the most important time in my life and were always there for me,' she reasoned. 'Not like your seven surf buddies, who will probably bring a partner each. You've only got to know them in the past three years, and only see them sporadically.'

'They are my friends,' he shouted. 'I'm not keeping a clock on how long I've known them! You know they are the guys I hang out with!'

'I started school with some of those girls!'

'You want to have people from college and work,

too!' he kept on. 'There's Jilly. She didn't invite you to her wedding! And Norah; you are always giving out about Norah.'

'Everyone gives out about their boss, but that doesn't mean that they don't want them to be there on their big day.'

'Well, I'm not inviting my boss or the partners from my firm.'

'There are at least fifty partners in your firm,' Amy retorted, getting annoyed with him.

It was stupid, because they were both sociable and had lots of friends from different parts of their lives. It was just whittling them down to the final few that was causing the rifts.

'Why have you put Laura on the list?' Amy went on.

'Laura and I have been friends since I was five years old.'

'She's an ex-girlfriend.'

'We were only fourteen when we went out!' Dan protested. 'Don't be so stupid, Amy! I thought you liked Laura?'

'I do,' she grudgingly admitted. Blonde, beautiful Laura O'Reilly was a next-door neighbour of the Quinns, and had been around, floating in and out of Dan's life, for years. 'But she's an ex.'

'Look, my parents will invite the O'Reillys, so I feel I should invite her, too,' he explained logically.

Amy sighed. She had a guest list file set up on her laptop, but no matter how many times she went over and over it with Dan they just couldn't seem to reach an agreement on all the names. Apparently Carmel Quinn was in a fury about the numbers she'd been given, and Amy's mum and dad – with so many brothers and sisters – were finding it really hard to decide which of the cousins they should invite. The whole thing was a nightmare, and Amy just wished they could make some sort of decision. Dan felt that their friends who were in pretty permanent relationships should be allowed to bring their partners, but that others – who were just on and off dating or seeing someone – should come on their own. It would cause ructions, but it probably was the only solution.

Dan was in a bad mood the next morning, and barely spoke to her when they were getting ready for work. She kept silent, too. They seemed to be constantly fighting about 'the wedding' or 'the guest list' or something stupid! Amy had never seen Dan in such bad form since they'd met and hoped his grumpy mood would blow over.

Norah was out of the office for most of the day, so Amy managed to get a chance to run down through all the names again. She phoned Jess and Sarah to see what they thought about it.

'I wouldn't expect you to ask my boyfriend if I was just dating someone between now and the wedding,' Jess declared. 'And I'm sure most of the girls will understand.'

187

'We invited a few friends with the people they were dating to our wedding,' admitted Sarah. 'We all knew they wouldn't last, and they all broke up literally a few weeks later. Do you remember Fiona and Terry? They broke up two days after! It was such a waste of an invite, as there were lots of other people we would have loved to ask!'

Realizing Dan was right, Amy took a few more names off their list. Also, seven of her school friends coming to the wedding was enough; apart from Faye, who lived in America now, they were the ones she saw the whole time. She managed to cull a few more people and emailed the changes to Dan immediately, before she could change her mind.

'Good work,' he emailed back. She reminded him they had an appointment that evening with a wedding film company in Leeson Street. She had searched the internet and they seemed to be one of the best. It cost a fortune to have a wedding filmed, but she wanted a memento to keep for the rest of their lives.

Dan was bored as they sat watching bits of other couples' wedding DVDs. Gerry Henderson explained how he worked and what equipment he used and where he set up his cameras.

'We have two in the church, as it makes it easier to get everything on film.'

'And more expensive,' muttered Dan, studying the price list.

'We are not shooting a movie where we can say "take one, take two",' explained Gerry. 'So we have only the one chance to capture something on film, whether it is the two of you walking down the aisle, or greeting your friends, or putting rings on each other's fingers.' Amy could understand it, but Dan was still sceptical, given the costs involved.

'We are very heavily booked already,' pressed Gerry. 'As your wedding is only three months away we would need to put it in our books now.'

'Dan, we need to choose a photographer, too,' Amy said, as they walked out, having failed to decide whether to use Gerry or not. 'Most of them are open on a Saturday. There's one in Dalkey and one in Sandycove, and Mum said the one who did Fran's daughter Katie's wedding was great and pretty reasonable. He's up in Dundrum.'

'I'm busy next Saturday,' Dan said obstinately 'I've got a tear in my wetsuit so I need to buy a new one. I'll go out to Wind and Wave in Monkstown to try and get one there. Afterwards I'm meeting the lads in Gleeson's for lunch and to watch the big Manchester United match.'

Amy bit her tongue. He'd be gone for the whole day! She was about to explode at him, because he seemed to think that he was still single . . . OK, technically he was, but he should be equally involved in organizing the wedding.

'Look, I'll come to the marine shop with you,' she said stubbornly, 'then we can run out quickly to Dalkey and Sandycove to have a look at the photographers.

I'll call over to Mum's on Saturday, too, and ask Fran if I can have a look at Katie's wedding album while you're watching the match, and hopefully then we can decide.'

'Amy, why can't you just choose a photographer and bloody book him!' Dan said, totally uninterested. 'I don't give a rat's ass!'

'Well, I do,' she said stubbornly, not wanting to let him off the hook.

Chapter Twenty-nine

Helen pulled her car up outside Bibi Kennedy's large house. She'd known Bibi for years and was delighted when Bibi had offered to make Amy's wedding cake.

'Helen, you know me, I love making cakes for my friends,' Bibi had insisted, when Helen and Paddy had been round in Bibi's house having dinner a few nights after the engagement.

'Are you sure she doesn't mind making my cake?' asked Amy as they stood at the door of the big red-brick house in Donnybrook.

'No,' smiled Helen, 'she says consider it a wedding gift.'

'Amy, it's lovely to see you,' Bibi said, as she came out and welcomed them. 'Come in and tell me all about your wedding.' She smiled, leading them through the long hall to her huge sunny kitchen overlooking an amazing garden. 'I love weddings and hearing all about them.'

Helen smiled back. Some women played golf, some

191

women played tennis or spent their time trawling around the shops or sweating it out in the gym, but Bibi's passion was for cake-making and icing! Helen had never met anyone who enjoyed their hobby as much as Bibi did. She was constantly trying out new recipes, challenging herself with different designs and coming up with fresh ideas and concepts for cakes. There was no one like her for making a special cake, a one-off original. To have a Bibi Kennedy cake for your wedding was like having a one-off designer dress!

Bibi had three fruit cakes baking in the oven of her large Aga, and the smell and the warmth of her kitchen reminded Helen of Christmas, when her mother used to turn out cakes and pies and puddings.

'Honestly, I don't know how you get the time to bake,' sighed Helen, enviously. She avoided it like the plague, and only made cakes for birthdays. Bibi was one of the busiest people she knew: always fund-raising for charities and entertaining in her huge house as well as looking after her kids and a load of grandchildren – and she made it all seem easy.

'Ask a busy person.' Bibi smiled. 'We tend to get things done.'

Helen agreed with her on that. She herself was rushed off her feet at the moment, between going back and forwards to her mother's and helping Amy with the wedding.

'What date are you getting married on, Amy?' Bibi asked.

'Saturday the sixth of June, and the wedding is down in Castle Gregory.'

'Lovely!' Bibi smiled again. 'Sean and I were at a wedding there about two years ago, and it was wonderful. Have you looked at any cakes, or got any ideas about what you'd like?'

'I looked in one or two shops: Les Gâteaux and the cake shop in Rathgar, to see the kind of thing that they do.'

'Did you see a design you like?' quizzed Bibi as she made a big pot of tea and they all sat down at the large kitchen table. 'Are you going to go for a very traditional cake, or do you want something a bit different?'

'I suppose traditional,' said Amy. 'But really, I'm not sure what I want.'

'Well, first off, you have to decide what cake base you want,' Bibi explained. 'For the cake itself, do you want a traditional fruit cake like those ones in the oven, or a chocolate biscuit cake, or a Madeira-type sponge? Also you have to consider if the cake is just for the wedding or if you intend to hold on to a small tier of it for a christening cake, which some couples like to do. The fruit is best for that.'

'We haven't thought that far!' Amy giggled. Dan and she had talked about kids and both were looking forward to having a family, but as to saving a layer of cake for the christening – that was a just a step too far!

'Bibi, what do people usually go for?' Helen asked, curious.

'The fruit cake is obviously the most traditional, but I find a lot of brides are going for the chocolate biscuit cake now, as their friends all love chocolate and it's almost like a dessert. Sometimes I mix them, depending on how many layers there are.'

'So we could have a tier of each?'

'Yes, if you want to.' Bibi laughed.

'The chocolate biscuit sounds yummy.'

'Do you want to try a bit?'

In a few minutes fingers of fruit cake, chocolate biscuit cake and sponge all appeared on a pretty floral plate.

'Go on, try them!' urged Bibi, as she poured the tea.

Helen loved the fruit cake, but she knew the chocolate would be Amy's favourite, as she was a total chocaholic.

'Oh my God! We have to get this one, Mum.'

'I thought you'd like it!' Bibi said, passing Amy another slice. 'Now, let me get my album and show you photos of some of the cakes that I've made.'

Helen was astounded. She'd seen some of the magnificent creations Bibi had produced for friends' weddings and anniversaries, but really had no idea of the impressive range of cakes her friend had created.

'I also do a variety of icings,' explained Bibi, as they looked at the album. 'There is the traditional white icing with marzipan, or a rich butter-cream or a kind of American frosting.'

The decorative icing work was intricate and time-consuming, and Bibi showed them sixty iced roses that she was making for a cake, with each individual petal piped and left to dry before the tiny rose was constructed and put in place.

'So much work goes into it!' said Helen, studying the photos, astounded by the delicacy of Bibi's work, and the patience needed to decorate the cakes.

Amy liked the pale-pink icing covered in roses, and another cake with a design of butterflies on every tier. There was also a stunning five-tier creation with a creamy-coloured icing made to look like old lace.

Helen loved the simple white cake with white iced flowers tumbling down the side of it.

'Bit plain!' Amy ventured.

They both liked a cake iced with a wickerwork pattern, and with a few daisies scattered around its tiers.

Bibi went through the book with them. As well as wedding cakes, there were cakes for other occasions. There was a cake wrapped like a present, with a stiff iced bow; a layered white house with a yellow veranda and flowers growing around the door.

'That was for a new home,' Bibi said.

There were round cakes and square ones. A cake edged in gold, a cake that looked like a pretty hat, a wonderful one like a hot-air balloon, another that was a knitting box full of multicoloured wool.

'My Aunt Gen loves to knit,' explained Bibi.

Amy adored a cake with blue icing and little surfboards and a marzipan figure on a board on top which reminded her of Dan.

'That was for my nephew's twenty-first. He had a surf-theme party.'

As they studied the photos they agreed that a cake with three tiers was plenty, and that they liked the option of having mixed tiers.

'But the biggest one has to be the chocolate,' insisted Amy. 'That's the one my friends will prefer!'

Mixing the layers was a good idea, as there would also be a tier of the light fruit cake and the top would be a sponge.

Now that was decided, choosing the design was next. Bibi showed them Celtic designs, and intricate lacy patterns. There were iced balloons, trailing ivy, twisting leaf stems, tight rosebuds, hydrangea flowers, daisies and daffodils – one couple had even had a little trail of sheep.

'The husband is a farmer.' Bibi giggled.

'It's so hard to choose.' Amy felt totally indecisive as she leafed through the book, studying all Bibi's amazing cakes.

'Some brides go with the theme of the wedding or their flowers or the colour of the bridesmaids' dresses,' Bibi suggested.

'I am going to carry roses and the bridesmaids are wearing purple.'

'Well, maybe not purple roses!' Bibi flicked the pages of the book. 'What about something like this? A layer of pink roses, with trails of leaves, if that's what you'd like.'

Amy studied a cake which was studded with pretty iced roses, with thin wisps of green leaves. Another cake she liked was covered in a pale pink icing with a neat ring of iced white roses.

'I like the roses, but I'd like them to be pink and maybe loosely tumbling down one side of the cake.'

'Bibi, can you do the roses in a different colour?' asked Helen.

'I'll do whatever colour Amy wants.' Bibi smiled.

'Oh, it's going to be lovely.' Amy was breathless with excitement, imagining their wedding cake covered in roses and Dan and herself cutting the first slice.

'I'm writing that in for June,' said Bibi. 'My cakes are all freshly made and it will be ready just before the wedding.'

'Oh, that sounds wonderful,' Helen said, thanking Bibi. 'It makes it so much more personal having one of your cakes.'

'Well, I'm delighted to be making it. I love family weddings, with all the fuss and fun and glamour! What colour outfit are you wearing, Helen?'

'I haven't found anything yet,' she admitted. 'I have been looking . . .'

'You haven't got your outfit yet, and you're the Mother of the Bride!' Bibi scolded. 'Honestly, Helen, you need to get your skates on. Most of the shops and their designer departments carry only one or two of the kind of thing you'd want to wear to a daughter's wedding, and, I'm telling you, they are snapped up very fast.'

'Bibi, don't tell me that!' she said, vowing to drag Fran shopping with her next week.

'Helen, I'll see you in Maeve's house next weekend. I believe we're all having dinner.'

'It should be fun,' smiled Helen, grabbing her handbag.

'Thanks so much, Bibi. We really appreciate you making the cake,' said Amy, her eyes shining as they got up to leave.

'Mum, thanks so much for helping me with everything,' said Amy as they drove home. 'I don't know what I'd do without you, as Dan has no interest in half the things I'm trying to organize. It's as if "the wedding" doesn't matter to him!'

'I'm sure that's not true.' Helen laughed. 'Dan's like most men, and may not be interested in flowers and cakes and dresses, but I'm sure his heart is very much where it is meant to be, planning for your future together. When your dad and I got married it was all very simple and no fuss; all your dad cared about was trying to get us a roof over our heads, or we'd have ended up living with your granny and granddad, or down in Cork with his parents, which wouldn't have been much fun! He hadn't a clue about what was going on with the wedding plans, but was doing everything he could so we would get a mortgage and buy our first house.'

'I suppose you're right.' Amy sighed.

'Let's call in and surprise Mum,' Helen suggested, as

they were only a few minutes' drive from Willow Grove. 'She'll be dying to hear all your news.'

Helen glanced over at Amy, trying to shake off the slight concern that her daughter's remarks had raised. Things were going fine between Amy and Dan, the wedding was only about three months away, and Amy was probably just a bit tired and excited with it all.

Chapter Thirty

Jess had hopped on the Luas and got off at Stephen's Green. She was meeting Amy for dinner later in Carluccio's and had no intention of driving. One of the main joys of teaching was the holidays, and she had spent all morning repainting her bathroom, which had been a nasty shade of turquoise and was now a lovely pale French grey. It perfectly showed off the old-fashioned white bathroom ware and silver taps. She would love to install a fancy power shower and new tiles, but that would have to wait until next year, as her budget was blown, and there was just so much work to do in the old cottage.

She had treated herself to a cut and a blow-dry and then spent an hour shopping on Grafton Street for something new to wear. Why everyone had to make you feel a freak because you wore a size sixteen or eighteen was beyond her! It was bizarre that all the shops had mostly the same clothes in the same small sizes, and anyone even a fraction larger was frowned on. She had found a great-fitting purple skirt, which showed off her long legs, and although it was a little tight in the waist had impulsively bought it. She was dieting like mad, and hopefully in another month or six weeks it would be perfect on her. Glancing at her phone she realized the time, and headed for the restaurant, where she grabbed a table near the window.

'Hey, your hair looks great!' Amy enthused, noticing the minute she saw her. 'You should keep it that length for the wedding.'

'Thanks.' Jess's hair, when it was long, went wavy – and not romantically, but in a crazy, standing-on-end way that made her look like she hadn't touched a hair-brush.

'You look great yourself.'

Amy always looked beautiful, and Jess noticed enviously her figure-tight black trousers worn with high-heeled fitted boots and a simple black top with a classic white shirt underneath.

'We were crazy busy in the office all day, so I've just come straight from work. We are putting in a tender for a big new client account and Norah and I were working on it.'

They ordered wine and decided to share a plate of antipasti, both opting for a pasta main course. Jess was tempted by the rich creamy pasta and chicken special but, thinking of her new skirt and being a bridesmaid, opted for the lower-calorie tomato and basil tagliatelle served with a salad.

'Did I tell you about the invitations that I am look-ing at?' Amy asked, producing a few samples from her handbag and passing them to her. 'The first three are the ones I like best. Which do you prefer?'

Jess studied the three cards. One was plain and sim-ple, classic black and white on expensive gold-edged card. The second had a raised design with Amy and Dan's initials entwined, and the last had a picture of a couple in silhouette, which was kind of different.

'I like the last one.' She smiled.

'That's my favourite, too.' Amy beamed. 'But what do you think of these font styles and sizes?'

She passed Jess a sheaf of pages with the same wedding invitation printed in a variety of ways: curly writing, Celtic style, looking like it was handwritten, Times New Roman.

'I wouldn't have a clue,' Jess admitted, passing the samples back to Amy.

'I'm torn between types five and eight,' mused her friend, putting them back into her big handbag. 'And I'm trying to decide on a colour scheme for the tables and whether we should put a touch of that on the invita-tions, too.'

Jess shrugged and took some Parma ham and asparagus. It was to die for.

'Honestly, there is so much to do I can understand why some brides hire wedding planners to do it all for them,' Amy murmured, taking a few olives.

Jess remembered her older sisters' weddings, which

seemed just to have happened. Deirdre's had been a big bash held in the local hotel, with every cousin and auntie and uncle imaginable. She herself had been forced to wear an awful pale-pink dress with a big bow at the back. She'd looked like a marshmallow. Her Uncle Jim had got so drunk he had fallen and broken his ankle, and her Auntie Patsy had screamed at her husband Tony about being unfaithful for half an hour just before the bride and groom cut the cake. And then everyone had cried and laughed and sung and danced till all hours of the morning, and her mam had taken to her bed for four days once Deirdre and Shay had gone on their honeymoon.

Her sister Ava had got married only three years ago, and had opted for a wedding in Spain with about sixty guests in a hotel on the beach in Marbella. The photos had been amazing, and they had spent four days in the sun celebrating.

'Are you listening, Jess?' reminded Amy, dangling paper serviettes in front of her. 'Which one?'

Over the next few hours all Amy talked about was the wedding!

The flowers . . .

The music . . .

The band . . .

The cake . . .

The speeches . . .

Naming tables . . .

Table places . . .

Jess tried to pretend she was interested, but when Amy began to discuss the colours on the place name-cards she frantically tried to change the conversation. However, unrelenting, Amy kept on and on . . .

Jess ordered a carafe of wine. She needed another glass. How had her best friend become like this? she wondered.

Amy was rabbiting on, all stressed and obsessed with minute details instead of focusing on the fact that she was marrying Daniel. Gorgeous, kind, funny Daniel; if she was ever lucky enough to meet someone like Daniel Quinn herself and get engaged to him she wouldn't give a crap what colour the place name-cards were or print-size the invitations came in!

'How's Dan?' she asked.

'Fine. But he wants us to take off and go surfing for Paddy's weekend in Lahinch! It's absolutely impossible when there are literally only a few weeks left to the wedding. There's no way we can go! Then he's got his stag night away with all the lads in Edinburgh, and then there's my hen weekend.'

'The hen is all in hand,' teased Jess. 'All I can say is that it is going to be great fun!'

Jess had told Amy they were going to a spa, but had secretly planned something completely different. It would be a hoot. The girls were all up for it, and she'd book two great restaurants, one for the Friday and one for the Saturday night.

'I'm so looking forward to it,' confessed Amy. 'The

spa and the hotel you booked sound brilliant. It should be so relaxing!'

'Yes, it's going to be really relaxing.' Jess laughed, trying to keep a straight face.

Mustering her willpower she refused the temptation of gelato and pannacotta, sipping her wine instead and ordering a frothy cappuccino.

She watched as Amy tucked into a big bowl of chocolate ice cream. How was it Amy never put a pick of weight on despite eating so much?

'For God's sake, Jess, take a spoonful!' urged Amy, offering her a delicious scoop.

Jess gallantly tried to change the conversation from boring wedding talk to the latest Colin Farrell film that was opening in the cinemas that weekend.

'That guy Dermot who was in college with us directed it!'

'That waste of space never turned up for lectures and smelled like a Moroccan bazaar!'

'Yes. I saw his photo in the paper. He's still got the hair and tatty jeans but he's in Hollywood now, working on some new horror film. A few of the college crowd were thinking of going along to see it.'

'Honestly, Jess, do you think that I have time to go to the cinema? I doubt I'll see the inside of the multiplex until I get back from my honeymoon. But, talking of the college crowd, these are the ones I plan to invite.'

As they lingered over their coffees Amy went through

all the mutual friends they had that she was planning to invite to the wedding.

'Wow, it's a big crowd you're having!'

'Of course.' Amy laughed. 'We both have lots of friends, and then there's the family and relations and the parents' friends, too. Do you think I should put Chloe and Orla on the same table, or am I asking for trouble?' she mused.

Jess rattled her brain. She remembered the girls having a big bust-up about some guy in first-year Law they both went out with.

'Chloe's back with him, and I heard they're talking engagement.' Amy giggled. 'But Orla adored him. He was her first love.'

'Well, I don't think they'll fight at the wedding!' Jess teased.

'I know, but if Orla has a few glasses of wine she's likely to fling herself at him!'

'Separate them! Put them as far apart as possible, and put a nice guy on Orla's table.'

'Jess, do you realize that every single girl I know wants me to put her on a table with a great single guy?' Amy sighed dramatically. 'Daniel and I are planning a wedding, not a matchmaking service!'

Jess laughed. Her own hopes plummeted. She was dreading spending so much time around Liam bloody Flynn and was hoping to ask Amy to introduce her to someone else from Daniel's work or old college crowd. People always seemed to meet other people at weddings!

That's how her mam and dad had met! And Deirdre and Shay had met at his cousin's wedding. It was a well-known fact that a happy occasion like a wedding was the perfect venue to meet someone; better than a night-club when you were both off your face drunk. What could be more romantic than a wedding!

'Jess, are you listening? I was trying to decide if we should give favours at each place-setting. They do it at some weddings.'

'Excuse my ignorance, but what the hell is a favour?'

'It's a little token gift for each wedding guest to show that they are special. It could be sweets, or biscuits, or a little toy, or a glass figurine. It's really big in America.'

'I don't think people will be expecting it at an Irish wedding!' Jess teased. 'They'd far prefer a few drinks at the bar.'

'I don't want the wedding to turn into a drunken hooley like your sister's wedding,' Amy retorted hotly.

Jess muffled her disappointment. She'd been hoping the wedding would be just as much fun as Deirdre's had been. They hadn't got to bed till almost 6 a.m., and the chef in the hotel had been bribed by her dad to cook an early-morning fry-up for those who could stomach it before they went to bed. Deirdre and Shay, happy and bedraggled, had headed up the queue for sausages and rashers and fried eggs.

'Jess, I want my wedding to be perfect. You under-stand, don't you?'

'Of course I do,' she reassured. Jess knew that

getting married and having a big wedding with all the trimmings had always been Amy's dream. She'd been talking about it since she was about eight, when they used to play Barbie weddings and dress themselves and their dolls up. That had been an age ago, and though Jess had firmly left those days behind, Amy was busy playing her own grown-up version of dress-up Barbie with her wedding plans.

'Jess, I'm so lucky to have you as my chief bridesmaid, as you know what Ciara is like!'

'I'm honoured.' Jess laughed. 'But Ciara's a good kid. She's just a bit different to you, that's all. Mam says sisters are either like peas in a pod or chalk and cheese.'

'Cheese, definitely, with that wild child! She has Mum and Dad worn out with her antics, and now she says that she is going to fail her exams.'

'Thought she was a clever clogs.'

'Yeah, when it suits her, but drama is her middle name. God knows what she'll do on the wedding day!'

'She'll be your beautiful bridesmaid and sister,' Jess reassured.

'Jess, you've always been my rock, and such a friend and support. I know that I can trust you totally on my big day, while Ciara will probably act up like she usually does.'

Good old reliable me, thought Jess to herself. Third time being a bridesmaid with not a sign of a romance of my own! Up and down church aisles like a yo-yo.

I've already got two godchildren, and no doubt when Amy has a baby I'll be a godmother again!

She tried not to be a little jealous as she thought how life was all mapped out for Amy – engagement, wedding and babies – while she had not even got one foot on the relationship ladder yet, and maybe never would . . .

'One more glass of wine and then we'll get the bill,' Amy called over to the young Polish waitress.

Forty minutes later, as they settled up and went to get their coats, Amy, almost as an afterthought, remembered to ask Jess about her life.

'Jess, what have you been up to?'

'Well, my class are making their First Communion in two weeks' time,' Jess smiled. 'So it's my job to turn twenty-seven little devils into angels so they won't let us down!'

Amy yawned.

Jess flushed. Having the First Communion class was a big deal in St Brigid's School. OK, her life might not be as exciting as Amy and Dan's, but to her mind getting her class of eight-year-olds through the minefield of first confessions and rehearsals in their local parish church without incident would be a minor miracle. Then she was trying to teach them to sing a load of hymns, and had to get involved with the parents organizing the post-communion class party back in the school. To top it all, she still hadn't found a suitable outfit to wear, given the fact that she was meant to look suitably stylish and professional on the day.

'It's a really nice thing to be involved in, but a lot of work.'

'Mmmm, I'm sure it is,' Amy said, putting her wallet back in her handbag. 'Listen, Jess, I'll give you a shout next week, as we have to get shoes for you and Ciara.'

Jess prayed that she wouldn't be expected to wear killer high heels or the like for the wedding, but thinking of Ciara knew that Amy's sister would point-blank refuse to put anything on her feet that didn't suit her. She'd probably want to wear trainers.

'Take care of yourself,' Jess urged, as they both walked up to catch the late-night Luas tram. She had never seen Amy so uptight and distracted. 'And remember to give my love to Dan.'

Chapter Thirty-one

Amy watched from the corner of her eye as Dan packed his large blue sports bag for the weekend. They'd had a massive row the night before, screaming so much at each other she was sure the couple in the next apartment must have heard them fighting. Dan was insisting that they go away for the weekend, while she had told him they were staying in Dublin.

'Amy, the surf report is good, so it's going to be a great weekend!' Dan begged, trying to get her to change her mind as he checked and packed his new wetsuit and his surf gear and equipment. 'Come on, Amy, you'd better get a move on, as we want to be able to leave first thing after work tomorrow!'

'I told you that I'm not going!' she said angrily. 'We can't go! There is far too much to do.'

Amy had no intention of wasting her time watching the lads surf in freezing cold water. It might be March, but the weather, as always for St Paddy's weekend, was bitterly cold, and when the sun did deign to make an appearance it was usually followed by heavy rain showers.

'Dan, the weather forecast is bad, and there are lots of things we need to do this weekend.'

'Lahinch was booked months ago!' he spat out, furious with her. 'Conor's girlfriend Kim is going, and Jamie is bringing Sophie, and Liam and Jade are going. We can't cancel now! It's going to be great crack, and the houses we've rented are literally on the beach.'

'OK, it sounds great,' she said grudgingly, 'but we've too much on: we need to meet that photographer we picked and run through things with him in person. And I promised to go with Ciara and Jess to look for shoes to go with their dresses.'

'You just don't want to go away with me to Lahinch!' he said, standing up. 'Admit it!'

''You're a hundred per cent right,' she said angrily. 'I don't want to go! I've got far too much to do with the wedding.'

'You are obsessed with the bloody wedding!' he shouted, glowering at her. 'It's all you ever talk about or think about! The wedding! The fecking wedding!'

'Dan, that's not fair!' she argued, hurt by his accusation. 'We're getting married in less than twelve weeks' time and there is so much to do!'

'Well, you just go bloody do it, because I've had enough of flowers and menus and invitations and music and readings and what kind of tie or waistcoat I have to wear, and all that crap! I'm sick of it.'

Amy stopped. She had never seen Dan so angry.

'Dan!'

'Don't Dan me!' he countered fiercely. 'I've had enough of this bloody wedding, morning, noon and night. It is all you ever talk about. You used to be fun, a laugh, but now you've totally changed. You're not the Amy I proposed to in Venice! You've turned into some weird kind of Bridezilla!'

Amy couldn't believe what he was saying.

'I should never have said that we would get married. We were happy as we were, now it's all changed.'

'What do you mean?' she whispered, conscious of a sinking feeling in her stomach.

'I mean, maybe we should think about this whole marriage thing, and if it is really what we want.'

'It's what I want,' she said firmly. 'I love you. I want us to be married and spend the rest of our lives together.'

Her sentiments were greeted by a yawning silence. What was Dan thinking! What did he want?

'I want to spend my life with you, too,' he admitted grudgingly. 'But I don't care about the rest of it! Listen, stay in Dublin! Do whatever silly thing you think needs doing, but I'm going surfing with the lads! There was a time all you wanted was for the two of us to pack up and head off to the West, surf, swim, laze on the beach, walk, just have fun and a few pints and a meal. Now it's all changed. You've changed.'

Dan sounded sad, as if they had lost something, something they would never get back.

Amy was tempted to say 'Feck the wedding', and all the plans, and just agree to go with him, fling a few things into her backpack and wrap up warm in her big red fleece! But her anxieties about not having perfect photographs of their big day, or her sister wearing the wrong shoes with her bridesmaid dress just seemed more important. Dan could surely understand that?

'Dan, just go with the lads. Surf all day. I'll stay here for the weekend. It's only two days, and I'll cook a lovely dinner for when you get back on Sunday,' she promised, trying to appease him.

Dan said nothing; he just bent down, fiddling with the spare runners and wet socks he had put in the bag.

'Whatever you want, Amy,' he said. 'Whatever! I'm going to bed.'

Amy sat stunned on the leather couch. OK, Dan was upset with her, but at least it was sorted. She went over, turned on her laptop and began searching on the internet for gold strappy sandals for her sister and Jess in some of the Dublin shoe shops they'd visit on Saturday. House of Frazer in Dundrum had a huge selection: maybe they should start off looking there. She also organized to meet Julien Marks, the photographer, to discuss the type of photos they wanted and the arrangements for Castle Gregory. Dan was asleep in bed, his back turned to her, when she finally slid in beside him. They slept side by side, without touching, all night.

In the morning he was in the shower and gone before she had time to say a word to him, just catching a flash of his figure with his sports bag flung over his shoulder disappearing out the door.

'Have a good time!' she yelled.

'See you Sunday,' he snarled gruffly, not even returning to give her a good-morning kiss.

She tried to shake off her sense of unease about his behaviour, but, not wanting to get in another fight with him, just let it go. She'd text him later.

She kept herself busy all weekend, watching a video with Aisling and Nikki on Friday night, and on Saturday going on a shoe-shopping blitz with Jess and Ciara, which resulted in the two most perfect pairs of high-heeled gold strappy shoes for the girls. She hadn't been able to resist a pair for herself, too, and planned to wear them on honeymoon.

She'd also met with the photographer in Sandycove. Julien Marks was great, very down-to-earth, but his prices were pretty steep. He showed her the various wedding packages he did, which ranged from the very formal to completely casual. She'd fallen in love with the type of wedding photos he took: some were classic, and others in black and white and colour, were just that bit quirky and different. She was glad that she'd had the chance to run through things with him and discuss the kind of album she wanted to order.

On Saturday evening she'd joined Tara and Sarah and a few friends for pizza and a few glasses of wine down in Dun Laoghaire, getting a taxi home on her own at midnight, as she had no interest in hitting the Leeson Street nightclubs. She had phoned Dan and sent him a few messages throughout the day and evening but his phone seemed to be off, or maybe he had just forgotten to recharge it.

On Sunday she had gone for a brisk walk on Sandymount Strand and tidied the apartment, washing the floor and changing their bed and cleaning the bathroom and shower until they were sparkling. She'd had lunch with her parents, and got two nice steaks and a bottle of Dan's favourite wine for dinner. He'd be ravenous after surfing all weekend, and she was dying to hear about the trip. The weather had picked up on Saturday afternoon and stayed dry on Sunday, so it would have been fine surfing weather. He should be in good form. He'd probably get home by 7 p.m.

She tried to dismiss her concern, and sat down to have another go at the invitation list, adding even more friends' names to the sheet in her bulging pink Filofax, and deleting a few cousins that she hardly ever saw. By eight she was panicking, and kept phoning and texting Dan, wondering where he was. At ten o'clock she rang Liam to ask if he was still with Dan.

'He's with me,' admitted Liam. 'He's staying in my place for the night but I'll get him to phone you tomorrow.'

Amy wanted to scream at Liam and demand that he

send Daniel back to her straight away, but instead she just said, 'I see.'

She didn't sleep a wink all night, and dragged herself into work the next morning, leaving her phone on all day – even when she went to meetings – in case Dan tried to contact her. She felt sick and panicky, and couldn't concentrate, snapping at Niamh Owens – the new junior in the firm – and doing her utmost to keep out of her boss's way. Norah had antennae about personal troubles, and Amy had no intention of discussing herself and Dan's problems with her. At ten past five she escaped the office and rushed home. She sat on the couch drinking coffee till almost nine, too nauseated and tense to eat.

A few minutes later she heard Dan's key in the lock and jumped up to greet him.

'We need to talk,' he said slowly. Amy noticed he had not brought home his bag. Like a zombie, she followed him into the sitting room.

Dan paced up and down the wooden floorboards.

'I don't think we should get married now,' he said firmly.

'What do you mean?' she demanded, her stomach lurching. 'Do you want to delay the wedding? Put it off for a few weeks?'

She could feel hysteria rise, threatening to engulf her, as if she had been hit by a tidal wave and was being swept under.

'No, Amy, I want to call the whole thing off. I'm not ready to get married to you at the moment.'

'That bastard Liam has put you up to this!' she cried furiously.

'Liam has nothing to do with it,' he said patiently. 'Liam was actually trying to persuade me to go ahead with things. No, this is totally my decision. I've had all weekend . . . more, to think about it. Funny, when you are out there on a board in the water on your own, things become clearer.'

Amy sat staring at the glass coffee table, tempted to kick it or fling it and have it break into a million pieces, to shatter it like her heart.

'Why didn't you say something?'

'I should have said something earlier, but you were so caught up in all the arrangements that I just didn't know what to do.' He ran his tanned fingers through his hair. 'Every time I did try to say something you just kept on going . . . it was like a big juggernaut powering ahead and I had no control or say over it.'

'Dan . . . I'm so sorry. I never wanted you to feel that way.' She sobbed. 'I love you.'

'I know,' he said, softening and giving her hope. 'I love you, too, but I still don't think we should get married . . . not till we both feel it is right.'

Amy sat stunned on the couch, not knowing what to say or do.

'I'm going to stay with Liam for a bit, give you time to sort things out. Maybe we should wind things down for a bit . . . just see how it goes.'

Amy felt like she couldn't breathe. She had to get up

and go to the balcony window for air, trying to suck it into her lungs.

'I'm sorry, Amy, honest, I am.'

She fiddled with the ring on her finger.

'Do you want it back?'

He didn't answer her, and, wordless, Amy slipped the diamond off her finger and put it on the coffee table between them.

They both stared at it, and Amy watched as almost in slow motion he picked it up and held it.

'It's still yours,' he said, holding it in the palm of his hand.

'Well, you keep it, then,' she said. 'You paid for it.'

He reeled, as if she had punched him, and she wondered when they had started being so cruel to each other.

He slipped the ring into his pocket, and Amy was immediately filled with regret, noticing the pale circle on her ring finger and aware of the gaping hole that had been torn in her heart by the man she had thought she was going to marry.

'What will we say to people?'

'I don't know,' he shrugged. 'Whatever you want to tell them is fine with me.'

She sat totally still as Dan went to the bedroom and grabbed some clothes from the wardrobe: his good jacket and trousers and a few shirts and ties.

'Dan, please don't go. We can work things out,' she begged, losing control and standing up in front of him, like a small child trying to block his escape.

'I'll talk to you in a day or two,' he said calmly, side-stepping away from her. 'Take care of yourself.'

She stood like a statue for half an hour after he'd left, listening for the sound of his door key, the door reopening, imagining that somehow she had made a mistake, dreamed this, and that Dan would walk in and hug her and kiss her and never let her go . . .

Chapter Thirty-two

Amy sat in the apartment as it got darker and darker, too shocked and scared to move.

It felt like she had been in some sort of accident: a head-on collision with some huge vehicle which had left her broken and battered and unable to stir. She was like a bird that had been hit by one car and sat waiting for another to come along and finish it off.

She was breathing; she could hear the raspy gasp of her breath, and feel her heart beat, but hadn't the courage or energy to move or do anything but sit there.

The bedroom seemed miles away, and she somehow pulled the woollen throw from the back of the couch over herself and huddled there as hour after hour passed.

She heard the sound of midnight sirens and lonely middle-of-the-night cars, busy taxis, grinding street-cleaners and bin lorries, and gradually the rumble of early-morning traffic. She ignored it all, just sat there.

Her mobile rang somewhere in her handbag in the bedroom . . . she ignored it.

Dawn's first light gradually forced its way into the living room, sneaking over the balcony and through the curtains, and she retreated to the bathroom, where she was violently sick. She sat there as wave after wave of nausea washed over her. Eventually, clammy and exhausted, she staggered to the bedroom, where she fell into bed and the glory of oblivion.

It was late afternoon when she finally woke: to the dreadful realization that Dan was gone and their wedding plans had just been some silly dream that she had believed in.

What was she going to say? What would she tell people? How could she explain that she had let the man of her dreams, her soulmate, slip through her hands because of her own crass stupidity?

She longed to turn back time to last weekend, to pack her bag with her wetsuit and togs and jeans and fleece hoodie and join Dan and his friends. To walk the beach, surf, swim, play! To have the wind whip through her hair and cover her with sand, Dan and herself making a game of kissing and rubbing it away at night in the little house overlooking the beach!

'No . . . noo,' she cried, frightening herself with the moan that escaped her.

Her phone rang again. She reached for it, hoping that Dan's name would come up. There were a load of missed calls and text messages but nothing . . . absolutely nothing from him. Pain assaulted her again, and she ran to the bathroom.

She barely recognized the girl staring back at her in the mirror: she was a mess, eyes red-rimmed, nose snotty and streaming, skin ghostly white, hair all over the place. She looked mad, crazy! Back in bed she curled up, wanting to die. Wishing the pain would stop and that she could break free from it.

The phone rang again. It was Jess.

'Amy . . . I've been trying to get you all day. Are you OK?'

Good old Jess, who always knew when something was wrong with her, when she was upset or frightened or scared.

'No!' she blurted out, beginning to cry. 'Dan and I have broken up. The wedding is off.'

She could hear Jess's shocked intake of breath.

'You've had a fight,' Jess said calmly. 'You'll get over it!'

'No, Jess, it's over,' Amy bawled, breaking down. 'He's gone to stay at Liam's . . . I don't know what to do.'

'I'll be there as quick as I can,' Jess said, putting down the phone. Amy could imagine Jess grabbing her car keys and going out to her green Golf and driving determinedly to her apartment.

Thirty minutes later she opened the door for Jess, who seemed to take the situation under control almost straight away, putting on the kettle and opening the curtains to let some light and air into the place.

'Sit down!' she ordered in her teacher's voice. 'You need a cup of tea and something to eat.'

Jess made her eat soft fingers of buttered toast, and sweet milky tea laden with sugar. 'You've had a shock,' she said.

Amy's mouth felt dry as she tried to speak and recount, step by step, what had happened the night before. And her refusal to go to Lahinch with Dan, and the litany of cancelled nights and days and weekends that had built up over the past few months.

'Am I that bad, have I been such a cow to Dan because I wanted everything to be perfect for our wedding day?' she anguished.

'You have been obsessed with the wedding,' Jess said carefully. 'It's as if nothing else mattered to you for months. Maybe Dan felt even he wasn't that important to you any more, you had got so caught up in it all.'

Amy howled again.

'I still love him, Jess, I love him so much.'

'I know you do. And I'm sure Dan still loves you, too. It's just that you have got yourself into a mess.'

'Why didn't I go away with him?' Amy sobbed. 'If only I could turn back time.'

'OK, you should have gone with him,' Jess agreed, taking Dan's side. 'But I'm sure Dan will get over it. Everyone knows he's mad about you.'

'Not any more,' Amy whispered in a small scared voice.

Jess put her arms around her.

'Have you told your mum and dad yet?'

Amy shook her head slowly.

'What will I say to them? They both love Dan as if he was their son already. They'll be heartbroken!'

Jess knew that Paddy and Helen O'Connor were delighted with their future son-in-law and the upcoming wedding, and she could understand Amy's reluctance to tell them.

'I don't think you should stay here in the apartment on your own,' Jess murmured aloud. 'You are welcome to come and stay with me, or I can drop you back home to your parents' place.'

Amy tried to think straight. This apartment was actually Dan's. He had bought it two years before they had even met, and shared it with one of the guys he was studying accountancy with. She had moved in about a year after they started dating.

Pre-Daniel she and Jess and two other friends had shared a house in Ranelagh for two years, but once she had moved in with Daniel Jess had decided she'd had enough of renting and sharing. She'd bought a place of her own: a renovated, quaint red-brick cottage near the canal in Harold's Cross. With its tiny courtyard garden and an open-plan living room and kitchen it wasn't very big, but Jess did have two bedrooms. Amy couldn't bear the thought of facing home, and the massive upset of her mum and dad's bewildered questions and need for an explanation.

'Please, Jess, can I stay with you?' Amy whispered.

'Sure,' said Jess, giving her a big comforting hug.

The two of them flung a few of Amy's things into her bag, and she grabbed her make-up and shampoos and toiletries from the cabinet in the bathroom. She was trying not to cry as she closed the door of the apartment and followed her best friend to the car.

The tears came again as she left the apartment behind. Jess said nothing and kept driving, the news on the car radio blaring as Amy tried to compose and calm herself.

In Harold's Cross Jess settled her in front of the gas fire with her pyjamas on and a big blanket wrapped around her. She gave Amy a bowl of pasta with chopped-up rashers in it.

'You have to eat!' she bossed, passing her a glass of red wine.

Amy's stomach flipped, and she found herself talking and talking as she sat there with Jess patiently listening.

'Jess, what am I going to do without him?'

'Amy, I'm no expert, but I do know Dan loves you. OK, so you've had a massive bust-up and really hurt each other,' she said, trying to be consoling, 'but I think in time that you'll get over it, get back together again.'

'You do?'

'Honestly, I do. I can't see you living your lives separately. You both love each other far too much.'

'Oh, Jess. I hope that you are right!' Amy sniffed. 'But what am I going to do about the wedding? It's only a few weeks away!'

'You are going to have to tell someone,' said Jess pointedly. 'Because if the wedding is really being called off you will have to start cancelling things.'

Amy felt overwhelmed at the thought that things could be finally over with Daniel. She burst into hysterics and cried and cried. She blew her nose and tried to get her breath back as Jess passed her a box of tissues.

'You have to tell your mum and dad,' Jess advised, serious. 'Phone them tonight. They deserve to know.'

Amy thought and thought about it, deciding that she'd definitely wait until tomorrow to break the bad news to her parents and family, just in case Daniel changed his mind and phoned her and this nightmare she was caught up in somehow resolved itself.

'I'll do it tomorrow,' she promised, praying that this was just some weird kind of bad dream, and that in the morning she would wake up and things would be miraculously back to normal again.

Chapter Thirty-three

The minute Amy stepped through the front door Helen O'Connor knew something was seriously wrong with her daughter. She could see the utter misery written all over her face. Jess, good friend that she was, came in with Amy, holding her hand as if she was six years old, and signalled for Helen and Paddy to sit down on the couch. Then Amy, almost in a whisper, began to tell them the bad news.

'What did she say?' asked Paddy, straining to hear.

'Amy, are you telling us that your wedding to Daniel is off?' Helen couldn't control the quaver in her own voice.

Amy nodded, so upset that she could hardly get a breath, let alone speak.

Jess, sitting near her, filled them in quickly on how she had phoned Amy and, discovering what had happened, called over and had taken her friend back to her place the previous night.

'Thank you, Jess,' said Paddy. 'You've always been

a good friend to Amy. Helen and I appreciate it, and everything that you have done.'

'We're friends,' Jess said, tears welling in her own eyes. 'But I think I should go, let Amy talk to you alone. I'm around if you need me, OK?' She hugged Amy before discreetly letting herself out the front door.

Helen sat holding her breath, not sure what to say.

'Yes, it's off!' shuddered Amy, hunched forward on the armchair in the sitting room, her fingers gripping the red cushion as if it was a lifesaver. 'Daniel says that he doesn't want to go ahead with the wedding.'

'He doesn't want to go ahead with the wedding!' Helen gasped in disbelief, a look of incredulity darting between herself and Paddy as they gazed at their daughter and the state she was in.

'He says we need to consider before taking such a big step, and not rush into things,' Amy gasped, trying to control her breathing.

'The bloody bastard!' shouted Paddy angrily.

'He says that we've just got so caught up with planning the whole big wedding thing that we've lost us. It's just got too much, the last month or two, and he thinks we should cool things, think about it and slow down and take our time. He said that maybe now is not the right time to get married!' she wailed.

Helen stared at the paleness of her daughter's skin, the red rims of her eyes, sore from crying, the shadows underneath them. She could feel her own heart pounding in disbelief at the utter nightmare that was being laid out before her. One minute she'd been relaxing, doing the crossword in the newspaper in the kitchen, worrying about some stupid anagram clue while Paddy caught up with the *Sports News* on TV, and the next their whole world had turned upside down.

'I don't know what to do,' sobbed Amy, losing control totally as Helen jumped forward and wrapped her in her arms, letting her cry her eyes out.

'Maybe he's just got cold feet! You hear about it happening. It's always in the films!' Helen murmured, trying to calm the situation down.

'Has he someone else, is that it?' raged Paddy, looking like he would burst a blood vessel as he stalked up and down the carpet.

'No, Daddy! No.'

'Tell us what happened, pet,' urged Helen, trying to discover what had led to this calamitous situation between two people who loved each other so much. 'Is there someone else involved?'

'No!' shouted Amy angrily. 'It's nothing like that. We've been fighting . . .'

Thank God, thought Helen silently. Couples always fought. Paddy and she had endured umpteen battles over the years. Age was ensuring that the skirmishes between them were fewer now, but in the early days of their marriage they had had some massive fall-outs. She remembered one time packing up the kids into their old Toyota and taking them to her mother's for the night. Another time, before the children had been born, she had locked Paddy out of the house. All couples fought! It was normal.

In between sobs and hiccups and much nose-blowing, Amy gulped out about not going surfing and the build-up to the whole sorry saga.

'I've been such a cow, no wonder Daniel hates me!' she wailed, in tears again.

'I'm sure that's not true,' Paddy said, taking her hand and squeezing her fingers. 'No one hates you.'

'It is! It is,' she shouted. 'Dan wouldn't even talk to me. He went to stay in Liam's when he came home on Sunday. I just can't believe it. But it's his place, so I've moved out of the apartment, and I've gone to stay in Jess's until I sort something out.'

'You know that you always have your room here,' reassured Helen, remembering how Amy had told her about the tiny cottage that Jess had managed to buy and was busy renovating. 'You are welcome to move back home if you want.'

'Thanks, Mum.' Amy sniffed, taking some tissues that Paddy offered her.

'And what has Daniel to say about all this?' enquired Paddy. 'Maybe I should phone him, talk to him man to man.'

Helen had to agree with Paddy. She would gladly have got hold of her future son-in-law and throttled him for the upset he was causing and the pain he had inflicted on their daughter.

'Daddy, please don't do that!' beseeched Amy. 'He's

made his decision and you are not going to change his mind.'

'What are you going to do?' urged Helen softly. 'What do you want us to do?'

'Jess says that I should start to cancel things . . .'

'She's right, of course,' agreed Helen, stroking Amy's light brown hair, and wishing for all the world that things could be different. 'There's the castle, and the caterers you've hired, and the photographer.'

'And the band and the car and the flowers and a hundred other things . . .' Amy cried hysterically, giving into the utter dejection she felt.

Helen watched uselessly as Amy broke down and curled up on the couch.

'We'll make a list tomorrow,' she soothed. 'It will all be taken care of. Don't worry, love.'

'What about work?' Paddy asked, concerned.

'Jess phoned and told them that I had the flu and wouldn't be in for a few days,' Amy sniffed. 'I don't know how I am ever going to face going into work again—'

'Let's not think about that tonight,' interrupted Helen.

'I've made a mess of everything. You must all be mad at me,' Amy whispered.

'We're not mad at you,' Paddy hushed. 'Obviously we're disappointed about the wedding, but it's not the end of the world.'

'It is the end of mine,' she said vehemently.

'I know you'll think I'm an old fuddy-duddy,' said Helen gently, 'but time generally works things out. You and Daniel just need time to think and get your heads straight. You are both so young.'

'Mum, I'm thirty years of age,' Amy said. 'I'm not young, and Dan is thirty-three. You and Dad were married years at this stage and already had the three of us.'

'Things were different then,' Helen tried to explain. 'Very different.'

Paddy smiled at her, and Helen knew she wouldn't have changed a thing about jumping into marriage so young and having her family so quickly.

Amy was sipping a cup of coffee when Helen heard Ciara coming through the front door, junking her jacket in the hall and flinging her backpack on the floor.

'Hey!' she called, coming into the kitchen. 'What's for dinner? What's everyone doing?'

'The wedding has been cancelled,' Amy spat out fiercely, glancing up at the look of utter confusion in her young sister's face.

'Cancelled! What are you talking about?'

'Amy and Dan have had a fight, a disagreement over a few issues,' Helen tried to explain. 'But I'm sure that it will all blow over.'

'UUUEEE!' Ciara whistled, unbelieving. 'You and Dan aren't getting married?'

'No,' said Amy forlorn, closing her eyes.

'I don't believe it! You're spoofing me.'

'Unfortunately not,' said Paddy, in a serious voice. 'Your mother and sister will have to phone and start cancelling everything tomorrow.'

'Amy, I'm so sorry.' Ciara ran over and squeezed on to the chair beside Amy. 'What did Dan do? Men can be such stupid assholes.'

'Dan did nothing. This is all my fault for being such a stupid self-centred cow.'

'There's not going to be a wedding?' Ciara asked, hesitant.

'Ciara, I suppose you must be delighted not to be my bridesmaid,' Amy cried out angrily. 'You and Carmel Quinn must be jumping for joy that the wedding has been called off.'

'That's an awful thing to say,' responded Ciara, hurt. 'Just because I don't want to dress up like a dork doesn't mean I don't want you and Dan to get married.'

'Honestly, Amy, how could you think such a thing about your sister?' objected Helen. 'And I'm sure the Quinns are equally upset about what's happened!'

'Sure,' said Amy sarcastically.

Helen got up and went into the kitchen to check on the spinach lasagne that she had put in the oven almost an hour and a half ago. With all the fuss, she had totally forgotten it. The topping was burned, the cheese black, and the creamy white sauce all dried out. She turned off the oven and left the dish on the draining board.

'The dinner's destroyed,' she said, rejoining the others.

'I'm not hungry anyway,' said Amy.

'I'll make us something,' offered Ciara, disappearing into the kitchen.

Helen didn't understand it. Some days Ciara wouldn't as much as look at the plate in front of her, and here she was offering to cook. God knows what she'd make.

Helen listened as Amy went back over all that had happened again and again, not knowing what to say or do to ease the pain she was in.

Forty minutes later Ciara produced a dish of stuffed peppers with rice and a side salad.

'That's not bad,' Paddy said, tucking in.

Amy sat at the table, disinterested, playing with the food on her plate.

Helen tried to remain calm as she passed around the salad, unable to disguise the fact that she too was distraught about the wedding that she had looked forward to so much not going ahead. Poor Amy! She and Dan were meant for each other, anyone who knew them could see that. How had they managed to lose track of what was important to them?

Marriage was a constant give and take; all couples knew that, and were prepared for it. It was how marriages – well, the good ones – worked, and here were Amy and Dan falling at the first hurdle. Vows and the legally binding marriage contract that a couple signed all seemed to act as a safety net when things got ropey and seemed to fall apart, but it was love that kept a couple together. Love. She had thought that the love between Amy and Dan was strong enough to withstand the stresses and strains of their upcoming marriage, but maybe she'd been wrong. Maybe they were not the couple she and Paddy had thought they were.

They all sat at the table silent and gloomy, not knowing what to say.

'I have to study.' Ciara, having wolfed down her meal, jumped up and put her plate in the dishwasher, something she rarely did.

Helen couldn't blame her for wanting to escape.

After dinner Helen cleared up, glad of the peace and quiet of the kitchen as Amy and Paddy retreated to the sitting room. She was at a total loss as to what to say or do. It was like having a bereavement in the family, with all their expected happiness suddenly wiped out. She put on a small saucepan of milk and made a big mug of creamy hot chocolate, dropping a marshmallow into it, and carried it into the sitting room with a few spare marshmallows for Amy.

Paddy had her lying up on the couch wrapped in the rug like an invalid; it reminded Helen of the time when Amy was younger and had had pneumonia.

'Here you go, pet,' Helen urged.

'Thanks, Mum.' Tears welled up again in Amy's eyes.

'It's OK, love,' Helen said, sitting down near her. 'Your dad and I are here. It will all get sorted out, promise.

You are not to worry. Maybe you should stay here just for a night or two until you are feeling a bit better . . .'

'Is that OK with you?'

'Course it is,' mumbled Paddy, trying to control his emotions.

'What about Castle Gregory? And the church?' Amy said, panic creeping into her voice.

'We'll sort things out tomorrow, pet, promise we will,' soothed Helen as she desperately tried to conceal her own sense of panic. 'We'll sit down and go through it all in the morning, but you need a good night's sleep tonight.'

It was eleven before they finally persuaded Amy to go up to bed. She looked absolutely wrecked, and Helen prayed that somehow she would sleep.

Looking in the bathroom mirror as she cleansed her face and applied her expensive night cream, Helen felt ancient. There was no escaping the sound of Amy sobbing heartbrokenly in the room near theirs.

'What are we going to do?' she asked Paddy as she climbed into bed beside him.

'I suppose you and Amy should start cancelling things, but first of all let me phone that fellow my lad, and hear his side of the story. I'll give Eddie Quinn a ring, too. He struck me as a decent type of man, not the sort to let his son treat a girl like this.'

'Paddy, you can't force Dan to marry her! Amy wouldn't want that.'

'I know. I know,' Paddy said stubbornly. 'But I want

to find out what the hell is going on. Daniel is a decent type of guy and I just want to talk to him.'

Helen sighed as she rolled down in the bed and wrapped herself in the quilt. Paddy began to snore slightly beside her. How could he sleep? Her mind was racing, worried about Amy, worried about cancelling the arrangements, and worried about what exactly she should tell people!

Chapter Thirty-four

Ciara lay wide awake in bed listening to Amy cry. Hour after hour it went on. The house was silent except for her sister's shuddering sobbing. Ciara stared at the bedroom ceiling listening to the true sound of heartbreak. It was unbearable. She thought when she had caught Jay with another girl that she had experienced pain, but now she knew that it had been nothing compared to what Amy was going through. Jay had been a shit, a bastard of a boyfriend, and probably she had known that all along; facing it had been the thing that had hurt, the thing that had pained her and wounded her. But Dan was good and kind and funny. OK, he wasn't her type, but he was Amy's, and Amy loved him. How in hell was Amy ever going to get over losing someone like him? She wasn't strong enough.

Troubled, Ciara sat up and slipping out of bed went and stood at the door of her sister's room. Amy used to ban her from her room, and had made signs saying 'Keep out Ciara' which she had stuck up on her door.

Amy always accused Ciara of stealing her lipsticks and using her perfumes when she was smaller. Ciara used to ignore the signs and still creep in and steal and use her sister's stuff and try on her clothes and read her magazines.

She hesitated at the doorway, seeing the crumpled figure hunched in the bed. Then, unable to bear it any longer, she went over and eased back the quilt and slipped in under it. She put her arms around her sister and let her cry and cry till she was wet and covered in snot and Amy began to quieten as she stroked her hair.

'It's all right, Amy, I'm here. I'm here,' she whispered, rocking her and soothing her till finally Amy began to relax, the two of them curled up together. She held her breath as her sister began to let go and finally breathe deeper and deeper as she slept. Ciara cuddled beside her, like when they were little and she had sneaked into Amy's bed when she had a nightmare.

It was after 7 a.m. when she woke and realized where she was. Amy was still asleep beside her. She was about to get up when Amy reached over and hugged her.

'Thanks.'

Ciara gazed at her. Amy's eyes were raw and she looked awful.

'I'm not used to sleeping on my own,' Amy said, trying to control the shake in her voice.

'It's OK.'

'When did you get the dragonfly?'

Ciara tried to pull down her T-shirt.

'I've been looking at it for the past fifteen minutes.' Amy smiled shakily.

Ciara tried to guess what she was thinking.

'It's kind of cool,' Amy said. 'Dan's got a dolphin near his coccyx. I was never brave enough to get one. You know me and needles.'

'I hate them too,' Ciara admitted, 'but a guy I was going out with was really into them. It was pathetic because I got it for him. I thought it would make him like me more. It was stupid. He was stupid.'

'Do I know him?' Amy asked.

'Nope,' said Ciara. She had no intention of discussing Jay. He was gone from her life and the shagging tattoo was all that was there to remind her of him. 'How are you feeling?'

'Shit. No, make that double shit!'

'Are you going to move back here?'

'I'm not sure if that's a good idea.' Amy sighed. 'You know what they're like.'

Ciara knew her parents would wrap Amy in cotton wool and fuss and baby her terribly. Mum and Dad might mean well, but it would probably drive Amy mad to have them hovering over her.

'I'd better get up, I've college,' Ciara said, easing herself out of the bed.

'I'm not getting up,' Amy said doggedly. 'I don't want to think about things. I wish that I could stay asleep here for ever like Sleeping Beauty, with everything frozen in time.'

'Till a handsome prince called Daniel comes riding by,' said Ciara without thinking. She immediately regretted what she had said, as Amy curled up into the pillow. 'Sorry.'

'It's not your fault,' said Amy tonelessly, retreating under the duvet.

Chapter Thirty-five

Helen felt like every bone in her body was sore, she had slept so badly all night. For hours her mind had been racing, going over all the implications of Amy and Dan not getting married. Dan had been like another son in their house, and now suddenly he was no longer going to be part of the family. She felt awful about it, and could only imagine how poor Amy must feel. She should be angry with Dan and curse him for hurting their daughter, but she knew that he was probably equally hurt. She felt so sad for both of them. They had seemed such a perfect couple. But now herself and Paddy had to be practical, and start unravelling the mess and cancelling the wedding in ten weeks' time.

Paddy came slowly down the stairs to breakfast, too, looking like an old bear in his wool dressing gown, barely glancing at the morning newspaper and picking at his toast and rashers.

'I'll try and talk to Dan and Eddie later. You'd better phone the castle and find out what the procedure is if we need to cancel everything,' he reminded her as he went upstairs to shower and shave before going into the office. 'They are liable to charge us a hefty cancellation fee.'

He sounded worried, and Helen couldn't blame him. As she sipped on a mug of coffee she grabbed a pad, and started to make a list of all the places she and Amy had to phone today.

It was mid-morning when Amy finally appeared. She had violet shadows under her eyes, and didn't look like she'd slept a wink either.

'Some cereal?' Helen asked. 'Or what about toast?'

'I'm not hungry.' Amy filled a mug with coffee.

Helen felt so sorry for her. Paddy had phoned an hour ago after speaking briefly to Dan. 'The lad is upset, worried about Amy, but the wedding is definitely off as far as he's concerned,' Paddy explained. 'I offered to meet him for a pint and to have a chat, but he said to leave it for the moment. Eddie's secretary said he's busy but that he'd phone me tonight or tomorrow.'

Helen sighed. It all sounded so final.

'Love, I've made a rough list,' Helen ventured, 'and the sooner we both start phoning everyone to cancel the wedding, all the better.'

'Sure, Mum, whatever you think.'

Helen had the pity of her heart for Amy as they both ran through the telephone numbers and contact details that she had amassed in her pink wedding Filofax.

'Let's start with contacting the castle?' she suggested.

'Please, Mum, can you do it?' beseeched Amy. 'Can you phone Castle Gregory? I'll just get too upset.'

Helen steeled herself for embarrassment as Hugo Robert's quiet, educated voice came on the phone. Taking a deep breath Helen told him that the O'Connors would no longer need to hire Castle Gregory for their daughter's nuptials on 6 June.

'Do you want to change the date of the booking?' asked Hugo.

'No, I'm afraid that we have to cancel it,' insisted Helen, trying to remain calm. 'The wedding will not now be taking place.'

'Oh dear!' Helen could tell that Hugo Roberts was unused to people cancelling the castle. 'I'm so sorry to hear that.' Then he said, sounding more understanding, 'You must be all so upset.'

Helen could feel herself being less defensive as she unrolled the sorry saga, hoping to appeal to Hugo's more generous nature.

Amy, white in the face, listened as Helen made it 100 per cent clear that the O'Connor family had no need of Castle Gregory and its services any longer.

'You have paid a large deposit for this booking,' reminded Hugo. 'And you do know that we are entitled to it in lieu of a cancellation? That is our policy.'

Helen couldn't hide her intake of breath as she imagined Paddy's reaction to the loss of such a large amount of money.

'However,' Hugo's voice softened, 'we have had

an unusual request in the past ten days from a well-known radio star with regards to hiring the castle for his wedding. We had told him that we were booked out totally until late October, but he asked to be kept informed of any cancellations, as he is really hoping to marry during the summer. June was his month of preference.'

'Oh,' gasped Helen, seeing a chink of light in a very dark tunnel.

'So if you are sure that your daughter Amy and Mr Quinn are definitely not going to go ahead with using the castle on that date, I may be able to find an alternative booking for it.'

'Oh, that would be wonderful,' gushed Helen.

She felt relief wash over her as she put the phone down.

'What did they say?' quizzed Amy, frantic to find out what was happening.

'We will lose ten per cent of our deposit only, not the full amount, and they will return the balance by cheque once they receive an official letter from you cancelling everything.'

'Oh thanks, Mum!' Amy sighed, relieved.

The caterers, Lainey Sullivan and Company, weren't quite so accommodating about losing the fee for a big event on a summer Saturday.

'I think there is a possibility of another big wedding on that day,' Helen suggested, 'but you need to check with Hugo up at the castle.'

'If I have another wedding on that day all is not lost,' the caterer told Helen, phoning back and eventually agreeing to return the full deposit.

Father Tom Doorly was sad when Amy herself told him that there would be no wedding in the little chapel near the castle.

'I hope that you and your young man can find the good grace to get over this disappointment,' he urged. 'You know it is far better to cancel the ceremony than to get married if you are not sure about it. I can't tell you how many couples I see who break up within only a year or two of big fancy weddings.'

The band and the DJ were less generous and refused to return the deposits paid to them. 'We have no other gig booked in for that night, and Saturdays are always a big night for us. We can play another Saturday if you need us to instead.'

'That won't be necessary,' explained Amy, 'as there will be no wedding.'

The florist was peeved with them, but as they had only paid a small deposit agreed to return it, given the circumstances.

'I only do three weddings a day,' she confided. 'So hopefully I'll be able to pick up another bride or event.'

Amy couldn't imagine anyone organizing a florist at this late stage, but Helen reassured her that loads of people left things till the last minute.

Julien, the photographer, was narky in the extreme,

but reluctantly agreed to return the deposit, which he had literally just been paid.

'I have lost a day's work at the height of the wedding season,' he told Amy, over and over again, and it was no good her reminding him that she'd only booked him that week. Amy secretly vowed that hell would freeze over before she would ever use him for anything again, or recommend him to her friends.

Luckily Jeremy, Dan's friend from college, who had his own small film and advertising company and who had agreed to make the DVD of their wedding, was much more understanding. He couldn't believe that she and Dan were cancelling the wedding.

'That's so crap for you, Amy,' Jeremy blurted out. 'Do you want me to talk to Dan?'

'Please, Jeremy, don't say or do anything,' she begged. 'Things are bad enough.'

Amy was almost shaking when she phoned Judith Deveraux, the designer whose dress she'd ordered. She couldn't face going in there in person and telling her what had happened.

'Oh, Amy, I'll have your dress ready in about five weeks' time,' Judith reassured. 'That gives us plenty of time for any last-minute fittings and alterations needed.'

'That's just it.' Amy began to choke up. 'There won't be any need for fittings or alterations, as I'm not getting married. The wedding is off.'

'Your wedding is cancelled!'

Helen took over the phone immediately, and the two women, over a long conversation, agreed on a course of action over the dress.

'Judith has kindly agreed to refund the full amount that I paid for your dress,' she explained gently. 'The dress was obviously being fitted for you, but I'm sure Judith will have no problem selling it as someone else will probably love it.'

Amy nodded silently, her eyes welling with tears. Moments later, 'There's the bridesmaid dresses, my shoes, the invitations.' She sounded panicked. 'They are meant to go to print in ten days' time!'

'It will all be sorted,' soothed Helen, trying to calm her down. 'I'll phone the printers straight away.' She took a deep breath as she saw the huge number of people they still had to contact: the jewellers, organist, church singer, car hire, the Arnotts wedding list organizers and, of course, Bibi. It was endless!

'It will all get done!' she promised. 'Honestly it will.'

Helen felt like a dead duck. Fit for bed. Amy had gone upstairs for a rest and Paddy had announced that he was off playing golf, would have a bite to eat in the club house and wouldn't be home till late. Who could blame him for wanting to keep out of the place and the pandemonium they were immersed in!

She had phoned Carmel Quinn, who was strangely distant with her.

'Helen, this has been just as big a shock to us as to

you, I assure you,' Carmel had said politely. 'Eddie and I are naturally upset for the two of them, but it is their decision. Marriage is a very big commitment and maybe the two of them weren't suited to it.'

Helen was annoyed with her reaction and wondered what kind of mother Carmel was!

'*What's up?*' Helen looked at the text from Fran. '*Trying to phone u all day. Are we going MOB shopping?*'

'*DISASTER,*' Helen replied.

Ten minutes later Fran was at the door.

'What the hell has happened?'

'Sssh,' Helen whispered, dragging her into the kitchen. 'Amy's upstairs asleep. I don't want to wake her.'

For the first time Helen found herself getting tearful as she sat down at the kitchen table and told Fran the whole saga.

'You poor old things, having this happen, but thank heaven Amy is all right. It's awful, but at least you had a few more weeks until the wedding, and the invitations hadn't gone out yet.'

'I suppose so,' admitted Helen, relieved that Amy's perfectionism had delayed the printing. An hour later, at Fran's insistence that this crisis definitely qualified as Martini Time, Helen was sitting on the couch sipping a large Martini and beginning to feel a bit better.

'No one has died,' reminded Fran. 'Couples these days are always fighting and making up and getting married and divorced and remarried. There's none of that you-made-your-bed-you-must-lie-on-it attitude that we used to get! God knows how many times Tom and I broke up before we actually made it to the altar.'

'But you hadn't booked Castle Gregory and the whole shebang!' Helen argued.

'I'll give you that Amy and Dan's situation is a bit more public, but a break-up is a break-up! That's what we are talking about. It happens!'

'It's been so awful. I've been on the phone since break-fast. What are people going to think?'

'People will get over it. Like me, they'll be a bit miffed about not getting to dress up and have a day out seeing Amy getting married in a big castle courtesy of the O'Connors, but they'll cope,' Fran teased.

Fran was a good friend. She had the rare ability to keep her head in a crisis, and make things seem better than they were. Helen remembered when Amy was two and had slipped in the garden and hit her head on the paving stones and gashed it open. Fran had calmly driven them both to the hospital, and kept telling Helen it was only a scratch. She was the one who had held Amy as the doctor had stitched her head; Helen had almost fainted at the sight of all the blood.

'Now, what about another drink?' urged Fran, getting up and fetching more ice from the fridge. 'Have you eaten?'

'Not yet. I'll wait till Amy wakes up and see what she feels like.'

As she sipped her drink Helen agreed with Fran that a big take-away pizza with all the trimmings was exactly what they all needed.

Chapter Thirty-six

Amy stared blankly at the computer screen, barely able to work. She couldn't concentrate or even think about what she was meant to be doing. She was sitting at her desk, but her mind was a hundred miles away.

She had stayed out of work for four days. Any longer and she would have needed to get a doctor's certificate to say she was sick. Somehow, with her parents' and Jess's help, she had managed to pull herself together enough to get into the office and look presentable.

'I look awful,' she had grimaced, studying herself in the mirror.

'You are meant to have been off sick,' Jess had reminded her before she left for St Brigid's. 'No one is expecting you to report back into the office glowing with health and looking good.'

The past few days had been a total blur of being at home at her parents', and then at Jess's, and Amy felt like she really had been hit by some awful illness that had absolutely floored her and left her barely able to stand or talk or function like a normal person.

'Just thank your lucky stars that you don't have to face twenty-seven curious eight-year-olds trying to prise information out of you about why you were sick, and asking you if you had chicken-pox or worms!' Jess said.

Daniel had texted her, saying '*THINKING ABOUT YOU*'.

'*ME TOO!*' Amy had answered, but there had been no more communication. She longed to phone him or email him but her pride just about stopped her. If Daniel wanted to talk to her he knew where she was!

She'd gone into work slightly early, as she couldn't face the thought of crowded rush-hour buses, and had slipped behind her desk, then checked the raft of company emails that awaited her. She put the photo of Daniel in a pair of Hawaiian-print shorts and with a cheeky grin on his face, taken in Dingle last summer, into her drawer alongside two copies of *Beautiful Bride* that she had been reading. She watched from the corner of her eye as her boss Norah arrived into her office and got on the phone straight away. Hopefully she would manage to keep off Norah's radar until lunchtime at least.

Amy took out the Gordons' file and began to go through it. They were a family of a father and three sons who ran a chain of busy garden centres in the suburbs, and had come to Solutions with the idea of trying a coordinated marketing campaign to attract more customers and tell them about the landscaping services they offered. Fintan Gordon was a nice man, and he'd insisted on giving Amy a beautiful potted magnolia tree the first time he'd come to the office for a meeting. It had pride of place on Dan's balcony and was just about to come into bud.

Amy looked at some of the design work that Jilly had done on the campaign, and really liked it. She herself still had to work out the costing on various avenues of the promotion, which included advertising banners on the back of local buses. What a triumph it would be, too, to get a piece on the family business in the *Sunday Times*! And a lovely double-page spread about the firm in the new *The Gardener* magazine – if they took out an ad on the back page. It would be money well spent as far as she was concerned. She'd noticed that her dad had a copy of the magazine, and had spotted one in the hairdresser's and the dentist's in the past few weeks. It had a perfectly targeted circulation! She rang a few places to get rates, and was busy writing up her proposal when Norah came down to the desk with her usual mug of black coffee in her hand.

'Good to have you back, Amy.'

'Thanks.' Amy glanced up from what she was doing.

'You're still looking a bit peaky.'

'I still feel it,' Amy said slowly.

'Hope that boyfriend of yours is taking good care of you.'

Amy didn't trust herself to speak and just nodded dumbly.

Norah hesitated for a second as Amy stared fixedly down at her keyboard, wishing that her boss would disappear.

'Everything OK?' Norah said.

'I'm fine.' Amy smiled, trying to avoid Norah's scrutiny.

She breathed a huge sigh of relief when Norah passed along and turned her eagle-eyed attention on Gary Cole, the new guy who had come to work with them last year. He was getting a lot of the crappy jobs, but everyone had to start at the bottom, that's how it worked. As Norah pulled a chair up at his desk poor Gary's pimply skin flushed a deep red.

At lunchtime Amy left early and escaped to Grafton Street, moping about on her own in Marks & Spencer's and BT's and grabbing a quick sandwich and a smoothie. The afternoon was spent going over the figures on the Chippos' crunchy corn snack campaign with Jackie from their accounts section, and sending replies to about six new potential customers telling them about the services that Solutions offered.

'Hey, won't be long till your wedding,' teased Jackie, who had got married last year in Clare. 'Where are you two lovebirds off to on honeymoon?'

'Not sure yet, but I expect it will involve surfing and snorkelling,' Amy fibbed, feeling herself redden as much as Gary had. She printed out another sheet of figures quickly to distract Jackie from asking any more questions.

She was wrapping things up on the predicted spend on the Chippos' snack account when Norah called her into her office.

'I just want a word, Amy.'

What the hell did her boss want?

'I couldn't help noticing you weren't yourself today, Amy,' said Norah, gesturing to the seat across from her big oak desk. 'Is everything all right?'

Amy swallowed hard. 'I'm fine,' she lied. 'Just a bit tired after being sick, that's all.'

'Are you sure that is all it is?' asked Norah kindly, coming over to sit near her, perching on the corner of her desk in her classic black shift dress and black opaque tights.

Damn her boss's perceptiveness! Nothing could get by her.

'I noticed that the picture of your fiancé seemed to have disappeared from your desk.'

'My fiancé Daniel?'

'Yes. He's a pretty cool guy, judging by that photo of yours. Besides, I didn't spot you up on any wedding or honeymoon websites even once today.'

Amy sighed. The woman really did have eyes in the back of her head. Jackie and Nadia were right: she must have cameras hidden all over the place.

'Is everything OK between the two of you?'

Amy heard a sob, and realized suddenly that it had escaped from her mouth. Was she mad, letting her guard down in front of Madame Perfect, her boss Norah Fortune?

Norah, the forty-year-old head of Solutions marketing, with her immaculately styled shoulder-length blonde hair, manicured nails, and round face with piercing blue eyes, was staring at her inquisitively.

'No, actually, it's not,' Amy admitted, her voice breaking. 'We've split up. Daniel doesn't want to get married.'

'Oh, Amy,' said Norah softly. 'I'm sorry. How awful for both of you!'

'Yes,' said Amy glumly. 'AWFUL!'

'I remember when I broke up with my fiancé, I thought that I would die and that nothing would ever go right again in my life,' confessed Norah. 'It was about four weeks before my wedding, and there was uproar in the family about George and me splitting up and everything having to be cancelled.'

Amy was confused. What was Norah talking about? She was married to a composer called George, a gentle bald-headed man with glasses who was said to have written the music for a big American airline advertising campaign that had netted them enough money to buy a massive house out in Dalkey. They had eight-year-old twins called Charley and Henry who'd been born with the help of IVF. Norah made no secret about it.

'But you're married to George!' Amy said, incredulous.

'Now I am, but after we broke up I went out with other men. First of all there was a disastrous two years when I was involved with a charming French lawyer called Marc, who slept with every legal apprentice who crossed his desk; and then I had an ill-advised fling with a client. Then, luckily, fate intervened and George and I met up again, when we weren't so scared and stupid and both knew what we wanted. I adore that man, and he is a wonderful father.'

Amy sighed heavily.

'I guess what I am trying to say,' explained Norah, 'is that you should believe in fate! That in the end we marry the people we love and, if we are lucky, get to spend the rest of our lives loving them. Wait and see what happens. It's called LIFE! You and your Daniel are both so young.'

All the way home on the bus Amy thought about her conversation with Norah. She didn't want to be like Norah, and wait years, and waste half her life, with only a slight chance that she and Daniel would ever find each other again. She wanted Daniel now!

Chapter Thirty-seven

Helen didn't know what possessed her, but she phoned Carmel Quinn again and asked if they could meet for coffee. Carmel immediately suggested The Shelbourne Hotel.

'I have an appointment in town on Wednesday, so that would suit me best.'

Helen didn't know what she would say to Dan's mother, but she knew that something had to be done. She had never seen Amy so unhappy. Amy had moved temporarily to Jess's house and was back at work, but, as Ciara so aptly put it, she was like a robot going through the motions. She knew that Paddy had phoned Eddie, and that both fathers had been equally puzzled about what was going on between their offspring and had commiserated with each other.

Carmel was sitting on a couch near the window in the hotel's magnificent lounge overlooking St Stephen's

Green, elegant as ever in a cream jacket and tan-coloured trousers.

'It's lovely to see you,' she said, as Helen joined her and ordered a pot of tea.

Helen sat down beside her, unsure of how to start.

'How is Amy?' asked Carmel.

Helen would love to have lied and said Amy was fine and had a wonderful new boyfriend, but she was brutally honest instead.

'Miserable.'

'Dan's the same,' Carmel said slowly. 'He tries to pretend that he's fine, but it's obvious he really misses Amy. Eddie and I are baffled as to what this is all about, and believe me, Helen, we are highly embarrassed at our son's behaviour.'

'Has he said anything to you?'

'Obviously there was some big row about a surf weekend, but Eddie says that there was more to it than that. Dan wouldn't say much to me, but he does talk to his father. Eddie's close to the boys.'

'Amy blames herself,' Helen said calmly. 'She says that she was too caught up in planning and organizing the wedding and all the arrangements, and drove Dan away.'

'For heaven's sake, a girl has to organize a wedding and make arrangements!' Carmel sighed with exasperation. 'Dan should have thanked heaven he had a girlfriend who *could* organize things. What kind of wife would she be if she couldn't? Honestly, men haven't a clue.'

Helen was surprised that Carmel was not just taking her son's side.

'I don't know what is going on with my boys,' Carmel ruminated. 'Rob was going out for years with Hannah, a nice girl but clearly not the right person for him, and the two of them finally decided to break up. Then there's Dan, getting cold feet about marrying Amy – and Dylan, who seems to have a string of unsuitable girlfriends. The boys don't talk to me very much, and I try not to interfere in their lives, they are young men after all, but this situation is unfortunate, to say the least.'

'The past few weeks have been a nightmare,' Helen confided. 'But at least we've cancelled everything. Sent the wedding gifts back, and told everyone.'

'It must be awful,' Carmel commiserated with her. 'I myself found it so embarrassing telling our friends and family. And it's so humiliating.'

'Anyway, it's all done now, and I guess we just have to get over it!' said Helen sadly. 'Paddy and I were always very fond of Dan; we still are. Amy is young, and she will just have to get on with her life, even if it is without him.'

'Helen, I wish I could say that I could do something to change things, but unfortunately I cannot,' said Carmel firmly. 'We cannot interfere where Dan is concerned; he is thirty-three, after all. Eddie and I have a policy not to intrude in our sons' lives. There is nothing worse than a man who constantly seeks the approval of his parents!'

'Of course not.'

'Amy might think that Eddie and I had some hand in this, but I promise you we had nothing to do with it. Both of us think that Amy and Dan were very suited and we were looking forward to having her as a daughter-in-law.'

Helen could sense regret in Carmel's voice, along with an unwillingness to say any more about the situation.

Awkwardly, they finished their tea and made some small talk before Helen paid the bill.

'Please give Amy my regards,' said Carmel, as she took up her handbag and left.

Helen considered staying on in town and doing a bit of shopping, but she was in no mood for looking at clothes or shoes, and instead decided to call over to see her mother.

Sheila was a big worry at the moment. Last week she had taken the DART train to Malahide for no apparent reason, using her old-age pass. Her mother didn't know a soul in Malahide, and luckily a Good Samaritan called Alice Scanlon had noticed her sitting on a bench down near the marina in the spitting rain and gone over to check if she was OK. Sheila hadn't been able to remember where she lived, and had been persuaded by Alice to go to her house for a cup of tea while she tried to discover who to contact.

Alice had found Helen's name and phone number

under 'next of kin' on the donor card in Sheila's handbag and had phoned her.

Filled with trepidation, Helen had driven over, only to discover Sheila out admiring Alice's roses in the back garden. Sheila had seemed as right as rain after her adventure. She'd been like a little kid, and Helen had hugged her, trying not to let her mother see how overwrought she was as she thanked Alice and her husband. Her mother's memory lapses were getting worse, and Helen knew the situation was something that had to be tackled. She'd had reports of Sheila not having enough cash to pay in the local shops, and forgetting to collect her pension. Honestly, her mother was half daft!

The family were all concerned, and knew that something was going to have to be organized if Sheila was to continue living safely in Willow Grove. They decided that her mother's home help Sylvie – who'd been persuaded to return – would come in for a few extra hours during the week, and that at weekends they would all take turns looking after Sheila. Paddy was the best in the world and made Helen's mother welcome almost every weekend, but now her brothers would have to give a hand, too.

Chapter Thirty-eight

Helen O'Connor was determined that their weekend away in Wicklow would be relaxing. The past few weeks had been total calamity, between the situation with Amy and Dan, the constant worry of her mother, and Paddy having to work longer hours to make up for the reduction in staff at his firm. Paddy and she were both in dire need of a holiday from the stress and strains of the family. A break at Glebe House was definitely what they needed!

Amy, to all outward appearances, seemed to be coping with her break-up from Dan but Helen couldn't help worrying about her. Ciara was demented, studying for exams and warning that she was going to fail them; and Sheila had given them all another scare when she had tripped in the back garden as she was putting clothes on the washing line. Helen had just called in at Willow Grove with some shopping when she'd discovered Sheila sitting on the grass with cuts to her knee and hands, and a bit of bruising. The injuries were minor, but yet again

Sheila hadn't been able to remember exactly what had happened.

The local GP had been fantastic, but had confirmed that Sheila's age was beginning to take its toll, and that she definitely had the gradual onset of a dementia-type illness. Helen found that she was visiting Sheila almost every day or bringing her over to their place. Despite Sheila's health and memory beginning to fail, she was insistent that she was fine. This weekend, at least, Helen's brother Tim and his wife Linda were on duty and responsible for keeping an eye on Sheila. Old age was awful and Helen dreaded watching her mother's decline!

Driving through the Glen of the Downs she could feel herself begin to unwind. It was good to escape to their favourite haunt and leave the family and work and the city behind them. Paddy had to be forced to take a break from the office, even though it was only for a weekend, and she had insisted he leave his laptop at home. For the past six months he'd been working far too hard, trying to chase down contracts and get money in to the small firm he ran. Glancing at him, she could see how tired he was. Two of his staff were on a three-day week. Business might be cut back, but thank heaven boilers and machinery still needed fixing and replacing, and the business was holding its own.

'Isn't the countryside glorious?' she remarked as they passed green field after green field, and a wooded copse speckled with sunlight.

'The weather forecast is good, so we should be able to get a few walks in,' Paddy answered.

She loved the way she could always rely on Paddy to watch the weather forecast and tell her what to expect. Funny how a few nice walks, some good food, two or three bottles of wine and the chance to spend some time together was paradise at their age. Simple pleasures: those were what they both enjoyed, and her heart lifted as they turned off the busy roadway and up into the drive of Glebe House, its avenue flanked by a border of rhododendrons and tall elegant oak trees.

The pale painted walls of the old manor house welcomed them, shining through the greenery as they came to a halt on the gravelled car park to the side of the house. Everything looked the same as ever, she thought, as she reached for Paddy's hand. Bluebells danced on the lawn, and bright red tulips spilled from the beds and tubs and stone containers around the old house. They grabbed their bags and headed inside. A fire glowed in the grate in the hallway as they made their way to the small reception desk at the back. Helen smiled, noting the piles of walking shoes left near the front door.

'Hello, Mr and Mrs O'Connor,' welcomed the owner's daughter, Trudy Hanlon. 'It's good to see you again.'

'It's been about six months since we've been here, but it's lovely to get the chance of a break away.'

'I've put you in one of the lake rooms, the corner one,' smiled the petite dark-haired young woman, who was so like her mother, Eve.

Helen smiled back. There was nothing like having a beautiful big bedroom with a magnificent view of the rippling water and lakeshore even from the bed.

'That's wonderful, Trudy. Thanks.'

'Will I book you in for dinner tonight?'

'Of course,' said Paddy, passing back the registration form and his credit-card details. 'You run the best restaurant in these parts. It's well worth the drive.'

Upstairs in the room they unpacked quickly, and Helen noticed that Paddy was out of breath after insisting on carrying their bags himself. Their room, with its enormous double bed, pristine white bedlinen and plush aubergine-coloured throw, had recently been done up. The faded rose-patterned chintzy look had been replaced by a far more modern decor, which somehow made the place more stylish and elegant. There were two cosy armchairs in an olive-green colour, with purple and green cushions, and an oak writing desk with a bunch of tulips in a clear glass vase.

'The place looks great,' said Paddy approvingly, as he hung his jacket in the wardrobe.

'It's lovely. We must congratulate Eve when we see her,' Helen agreed, taking in the power shower and shiny new white-tiled bathroom.

'What about a stroll down by the lake? And then we can have some afternoon tea,' Paddy suggested. 'A bit of a walk will do us good.'

*　　　*　　　*

It was quiet down by the lake. The water reeds danced in the light breeze and a busy heron was flying over the water occasionally diving in his quest for fish. Helen could feel Paddy relax as they walked along hand in hand. Lately he had looked tired and pale, and she hoped the break away together would give them both a chance to unwind. He was so caught up with work, but she had been equally at fault: preoccupied by all that was going on with her mother and Amy. Paddy and she barely got any time together, and if they did seemed to spend it talking about family problems.

No, this weekend she was determined there would be no talk of Amy and Dan or her mother, or worries about Ciara going off to Thailand with her weird friends, or about how Ronan and Krista were ever going to afford to buy somewhere instead of renting. This weekend was going to be theirs, not their children's!

'There're the swans,' nodded Paddy. 'That pair are here every year, always together.'

They watched the swan pair gliding on the small lake, ignoring the other waterfowl as they dabbled in the water with their long white necks, regal heads and sad dark eyes.

Helen felt Paddy squeeze her hand.

'They mate for life,' she said. She'd read it in some magazine and been struck by the beauty of it, and by the thought of how awful it was when one of a pair was killed or mistreated by cruel young hoodlums.

'They're good and safe here, it's so quiet,' said Paddy, almost reading her mind.

They continued to walk along by the lake, then turned back across the bottom of the meadow in the direction of the kitchen garden with its rows of early vegetables and herbs.

'Look at the size of those cabbages!' admired Paddy. 'And not a drop of those chemical fertilizers on them, all organic.'

Helen could see row after row of rich green cabbage and curly kale and spring onions. The garden here provided a range of homegrown produce for the kitchens, everything fresh. The herb garden was a special joy, with it enticing range of parsley, rosemary, sage, chives and other culinary seasonings.

They trooped back up towards the house, both ready for the Glebe speciality of afternoon tea. The large drawing room hadn't changed, with its fading floral print-covered chairs and old mahogany coffee tables, and they passed through it and out to the Victorian-style conservatory with its white wicker tables and chairs overlooking the side lawn and rose garden.

After a plateful of home-baked scones served with a delicious plum jam, and a selection of baby éclairs and home-made macaroons served with a reviving cup of tea, they both felt their cares slip away.

'Well, it's lovely to see the two of you back again,' beamed Eve Hanlon, welcoming them warmly. With her immaculately cut short hair framing her pretty face, and her petite figure clad in the usual black jeans, black shirt and cashmere cardigan, she was a stylish woman. She had created the unique ambience of the old house with her impeccable taste and sense of style.

'And it's good to be back,' beamed Paddy, unable to resist the charms of another miniature éclair.

'Eve, our bedroom is gorgeous,' praised Helen. 'Have you redone them all?'

'Yes. We started with the bedrooms,' Eve said, sitting down to join them. 'Trudy and Sean persuaded me that the place was getting a bit too faded and we needed to give it a lift in style. We've been working on the refurbishment, and have had the decorators in since we closed up in late November. They've done a great job. Wait until you see the dining room tonight – it's certainly got a new lease of life! By May it will all be finished: this place and the sitting room are next. You've got to keep up a bit with the times even in an old place like this, people expect it.'

Helen was filled with admiration for Eve, who had taken over the running of Glebe following her husband Peter's death almost twenty years earlier, and had turned the old house into a country retreat providing classic good food and wonderful accommodation for those looking for a few days' break. Year after year the same couples and families returned to the place, glad of Eve's guaranteed welcome.

'Listen, I'd better go,' said Eve, getting a message on

her phone. 'I'll see you two later on tonight. Sean's got a lovely roast shoulder of lamb on the menu.'

'My favourite,' said Paddy happily.

Helen looked out over the garden. A few early roses were beginning to open, the tulips creating a great display. She took a bite of a melt-in-the mouth macaroon. This was bliss, and she was so glad she had persuaded Paddy to come away to unwind.

The dinner was perfect; they ordered different dishes for each course and tried each other's. Prawns and duck were followed by monkfish and lamb and a mixture of puddings from the mouth-watering dessert trolley. Two glasses of Chablis and a bottle of Bordeaux helped to complement the food. Afterwards they sat in the small bar with its cosy fireplace till after midnight, sipping port before heading off to bed.

The huge Irish breakfast the next morning included pancakes, and Helen laughed to see Paddy layering them on to his plate with maple syrup. She loved the home-made muesli that Eve served, and the two of them agreed that a massive walk was called for if they wanted to work up an appetite for lunch. They decided to head down towards the beach, which was about two miles away.

No longer kids, they both huffed and puffed as they slowly climbed up the tall sand dunes before rushing down on to the golden sand. In summer this place would be crowded with holidaymakers and swimmers, but today it was quiet except for one or two other couples and a few people walking their dogs.

The beach held so many memories for both of them, and they walked along the strand hand in hand. The tide was out and they watched as a wizened old man swam in the choppy water.

'He's a brave soul,' declared Paddy.

'I remember when you used to swim all the time,' Helen reminded him. 'Summer or winter, you'd be down in Seapoint or Sandycove or Brittas Bay when we were on holidays.'

'That was a long time ago,' he laughed. 'I've got sense now.'

'The children used to think that you were like the Man from Atlantis,' she teased. 'You were always in the water and were such a strong swimmer.'

'I remember Amy and Ronan trying to swim out to me from the beach here one time when they were small. Ciara wanted to come, too, but she was only a baby, and she bawled and bawled and yelled "DA DA", and you had to walk out into the water with her in your arms.'

'We got them ice cream and lemonade afterwards from the Mr Whippy van that used to park beside the dunes, and I remember I fell asleep in the sun and got sunburn on the back of my legs. Oh, the pain of it!'

'They were the good times!'

'We hadn't a minute with three of them. I always seemed to be changing nappies and washing faces and wiping noses, and spent my life making dinners and trying to get clothes dry.'

'It seemed a lot of work, but it was a lot less compli- cated then. They were such good kids! Great fun!'

'They still are,' she reminded him gently. 'It's just that they've grown up.'

'Hate that!' he grimaced. 'It makes me feel old and useless and crotchety like my father!'

'You are not a bit like Seamus! Besides you're only sixty-one, so a bit less of the old man!' she teased.

'Some days I feel old and tired,' he admitted. 'Over the hill. Isn't that what they call it?'

'Paddy O'Connor, don't you dare say that you are over the hill, because what does that make me?'

'Twenty-one for ever,' he shouted, swooping her up in his arms and swinging her wildly around. 'Twenty-one in my eyes, like when we first met.'

She touched his handsome face, his dark hair now grey, wrinkles around his eyes.

'I love you,' she said, kissing him.

'And I love you, too.'

The weekend passed far too quickly, with the afternoon spent reading the papers and the evening enjoying another fine meal. As they packed up the next day and left their bedroom with its view of the lake they decided to come back to Glebe House before the summer's end.

Refreshed and re-energized, down at the desk in the

hall they both thanked Eve for her wonderful hospitality and promised to return.

'I want to see your roses in full bloom,' Helen said, taking a last glance around.

'And I'll be back for more of those breakfast pancakes,' Paddy joked, taking their bags out to the car.

Chapter Thirty-nine

Amy's hopes had risen like a kite in the sky when Daniel phoned her when she was in the middle of Supervalu getting a few groceries.

'We need to talk,' he said, keeping the conversation brief. 'Do you want to meet in McSorley's tomorrow after work at about seven?'

She had hoped that he would suggest meeting at the apartment, where they would be back on familiar territory, and was surprised that he had opted instead for the local pub in Ranelagh.

'Great,' she said, unable to keep the hope and excitement from her own voice despite his rather distant tone.

She blow-dried her hair and sprayed herself with Dan's favourite perfume. Pulling on her pale denim jeans she noticed that she had dropped a few kilos, not just from the stress and upset but because, despite the wedding being called off, Jess had still insisted on sticking to her new healthy eating regime, and wouldn't let a square of chocolate or a packet of biscuits or cheese and onion crisps past the hall door. No comfort eating allowed! The salads and fruit and crunchy nibbles in the fridge were working for them both, Amy thought, as she slipped into the pink chiffon top with the tie front that Daniel loved to play with, and her grey suede ankle boots. She had worked all through lunch and finished up at 5 p.m. so that she could chase to Jess's place and get ready to see Dan again.

It was two weeks since they had seen each other, and she was dying to look at him and touch him. There was so much she wanted to say.

'Amy, please don't go building it up in your mind too much!' warned Jess. 'Daniel's hardly bothered to contact you. He might just want to sort out stuff about the apartment and things.'

'I'm sure there's more to it than that,' Amy laughed. 'Honestly, Jess, you are such a pessimist!'

'Please, Amy, take it easy,' warned Jess, before disappearing to her weekly yoga class.

Dan was already sitting in the back section of McSorley's, nursing a Guinness, something he rarely drank. When he did he usually only took one or two pints.

'Hi,' she smiled, resisting the urge to lean forward and kiss him or touch his hair.

'What will you have?' he asked, jumping up to go to the bar.

'A glass of white would be great.' Daniel knew the kind of wines she liked and hated and he returned a few seconds later with a wine glass and a small bottle of her favourite.

'How have you been?' she asked.

'Fine.'

'Great.' She took a sip of wine and tried to control the hysteria she felt bubbling inside her.

'I'm sorry about what has happened, Amy, really sorry, but I just couldn't go through with the wedding the way things were between us. It would have been like a big lie, pretending everything was OK when clearly it wasn't! We were taking such a big step and it was clear that we weren't ready for it . . . Well, I wasn't ready for it.'

'I see,' she said, trying to focus on the French label of her wine bottle as the words swam in front of her eyes.

'What have you been up to?'

'Well, obviously I've been kind of busy getting in touch with everyone to cancel all the wedding arrangements.' She made no attempt to hide her sarcasm.

'I'm sorry,' he apologized, embarrassed. 'But is that all done?'

'Yes,' she sighed. 'Everything is done. Mum has been great. You've no idea how embarrassing it was phoning everyone and trying to explain. But all the arrangements we had made are totally sorted and wiped away. We returned some of the wedding gifts that had arrived early. And you'll be glad to know that another couple were delighted to get our date to get married in Castle Gregory!'

'I see.'

She looked at his face. He was pale, with a few zits around his chin. His polo shirt hadn't been ironed, just folded over, Daniel-style, and flung on.

'Let's hope it is a luckier day for them than for us!' she said bleakly.

'I really am sorry, Amy. I can only imagine how hard it has been for you.'

'Pretty shit!' she said bitterly. 'But as they say, shit happens!'

'I'm sorry.'

'Stop it!' she found herself saying loudly. 'I'm fed up of you saying sorry when you are the one that ruined everything.'

'Amy, I still love and care for you,' he said, staring at her. 'That hasn't changed!'

'Then what is all this about, Dan? What in God's name is this all about? Please just tell me! Give me some explanation for the shit that has happened.'

'Amy, I still want a relationship with you but one that is about us, and the things that are important to us. We got caught up in some kind of wedding frenzy. We both let it get out of hand. Maybe we were rushing things too quickly, and lost track of what is important to both of us. The only explanation I have is that we changed – we both did,' he said sadly. 'I didn't like what we were becoming. It was as if we were the least part of the wedding! It was meant to be about us loving each other but it became this big show! I didn't want to be part of it any more. I felt you didn't want me . . . didn't need me . . .'

'But I did,' she whispered. 'I do . . . And you were the one who proposed,' she reminded him.

'I know. I know.'

Pensive, they both sat silent, staring at the table.

'Do you want to move back in?' he said, the tips of his fingers touching hers; so intimate and yet so distant. 'See how things go between us?'

'What do you mean?'

'Amy, I miss you. I want you to come back, and for things to be the way they were before!'

She held her breath. They were the words she had been waiting every day for the past few weeks for him to say. But he wasn't saying what she expected, hoped for! He wasn't saying that he was heartbroken without her, loved her madly and passionately and couldn't live without her in his life. She could tell that Dan just wanted things to go back to the way they were pre-engagement: easy-going and relaxed, having fun together, hanging out, just being a couple again and slipping back into the comfortable routine they had enjoyed for the past two years.

But everything had changed in the past few weeks, *everything*. Couldn't he see that? Nothing was the same. She certainly wasn't the same. He had broken her heart, turned her world upside down.

'Daniel, I'm not ready to move back yet,' she found

herself saying. 'I need more time to think about things, to think about us and what we should do.'

She could see the disbelief register in his eyes.

'I'm sorry, Dan.' She regretted the utter stupidity that had driven them apart, but knew that moving back in together and pretending everything was back the way it was before would be a big mistake. 'I'm staying with Jess at the moment, and she says that I can stay on there for a while longer if I need to. She's been great. Everyone's been great: Mum and Dad, Ciara and Ronan – even Norah in the office and Jackie and the crowd there.'

'I see.'

'But I do need to take some things from the apartment if that's OK with you, so maybe we can organize that.'

'We can go over there now if you want,' he said, brightening up, hoping that proximity and familiarity would help her to change her mind.

'No,' she said, determined not to weaken her resolve. 'It's better if I go on my own. Are you still playing football tomorrow evening with Liam and the lads?'

'Yeah,' he nodded.

'Right. I'll go over to collect some stuff then.'

'Listen, will you have another wine?' he asked.

She had already gone through two glasses. She didn't need a third, didn't want alcohol to fuzz her thinking. She was tempted, but didn't want to stay.

'No, I'm fine, thanks,' she lied. 'I've a big presentation tomorrow. So I'd better go.'

'Christ, Amy, what have I done to us?' he said, looking forlorn as she stood up to go. 'What have I done?'

Not trusting herself to speak, she managed to compose herself enough to get out of the bar and, turning left, began to walk along the familiar road towards the canal.

She had no intention of being over-dramatic and chucking herself in the water, but knew that a long fast walk along the deserted canal bank where she could scream at the seagulls and swans and the water would do her good!

'Feck him!'

'Feck you, Daniel Quinn, for ruining my life!'

She yelled and shouted as loud and as hard as she could, letting the dark muddy water claim her words.

Chapter Forty

'I can't believe it, Amy!' Jess was incredulous when she returned from yoga in the parish hall to discover that Amy had been asked, but yet refused, to move back in with Daniel.

'Do you think that I've gone mad?' Amy asked, in a quivering, small voice. 'I don't know what possessed me, but I just knew that I couldn't move back the way things are now, with Daniel thinking everything is OK again, when it isn't.'

'I can't believe that you didn't cave in,' Jess said, seeing a side to Amy she had never known existed.

'I was tempted. I really was . . . I love Daniel, you know I do, but I'm not sure that he loves me enough,' Amy said in a small voice. 'I couldn't bear that. Imagine how bad it would be if I went back and it didn't work out. Jess, I'm not sure that I could take it.'

Jess knew just how fragile Amy really was, but yet some kind of miracle had happened and she had managed to retain her composure around Daniel, and to think clearly.

'I'm so proud of you,' Jess said, giving Amy a big hug.

'Do you have any wine?' Amy asked. 'I think I need a drink.'

'Sure, there's a Prosecco in the fridge and a Shiraz in the press.'

'Prosecco, please.'

They stayed up late talking, wrapped in the big brown rug. Finishing the Prosecco, they opened the Shiraz as Jess drunkenly demonstrated to Amy the two new yoga positions she had learned: the Cobra and the Bull Frog.

'You have to stick your tongue up towards your nose and stretch it up and down like a snake!'

The two of them collapsed in a heap of giggles as they squatted on the floor.

'Maybe I should take up yoga, too!' teased Amy.

'No, you'd make me laugh too much.'

An hour later at 2 a.m., they went to bed, having talked and talked about Daniel and Amy's relationship from every angle.

'I promise I'll try and get a place of my own,' slurred Amy.

'You have a bed here for as long as you need it,' Jess insisted. Although she loved her own space in the cottage and the spare room was tiny, she didn't want Amy to go back to live with Daniel just because she felt she needed somewhere to stay.

*   *   *

Jess was suffering, totally hungover, the next morning, and even after a blasting hot shower to wake her up and revive her felt like she had been eating a bag of feathers all night. She felt ill when she opened the fridge, and just managed a cup of tea and two dry Ryvitas. She couldn't believe it when she checked in on Amy in the spare room and discovered that she was already up and gone to work. Her mug and plate were packed in the dishwasher.

Somehow Jess managed to drag herself to school. Second class would definitely be having Reading Time today, Art Time and anything quiet that she could think of. Trying to keep a bunch of eight-year-olds quiet was a nightmare even at the best of times, but today, with this constant feeling of nausea which made her think she was going to puke, it was essential. She prayed that Bernadette Carroll, the principal, gave her a wide berth today and didn't come near her class. Roll on three o'clock and home and her *leaba* . . . her big comfy bed, which had cost a fortune but was well worth every penny.

Tonight she had no intention of going anywhere, and would be happy to veg out in front of *Friday Night with Jonathan Ross* or *The Late Late Show* on the TV. Tomorrow night Amy and she were heading out with the girls for drinks in town before hitting a nightclub. It had taken a bit of persuasion to get Amy to agree to going out without Daniel in tow, but a night with the girls was just what her best friend needed.

Chapter Forty-one

Amy pushed through Kehoe's, the packed bar on South Anne Street, trying to get a drink. Why was it that one of the city's hottest bars – which spilled on to the streets outside – was also one of the smallest?

'I'll have a vodka and Coke,' yelled Tara to her. 'Lisa wants a Bacardi and orange, and Aisling wants a Bacardi and Diet Coke.'

Amy shouted their order to the barman over the sea of heads and shoulders, and battled to get the glasses and pass the money towards him. Then she retreated to the place they had managed to find, standing in the middle of a gang of people.

'Here, Jess, take your vino!'

How Jess was drinking tonight was beyond Amy. She had been dying yesterday, but had somehow rallied.

'You OK?' asked Lisa.

'I'll live.' Amy did her best to change the conversation. Tonight she just wanted to relax and have fun. She'd had enough of misery over the past few weeks.

'Well, you are looking great,' whispered Aisling. 'I love that skirt on you.'

Amy grinned. She'd found the short vintage swirly cotton skirt with its fifties print in the Camden Street market, and had teamed it with a black string top.

'God, every time I go to the market it is just full of tat. I can never find anything,' moaned Lisa.

'Amy could make a potato sack look good,' laughed Jess.

Amy was intrigued as Tara filled her in on her new job in a small film production company.

'I'm working crazy hours, but I love it. The money is shite but the people are great. We are going to be doing a big new advertising campaign for one of the children's charities, and lots of celebs are going to be involved. My job is to look after the arrangements for some of them.' She grinned. 'Then next month the crew are filming the music video for the new album by Roisin, the traditional singer. It's going to be shot down the West so I'll be in Kerry for a week or two helping out.'

'Sounds great!' Amy was glad for her friend, as for the last year and a half she'd had a nightmare of a job in a small insurance company, working with a crowd of bitchy wagons who had made her life hell.

'I'd prefer to be earning half nothing than to be working for that shower in Mulligan's and Molloy's again,' insisted Tara as she knocked back her vodka. 'Rua might only be a small company but Dave, the boss, has big plans for growing it.'

At closing time the five girls finished their drinks and headed towards Harcourt Street. Tara and Jess and Lisa were arguing over which of the nightclubs they should go to.

Amy wasn't particularly in the mood for clubbing and would have happily gone home, but she didn't want to be a wet blanket.

'Where do you fancy?' asked Lisa.

'I really don't mind.' It was stupid, but Amy found it hard to think straight and make decisions about anything at the moment.

'We're going to Roxy's.' Jess and Lisa beamed. 'Orla and the others are already there.'

The club was heaving, the dance floor packed, as they made their way up to one of the lounges with its trademark striped couches and glass bars. Amy could feel herself relax as the music beat enticed them to dance.

Orla was with Nikki, and they were up dancing like crazy people. After another glass of wine they all got up on the crowded floor.

'This is like when we were kids and used to go to Wesley disco,' teased Jess. 'All dancing together!'

Amy remembered those days, and how innocent they had all been. Sneaking sips of gin or vodka or brandy from their parents' drinks cabinets, or a small bottle they'd all bought and shared, before legging it to the famed Southside junior rugby club disco, which ended,

Cinderella-style, before midnight with the mums and dads coming to collect them all. When the DJ played 'Light my Fire' by Take That they all gave a roar, laughing their heads off, remembering.

In the bathroom Amy tried not to comment when Lisa drunkenly went on about Dan. 'Marriage is not the be-all and end-all, Amy. Simon and I think that living together is what is important. Not some stupid piece of paper!'

'Butt out, Lisa,' warned Jess, who was trying to reapply a fresh coat of lip gloss.

Back outside Amy couldn't believe it when she spotted Liam Flynn on the dance floor.

'Oh my God, Jess, what am I going to do?' she wailed. 'Please go and see if Dan is with him.'

Jess had no interest in talking to Liam herself but grabbed Aisling, and the two of them went off in his direction while Amy turned the other way. She didn't want to meet Dan tonight.

A few minutes later they reported back.

'They're with a big gang of guys, it's some sort of stag night. Will and Oisin are with them, too.'

'What about Dan?'

'I asked Liam,' said Aisling, 'but he's too bombed. But I don't think Dan is with them, unless he's in the upstairs bar.'

Amy did her best to try not to think about it, but she was too conscious of Dan's friends being around her. The night was ruined as far as she was concerned, and a half-hour later she'd had enough and decided to head home.

'Don't go!' pleaded Jess and Tara. 'Just ignore them.'

'Listen, I want to go,' Amy insisted. 'Aisling wants to, too, so we'll share a taxi. I'll be fine and don't worry, Jess, I've your spare key.'

'OK then, honey bunny, see you in the morning or whenever I get up.' Jess hugged her, then went back to chatting to a guy who used to be in college with her.

Outside the temperature had dropped and a row of taxis filled the street. Amy wrapped her jacket around her, glad of its warmth.

'Hold on a second, Amy, I want to have a smoke,' pleaded Aisling, lighting up.

Smokers! thought Amy. The cold weather was absolutely no deterrent to her friend as she lit up and started an immediate conversation with two fellow smokers. Amy rested against the railings near the steps, waiting for her. As she glanced around she froze, disbelieving, as she recognized the familiar figure of Matt Kerrigan, just as he turned, too, and spotted her. She tried to hide, but there was no bloody escape.

'Amy.' He grinned, moving away from the door and coming towards her.

Amy's knees almost buckled. She hadn't expected to see Matt Kerrigan, her old boyfriend, ever again. The last she had heard he was settled in Sydney, living the good life.

'Matt!'

Matt Kerrigan kissed her on the lips before she could stop him. He tasted of cigarettes and beer, and gave her that warm full-lipped sensation that he always used to. She felt herself flush. She hadn't seen him in over four years, and now he was standing right in front of her. Her ex-boyfriend: the guy who had dumped her and humiliated her and taken off to the far side of the world with barely a goodbye! Would this fecking nightmare of a night never end? Why hadn't she stayed home? Just sat in, watching crappy TV! This is what she got for trying to go out and pretend she was having fun!

'You look great, Amy!' Matt said, and she knew he meant it. 'I heard that you are getting married. He must be some lucky guy!'

Amy stuffed her hand in her pocket.

'Is he with you?'

'No!' she said abruptly. 'It's just a girls' night out with Jess and Tara and some friends.'

'The Famous Five, the old crew!'

'Yeah!' She stopped talking, hoping he would move away, but instead he came and stood beside her.

'You look more beautiful than ever,' he said, staring at her intensely.

'You look well, too,' she said, trying to keep it light and wishing Aisling would finish her cigarette so they could go. 'Life in Australia suits you.'

'Oz is a great place.' He laughed. 'But it's nice to be

back in the old town for a while and catch up and see some old friends.'

Amy wondered if she qualified as an old friend. For eight weeks after Matt had left for Australia she had emailed him almost every day, without even a word of an acknowledgement from him. She'd been so hurt and upset. Eventually she had got the message when she had seen his photo up on Bebo with some beautiful beach babe – his new girlfriend!

'Hey, do you want a drink?' He gestured for her to join him back inside.

'No, thanks,' she said stiffly. 'I'm just heading home.'

'The night is young,' he coaxed. 'I know it's been a long time, Amy, and I was a right bastard to you, but it would be really nice to catch up.'

He was standing so close to her that Amy could feel the strong familiar beat of his heart. This was definitely not part of the plan.

'I'm sorry, Matt, but I'm just going to get a taxi with Aisling,' she explained, calling to her friend, who looked suddenly like she had no interest in going home and was deep in conversation with another smoker, a thin weedy guy wearing a trilby.

'Hey, Amy, this is Rory,' she said. 'Imagine: he works in the computer section of the bank, and we've never even met before! He said a few of the guys from work are in Legs so we might go join them. Do you want to come along, too?'

'No, Aisling, it's fine, you go, honestly.'

'Are you sure?' Aisling's eyes widened when she recognized Matt, and she hesitated.

'Hi, Aisling.' He grinned.

'I'm fine,' assured Amy. 'I'll get a taxi home. Matt and I just bumped into each other. I'll talk to you to-morrow.'

Watching her friend walk down the street, it never ceased to amaze Amy how smokers always met up with people when they were outside in the smoking areas of bars and hotels. God knows how many romances must have started that way!

'Come on, Amy, forget going home,' enticed Matt. 'If you don't want to go back inside the nightclub, fair enough, but there must be other good places to go! Is that great late-night Greek place we used to go to still open?'

'Shut last year.'

'What about the Chinese place?'

'It's Thai now, and closes at eleven.'

'What about Freddy's? Is that still there?'

Fifteen minutes later, despite her better judgement, Amy found herself sitting opposite her old boyfriend in Frederico's, the small late-night café on Dame Street, perusing the menu after ordering a bottle of Chianti.

I must be utterly stark staring mad, Amy told her-self. Why am I giving Matt Kerrigan the time of day, let alone talking to him and sitting down to eat with him?

He broke my heart and stomped all over my emotions, and fecked off to Australia with never a care about me or our relationship.

'It is so good to see you again, Amy,' Matt admitted, slowly filling her glass. 'I often wondered how things were with you, and what would have happened if I hadn't gone away.'

'That's water under the bridge, Matt,' she said quickly, not wanting to admit she was thinking the exact same thing.

'We were such a couple,' he mused. 'But we were so young – I wanted to get out of Dublin, to get away from my boring job and all the old crowd and places, see the world and have an adventure.'

'And I wasn't part of it?'

'No. I was a stupid, self-centred bastard,' he admitted. 'I didn't want baggage like a lovely girlfriend.'

'It was a long time ago. You made your life in Australia and I made mine here.'

'So I gather,' he said, saluting her.

She felt a pang of déjà vu as they both ordered the pepperoni pizza, a house speciality, opting to share a side-order of tomato and olive salad.

Sitting here with Matt felt strangely comfortable as she asked him about Sydney.

'Your mum told me that you work in one of the big banks there.' She smiled. 'She's so proud of you.'

'Ma loves coming out to stay and escaping the winter here. I work for Bank West. I'm one of their IT guys.

The market is still pretty good there, and the lifestyle is great. I've got into water sports and I'm into sailing and surfing.'

'Tell me about it!' she laughed. 'My boyfriend is addicted.'

'Good on him.'

Amy scooped a large slice of pepperoni into her mouth, conscious that Matt was looking at her.

'When are you two getting married?'

'That's the million-dollar question.' She shrugged. 'And I wish that I knew the answer.'

'I'll never figure you out, Amy.' Matt shook his head.

'What about you?'

'I got divorced last year.'

'I'm sorry,' she said, feeling bad for him. 'I'd heard rumours.'

'It was mutual,' he said. 'People make mistakes.'

She could feel him staring at her, just like he used to, as they finished off the Chianti and chatted about old times.

'Matt, it's really late. I'd better go.'

'I suppose I'm keeping you from that boyfriend of yours,' he groaned.

'Not really,' she said slowly. 'It's complicated.'

'Let me take you home?' he offered as he paid the bill and tipped the waiter.

'No, thanks, Matt, you're staying with your family. I'm in the other direction. I'll just get a taxi out on the road.'

She didn't trust herself to be alone with him, not when she felt so vulnerable and angry with Daniel. But still, bizarrely, Amy found herself giving Matt – the guy she had fallen for when she was twenty-two – her new mobile number as she waved down a taxi-cab. Fate had thrown them together tonight for a reason! Meeting up with Matt had happened out of the blue, and she had to admit that in the few hours she had spent with him she hadn't given a thought to Dan. Not one!

Chapter Forty-two

Amy smiled at the text message on her phone. Matt had texted her twice or three times a day for the past four days. She read it, not bothering to reply. Two can play at that game! She grabbed the graphics that had been done for the new cough medicine. She liked them, but they had to pass Norah's scrutiny before going to print.

She sipped some water before putting the folder together, and then got up and went into her boss's office. Norah was busy on the phone, but gestured to her to sit down. Norah had been away last week in Gran Canaria for a bit of sunshine with her family, and looked tanned and relaxed. Amy listened as she dealt with a major client, wondering if she herself would ever get to have an office of her own and be the one to make the big decisions about campaigns.

'Hey, that work is great!' congratulated Norah, studying the green and pink graphics for the new peppermint-flavoured medicine. 'The company should be really happy with that. It looks good, and gets the message across. I'm having lunch with the MD and their marketing people tomorrow, if you'd like to join us.'

'Yes, please.' Amy grinned. Getting invited to a client lunch was a massive pat on the back, as Norah usually grabbed all the glory herself and refrained from letting clients deal too much with junior minions.

'Just between ourselves, Jerome Laboratories are thinking of launching a new range of over-the-counter vitamin products. It will be a huge spend and they'll probably want to sound us out on it tomorrow. Maybe you can do a bit of research on it tonight, check out competitors, market share and pricing before we meet them in Harvey's tomorrow.'

'Sure.' Amy smiled, trying to hide her annoyance that the night at the cinema she had planned with Jess and Tara to see the new Jennifer Aniston chick flick would have to be postponed.

'Good. I'm glad that I can rely on you.' Norah beamed, turning back to her computer.

Amy was just sitting back at her own desk when she got another text message.

Maybe it was Daniel! Disappointed, she realized it was only Matt. Matt, undaunted, was texting her again and again. How long could she keep this up, ignoring him and treating him like he'd once treated her? Why hadn't Daniel phoned or texted her? He was the one she wanted to hear from. Turning back to work, she tossed her phone into her handbag.

*　　　*　　　*

She was working on her laptop at the kitchen table when Matt called again.

'Don't hang up on me, Amy,' he pleaded. 'I just want to talk to you.'

Saving her work, she gave in and found herself laughing as he told her of his visits to some of the old places they used to frequent.

'Bewley's is a bloody fancy pasta restaurant now!' he complained. 'You can't get even a sticky bun or a slice of coffee cake there any more.'

'Things change,' she teased, 'nothing stays the same; besides, they do a great spinach fettuccine and seafood tagliatelle there now.'

'Then will you join me for a bite to eat there tomorrow?' he begged. 'And we can go for a drink after?'

She froze, wondering was she mad to be even speaking to him, let alone considering meeting him? He guessed her hesitation.

'Come on, Amy, for old time's sake,' he cajoled. 'We used to be best mates, you and I, or have you forgotten that?'

She hadn't forgotten it, the friendship and the fun and the romantic whirlwind that ensued when she was with Matt. She remembered the minute they had met and started dating in college, and all the highs and lows of their relationship. She had missed him so much when he had gone to Australia, and had been bereft without him. She had started saving madly for the airfare to go and join him, until she'd discovered that she did not figure at all in his plans for his down-under odyssey! So she had been sensible, and listened to her mum and dad and Jess and the girls, and got a grip, and in time gotten over him.

That was ancient history because then, almost two years later, Daniel had come along, and she had realized what love really was. Matt wasn't a patch on Daniel, but Matt was the one texting her now, and what was the harm of seeing him before he went back to Australia?

'OK, OK,' she gave in. 'I'll meet you.'

'Are you gone mad?' raved Jess when she told her. Jess had already bitten the head off her for going to Freddy's with Matt the previous weekend.

'Don't you know what a conniving cheat he is? How do you know he's divorced? I wouldn't believe a word he says. He's a charming bastard, and he's probably left that poor wife of his back in Australia. Keep away from him, Amy. Don't you think that you have enough on your plate without getting involved with him again?'

'I'm not involved,' she argued hotly. 'Honestly, I'm not.'

Jess flounced out of the room and disappeared up to her bedroom.

Amy sighed to herself. Jess was the best in the world, but she was definitely beginning to feel that she was outstaying her welcome. She had to find somewhere of her own to live. Jess was smothering her.

*   *   *

'Hey!' Matt grinned, gesturing to her from a quiet table under the stained-glass windows near the back of Café Bar Deli.

Amy slid on to the seat across from him. The large noisy city-centre restaurant was busy. It was certainly not a place for a quiet intimate romantic dinner, but that was fine by her.

The waitress took their orders, and she giggled as Matt filled her in on his attempts to connect with old friends.

'Do you remember DJ? He's married to a dragon of a girl. They have two kids and he's living in a shoebox of a house up in Sandyford. When I met him the other night he was literally crying into his pint.'

Poor girl! thought Amy, remembering what an obnoxious creep Matt's friend had been, always full of his own importance and bragging about his job in IT.

They were easy with each other through dinner, and Amy relaxed. She remembered that Matt had always been good company, as he regaled her with stories about Australia.

'I've told you loads about Oz and breaking up with Libby,' he said softly as they ordered coffee. 'And you have barely mentioned anything about you and your Daniel.'

Amy took a deep breath and began to tell him about the collapse of her engagement.

The humiliation and embarrassment of cancelling the

wedding, and the no-man's-land situation that she now found herself in.

'I honestly don't know where I stand any more with Daniel,' she confessed.

When Matt reached for her hand and held it, she was overwhelmed with gratitude at the fact that he had simply listened.

Finishing up in the café they paid the bill and went for a walk. It was mild outside and they fell into step together, Matt with his head bent listening to her as she talked and talked.

'Come on, let me buy you a drink,' he insisted.

They walked up towards Baggot Street and sat in Doheny and Nesbitt until closing time, talking and talking. Amy was glad of his company and reminded just why she had always found him so attractive.

'Can we do this again?' he asked as the two of them shared a cab. It had started to drizzle.

'Of course.' She'd laughed, unable to stop herself enjoying the sensation of being held in his arms as they drove along towards the canal.

Matt didn't hide his disappointment when the taxi stopped outside Jess's place and she made it quite clear that she wasn't inviting him in.

'I'll call you,' he promised, kissing her goodnight briefly.

Amy was relieved that she didn't have her own place, as she would have been sorely tempted to prolong the evening and ask him in for coffee.

The light was still on in the sitting room, and Jess was waiting up for her, pretending to watch TV in her dressing gown and fluffy pink slippers, a big mug of coffee at her side.

Amy made a mug of decaf for herself and sat on the sofa near her. Poor Jess, to be so worried about her. Honestly, you'd think Matt was some kind of axe murderer the way that she was going on.

'What happened?' Jess asked.

'Nothing,' Amy protested. 'We had dinner. I had the creamy chicken and pasta. And then we went for a drink in Doheny and Nesbitt.'

'Nothing?'

'Absolutely nothing! We talked. I told him about Dan and he was very understanding.'

'I'd say he was! Amy, please be careful!' Jess warned. 'Matt still has a hold on you. You know what he's like.'

'Matt's an old friend.' Amy blushed. 'That's all. It's nice to catch up with him before he goes back to Australia.'

'Sure,' harrumphed Jess disapprovingly. 'But just be careful about falling for him again.'

'Jess, how can you say that?' Amy protested. 'Falling for him doesn't come into it. I'm in love with Daniel, you know that.'

Jess took a slow sip of her coffee and said nothing as Amy checked her phone again. Not even one word of a message from Daniel. What was she going to do?

Chapter Forty-three

Jess came home from work and cooked dinner quickly. Amy and herself had managed to get tickets for the production of a new Roddy Doyle play in the Abbey, and had agreed to eat and then get a bus into the city.

Where the hell was Amy? At this rate they'd be late! She hated getting to the theatre after it started and disrupting everyone in their seats, or having to stand in the back row until the interval. She'd give Amy a piece of her mind when she saw her. She tried to text and phone Amy again, but her phone was off.

She went upstairs to get ready and glanced inside Amy's room. She couldn't believe it when she saw that Amy's pink and grey patterned suitcase, which was usually flung on the floor in her spare bedroom, was missing. She didn't mean to be nosy but even at a glance she could see that Amy's hair straightener and make-up and wash bag were also missing. Flummoxed, she sat on the bed. Amy had made no mention of going away for a night or two. The rest of her clothes still hung in the wardrobe, the floor was covered in her shoes, and her expensive Mulberry handbag was sitting on the dressing table, so it wasn't like she had decided to move out!

Maybe she had gone home. Jess punched the O'Connors' number into the phone but there was no reply there. She tried Tara and Aisling and Sarah, but none of the girls had heard from Amy or had a clue where she was. She even sent Dan a text. Maybe Amy had gone back to the apartment.

Dan phoned her immediately. 'Jess, is Amy OK?' he asked, his voice filled with concern.

'Everything's fine,' she lied. 'I was just wondering where she was. I think she's actually gone to Tara's. Sorry to have hassled you.'

'Jess, thanks for being such a good friend to her at the moment. I know how much support you've been to her, and I really appreciate you letting her live with you,' he said. 'This has been an awful time, but I know we'll get through it . . . we still love each other and that's what matters.'

As she was listening to Dan Jess got a sudden appalling feeling that maybe Amy had arranged to see Matt. Shit! Don't say she was with him!

Jess hadn't Matt's number, but she did know where his family lived, and a quick call to directory enquiries put her through to Marie Kerrigan's home in Clontarf.

'Hi, Mrs Kerrigan, is Matt there?' she asked. 'I'm a friend of his.'

'I'm sorry, dear, but Matt's not here,' replied his

mother. 'Do you want to leave a message and I'll tell him when he gets back?'

'Gets back?'

'Yes, dear. Matt's gone down the country for a night or two with a friend.'

Jess almost dropped the phone. Surely Amy wasn't stupid enough to go off with Matt? Shit! She had to stop her from destroying her life with someone like that!

'If I want to contact him, do you know where he's staying, by any chance?' she probed.

'Well, Matt didn't actually say, but I know it's one of those big hotels in Kilkenny.'

'Thanks,' Jess said, almost dropping the phone as she considered what to do.

1. She could stay here and do nothing and go to see the play on her own.

2. She could try to do something to stop her best friend making the biggest mistake of her life!

There was no contest. She had to interfere for Amy's own good! Anyone with eyes in their head could see Amy and Dan were meant for each other and that it was just a matter of time before they both got sensible and got back together. Matt Kerrigan turning up like a proverbial bad penny could ruin everything, and Jess Kilroy had no intention of letting that happen.

She dialled the O'Connors again to make sure that Amy hadn't just gone home for a few nights. She let the phone ring and ring and eventually Ciara answered it.

'Ciara, it's Jess,' she shouted. 'Is Amy there?'

'Don't think so.'

'Can you go and check?' she demanded. 'Go and see if she's left her pink case there, or moved stuff into her old bedroom?'

'What?' Ciara sounded peeved that she had to go and do anything.

'For heaven's sake, Ciara, will you run up and check Amy's bedroom!'

Ciara sounded half-asleep and Jess could imagine her slowly walking up the stairs.

'Hurry up,' she yelled down the line.

'She's not here,' Ciara said, puzzled. 'Mum and Dad are gone to Cork for the night for Auntie Sinead's sixtieth birthday party, so there's no one here except me and the dog.'

'Shit!' Jess couldn't disguise the mounting sense of panic in her voice.

'What's wrong?' asked Ciara. 'What's the matter?'

Jess hadn't intended to, but she found herself telling Ciara all about her concerns for her sister and Matt Kerrigan.

'Matt Kerrigan's back? I don't believe it!'

'He's back in Dublin and Amy's already met up with him a few times.'

'Feck! I don't believe Amy'd be so stupid as to give that wanker the time of day!'

'Well, they've had dinner twice and he's always texting her,' informed Jess. 'Also, I know for definite that he's gone away for a couple of nights, and I'm really worried because Amy's not answering her phone, and her case is missing, and her make-up bag.'

'Double feck!' said Ciara succinctly, summing up the situation. 'Where are they?'

'I think that the two of them are in Kilkenny,' said Jess firmly. 'I'm not going to let Amy make a fool of herself with Matt again and screw things up with Dan!'

'But what can we do?' Ciara grasped the urgency of the situation, too.

'Stop her,' said Jess firmly, making a decision. 'She's not answering her phone but they are only in Kilkenny, it's not that far away. I'm going to drive down and try and get her to see sense.'

'Can I come, too?' asked Ciara.

'Sure. I'll collect you in about fifteen minutes, so be ready!'

Jess was glad that Ciara had agreed to come with her. Heaven knows what kind of reception they'd get from Amy. It was only because she cared so much for her best friend that she was prepared to do this and intervene. Amy might never speak to her again, but she had to somehow try and stop her making such a catastrophic mistake!

Ciara, in black jeans and a T-shirt and grey hoodie, was ready. Jess chatted to her about college and discovered that her friend's sister was a lot more interesting than Amy usually let on. Ciara was studying Philosophy and Classical Studies at UCD, and despite appearances seemed to be a good student.

'Sometimes I feel my brain is going to burst with all the thoughts and ideas that fill it!' she confided. 'It's kind of weird, as I expected to hate college. I detest all that D4 snobby crowd that always hang out in the canteen, but the rest of the students are OK. I'm in an experimental dance group, and at the moment we are working on a piece about global warming and its effect on mankind. We have rehearsals all week in college and hope to perform it in about a month's time.'

'Ciara, that sounds really interesting.' Jess praised her, realizing that the awkward crazy kid who used to be the bane of herself and Amy's life was actually growing up to be pretty decent. 'I wouldn't mind seeing it. I'm sure that something like that would be great for the kids in the school where I teach: get them to be more aware of the world around them.'

'We haven't performed much to audiences yet, but kids would be great as they'd get it, and we could show them some of the moves and routines we've created.'

Jess smiled. She remembered when Ciara used to dress up in a pink ballet tutu and go to ballet lessons. She'd waltz around the O'Connors' house doing constant pliés and pirouettes. She'd always been good at dancing, and here she was taking it on to the next stage.

'What do you think Amy's doing?' Ciara mused aloud as they saw a road sign for Kilkenny.

'She's probably having dinner or a drink with him,'

sighed Jess, putting her foot on the accelerator. 'With any luck we should be there in about half an hour or so.'

As they neared Kilkenny they both fell silent, unsure of what the plan ought to be.

'Do you even know what hotel Matt and Amy are staying in?' asked Ciara.

'No, but we'll find them.'

They drove around for a bit. They stopped at a massive hotel on the outskirts, but discovered that there was no Matt Kerrigan registered there. They tried two smaller places and drew a blank, but then, when Jess asked in the Castle Hotel overlooking the river near Kilkenny Castle, they got a response.

'Mr Kerrigan checked in here a few hours ago.' The receptionist smiled.

'Has he gone out to dinner?' asked Ciara. 'Or is he still in the hotel?'

'I think Mr Kerrigan and his partner had dinner earlier in the dining room, and they might still be in the bar.' The receptionist smiled again before turning to answer the phone.

Ciara and Jess raced to the bar. There was a big group of business men in one corner, and a few couples, but no sign of Matt and Amy.

The barman was helpful, and told them that Matt and his partner had been sitting at the table over near the window only a few minutes earlier, but must have just finished their drinks.

Jess sauntered over to the table he'd pointed out. Matt's signature, she saw, was on the hotel docket for room 305. She signalled for Ciara to join her in the lobby.

'They're here, on the third floor!' whispered Jess. 'But what should we do?'

They'd come here so impulsively, and now neither of them was sure what their next move should be.

'We've got to stop Amy making an utter prat of herself,' insisted Ciara. 'That's our mission.'

Nervous, they got into the lift, and found the room easily on the third floor. They could hear talking and laughter coming from inside.

'What are we going to do?' whispered Ciara. 'It sounds like Amy's there.'

Jess took a deep breath and knocked on the door. She felt like a private detective on a case. She held her breath, terrified, as Matt came to the door and answered it wearing a pair of pale-blue boxers.

'Jess, isn't it? You're Amy's friend. What the hell are you doing here?' he demanded.

'I need to talk to Amy,' she said, standing her ground. Ciara was like a mute statue beside her.

'Amy?' Matt seemed puzzled. 'What are you talking about?'

Suddenly the door opened wider as Matt's girlfriend appeared, curious. Her dark eyes flashed as she asked in a strong Belfast accent: 'Who are these two?'

'I'm sorry, Matt, there's been a misunderstanding,'

said Jess, praying that the ground would open up and swallow her. Ciara was trying to stop giggling, and had run off down the corridor leaving her to take the flak.

Making up a story about being there for an annual teachers' conference and spotting him in the distance in the lobby, and presuming that Amy was with him, Jess somehow managed to extricate herself from the situation and get back out of the hotel and to the car park, where Ciara was laughing and smoking.

'Jess, you are so crazy!' she teased. 'Now I know why Amy likes you so much. You are a blast!'

Jess began to laugh herself. It was so ludicrous that she had to see the funny side of it. Amy would kill her when she found out. The problem was, they still had no idea where Amy was and who she was with!

They stopped off in a small café for coffee and a snack, going over the humiliation of what they had done and reliving every awful detail, before the long drive home.

'Try texting Amy again,' Jess suggested as they drove back to Dublin.

Thirty minutes later, a relieved Ciara said, 'Hey, she just texted me back. You won't believe it, but she's at my gran's. Gran had some kind of a turn and was in hospital, but they are back in Gran's house now and Gran's asleep. Amy said that she's going to stay there tonight with her. Poor Gran. I'll call over to her tomorrow.'

'Phew,' said Jess, wondering how she was ever going to explain what she had done to her best friend.

'Remember, nobody knows about us being down in Kilkenny,' Ciara warned, 'and that's the way to keep it!'

Jess glanced over. Amy was always saying that Ciara was like a sphinx and that sometimes you could get nothing out of her.

'What about Matt?'

'He's not going to tell Amy he's off in a hotel with some girl from Belfast!'

'I suppose not!' Jess agreed.

'Did you see the look on his face?' teased Ciara.

'Did you see *her* face?' laughed Jess, and the two of them got hysterics replaying it over and over again in their heads, both swearing to each other to keep it a secret.

Chapter Forty-four

Amy stared at the text again. All day long Matt had been phoning and texting her at work, begging her to come down to Kilkenny for the weekend with him. He kept pestering her about the two of them getting away from everything and everyone and having the chance to be together like the way they were before.

Despite finding Matt as attractive as ever, Amy had no intention of turning back the clock. What part of 'no' did Matt Kerrigan not understand? She had texted back, irritated, wishing that he would just leave her alone with her broken heart!

Concentrating on a press release she was about to send out, she ignored her phone ringing again. It was a number she didn't recognize and she let it ring out. The number rang yet again. About to give Matt a piece of her mind, she answered.

'Matt, I—'

'Hello, is that Amy O'Connor, Sheila Hennessy's granddaughter?' asked the voice.

'Yes,' she replied, suddenly worried.

'This is Cathy Jordan; I live next door to your granny.'

'Is she all right?' Amy asked, panicked.

'Well, actually, no,' explained her gran's neighbour. 'I'm in St James's Hospital with her. She's had a bit of an accident. She fell and cut her head, and she's had a few stitches.'

'Oh my God. Poor Gran!'

'She's going for X-rays as the doctor thinks she may have broken her wrist, and they are checking her ribs, too. But you know Sheila, all she wants is to go home.' Cathy Jordan sounded worried. 'I tried to phone your mum, but there's no one at home, and there's no answer from your Uncle Tim's either. They are the only numbers that I could find. But I remembered that your granny told me where you worked one day when we were having a cup of coffee.'

'What happened to Gran?'

'She was up at the local shops and she was in a bit of a state. She didn't seem herself, and didn't even say hello to me! She was outside the chemist's when she suddenly stepped out in front of the traffic, and a young lad on a bike nearly knocked her over. She fell in the roadway and hurt her head. I called an ambulance and took her to hospital.'

'Cathy, thanks so much,' said Amy gratefully. 'My mum and dad are gone to my aunt's sixtieth birthday party in Cork, and my uncle is in France. Listen, I'll be

315

over to St James's as quick as I can,' she promised.

Norah had taken the afternoon off as there was a parent–teacher meeting in the twins' school and Jilly and Gary had already left. Amy could see Niamh and a few others were busy on a presentation, but there was nothing to hold her, so she turned off her computer and grabbed her things. She'd race back to Jess's and get her car and a few things en route to the hospital, as she'd probably stay in Willow Grove if her granny was sent home.

To say the busy Accident and Emergency department in St James's Hospital was crowded was an understatement, and Amy could see two ambulances waiting to discharge patients as she walked into the reception. She searched around, looking for any sign of her grandmother, the receptionist pointing her towards the back row of cubicles.

Sheila Hennessy looked pale and exhausted lying on the trolley bed, a big gash in the centre of her forehead stitched and covered lightly with a piece of gauze. Her hair was in a white halo around her face, her skin drained of colour, and lined like old paper.

'Gran, what have you done to yourself?' asked Amy, rushing over to kiss her.

'I was just doing a bit of shopping,' Sheila said emphatically. 'I need to get a new coat and some boots!'

'Gran, you were up at the shops! Do you remember that?'

Her grandmother clammed up like a small kid.

What was her eighty-four-year-old gran up to, walking almost a mile to the shops? What was she thinking of with her talk of buying a new coat and boots when there was only a supermarket, a butcher's, a chemist's, a hairdresser's and the post office in the small crescent of shops?

'Hello, I'm Cathy,' the pretty dark-haired young woman sitting on the far side of the bed introduced herself. She was only a few years older than Amy and looked pregnant.

'We bought the old house next to Sheila's and moved in about six months ago when all the building work was done. We've become good friends,' she said, patting Sheila's hand.

'Cathy, thanks so much for being there, and helping Gran, and going in the ambulance and everything.' Amy was filled with enormous gratitude towards this stranger who had taken care of her grandmother.

'That's what neighbours are for.' Cathy grinned. 'But I'm glad that you're here now, because I've to collect my four-year-old from a friend's house. She was able to hold on to her. My husband said that he'd pick me up here once someone came for Sheila.'

'Where are you going?' asked Sheila, getting all fretful when Cathy stood up to go.

'I have to go home, Sheila, but I'll see you tomorrow,' Cathy promised, leaning forward and giving the old lady a hug. 'Amy's here to look after you now.'

Amy sat for hours beside her grandmother waiting for someone in the busy Accident and Emergency department to organize for Sheila to go for her X-ray.

'Where's your young man?' asked her gran, who had a soft spot for Dan.

'He's not here, Gran. He's in work.' It was much too complicated to explain again to someone like her gran what was going on between them.

Amy was relieved when they were finally brought down to X-ray. Her grandmother, who was mad on medical programmes on TV, plagued the nurses and young doctor in the X-ray department with questions, displaying an encyclopedic medical knowledge few eighty-four-year-olds could match!

An hour later Sheila Hennessy's broken left wrist was in a cast, and she had been told to take things very easy as she had a broken rib on her left side, too. There were no spare beds in the hospital so they were discharging her.

'Thank heaven,' said Sheila loudly. 'I don't want to catch MRSA.'

'No more gallivanting, young lady!' warned the A & E consultant, as she gave Sheila a letter for her GP and an appointment for the hospital the following week.

'Come on, Gran, let's get you home to Willow Grove,' urged Amy, helping her.

It was late by the time Amy got her grandmother home and safely upstairs to bed. She made them both a toasted sandwich and gave Gran a big mug of milky cocoa. Sheila was exhausted, and half an hour later was fast asleep, snoring. Amy slipped back downstairs and made herself a cup of coffee, deciding there was no point ruining her parents' night at the party. She'd phone them in the morning. Gran was safe and as comfortable as she could be, asleep upstairs in the bedroom. She'd text Ciara and Ronan to tell them and would text Jess to apologize for letting her down about the theatre.

Amy looked around the old-fashioned messy kitchen and began to tidy it: sorting out papers for recycling, bottles for the bottle bank, and chucking all the out-of-date jars and cans and packets from her gran's larder and fridge firmly in the bin. It was a wonder that her gran wasn't in hospital with food poisoning! How did old people live like this? she wondered. She stacked the new dishwasher her mum and her uncles had brought for her gran at Christmas with all the grimy mugs and bowls and plates and pots that were around the kitchen, then put it on to an intensive wash cycle. It was 2 a.m. before she realized the time, and with fresh sheets taken from the hot press, she made up a bed for herself in the back bedroom.

The next morning, as the sun streamed in, Amy couldn't believe how well she had slept. It was her first proper night's sleep since she had split up with Dan, and she felt drowsy and relaxed as she looked at the faded pink floral wallpaper and old velour curtains.

Cathy from next door called in an hour later with her little girl, Emily, to see how Sheila was doing.

'We made some buns, and I know Sheila is partial to them.' She set the buns on the table and seemed delighted to be asked to stay for coffee.

Sheila showed Emily her cast, and ate two of the soft sponge buns with their pink icing straight away, and chattered away to the little girl, who was obviously a favourite. Ten minutes later Sheila's elderly friend Florence Byrne from across the street came over to find out how she was, and Sheila relished the attention as she told Florence all about her trip in the ambulance.

'These old houses are great,' remarked Cathy, looking out at the garden, where Emily was stomping around and picking daisies from the lawn. 'They have plenty of space for kids, and to build an extension like we did. Most of them are being sold and done up, so there is a great mixture of neighbours.'

Amy looked around at her gran's small cramped kitchen with its tired beige tiles and green kitchen presses, which could certainly do with being done up!

'Mum was in hospital!' Helen was upset when Amy phoned to tell her what happened. 'Your dad and I'll be there in a few hours,' she fussed. 'We'll check out of the hotel and be on the road to Dublin as soon as we can.'

'Mum, Gran's fine,' Amy reassured. 'Take your time, there's no rush back. She's broken her arm and a rib and she's had a few stitches, but honestly she's OK.'

Amy had a slightly bizarre phone conversation with Jess, where her best friend mentioned the wasted theatre tickets, but actually seemed more upset that she had taken off somewhere for the weekend without telling her. Maybe staying here in Willow Grove with her gran for a while wouldn't be a bad idea!

Her parents arrived mid-afternoon. Her dad looked tired from the long drive on the motorway.

Amy watched, bemused, as her mum fussed over her grandmother as if she was a child.

'What were you doing walking all that way to the shops on your own? You know that I'll always bring you shopping or get anything you need.'

'I just wanted to get one or two things,' replied Gran stubbornly.

'Mum, there are enough people to help if you want something.'

'I'm perfectly able to get shopping for myself,' said Sheila calmly. It had always been her habit never to depend on others.

'Mum, why don't you come and stay with myself and Paddy for a bit. Till you're feeling better, at least?' cajoled Helen.

'I'm feeling fine, Helen, just a bit stiff and sore from the broken rib and the bruising. But I'll mend,' Sheila said stubbornly. 'I'm not going anywhere.'

Amy could understand her grandmother wanting to stay in the familiarity of her own home with all her clutter of things around her. So much was changing around the old woman that this was probably the only place she felt safe.

'Gran, would you like me to stay here with you for a bit?' she found herself offering.

'That would be grand, Amy love,' nodded Sheila.

'Then I'll stay here for the moment,' Amy volunteered. 'I need somewhere to live. Jess's is great, but I can't stay there for ever. I've been trying to find somewhere, and being here with Gran is fine.'

'Are you sure?' asked Paddy, concerned.

'Yeah, it suits everyone.'

'Amy, it would be great if you were here at night to keep an eye on things,' said Helen, unable to hide the relief in her voice. 'But what will happen during the day when you are out at work?'

'Doesn't Sylvie already come in three days? Maybe you could ask her if she could manage five mornings for the moment? Also, Gran's neighbours are great.'

'There's no harm asking,' agreed her mother, 'and at weekends Brendan and David and Tim and all the family chip in.'

'Well, if that's settled, then,' said Sheila, 'I'm going to put my feet up and have a nap in the front room.'

Chapter Forty-five

Paddy O'Connor checked in with the pretty young receptionist at the Oaklands Medical Centre. It had been over two years since he had graced the place, and he shifted nervously in his seat in the large waiting area, seeking refuge in a copy of the daily newspaper. He was mostly surrounded by women: some with babies, some with elderly parents, and Bernice Patterson, a neighbour from down the road who was on crutches. An old geezer in the corner coughed his lungs out and was given a wide berth by everyone. A forty-a-day man, by the sound of it, and as evidenced by the brown nicotine-stained fingers that trembled as he pretended to read a magazine. Paddy hated coming to the surgery, dealing with doctors and nurses and medical people, but lately he had been feeling unwell. He believed that health was wealth. He ensured that his car was serviced regularly and passed the NCT test, so it was the least he could do to make sure that his own engine wasn't developing some kind of problem.

To be honest, for the last few weeks Paddy hadn't been feeling right. He'd felt awful down at his sister's sixtieth party in Cork and was tired and out of sorts. He found that even doing simple things was making him breathless. He hadn't mentioned a word to Helen, who had enough on her plate: dealing with Sheila – who seemed to suddenly have developed some form of mild dementia – and getting over the disappointment and upset of Amy's wedding. No, he would go calmly and quietly to Tom Galligan and find out what was what!

He scanned the sports results and the business page, unable to concentrate. In the distance a baby roared, the sound filling the silence. Poor wee thing, being vaccinated and subjected to a needle! He was a grown man, and yet he hated needles!

'Mr O'Connor!' The receptionist called his name. 'Doctor Galligan will see you now in room three.'

Paddy got up, abandoning the paper, and tried to compose himself as he walked along the cream-painted corridor.

'Come in, Paddy, and sit down,' Tom Galligan said warmly, pointing to a leather chair opposite his desk.

His office was bright and neat, with a slim computer and screen sitting on the modern desk with its silver legs and wooden top.

'How are you?' said the doctor.

'I don't know. I've been a bit off sorts lately,' Paddy said.

'In what way?'

'Well, I'm finding it harder to lift things . . . even to go up the stairs to the office sometimes.'

'Any shortness of breath?'

'A bit, I suppose, but it's probably just my age. My office is up on the second floor, and even though I'd consider myself fit, recently the stairs take it out of me. Then at the weekend I thought that I'd do a bit of work in the garden, digging, clearing the back up near the shed – and I had to stop.'

'Any pain?'

'I suppose a bit. I just didn't feel right.'

'Hmm,' said Doctor Galligan. He stood up and asked Paddy to remove his jacket and shirt. Then he took his blood pressure and pulse before getting Paddy to lie on the white couch while he examined him and listened to his chest.

'Paddy, when someone like you, who rarely darkens my door, tells me he's not feeling right a little alarm bell rings,' said Tom Galligan. The doctor examined him literally from head to toe. Paddy was embarrassed when he hooked him up to the surgery's ECG machine and stuck pads to his chest so that he could examine his heart.

'Hopefully, it's nothing, but I'd prefer to have you checked out properly. I think that we should do a few blood tests here today, and then Elaine, my receptionist, will set up a few more tests for you in the morning. Also, I want to get Elaine to book you in for a more detailed test of your heart – an echocardiogram – which is an ultrasound of your heart, down in the Blackrock Clinic tomorrow, if she can get an appointment.'

'Tom, do you think there might be something wrong?' Paddy asked, suddenly alarmed.

'I think we need to do a few more tests to see what's going on!' the doctor explained calmly. Paddy tried to mask his dismay as he thanked him and paid his bill before driving back into town.

Two days later Paddy got an appointment for the cardiology department in Blackrock Clinic. Luckily he had good medical cover and could get all the tests done on the same day. He filled in a detailed form which asked a load of questions about his health and his family history. His father, Seamus, had died of a stroke at seventy-two years of age. A fit, strong man, he had stepped out of bed one morning and collapsed, unable to speak or move, Paddy's mother finding him when she returned from ten o'clock Mass. There had been hospitals and doctors and scans, but his father had not recovered, and he had died about eight days later.

The first test was the echocardiogram: an ultrasound of his heart. The young male technician explained it to Paddy as he made him lie down on his side on the narrow bed. He firmly pressed the scanner down hard on to his chest and sides: the ECHO would help show up any weakness or abnormality in his heart. It was strange listening to the gushing and thumping sounds of his own heart.

Everything seemed fine, and Paddy felt he was a fraud, wasting medical people's valuable time.

Afterwards he was asked to do an exercise stress test on the treadmill. He wasn't much of a one for the gym, preferring eighteen holes of golf or a good walk in the fresh air, but he had been on a treadmill a few times before and felt confident enough as the machine started. The pace was slow and steady and it increased very slightly, but after only a few minutes Paddy felt he was struggling; the nurse stopped the machine. A few more blood tests and he was finished. He chased back into town for a meeting with a new client who was converting a warehouse to a manufacturing unit.

Doctor Galligan's secretary phoned him two days later, and Paddy returned to the surgery for his test results.

'The results of your tests are back and there are a few things that are causing some concern,' the doctor explained. 'Paddy, your cholesterol is high and the results of your stress test, the ECG and ECHO, and some of your blood-tests, are flagging up that something is going on. I'm referring you to a cardiologist, Paddy, as the ECHO shows there are some definite changes to your heart and there may be some blockage of two arteries.' Paddy sat in the chair feeling as if he had been punched. He had never really been sick in his life and now he had to go and see a specialist. Paddy listened as the GP tried to explain it all to him and gave him a letter for Doctor Clancy, the cardiologist he was to see.

Doctor Brendan Clancy, the cardiologist, saw him five days later. He was a small, dapper man and he studied the results of Paddy's tests carefully and read the letter from his GP.

'Paddy, I'm afraid that the result of the echo and your other tests indicate that there is a problem with the arteries, and we need to investigate further. I've scheduled you for an angiogram on Monday morning, here in the clinic.'

'An angiogram!' Paddy couldn't believe it, and listened as Doctor Clancy explained how they would inject dye into the top of his leg and it would show up the arteries in his heart so that they would get a much clearer picture of what was going on. It sounded awful, and Paddy was scared, petrified. He didn't know what to think.

'Once we see the angiogram we can decide what treatment you may need,' said Doctor Clancy.

'Treatment?'

'Well, if you need a stent or even a bypass.'

Sitting out in the car afterwards Paddy felt suddenly afraid. He was as healthy as a horse, had been all his life, and yet now there were doctors and tests and this bloody angiogram thing. He hated doctors, no matter how nice they seemed to be! What the hell was he going to do?

*   *   *

On Saturday night he persuaded Helen to go for a drink in Fitzgerald's. God knows, he could do with a drink after the strain of the past few days. He set her up with a vodka and orange and himself with a pint of beer. The pub was fairly busy and the barman, Ambrose, came over to say hello to them. Paddy wanted somewhere safe and quiet to tell Helen about his appointment on Monday. He knew her mind would be racing once he told her about seeing a cardiologist, and she would have lots of questions. Likely she would be furious with him.

Helen rambled on about Amy. 'I'm still so worried about her, Paddy. She's trying to put on a brave face but you can see she's heartbroken.'

Paddy took a long sip of his pint.

'Then of course there's Sheila. We need to know what's facing us!'

Paddy took another sip of his pint.

'Nursing homes and hospitals and doctors and carers, that's what the Hennessys and the O'Connors are facing!'

'Talking about doctors,' he began slowly, 'I was with Tom Galligan the other day and he sent me for a few tests.'

'I thought you had your health check done a while ago?' Helen put down her drink immediately.

'I haven't been feeling that well recently. Anyway, my cholesterol is raised and a few of the tests came back as abnormal so Tom sent me for an ultrasound and organized for me to see a heart consultant. A nice chap in Blackrock Clinic called Brendan Clancy.'

'Paddy, I don't believe it. You went and saw a consultant in hospital without telling me!' Helen whispered. 'Why?'

'You've had so much on your plate with Amy and Sheila that I didn't want to worry you,' he explained. 'It's bad enough one of us worrying about it, without the two of us going up the walls!'

'Paddy O'Connor, if we weren't in a public place . . . I'd kill you,' Helen blurted out. 'I bet that's why you brought me down here to tell me!'

'Too right,' he laughed, taking her hand.

'So what did this doctor say?'

'He said that I need to have an angiogram done of my heart.'

'When?'

'On Monday.'

'This Monday?'

'Yes, I have to be in Blackrock Clinic by nine in the morning, and I'm not allowed to drive.'

Helen was furious with him for not telling her that he was going to the doctor, and, worse still, that he had been sent to the Blackrock Clinic.

'You could have keeled over, Paddy, and how do you think that I would have felt – or the kids?' she demanded, all emotional.

He held her hand.

'Paddy, we're in this together. No more secrets, promise me!'

Paddy leaned over and kissed her, stroking her cheek with his finger. 'No more secrets,' he promised, relieved that everything was out in the open.

Chapter Forty-six

As Paddy lay waiting to be brought down for his angiogram, Helen sat beside his bed. Helen sighed; Paddy was being his usual protective self, trying not to worry her. He was such a good man, and without thinking she reached over and hugged him.

'I'll be fine, love,' he said, stroking her back with his hand.

Paddy was talking to the nurse as she took his blood pressure. The nurse explained everything to them, and said that Paddy would likely get a hot flush when the consultant injected the dye into him, and would be able to see what was going on on all the screens around him as they tried to find the source of his problem.

'Now you'll know what a hot flush feels like,' Helen teased, squeezing his hand.

Minutes later a porter came to collect Paddy in a wheelchair, and he went downstairs to the cardiac catheterization lab.

Helen didn't even want to think about the procedure

he was facing, and got up and went for a walk, glad of the big glass windows and the views from the hospital, which overlooked Dublin Bay and the bird sanctuary at Booterstown. The waves rolled in one after another, their rhythm strangely soothing and calming as she waited for Paddy to return.

Paddy was tired when he got back, telling her about the miracle of modern medicine that had let him see inside his own heart.

'What did Doctor Clancy say?' she asked.

'He said that he wanted to show the films to Mr Mulligan – he's a surgeon,' Paddy said, unable to keep the concern from his voice.

Half an hour later Doctor Clancy appeared, with another tall grey-haired doctor dressed in blue scrubs.

'Paddy, this is Mr James Mulligan: he's one of our finest surgeons here,' he said, introducing the other doctor. 'I asked him to review the film from your angiogram, and we are both agreed that the best mode of action is for you to have immediate bypass surgery.'

Helen could see that Paddy was shocked, as she fought to control the sinking feeling in her own stomach.

'You have severe blockages in three sections of arteries and we need to urgently bypass them,' explained the surgeon, calmly sitting down beside Paddy. 'We use grafts taken from veins in your legs or chest to bypass the blockages. I attach them above and below where the blockage is so that the blood can flow freely into the heart. It is the only way that your heart will regain its normal function. That is why you have been having some pain and difficulty exercising, lifting and doing things.'

'I see,' said Paddy, totally overwhelmed by the news.

'When does he need to have the operation?' Helen asked.

'He is scheduled for first thing in the morning,' said Mr Mulligan, serious.

Helen and Paddy couldn't believe it. How had this all happened so quickly, and become so urgent?

'Paddy is in the best place for this kind of surgery,' said Mr Mulligan. 'Our cardiac unit is world class. He was lucky that his GP suspected what might be going on and sent him here to be checked out.'

'Yes,' said Helen, trying to smile when inside her world was collapsing.

'What about the risks?' Paddy asked quietly.

'There are always some risks associated with any surgery,' Mr Mulligan explained. 'But with bypass surgery there are slightly more. However, the benefits of the surgery far outweigh any of the risks, which is the important thing.'

'I see,' Paddy said slowly. 'So you think that I need to have the operation?'

'I'm afraid you have no choice,' said the surgeon. 'You need an urgent triple bypass operation.'

Helen took a big shuddery breath, trying to control her fear. It had all been taken out of Paddy's hands and they both had to trust the two men standing beside them.

'Paddy, I'll see you in theatre first thing tomorrow morning,' James Mulligan excused himself. 'If you have any questions, Doctor Clancy or my registrar, Doctor Lennon, will explain things to you and your wife.'

'Thank you,' said Paddy.

They sat in silence after the doctors had left, both stunned by the results of the tests. Doctor Lennon, the registrar, had explained things further, going into more detail about the surgery and Paddy's post-operative care and long-term treatment.

'Well, I just have to have the operation tomorrow morning and get through it,' Paddy said, trying his best to sound calm and matter-of-fact.

'Of course you'll get through it,' Helen encouraged, trying to disguise her own fears. 'You are strong and fit and have had no health problems up to now.'

Later on that evening Amy and Ciara and Ronan all came to the clinic together. Helen could tell the girls had been crying.

'I can't believe it, Dad!' Amy said, throwing herself into his arms.

'It's a bit of a shock,' he admitted. 'But at least they discovered it, and I didn't just go and drop down dead somewhere!'

Ciara was quiet, watching him and stroking his wrist with her fingers.

'Dad, if there is anything you need me to do, let me know!' urged Ronan, his dark eyes filled with concern.

'I'm going to be tied up here for the next ten days or so,' said Paddy, 'and I'll need you to keep in touch with the office and give a hand to your mum and the girls. Most of my affairs are in order, and details of my bank account and insurance policies are all in my study.'

'Paddy, don't talk like that!' pleaded Helen.

'I have to tell you what's what,' Paddy said firmly, 'just in case things don't go well tomorrow.'

'Everything will go well,' she said fiercely, not wanting to contemplate the alternative.

The children stayed for about two hours. Paddy eventually sent them packing.

'You lot need to go home and go to bed. We all have a long day ahead of us tomorrow.'

'Ciara's taking your car home, Mum, so give me a shout when you are ready and I will come back and collect you,' offered Ronan, saying goodnight to his dad.

Alone at last, Paddy and Helen chatted easily about the time they first met, the first kiss and their struggles to save to buy a house and get married.

'The kids had us worn out,' he laughed. 'I remember when I used to come home from work I didn't know how you stuck it all day.'

'It was a bit crazy,' Helen admitted, 'but we had such

fun. How time has flown, and now they're all grown up!'

'They are the best thing we ever did,' said Paddy, serious, holding her hand. 'And I'm proud of each and every one of them. They have grown up into fine young people. But now we have time for each other – time to do the things we couldn't afford to do when we were younger. Time to go to all the places I promised to take you to, Helen – Rio, Cape Town, Sydney, Bath, Cornwall . . .'

'Paddy!' she laughed, 'we'll get there.'

'I know.'

Helen's eyes welled with tears. Paddy gave out to her for crying as she blew her nose.

The nurses were in and out and she knew she had to go when they started turning off lights in the corridor and in the room. Paddy needed to rest.

'I'll see you first thing in the morning,' she promised, kissing him.

Ronan had texted her to let her know that he was outside.

'Sleep well,' Helen said, and Paddy held her close. Helen felt such tightness in her own chest as they said goodnight, that she could have been the one with the heart problem.

At home, Amy and Ciara and Ronan were full of questions, and they all sat up eating toasted cheese-and-onion sandwiches and drinking coffee and talking till all hours. Helen was glad of the company and of having the people she loved the most in the world around her.

When the girls and Ronan had gone to bed, Helen crept downstairs because she couldn't sleep. She spent two hours on the internet Googling for information on heart surgery. Reading about the surgical procedure, and scrolling through accounts from patients and patients' families somehow made her a little less anxious. Think positive, that's what Paddy believed, and what she had to believe, too. Switching off the computer and the lights she eventually went back to bed, checking that her alarm was set for 6.45 a.m.

Chapter Forty-seven

Helen slept badly, tossing and turning for the rest of the night. She kept thinking of Paddy's operation.

She rose early and downed a full pot of tea, her stomach too sick to eat. Then they all showered and dressed and got ready to go to the hospital. Paddy's operation was scheduled for about 8 a.m. and she wanted to see him before he went down.

Ciara appeared in tight-fitting jeans, a pale-blue buttoned grandfather shirt, and a black cardigan.

'Did you sleep, pet?' Helen asked.

'No!' Ciara admitted as she filled a giant glass with orange juice and munched on two slices of brown bread and butter. She still looked half-asleep and had forgotten to line her eyes with their usual kohl.

Amy and Ronan both had to go to work, but wanted to see Paddy before his operation; Ciara had decided to stay with Helen. Helen checked that her phone was charged as they all went to the hospital. Ciara was driving her car for her, as she didn't trust herself on the roads today!

Paddy was already dressed in a hospital gown, ready for theatre, when they made their way to his room. He looked tired and had a scared look on his face, something they had rarely seen. He had been washed with a special antiseptic soap and his legs, arms, chest and underarms were shaved.

'I feel like a big turkey being got ready to put in the oven,' he joked, as they sat with him.

The nurses were busy and kept coming in and out, checking on things.

'I even had a priest in last night to give me a blessing after you'd all gone home!' Paddy joked.

Ronan was great, telling him about the football results and about his plans to go on holiday to Poland with Krista.

Ciara told him that she was glad to miss lectures today as their new lecturer was like a Nazi and constantly shouted at them all. 'Honestly, Dad, it's a wonder people take his class on Ancient Mesopotamia, as he hates it when anyone asks a question, and shouts at them if they try to ask someone else! It's a nightmare.'

'Ciara, don't you let that fellow my lad of a professor, or whatever he is, think he can walk all over you. You should all write out your questions, and put them in his inbox in the college. He couldn't ignore a hundred student questions!'

Doctor Puri, a young Indian doctor in blue theatre scrubs, came in, listened to Paddy's chest briefly, and gave him the consent form to sign.

'I am your anaesthetist,' he explained, 'and we will be ready for you in theatre in a short while.'

'That's good,' said Paddy, wanting to get it over with.

Helen tried to control her nerves when Staff Nurse O'Donnell came into the room to tell Paddy that it was time.

The nurse checked Paddy's wristband as they all hugged him and wished him luck.

'Daddy,' said Amy as she flung her arms around him. Ronan gave him a big bear hug, unable to say anything, while poor Ciara was crying as she hugged him tight. Paddy fought to control his emotions.

'You keep an eye on your mum!' he teased. 'I don't want her moping about the place just because I'm laid up.'

'Will do!' sniffed Ciara.

As the porter wheeled his bed away Helen was the last one to kiss him.

'Don't worry, love, everything will be OK,' he said.

Helen could have wept. There was Paddy going to have awful surgery, and his concerns were for her.

'I love you,' she whispered.

'Love you, too,' said Paddy.

'Mr O'Connor!' called Staff Nurse O'Donnell. 'Paddy O'Connor!'

The porter wheeled Paddy down to the theatre on the first floor, where another nurse checked his name bracelet and his chart.

Helen stood watching them push his bed down the corridor to the lift, praying that in a few hours he would be safely returned to them. She tried to compose herself till she was sure Paddy was well and truly out of sight.

'What will I do if anything happens to him?' she cried, searching for a tissue in the black hole of her handbag.

'Dad will be all right,' assured Amy, hugging her. 'He said that he's got the best medical team going, and he's been fit and strong all his life. He'll sail through the operation. Just you wait and see.'

The staff nurse reappeared.

'Are you OK, Mrs O'Connor?' she asked kindly.

'Yes,' said Helen, blinking away the tears. 'How long will he be in theatre, do you think?'

'It's usually four to six hours,' the nurse explained. 'You do know that he won't be coming back here to this room, but will go directly into intensive care?'

'Yes,' said Helen dumbly. Doctor Lennon had explained that to them yesterday.

'You should go for a walk or go shopping or do something else to take your mind off it, if that's possible,' suggested the nurse. 'We have your mobile number and will contact you when there is any news.'

Helen knew that she couldn't bear to stay in the room

342

or the corridor and wait. She needed to get some fresh air.

They walked outside. It was a bright breezy morning.

'I'd better go to work for a few hours,' said Ronan, 'but if you need me, Mum, just give me a shout.'

'I'd better head off, too,' apologized Amy. 'I told Norah that I'd come in for a few hours. Are you and Ciara going to go home?'

'What I need is a walk,' Helen sighed, 'along by the seafront, and then I'd like to go to the church there in Booterstown and have Mass and say a few prayers. Ciara and I can decide then if we want to go home for a while or go back to the hospital. You two go on ahead, and we'll keep in touch.'

Lost in thought, she and Ciara left the car parked and went for a walk down along the seafront, watching the sea horses run to the shore and the huge Seacat ferry head out across Dublin Bay. It was beautiful and sunny, and she found it hard to believe that Paddy was having his bypass operation while everything seemed so normal. People were flashing past in the DART trains heading in and out of the city, and driving along Rock Road in their cars to school and work and college, all unaware of what was happening to her husband in the nearby hospital.

The fresh air did her good, and she could feel her tension headache beginning to ease as she kept in step with her daughter. Turning up Booterstown Avenue they walked to the small local church, slipping into a pew to pray for Paddy. Helen was delighted when morning Mass began, and offered all her prayers for her husband, silently urging him to come through the operation.

Paddy was strong and healthy, and maybe he would sail through his surgery. In thirty-three years of marriage he had never been seriously ill, never had anything worse than bad flu or a toothache or stomach bug. One time he had fallen and broken his arm during icy weather when the children were small, and it had been a nightmare trying to cope while his arm was in a cast. She was the one who usually had the health problems. She'd had a hysterectomy seven years ago, and been so weak she could barely walk up and down the stairs of her home for weeks on end. More recently, she'd been having problems with her knees and had been told she was developing early signs of arthritis, a disease that ran in her family.

Paddy was strong as a horse, she reminded herself. He would get through this. He would.

'Mum, you've had no proper breakfast,' Ciara reminded her when Mass finished. 'Why don't we go down to a coffee shop in the village? Then maybe we can go for a drive, or, if you want to, just sit in the sun in the park near the hospital.'

'That sounds good. I want to be near by and be back in the hospital before your dad's operation finishes,' Helen insisted. 'I just want him to know that I'm there.'

*   *   *

Five hours later they seemed to have spent days waiting for news, walking the hospital corridors. They sat in the large hospital day room drinking tea and coffee from the vending machine in the corner.

The time ticked by so slowly that Helen felt like they were in some private limbo. Amy and Ronan and Fran kept texting her and she could only say no news . . . no news. She and Ciara took turns asking the nursing staff on the ward if there was any word on Paddy and his condition.

Helen felt the tight grip of fear ease a little when Staff Nurse O'Donnell eventually told her that Paddy was out of theatre and in the recovery area. At least he had come through the surgery and would soon be moved up to intensive care.

Ciara squeezed Helen's hand, her tense face twisting into a smile. 'Dad's going to be OK!'

An hour later they were dressed in gowns and masks and led into the intensive care unit, which was hushed and quiet, with patients asleep on narrow beds. These seemed almost suspended, and were surrounded by machines and attached to all kinds of monitors.

Oh my God! Helen thought, getting such a shock when the nurse who had been assigned to look after him, Nurse Breda Carey, brought them over to Paddy. He was covered in wires and tubes and looked as cold and white as a corpse.

'The operation went well,' assured Nurse Carey. 'Mr Mulligan will be in later, when he is finished in theatre, to check on Paddy. He'll be around again in the morning if you want to talk to him.'

Paddy looked so pale and old, his hair pushed back off his face, wrinkles across his forehead, and deep lines etched on either side of his jaw. Helen kissed him gently, almost relieved to hear his slight snore. She could see the dressing on the long wound on his chest: blood was oozing from it.

'You should go home and rest for a while,' suggested Nurse Carey. 'We will be closely monitoring him. The first twenty-four hours after surgery is critical.'

Helen stared at her husband, praying that he had the strength and energy to come through this.

'Is he in pain?'

'No, we have him sedated so he cannot feel pain,' assured Nurse Carey. 'Any change in his condition will be monitored, but we would hope that in twenty-four hours Paddy will be well enough to move from here back to the cardiac floor.'

Ciara was holding her dad's hand, stroking it gently.

'Can we stay here with him?' she asked.

'Only for a few minutes.' Nurse Carey smiled at her. 'We need to be able to move around him and make sure that he is comfortable, so unfortunately we cannot encourage family to stay sitting here around the bed, but you are welcome to use the family room across the corridor and we will automatically call you if there is any change in Paddy's condition.'

'Thank you,' said Helen, filled with gratitude for this young nurse who was helping to keep her husband alive. She was reluctant to leave Paddy, but knew that they were in the way of the high-tech medical team working in the unit.

'Come on, Mum,' urged Ciara. 'We can come back in and check on Dad later.'

Ciara was right. Paddy was in a deep sleep after the surgery. He needed the rest.

'I'll see you in a little while, Paddy love,' Helen whispered before leaving the intensive care unit with Ciara.

Amy and Ronan arrived about an hour later, Nurse Carey bringing them in to see their father. For the next few hours they all took turns going in and out to check on Paddy.

Amy fetched sandwiches from the hospital café. Helen was so glad that she had her family around her now when she needed them most.

'Mum, it's nearly midnight,' Amy announced. 'You've been here all day, maybe you should go home and sleep for a few hours. You must be exhausted!'

'How would I sleep with your dad like this?' Helen said, adamant about staying near Paddy. 'No, I'll grab a blanket and pillow and rest up on the couch there.'

'Listen, I'll stay here with Mum and you two go home,' offered Ronan. 'I'll phone you if there is any change. There's no point in us all being sleep-deprived.'

While Helen settled herself in a blanket on the couch, Nurse Carey showed Ronan where to find pillows for them both. Silently Helen thanked God for getting her husband to this point, and begged Him to let Paddy recover.

Chapter Forty-eight

Helen and Ronan were called during the night as Paddy's temperature had shot up. There was a fan positioned on his bed and Helen could see that he was shivering slightly.

'Unfortunately, he has developed a slight infection,' Nurse Carey explained. 'But we are giving him extra antibiotics and doing our best to get his temperature back to normal. Mr Mulligan's registrar saw him and will be back again in about half an hour to check on him.'

Poor Paddy, thought Helen, touching his clammy skin, hoping that the risks the surgeon had warned them about wouldn't overwhelm her husband.

Two hours later things appeared to have settled, Paddy's temperature was only slightly raised, and she had fallen asleep again, leaning on her son's shoulder.

Both of them were unable to hide their relief when, at 8 a.m., gowned and masked up again, they had gone back into the unit to find Paddy's colour was better and the awful blue tinge around his lips had disappeared. Helen grasped Paddy's hand, wishing that he could respond.

'Paddy, the operation's over!' she whispered, hoping that he could hear her, trying to control her emotions now that her husband had come through and survived.

'Dad,' said Ronan, standing beside her. She looked at her handsome son. He and Paddy were so alike. Not just physically, but also in terms of temperament and personality. Ronan was just as kind-hearted and soft as his father!

Mr Mulligan arrived up at the unit to check on Paddy at 9 a.m.

'He's doing well,' he told them. 'The high temperature is a bit of a setback, but hopefully we have the infection under control. I think we should hold on to him where he is for another few hours and review him again tonight. Hopefully by this time tomorrow he can move to the cardiac floor.'

'Thank you so much, Mr Mulligan,' said Helen, eternally grateful to the surgeon.

'Helen, we are not out of the woods yet,' Mr Mulligan warned, 'but looking at him, Paddy is making progress.'

The next twenty four-hours passed in a blur of worry and exhaustion. Ciara arrived, and insisted Helen go home for a few hours while she and Amy took over watching Paddy.

Helen remembered to feed and walk Barney. Then

Fran called over, and she bawled her eyes out for about twenty minutes as Fran listened to her fears. After that, she fell into bed exhausted, sure that she was having a bad dream. She woke up four hours later, horrified to find everything was real. But at least after she had showered and changed she felt more refreshed.

'I know he still looks very pale,' explained Nurse Carey when Helen returned to the hospital, 'but his temperature has settled and his colour and general condition and respiration have really improved over the past few hours. Mr Mulligan called in to check on him briefly before he went to his outpatients' clinic, and was very pleased.'

'Well, that's good to hear.' Helen smiled, silently thanking God and the universe for getting her husband to this stage, past the first critical twenty-four-hour period!

'Mr Mulligan said he'll talk to you tomorrow,' Nurse Carey said reassuringly as she checked Paddy's oxygen.

Early the next morning Paddy was transferred out of intensive care and back to the cardiac unit. Lucy O'Driscoll, a fresh staff nurse, welcomed him back and settled him into a private room near the nurses' station. Helen was so relieved that she almost wanted to shout with joy when Paddy finally opened his eyes and squeezed her hand.

'Your dad is going to be fine,' she told her children. 'He's going to be fine.'

She sat contently for hours watching as Paddy drifted in and out of sleep. She talked to him and chatted casually about everything, and at times he tried to talk back to her. He sipped on a long stick with lemon on it to damp his lips and mouth. Just before his medication he sometimes moaned in pain, but the nurses seemed so attuned to his needs that Helen knew that he was comfortable and in good hands. The dressing on his chest was saturated with blood, but Staff Nurse O'Driscoll assured her that was normal, as the dressings were only changed four days after the surgery.

'Then Paddy will be up and ready to have his shower,' she promised.

Ronan called in again for an hour before heading home. Amy and Ciara returned after going for something quick to eat in Eddie Rocket's. Looking at their two daughters, heads bent close together, chatting softly at Paddy's bedside, Helen gave silent thanks for their support and love.

Eventually, reassured by the night staff that Paddy was comfortable and fast asleep and that they would contact her if anything happened to him, Helen agreed to go home.

Amy was staying the night again. Thank heaven the problem of dealing with Sheila wasn't an issue, as she had gone off down to stay with Helen's brother Brendan and his wife Claire in Wexford for a few days' holiday. Helen was so relieved that on top of everything else she didn't have that responsibility.

The minute they got home, she and Amy collapsed on the leather couch in the kitchen.

'Do you want a drink, Mum?' asked Amy.

Helen would have loved a glass of something, but worried that she might be called back to the hospital again in the night and would need to be sober, so she opted for a big pot of tea instead.

'It's been such a long day!' She sighed as she took a sip of the reviving drink. Every bone in her body ached with tiredness, but she knew in her heart that the worst was over. She could see it in Paddy's eyes. It was early days, but he was a fighter. Paddy O'Connor was going to recover, get back on his feet and get on with his life!

Chapter Forty-nine

Amy had rushed through everything in the office, piling a load of work on to Gary Cole, the trainee, hoping to God that he was up to the responsibility and wouldn't let her down. All the art work for the new hotel that was opening on Ely Place was in, and looked fantastic, but she wanted it copied and packed in presentation folders for the directors and marketing people.

'Gary, everything must look perfect,' she warned, 'or Norah will have your guts for garters. She hates sloppy presentations.'

Gary at least had the good grace to look scared.

There was a meeting till 7.30 p.m. with the Ely Hotel management group, followed by a launch party for the brand-new crunchy corn snack called Chippo in the Laughter Lounge. She had worked on the campaign for the past three months and there was already a good, fun buzz about it.

'Norah, if it's OK I'll run and check in on my dad after the hotel presentation, and try and get back to say hello to a few of the Chippo reps and sales people afterwards,' Amy said. 'Apparently they are expecting a great turnout now that two of the members of that new boy band Dogz are attending. Rumour has it that they are bringing their model girlfriends.'

'Well, Chippo's team will be thrilled with that publicity, but, listen, go see your dad and don't worry!' insisted Norah, who to Amy's surprise had been very supportive since Paddy had got sick. 'You've put a huge amount of work into the campaign and everyone knows that. We'll have enough hands on deck tonight with Jilly and Gary and young Niamh there. The office will always be here, but your dad and your family need you now, so just go once we finish the meeting.'

Amy didn't need to be told twice, and once it was clear that the clients loved the glossy package she'd designed to promote their new classy city-centre hotel, she grabbed her things and set off for the hospital.

Amy yawned, suddenly tired. She had barely slept over the past few days, and had spent as much time at the hospital with her dad as she could.

Her mum was fit to collapse with all the worry and stress, and it was so incredible to see the closeness and love between them. The utter patience and care and understanding that her mum showed, as she sat at the side of the bed, talking and humming and keeping her dad company, even if he was almost unconscious asleep. Helen O'Connor refused to go home and sleep or let down her guard lest something happened to him. She was like a sentinel on constant duty watching over him. Paddy had come through major surgery, but the heart surgeon Mr Mulligan had made it quite clear that although he was making good progress he still wasn't out of the woods yet.

Amy had seen the haunted look in her mum's eyes, and had never prayed so hard for anything in her life as her dad's recovery.

She managed to find a place in the hospital's busy car park and rode the elevator to the third floor. She was exhausted, but would stay for a while with her dad. Ciara had been there most of the afternoon, allowing Helen to have a doze in the chair and go for a sandwich in the hospital's café. Ronan had promised to come in in a few hours and to stay as late as the nurses would allow him.

Amy was just sterilizing her hands when she spotted Dan coming out of her father's room. What was he doing visiting her dad?

'Amy!' he called, his eyes locking on to her.

She took a deep breath to steady herself as he walked closer.

'I was just in to see your dad,' he explained unnecessarily.

'Thanks, Dan. I appreciate it.'

'I couldn't believe it when I heard what had happened. I felt I had to come and see him.'

'Dan, you know how fond of you Dad is.'

'Even still?'

'Yeah, you know Dad!'

'He tells me he's weak, but that you can't kill a good thing!'

'Trust him!'

'He must have given you all a scare?'

'Sure did, but Mum's been great. She's barely left his side. She's just willing him to get better.'

'They're a great pair.'

'They sure are, mad about each other, still in love after all the years. I guess some couples never lose it . . .' She trailed off, trying not to cry and get upset.

'Amy!' He touched her shoulder.

'Listen, Dan, I'd better go in to Dad, see how he's doing.' Amy stepped away from him, conscious of other visitors passing them by.

'Amy, please can we talk?'

'I have to see my dad.' Amy didn't want to talk to Dan here in a hospital corridor.

She was tired and drained, and couldn't even think straight at the moment. She had been doing everything she could to avoid the embarrassment of meeting him or bumping into him. She'd shopped in different places, avoided their favourite bars and hadn't walked near Sandymount Strand for weeks.

'Well, what about after?' he pleaded, putting on that entreating hangdog expression that had always won her round in the past.

'Dan, I don't know if—'

'Listen, I'll wait for you downstairs.'

'I'm not sure how long I will be.'

'That doesn't matter,' insisted Dan. 'I'll wait.'

Amy pushed in the door to the small private room. Her dad was resting, eyes closed, his skin almost as white as the hospital pillows. It had been five days since his operation, and he still looked so fragile and weak. The oxygen tube was still in his nose, his legs were encased in white stockings, and he looked shaky and sick.

'Hey!' He smiled as she hugged him gently and kissed his forehead.

'How are you?' she asked, sitting in a chair positioned right beside his bed.

'Fine.' He nodded. 'Lucy, the staff nurse, had me out walking, and they got me into the shower on my own. I'm bunched after it. I slept for two hours I was so wrecked.'

'Dad, maybe it's too much for you,' Amy said, concerned.

'Amy, I have to get back on my feet. They get us up moving again as quick as they can. I'll have to be able to do the stairs here before they'll let me home.'

'The stairs!'

'It seems like Mount Everest,' he said, sounding dispirited. 'I don't know how I'm ever going to get back from this.'

'Dad, you're doing great,' she said, trying to encourage him.

'I feel shit,' he confided, 'but don't tell your mother.'

'Did you eat anything today?' she quizzed.

'I'm not hungry.'

She knew that her mum was really worried as Paddy had had absolutely no appetite yet.

'Dan was in with you?'

'Yes,' he nodded. 'He was in this afternoon.'

'Dad, it's night-time,' she reminded him gently. They'd all noticed he was totally disorientated about time. He had no interest in the news or what was going on, and had difficulty holding a conversation. The staff had reassured them that this was totally normal and told them not to expect anything much for at least two weeks.

'Someone needs to knock your two heads together,' he said slowly. 'I'd do it myself, but I'm as weak as a kitten.'

Amy looked at her hands, playing with the stiff corner of his starched sheet, not trusting herself to say anything. Her dad was sick and confused, and not even able to think or talk properly, but still Dan was in his mind.

'Mum is looking forward to you coming home,' she said, trying to change the conversation.

'She wants me to sleep downstairs.'

Amy didn't want to let him know that her mum had already discussed this possibility with them all. Helen was terrified of taking him home and what might happen.

'I'll sleep in my bed when I go home,' he insisted obstinately.

Amy smiled. Her dad was generally easy-going and the kind of man you could get around; it rarely happened that he dug his heels in, but when he did he could be as stubborn as a mule.

'Where's Mum?'

'She's gone to the café.'

Amy could see that he was tiring, drifting off to sleep again, and so she just sat beside him, picking up the newspaper that her mum had left on the locker. He looked so old, so vulnerable. Her dad had always been such a rock. They all needed him and depended on him so much. The thought of anything happening to him was unbearable. He had to get better and get over this operation!

'Hello, love,' said her mum, appearing about twenty minutes later. 'I was down getting a bit of dinner. They had some beautiful hake on the menu, you wouldn't get the like in the best restaurant in Dublin.'

Paddy woke up again at the sound of her voice. Helen pulled the other chair over beside his bed and took his hand.

'When you get home, Paddy, that is what I'll cook. Nice fish and vegetables and healthy brown stuff.'

'God!' he groaned.

Amy laughed.

'There'll be no more steak every night and fry-ups and mounds of butter. We've all learned our lesson!'

insisted Helen O'Connor, half-winking at Amy.

They were hilarious, thought Amy. Even with her dad sick, and after major heart surgery, they were able to laugh and tease each other.

Nurse O'Driscoll came in to check again on Paddy.

'Time for another go on the nebulizer, Paddy,' she said, starting it up and slipping the mask over his nose and mouth. 'We want to make sure to keep that chest clear.'

Paddy was using the nebulizer a few times a day and once during the night, as it was still very hard for him to cough.

'Amy, why don't you go home?' suggested Helen. 'You've got work in the morning.'

'Mum, I'm fine. I'll stay with you a bit longer.'

'No, Ronan's due in soon, and your dad and I might listen to the radio a bit. There's a concert from the National Concert Hall on Lyric: we'll have a listen to that.'

'Go!' signalled Paddy.

'OK, then, I'll see you tomorrow,' Amy promised, kissing his forehead, and leaving her parents together.

Walking back down the corridor, she was relieved that her father seemed improved since the day before. She'd heard all kinds of stories about people's reactions after major surgery, and so far it looked like her dad had come through with flying colours.

The lights in the hospital lobby were dimmed, the big reception desk closed, with only the porter at his small desk in the corner, when she spotted Daniel sitting in the deserted admissions area waiting for her.

'Dan!'

'I told you that I'd wait for you,' he said. 'Do you want to sit down here? It's quiet.'

'No, not here.' She'd had enough of hospital the past few days. 'Could we go somewhere else?'

'I'll drive,' he offered, as they walked out to the car park.

Chapter Fifty

Amy watched Dan's face. His expression was serious as they drove along the Merrion Road, crossing Merrion Gates, and parked by the familiar length of Sandymount Strand. She wondered what the hell he wanted to say to her. Hadn't they hurt each other enough? She sat silent and rigid against the car seat, staring out at the sea and Dublin Bay as darkness fell and the lights from Howth to Dun Laoghaire glimmered in the distance. The air was so tense between them that she was tempted to just jump out of the car and run away from both him and their situation.

'I'm sorry,' he said, looking at her. 'I'm sorry, Amy.'

She held her breath.

'I was dumb and stupid to do what I did,' he said, taking a breath. 'You don't have to go away for weekends with me if you don't want to. Just because I want to surf doesn't mean you have to! I was blaming you for all kinds of shit that was nothing to do with you and was about me . . .'

'What?'

'I was the one with cold feet, getting scared about the wedding and the people and the invites and the whole fecking thing! I just didn't know how to say it to you . . . so instead I blamed you.'

'Dan . . . I was awful! I was a right Bridezilla,' she admitted, acknowledging the obsessive drive for perfection that had broken them up. 'I turned into something I swore I would never be. It was some kind of obsession. I know that now. Even Jess said that I was unbearable, and that all I cared about was the wedding and other stupid stuff, instead of thinking about us. I'm so ashamed. No wonder you hated me.'

'I don't hate you,' he protested, his breath warm against her face. 'I could never hate you. You must know that. Amy, I love you. And, married or not . . . together or not . . . I still love you. I always will.'

Amy could scarcely believe what she was hearing. They were the very words she had waited and waited for him to say.

'I don't want to live my life without you,' Dan admitted. 'I want us to be together, whether we have rings on our fingers or a piece of paper or nothing. It doesn't matter to me as long as we are together. That's what's important! That's what matters!'

'You still love me?'

'Of course I do.' He turned her to face him. 'Tell me you know that.'

'I know that,' she whispered, realizing that she'd

always known that. Dan was a part of her as much as her heart, her breath, her skin. 'I love you, too, and I always will.'

'Good,' he whispered, pulling her into his arms, his lips and mouth claiming hers, making his feelings very clear as they kissed and caressed and touched. His fingers and lips were on her breast, and her belly, and they made her groan with pleasure as she tried to resist the temptation to climb on to his lap.

'Dan, we are in the car park,' she reminded him suddenly, glancing around. 'There is an old couple sitting two cars up from us listening to music and just holding hands. They're watching us.'

'Let them,' he said, pulling her closer again.

'Do you think we'll be like them when we are old, sitting here looking out at the sea?' she asked a while later.

'I hope so,' he said firmly. 'I'll love you when you are old.'

'When I'm grey and fat and have arthritis and can hardly walk?'

'Sure. Will you love me when I am old and bald and have no teeth and can't remember my name?'

'Of course I'll love you.' She giggled. 'Anyway, they can do great things for teeth nowadays, and I think you would look kind of cute bald.' She touched his face, tracing the outline of his cheek and jaw and nose and lips. 'What about when we have kids, and I'm pregnant and ginormous and have to rest with my feet up or spend half my time in the bathroom being sick every day?'

'I'll love you even more. I love pregnant women.' He laughed, tracing his finger along her stomach. 'But,' he countered, 'what about when I am a grumpy old fart playing golf and giving out to our kids and yelling at them to turn down the music?'

'I'll them that I love that grumpy old fart,' she said firmly. 'What will you feel when I'm sad and lonely and lost?'

'I'll love you,' Dan insisted. 'Even when I'm hooked up to machines and too weak to walk or talk, I'll still love you.'

'I will love you even more,' she whispered, blinking away the tears, thinking of her dad and her mum as she kissed Dan's eyes and eyelashes. 'It will never stop.'

'Marry me, then?' he asked.

'You already asked me that,' she reminded, 'and you know what happened.'

'I'm asking again,' he said. 'I love you and I want to marry you.'

'Yes, please.' Her voice was shaking, and she couldn't believe that by some miracle they had been given a second chance. 'This time it will be different,' she promised.

'No castle or two hundred guests!' he teased.

'Definitely not,' she answered.

'No gangs of Canadian cousins arriving over for our nuptials?'

'They won't be invited,' she was adamant. 'And none of your mum's gang of twelve golf mates, either?'

'Over my dead body,' agreed Dan.

'We could get married on a beach somewhere far away from everyone?' she offered. 'Or in the Register Office?'

He kissed her again. 'Amy, the wedding is to celebrate our love with those we love.'

Amy grinned. It was exactly what she was thinking. 'Wait till we tell Mum and Dad,' she laughed. 'They won't believe it.'

'Do you want to go tell them now?' he offered.

'Are you sure?'

'Yeah, come on,' he said, giving her a kiss as he started the engine. 'Paddy will be delighted that they're the first to know that we are back together.'

The hospital's night porter pretended not to see them as, hand in hand, they slipped into the elevator for the third floor. Her mum and dad were in the room, the lights low and Paddy dozing lightly.

'Dan! Amy?' Her mum was surprised to see them together, and noticed immediately that they were holding hands, and grinning like two crazy people! 'Paddy?' she called softly.

Paddy opened his eyes and smiled when he saw Dan.

'We wanted to tell you and Dad that everything is

OK between us again,' Amy explained. 'We're back together. The engagement is back on and we are getting married.'

'Oh, that is wonderful news,' cried her mum, jumping up to hug them both, tears welling in her eyes. 'God knows this family could do with some good news!'

Chapter Fifty-one

Amy studied the engagement ring, her fingers touching and twisting it. She enjoyed the familiar feel of it back on her finger and was so glad that Dan hadn't taken her advice to return it to the jewellers.

'I knew that you would be wearing it again,' he said, pulling her into his arms. Amy relished his touch and smell and the feel of his breath again, as she made her own feelings equally clear, the awfulness of the past few months without him forgotten.

'Stay tonight,' he pleaded. 'I need you.'

'I love you,' she said, wrapping her arms tightly around his neck, desperate to feel his body close to hers, and equally wanting to make love like they used to.

Amy saw the love shining in Dan's eyes as he led her back into their bedroom.

'Never leave me again,' he said huskily as he drew her close to him and they fell on to the soft quilt and pillows.

Amy silently vowed that she would never let angry

words or rows keep them apart again, as she began to let Dan know just how much she had really missed him.

Awaking beside Daniel the next morning, Amy watched the easy rhythm of his breathing as he slept on, a smile on his face. A few days ago she had thought that she was on the point of losing everything that was precious to her: Dan, her dad, and even her grandmother. Now, by some kind of miracle, she had been given a second chance. She swore silently never to take anything or anyone in her life for granted again.

They were both late for work, and Amy grabbed her phone and sent Norah a text to say that she wouldn't be in till after lunch. Then she lay back and dozed, realizing just how much the past few days of worry had taken their toll on her.

'Morning, gorgeous,' Dan said a while later, tickling her hips and stomach.

'Dan,' she laughed, as, ignoring the bedside clock, he dragged her under the bedclothes and they made love again.

They went for a romantic lunch in Picasso's, their favourite little restaurant in Ranelagh, and then both headed to work for a few hours. Amy was unable to keep the smile off her face when Jilly and Norah immediately spotted the ring was back on her finger.

'Back where it is meant to be,' said Norah, ignoring the fact that Amy hadn't appeared in to the office until nearly three o'clock in the afternoon.

After work Amy drove to the hospital to see her dad. He still looked awful, but seemed slightly brighter than the day before. He no longer needed oxygen, which was a very good sign.

'And he ate some porridge this morning,' said Ciara proudly, full of questions about how Dan and she had got back together again. 'I'm so happy for you, Amy. He is your other half, and you were lost without that missing piece.'

Amy wondered how her younger sister managed to sum up exactly how she had felt.

'Where's Mum?'

'She's gone over to Gran's for a while. Uncle Brendan is bringing Gran back up from Wexford tomorrow. He said they'd call to see Dad on the way.'

'Gran's coming back from Wexford!'

'Yes, that's what I said.'

'Gran's coming back,' Amy explained to Dan that night as they sat out on the apartment balcony and ate dinner. 'I've been staying with her for the past few weeks, ever since she had her fall. Sylvie, her home help, comes in during the day, and I'm staying with her at night to keep an eye on her.'

'Oh,' he said, unable to hide his surprise that she couldn't just move straight back in with him and have things return to normal.

'I'm sorry, Dan, but I can't just go and let her down.

Mum has enough on her plate at the moment with Dad coming home from hospital hopefully in a few days' time. I'm sure we'll get something sorted, but for the moment I need to stay in Willow Grove.'

'It's OK!' he said, smoothing the worry lines from her forehead.

Amy was relieved that he understood the chaotic state her family was in.

Trying to conquer his disappointment, Dan insisted on being a gentleman and calling over with her to her grandmother's house the next night. Amy had told her grandmother that she would be a little late, with having to visit her dad first.

'I'm sure that she'll be gone to bed at this hour,' remarked Dan, as it was past 10 p.m. when they arrived.

'Gran's a night owl,' Amy laughed. 'She doesn't go to bed till all hours. She stays up watching late films or documentaries or listening to the radio. Some nights I have to come down and make her go to bed or she'd be up till dawn.'

Sure enough, they could see the light inside, and Dan agreed to come in to see Sheila and tell her their news.

Sheila Hennessy was engrossed in the forensic examination taking place in Las Vegas in one of *CSI*'s more gory episodes.

'They always get their man!' she nodded, riveted to the autopsy table and barely glancing up at them as they came into the kitchen-cum-breakfast room.

'Gran, I've Dan with me,' Amy explained. 'We just wanted to tell you that everything is OK again, and that we are going to get married.'

'I know that,' the old woman said, turning around. 'Amy, you told me that before, and I told you I'm going to wear my peach suit and the hat with the roses on it I bought in Harrods for your wedding.'

'Sheila, that would be wonderful.' Dan smiled and kissed her. 'You'll look beautiful.'

'Would you two like a sherry or a drop of whiskey?' Sheila asked, enjoying the flattery, and suddenly remembering her manners

Amy smiled to herself. Her grandmother had a great stash of alcohol in the sideboard ready for little tipples. She was always asking visitors to imbibe with her.

'I'll have sherry.' Amy grinned, wanting to celebrate. She was getting partial to the sweet, sticky drink.

'I'll have a tot of whiskey with some water, as I'm driving,' said Dan, studying the range of malt whiskeys Sheila had accumulated.

'I'll join you.' Sheila smiled, and snapped off the TV. 'I've seen that programme before.'

Over the next hour she entertained them with stories of family weddings she'd attended: the disasters, the hilarious, romantic and beautiful ones.

'I think your Uncle David arriving at his wedding on his motorbike all dressed in black leather, and that girlfriend of his, Anna, turning up wearing a white leather top and a white leather skirt with biker boots, and coming on a Harley, was one of the ones that really stood out.'

Amy couldn't imagine her boring old Auntie Anna wearing leather, let alone riding a motorbike. Now all she did was knit big ugly chunky jumpers for her children and cook disgusting organic dishes made up of beans and lentils. A meal in Anna's house always upset everyone's stomach for days.

Amy remembered when her sister Ciara and herself were flower girls for her Cousin Terry's wedding, and the excitement of it all. They had had to carry baskets full of rose petals and scatter them.

'You can't beat a family wedding!' declared Sheila, pouring another sherry. 'There are enough sad things in life: illnesses, goodbyes, moving house, losing jobs, or emigrating. That's why this family believe in celebrating the good things when they happen. I saw Paddy today. Helen said that the doctor's fixed his heart. Isn't it amazing what they can do today? And what a celebration it will be when you two lovely people get married!'

Amy squeezed Dan's hand. She didn't want to wait another year, and there was no question of them running off to an exotic beach or far-flung destination to wed. Sheila Hennessy might be well into her eighties, but Amy wanted her beloved granny at their wedding.

Chapter Fifty-two

Helen O'Connor was so relieved to have Paddy back home again. It didn't matter that he was weak and shaky and quieter than she had ever seen him in her life. Paddy was back in his home where he belonged, and the nightmare of hospitals and doctors and the operation was over. Driving out of the Blackrock Clinic she had felt anxious about coping with Paddy being ill, but the staff on the ward had reassured her that he was making great progress and was totally fit to go home.

'We are throwing him out of here,' teased Staff Nurse Lucy O'Driscoll as they said their goodbyes. 'But he'll be back for his physio sessions and, when he is ready, he can join the Healthy Heart programme we run.'

At home, Helen felt like all the energy and adrenalin that had kept her going over the past eleven days had suddenly vanished, and she would have loved to crawl up under the bedcovers for about two days to recharge her batteries, but there was far too much to be done now that she had Paddy home.

She had read over and over the notes from the hospital dietician, and had totally restocked the fridge with healthy heart foods. Paddy's favourite butter spread on everything was a thing of the past, and his love of a decent steak a few nights a week was now going to be limited to once only. They both would have to get used to a new regime of fish and chicken and vegetables – and a new lifestyle. She had gone to the fishmonger's and got some salmon fillets to bake in the oven for dinner with some of the baby new potatoes he loved.

Paddy, true to his word, had refused to sleep downstairs, and in a way she was relieved. She couldn't imagine them not sharing a room or being together.

The first night he came home all the kids made a big fuss for his homecoming. Ronan, without complaint, cut the grass and weeded the flower beds, and Ciara had the house so spick and span and gleaming, it looked as if the Molly Maids had been in. Amy had bunches of flowers in every room, and had made a welcome-home cake with Paddy's favourite lemon icing.

As Helen looked around the kitchen table she could see the stress and strain of the past few weeks suddenly beginning to lift. Even poor Barney couldn't contain his excitement, and barked and wagged his tail for nearly twenty minutes when he saw Paddy walk through the hall door.

'There will be plenty of walks, boy,' Paddy promised the dog. He'd a strict exercise routine to follow now, which meant a long walk every day.

*　　*　　*

Helen tried not to get upset when she saw the changes that the operation had made to Paddy. He couldn't concentrate or read a newspaper or watch the TV, and she caught him crying a few times. Some days he didn't seem to want to do anything, and sat around like a sack of potatoes, irritating her. Mr Mulligan had reassured her that this was to be expected, and it would take a few weeks for him to return to normal. They had to be patient: his body had been through a major shock and was slowly trying to recover.

'Don't expect too much for the next five to six weeks,' Lucy O'Driscoll had warned when she was packing up Paddy's things to go home. Helen prayed that the Paddy of old would eventually be restored to her.

Fran and Tom and all the neighbours and their friends called to see Paddy, and Father Tom Doorly was a great support, spending time debating the meaning of life and change with him.

Paddy wasn't a very religious man normally, but he seemed to have found a new spirituality since the bypass. And, of course, he still had his good friends to fall back on: Fintan Byrne and Noel Phelan and Sean Kennedy brought him down to the local during his second week home.

'I'm on the mend,' he reassured her when he came home drunk after one pint of shandy.

The news that Amy and Dan were back together again, and living in Dan's apartment, had also lifted

Paddy's mood. Eddie and Carmel had phoned Paddy about it, equally delighted to see the young couple reunited. Because Amy couldn't be there all the time any more, a night roster of family to stay with Sheila had been drawn up. Amy, Ciara, Ronan and Helen's brother Tim's boys Rob and John all took their turn. For the future, Helen's brother David's youngest, Caroline, was hoping to go to college in Dublin in the autumn, and the offer of free accommodation in return for keeping an eye on her grandmother was certainly very appealing to the young student.

Amy and Dan were determined to get married, and were scouting for a new place to have their wedding, which they hoped might be some time before the year was out.

'We just want to be married,' they candidly admitted, as they made plans for the future.

Helen gave thanks for the life-saving surgery that meant Paddy would at least be well and strong enough to proudly walk his elder daughter up the aisle when the time came.

Chapter Fifty-three

The minute Jessica Kilroy heard the good news that Amy and Dan were back together she thanked her lucky stars that she had stayed on her diet. She was down by ten kilos, which made a huge difference: her jelly belly was flatter, her arms thinner and she felt so much healthier and trimmer.

'Jess, we'll be getting married as soon as we can,' confided Amy. 'So I hope that you will still be my bridesmaid.'

'Of course I will,' Jess promised. 'I wouldn't miss it for the world, and thank heaven I still have my dress!'

'You still have the bridesmaid dress!' gasped Amy.

'I told you that I loved it and would have bought it anyway.' Jess grinned. 'Though I did suspect – or hope – that I might get to wear it when my best friend and her boyfriend eventually came to their senses.'

Amy hugged her, tears in her eyes, so relieved that Jess had insisted on paying for it herself, as otherwise she probably would have returned it. It amazed Jess when she found out that Helen had also kept Ciara's brides-maid dress, and hidden it in the back of the wardrobe.

'Mum said that she couldn't face going through all that rigmarole with Ciara ever again,' confided Amy. 'She thought that maybe some day Ciara might need a dress, and that she would have it for her.'

Jess smiled, knowing that, like her, Helen O'Connor had been secretly hoping that Amy and Dan would get married after all, and that's why she had not returned the dress.

Jess was looking forward to the wedding. As well as losing weight, she had maintained her exercise regime. She was walking as much as she could: an hour at least every day before or after work. She went swimming with Tara once a week and, encouraged by her sister Ava, had signed up for the summer on a GI-type training session two nights a week in the local park. It was the toughest thing she had ever done, and she had had to force herself to get over the embarrassment of being surrounded by blonde skinny girls who didn't need to exercise and looked askance at her as, red-faced, she puffed and panted and sweated through one awful exercise after another. For the first time in her life her body was doing what it was meant to: stretching and jogging and moving, instead of lying or sitting around on couches and chairs.

Second class didn't know what hit them as she took them off on long nature walks in the nearby park and added an extra PE class to their school routine. If the weather was good Jess believed it was far better to have them exercising outdoors in the fresh air than being stuck in the classroom or the school hall.

Looking in the mirror as she got ready to go to lunch with Amy and the girls in the Canal Café, Jess could see that her hair had improved and her skin was actually glowing.

She might not have a boyfriend or a man in her life but she actually looked good.

The busy restaurant was packed and they all were shoved on to a table near the back.

The girls were all delighted for Amy and thrilled to know that Dan and she were back together again.

'We knew you'd get back!' they all shouted, as Amy showed them that her engagement ring was firmly back on her finger again.

'I'm never taking it off again,' she swore. 'Never!'

'True love always wins out,' insisted Tara. 'Everyone knows that you and Dan are totally meant for each other.'

'Is the wedding back on again, too?' asked Orla, curious.

'Yeah,' grinned Amy. 'We both want to get married before Christmas, but it's hard trying to get somewhere.'

'You're not going back to the castle, then?' Jess wanted to know.

'No, this time the wedding will be a lot smaller and more low-key,' Amy said, glancing over at Jess, who was delighted that Amy could talk about her wedding normally, instead of being a crazy Bridezilla!

They studied the tall menus, and Jess ordered a mustard and honey chicken salad while the rest of the girls went for lasagne and garlic bread and the chicken wings and wedges.

They were all just tucking in and chatting when Sarah fled from the table. Orla informed them a few minutes later that poor Sarah was throwing up violently in the Ladies. Her half-full wine glass was still on the table when she reappeared, looking pale and wretched.

'I'm ten weeks gone,' she said grimly as she downed the wine. 'And sick as a parrot.'

'Congratulations!' shouted Jess and the girls. 'Well done. That's great news!'

They all knew to a woman that Sarah was struggling to cope with her nine-month-old son, Sam, who'd had desperate colic and was an awful sleeper. It had put such a strain on her marriage that her husband Tom slept in the spare room during the week. That way, one of them could surface and work.

'It's not great news,' she admitted. 'It's shite news . . . the last thing Tom and I wanted was to have another baby so soon when we have Sam. It's a nightmare.' She began crying. 'A nightmare!'

'Babies who don't sleep a lot are usually really bright and intelligent in school,' Jess consoled, trying to think of something positive to say. 'Sam's great, and you and Tom are so lucky to be having another baby. My sister

Ava has been married almost three years and is dying for a baby, and she can't get pregnant.'

'Tell her she can have one in about seven and half months' time,' wailed Sarah. 'I'm sure I won't be able to manage.'

The rest of the meal was spent trying to cheer Sarah up and listening to the on and off saga of Tara's love life with Johnny, the rat she'd been dating for over a year.

'He's a disaster,' insisted Aisling, 'and he doesn't even treat you well. You should dump him!'

'I know he's not the best,' Tara admitted. 'But it's really hard being on your own and not having a boyfriend. I don't know if I could cope with being single like Jess.'

'Thanks a mill!' shrugged Jess, trying not to feel insulted.

'Ah, you know what I mean,' garbled Tara. 'Must be tough always doing things and going places on your own!'

Jess took a deep breath. She did know what it was like. She would give everything in the world to change it. To have a guy she cared for, and who loved her back, in her life. But she wasn't going to let the fact that there wasn't destroy her. There might never be someone special, and she just had to get used to living her life the way she wanted and enjoy it.

'You get used to it.' She smiled. 'Besides, I'm very in-dependent. I like things my own way and I couldn't see myself sticking with anyone who treated me badly just for the sake of it!'

An hour later they divided up the bill and said their goodbyes. Jess decided to walk home along by the canal and enjoy the sunshine . . . she was alone and there was no sign of that changing any day soon, but that didn't alter the bizarre fact that she was happy, and had a sense of contentment with her life.

Chapter Fifty-four

'This time let's have a smaller, more personal wedding.' Amy smiled as she lay curled up in Dan's arms. 'Let's keep it simple, so it's just about us getting married and making our vows to each other and celebrating with the people we care about.'

'The two of us in flip-flops on a faraway beach,' he teased.

'Tempting.' She giggled. 'But since Dad's operation I'd be worried about him being stuck out in some hot place, with no decent hospital. Besides I really want Granny to be there. She's says she's too old to fly!'

'Don't worry,' he agreed, kissing her shoulder. 'Sheila will be there. Anyway, I don't think we should be asking our friends and family to shell out a thousand euros, and waste their holiday time, just to come and see us getting hitched beside a swimming pool in some fancy hotel or castle in Spain or France. We've all been there, done that, and certainly don't need to do it again!'

'Dan, it would be nice to get married in St Mary's,

our local church, and have the reception fairly near by.'

'That sounds good.' He smiled, kissing her. 'Do you remember that awful B & B in Donegal we had to stay in, when we went to Sarah and Tom's wedding? Our room smelled of sick,' he reminded her.

'Just as well we were drunk when we came back to it, or we'd never have slept the night. It was disgusting!'

'We need some place pretty close to home, with good food and a bar, where we can chill and have a party with everyone.'

'A garden or nice views would be lovely,' she added. 'Do you think we should go for a restaurant? Or maybe even a small hotel?'

'I'm not traipsing the countryside again looking,' he warned sternly.

'I know that,' she said, kissing him. 'This time we are keeping it simple.'

Dan and she drew up a map of places that were approximately an hour or so from Dublin. Amy phoned a number of them to discover that they were booked out totally until the autumn of next year, and to her dismay found that they were left with a country house, a modern hotel with a golf course, and a quaint inn with a really good restaurant.

'Please, Dan, can we go and check them out this weekend?' she begged.

Tully House looked good in photos, but up close was pretty run down and ramshackle. All the weekend dates were gone until April next year, and looking at the shabby paintwork and upholstery Amy and Dan immediately said no.

The Carrick Ross Hotel and Golf Club had no Friday or Saturday available during the busy golf season, but could cater for a mid-week or a winter wedding. The hotel was modern and bright, with a fairly nice function room overlooking the golf course. Amy could feel a growing sense of panic and déjà vu. Then, as they drove along the road from Wicklow Town on their way to the Inn, Amy saw the sign for Glebe House.

'Let's stop in there for a drink or something to eat,' she suggested.

'Is it on "the list"?' puzzled Dan.

'No, they don't do weddings. But it's the place Mum and Dad love to escape to,' she reminded him. 'Ciara and Ronan and I stayed here twice when we were kids. I remember they had a little pontoon on the lake and Ronan caught a huge fish. He nearly fell into the water.'

Amy had forgotten how nice Glebe House was. She could see a lot of work had gone into painting and restoring it, and the gardens looked amazing. Dan and she found the bright airy drawing room and studied the menu. There was a good selection of afternoon tea, sandwiches, soup and crusty bread, a fresh salmon plate or prawns.

'I'll go for the prawns,' Dan said happily.

Amy opted for the same, and they went out through the French doors and found a small table outside in the sunshine, overlooking the gardens.

'Is everything all right with your meal, or do you need something else?' checked the young woman serving them politely, as they tucked into a huge plate of prawns and salad with fresh home-baked brown bread.

'Thanks, it's perfect.' Amy smiled.

'No wonder Paddy and Helen love it here,' joked Dan, tucking in. 'I can only imagine how good dinner must be.'

'Paddy and Helen?' The waitress looked at them inquisitively.

'My parents,' explained Amy. 'The O'Connors from Blackrock. They come here a lot.'

'How are they?' asked the young woman, introducing herself as Trudy Hanlon, the owner's daughter.

'Actually, my dad hasn't been well. He's had bypass surgery,' Amy explained.

Trudy was all concern for Paddy and Helen, and Amy found herself telling the sorry saga of Paddy's illness and her broken engagement and the renewed hunt now for a suitable venue. 'I know what it's like.' Trudy smiled sympathetically. 'I only got married three years ago myself.'

'Did you have it locally?' asked Amy.

'Actually . . .' Trudy hesitated. 'We had the wedding here and it was just perfect.'

'Here?'

'My mum insisted,' laughed Trudy. 'Have to be loyal to the family firm.'

'Lucky you,' Amy said enviously. 'It's so lovely here. I didn't know that you did weddings.'

'We don't normally,' confided Trudy. 'The dining room can only cater for about seventy guests, which is a bit small. We leave that kind of catering to the bigger hotels.'

An hour later they had walked around the small lawn and courtyard of the Drumlee Inn, near Wicklow, both of them disappointed by the inn's time-warp appearance, complete with Toby jugs and fire irons and copper pans. It was obviously geared towards its elderly regulars, and the menu was pure nursery-style with roast lamb, pork chops, rice pudding and bread and butter pudding a feature.

'It's quaint, and I know that it has a good reputation,' Amy declared as they had a coffee, 'but even Gran would think it's too old for her!'

'Why don't we go back to Glebe House and check it out for dinner?' suggested Dan, much to her surprise.

After booking in for dinner they both had a good walk around the grounds.

Amy was relieved to see the little pontoon was still there, and that a new jetty with fairy lights had been added, with a few places to sit and relax. The garden was overrun with colour, and the place was so peaceful.

'It's pretty special here,' said Dan, thinking aloud. 'There aren't many places like this.'

'It's lovely. I had forgotten how beautiful it was.'

'Great place for a wedding,' said Dan.

'But you heard Trudy! They don't do weddings, and the dining room can only hold seventy.'

'I'd prefer to have seventy people here than a hundred in the Carrick Ross or the Drumlee Inn or some fancy restaurant in town.'

'Are you sure?'

'Yeah. I think we should talk to someone about it once we've tested the dinner menu.'

The food was so good and the atmosphere perfect. Amy agreed with Dan: it would be great to have their wedding here. There was a fabulous view of the small lake and the grounds from the bay windows of the dining room; she could see blowsy pink rambling roses and lavender bushes swaying in the soft breeze.

Trudy, who was still on duty, came down to say hello to them again, her eyes widening when they asked if they could talk to someone about the possibility of holding their wedding at Glebe House.

'I think my mum might be in the kitchen,' Trudy said. 'I'll tell her.'

They had finished dinner and were sitting having coffee in the lounge when Eve Hanlon appeared and sat down beside them.

'I'm sure my daughter Trudy told you that generally we don't do weddings. We don't need to.'

Amy's hopes plummeted.

'But Paddy and Helen are old customers, and if it was just a small family wedding on a Friday later in the summer, when things have quietened down, we might just be able to manage it.'

'Oh, that would be wonderful!' Amy almost jumped out of her seat and hugged Eve, and she could see Dan's eyes shining.

'I'll have to check our bookings to see if we could give you the dining room and a reception room around September,' Eve continued. 'I'm busy now, but I will check it all out tomorrow and contact you, if that is all right.'

'Oh, Mrs Hanlon, we would be so grateful!' thanked Amy. 'We'd really love to have our wedding here. The place is perfect: just what we are looking for.'

'I'll come back to you,' she promised. 'Remember to give my good wishes to your mum and dad.'

'Do you think the search is over?' mused Dan as they drove back in the darkness to Dublin.

'I'm not sure.' Amy didn't want to get her hopes too high. Glebe House was one of those places that were always busy at weekends, all year round. It could well be booked up. They would just have to wait and see what Eve Hanlon said.

Chapter Fifty-five

Amy couldn't believe it when Eve Hanlon phoned her at the office on Tuesday to say that Glebe House would be delighted to host her wedding.

'As I mentioned, a wedding reception is not something we normally do, Amy, but I had a talk with your mother. Your parents have been coming here to Glebe House since we first opened, so we will do our best to accommodate you. Unfortunately I cannot offer you a Saturday, as it is our busiest night in the restaurant, but looking at our calendar we could possibly offer you Friday the twenty-eighth of August or Friday the twenty-fourth of October, before the Halloween break.'

'The last Friday in August is available?' Amy couldn't believe her luck.

'It's funny, but people are busy getting kids ready to go back to school or college and don't really want a weekend away then,' Eve explained. 'They will go out for dinner on the Saturday night, but not commit to the whole weekend.'

'Mrs Hanlon, the twenty-eighth sounds perfect for our wedding, but I just need to talk to Father Doorly, the priest who is going to marry us, to see if the date suits him.'

'Amy, will you come back to me the minute you know?' continued Eve. 'I'll try and hold those two dates until I hear from you. It's just that once we firm up on the date we have to get cracking on numbers, tables and menus pretty quickly. It will have to be organized well in advance so that I can take on extra serving staff and bar staff for the night. Also, can you work out a budget, and what accommodation you and your guests will need?'

'Of course,' agreed Amy, delighted. 'I'll check with Dan and Father Tom and come back to you immediately, Mrs Hanlon!'

'I look forward to hearing from you.' Eve added: 'And Glebe House will be delighted to be part of your wedding.'

'Yippee!' shouted Amy exuberantly as she put down the phone. Jilly and Gary wondered what the excitement was all about.

'Good news by the sound of it,' smiled Norah as she passed through the office.

'Dan and I have found the perfect spot for our wedding.' Amy laughed, ringing Dan straight away to tell him.

'Now we'd better go book the church!' he teased.

*　　*　　*

Father Tom Doorly was watching the golf on *Sky Sports* when they called at his door that evening. For a second the priest was worried that something was wrong with Paddy, and that he might be urgently needed, but they reassured him that Paddy was fine and they were here on wedding business.

Father Tom got out his parish diary, which was a booking record for every Mass, confession, funeral, wedding and christening ceremony held in the church.

'Now, let me see about dates,' he murmured, going through the calendar for August and September while keeping an eye on the twelfth hole. Padraig Harrington was playing, and was well up to the challenge of Phil Michelson.

'There isn't a free Saturday between now and Christmas, with all the weddings and christenings,' he said, turning the pages. 'But you want a Friday. Friday the twenty-eighth of August is the date you're looking for?' he asked, finding the page. 'Well, the church is free and I have nothing booked in for that afternoon, so I'd be delighted to marry you then.'

'Oh, thank you, Father Tom.' Amy felt almost like kissing him. 'We're so happy that you'll be marrying us, and that the wedding will be here in St Mary's.'

Amy remembered attending Sunday Mass at St Mary's with her family year after year, surrounded by neighbours and friends. She'd sung in the school choir at the twelve o'clock Mass for about three years, and had helped fund-raise for the parish youth centre and sending a group of local kids to Lourdes.

'Well, I'll write it in the book and that makes it official.' Father Doorly nodded. 'Your wedding banns were already up, but we'll put them up again. You can let me know what time you want the ceremony. Most couples go for two or three o'clock.'

'What about the readings and prayers for the ceremony?' Dan asked.

'I'll run through it with you both, but you should have a look at the Bible or one of those wedding books you can buy, to see if there is a reading you would like.'

'And the music and flowers?'

'That's our parish secretary's department. Jan can fill you in on all that.'

Father Tom offered them a cup of coffee, but they could see that he was engrossed in the golf, and they didn't want to disturb him any more.

Saying goodbye, they promised to get back in touch with him in about three weeks' time.

'I can't believe it,' said Amy, grabbing Dan's hand as they walked back down the pathway. 'We've a priest to marry us, a church and the perfect venue.'

'Now we just have to squeeze our guest numbers down from a hundred and eighty to seventy!' Dan reminded her.

Both of them remembered the awful arguments they'd had already over the original guest list, and how the numbers, despite their best intentions, had spiralled upwards.

'Dan. It's our wedding, and we just have to keep it simple.'

Amy dreaded telling her future mother-in-law about the drastic restrictions on numbers now that the wedding was at Glebe House. This wedding was going to be much smaller and more personal than the one they had originally planned, but in her heart and soul Amy was glad of that. This time both she and Dan were both very much in agreement on what they wanted.

Chapter Fifty-six

Helen O'Connor was so relieved to see the sparkle in Amy's eyes again now that she was back together with Dan.

The wedding was on.

The wedding was off.

And now, thank heaven, the wedding was on again!

They were both full of plans, and Paddy and herself were delighted when they found out that Amy and Dan had fallen under the spell of Glebe House and had booked to have their wedding there in only twelve weeks' time! It all seemed a bit of a rush, but Helen knew that Eve Hanlon could be relied on to do things perfectly.

'Mum, you've got to help me find a dress,' pleaded Amy, aware how tight the time was to get one. 'I'm taking tomorrow afternoon off work and going back to Judith Deveraux's. I really love her stuff and hopefully I'll find something!'

Helen knew how difficult it must be for her daughter

to get over her embarrassment and return to the bridal designer where she had first ordered a dress.

It drizzled rain as they descended into the basement studio, and Judith herself immediately recognized them. It was quiet midweek, and they had the place to themselves.

'Amy, it's so good to see you again,' smiled the pretty young designer, welcoming them. 'How are you?'

'Happy again,' laughed Amy, showing Judith that her engagement ring was back on her finger.

'So you and your boyfriend are getting married after all!'

'Yes,' said Amy, her eyes filling with unexpected tears.

'I'm glad to hear that,' said Judith, her voice sincere.

'The wedding is at the end of August.'

'So soon? Why, it is only a few weeks away!' She smiled. 'So you want to see a dress?'

'Yes, please,' Amy said, unable to disguise her eagerness.

Amy started to look at some of the dresses on display. Within minutes it was clear that there was no sign of the beautiful bow dress that she had originally selected. There were lots of other wonderful designs and styles but nothing like the one she had picked out before. That dress was gone, and they both had to accept it.

Helen sat in one of the floral-patterned chairs that had been upholstered in a cheeky pattern of colourful bouquets as Judith excused herself a minute. Amy's disappointment that the dress that she had chosen was gone was swept away when Judith returned with it in its protective wrapping, on a satin hanger.

'Oh my God!' screamed Amy, instantly recognizing it.

'I finished it a few weeks after you phoned me,' explained Judith. 'So I put it by for you.'

'Thank you, Miss Deveraux,' said Helen, as she saw the utter joy light up her daughter's face.

'Often, where I trained in France, there are hiccups before a marriage, but a good bridal shop tries to be thoughtful, and keep that special dress for the person it is designed for . . . so I've had your dress here all the time, waiting for you.'

'Oh, Judith, thank you, thank you so much,' declared Amy, deeply moved, as the designer took the dress out for her and helped her try it on in the fitting room.

It was even more beautiful than Helen remembered it, and she thanked heaven for the young designer's romantic foresight. The dress, with its classic bodice, simple skirt and unusual bow detail at the back accentuated her daughter's slim figure and elegant style. It fitted Amy perfectly, and there were tears in Helen's eyes as Amy slowly twirled around in it. She couldn't imagine Amy wearing anything else going up the aisle.

'I think the hem is still a little bit too long on you.' Judith considered. 'But maybe if you can bring the shoes you will be wearing I can measure it exactly.'

'Thank you so so much for keeping the dress for Amy,' Helen said gratefully.

'Judith, it's just wonderful.' Amy's eyes shone with relief that she could wear the beautiful dress that she had set her heart on.

'You will be a most beautiful bride,' assured Judith as she fitted the crystal bow headpiece in place and stood back to gauge the effect. 'Beautiful,' she said again.

'Well, Mum, you're the next person to get an outfit!' warned Amy as they walked back towards Kildare Street. 'The wedding's only round the corner and you still haven't got anything.'

Helen knew that she should be looking, but Paddy's recuperation seemed to have put everything on hold. The past few months had been horrendous: filled with calamity and chaos, and so much emotion that she had felt drained as she'd tried to juggle and cope with everything. But at last, seeing Paddy get a little stronger every day, seeing how happy Amy and Dan were together, and knowing that the care plan they all had worked out for Sheila was a success, she felt an enormous sense of relief and immense gratitude that fate was somehow working things out. Now all she had to do was to find a Mother of the Bride outfit!

Chapter Fifty-seven

'The wedding is a hundred per cent back on!' Helen laughed. 'Amy has even got her dress. Wait till you see it, Fran! It's beautiful.'

'I told you those two were meant for each other!' said Fran smugly. 'When is it?'

'It's all booked and organized for Friday the twenty-eighth of August, and you will never guess where!'

'Don't tell me, some other bloody big castle down the country!'

'No.' Helen laughed. 'They're getting married down the road in St Mary's. Father Tom Doorly is marrying them, and then the reception afterwards is going to be at Glebe House.'

'Glebe House, that hideaway place in Wicklow you and Paddy are always on about? How did they swing that? I thought they didn't do weddings there.'

'They normally don't, but Eve, the owner, has agreed it. Paddy and I are over the moon, as it is the most perfect spot for a family get-together. Wait till you see it, Fran.

The place is just beautiful, and the food is always good. We're all so excited about it.'

'So you being Mother of the Bride is back on!' cheered Fran. 'Now, you need to get an outfit . . . immediately. Soon the shops will be full of heavy winter stuff.'

'God, I didn't think of that!'

'We need to go shopping pronto. I'm free this Thursday and Friday, so what about spending the whole two days trying to find something?' Fran offered. 'We could hit the shops in Dundrum and the city centre on Thursday, and if we've no joy then on Friday we can try those big out-of-town places in Athboy and Kildare that specialize in bridal outfits. Remember? I got my outfit in McIlhennys.'

'Sounds great! I'll see if Ciara will agree to be here with Paddy.' Helen wasn't much of a shopper, and more often than not ended up returning purchases to the places she'd bought them. She certainly could do with having Fran along to help her choose. After all, Fran had already been through the whole thing with her own daughter's wedding.

Fran was a woman on a mission, and had Helen up in the massive Dundrum town centre almost the minute the place opened.

'We need to get in and out before the place gets busy,' she said sternly, refusing to be distracted by all the beautiful shops.

They spent three hours wandering in and out of

Harvey Nicks, House of Fraser, and a load of boutiques. Fran directed operations as they went through the racks and racks of clothes, choosing a few things and then sending Helen into the fitting rooms laden down with dresses and suits and outfits.

'Wrong colour! Wrong shape! Too mumsy! Too mutton dressed as lamb! Too hippy chic!' commented Fran, like a drill sergeant ordering her about. 'Too weddingy!' was another complaint.

'Hold on,' argued Helen, turning around in the bright mauve-and-cream patterned dress and wrap-over jacket. 'I want to look weddingy.'

'Not that way, not like you are on a day out and up from the country,' tutted Fran, making her put it back.

Helen really liked a classic black-and-white shift dress with a neat white jacket in Harvey Nicks.

'It's lovely, Fran, and I feel good in it,' she reasoned. 'And afterwards I know that I would wear it again and again to things.'

'It really suits you, Helen, and it would be great for parties and dinners, and even going to other weddings, but this is your daughter's wedding!' exclaimed Fran. 'It just is not Mother of the Bride material! You need to make a splash. Be a bit of a wow on the day!'

I don't know that I am a 'wow' kind of person, thought Helen to herself, as Fran led her upstairs to one of the smaller shops, with an exclusive French range. She immediately fell in love with a lace-patterned beige-

and-cream wrap-over dress. It was gorgeous, and fitted her perfectly.

'I can't believe that I fit into a size fourteen,' she thrilled, as she studied herself in the mirror. Obviously, the stress of Paddy's heart operation and the new healthy regime at home was beginning to pay benefits, and she had slimmed down without even trying.

'I do like that, but I'm not sure if the colour is you.' Fran sighed.

'Well, I really like it,' Helen insisted, thinking that it was a very definite possibility. She asked the shop owner to hold it for her. 'I'd really like my daughter to come and see it, too.'

Exhausted, they took a lunch break, beating the crowd into Café Mao. They ordered a tossed chicken salad with chilli and lime dressing.

'Let's head for town,' said Fran as they finished up, and downed two creamy cappuccinos.

'I'm exhausted,' Helen pleaded. But Fran was too hard a taskmaster, and insisted they head for town.

'We've got Arnotts, BT's, Pamela Scott's and Clerys to go through, plus the boutique in the Westbury Centre and a few other places . . .'

'We'll never get through all that!' protested Helen.

'There's late opening tonight,' reminded Fran, as they pulled into the busy city-centre car park off Grafton Street. 'So we've plenty of time.'

As they walked through BT's, looking at the expensive

designer ranges, Helen admired them but couldn't see herself wearing most of them. Besides, Paddy would freak out if she paid that kind of money for an outfit.

'This Louise Kennedy two-piece is gorgeous,' said Fran, passing it to her. 'Try it on, and try this Italian one, too.'

The Italian fitted dress was far too tight on Helen, and the assistant made it quite clear that it didn't come in a bigger size. The Louise Kennedy was in a warm gold colour, and was absolutely beautiful. Helen studied herself in the dress with its matching coat, both in a light satiny material. She really did like it, and to her surprise could imagine herself wearing it.

'Wow!' said Fran admiringly when she came out of the fitting room. 'That is really lovely on you. It's exactly the kind of thing you need.'

'I really like it, but I'd love Amy and Ciara to come and see it, too.'

'We have only one in your size in this colour,' explained the assistant, 'but I'd be pleased to hold it for you till the weekend.'

Helen agreed as she took the dress off and put it back on the hanger. She was dying to see the girls' reaction.

'Now, let's head downtown,' bossed Fran.

'But surely we don't need to?'

'We are leaving no stone unturned,' laughed Fran. 'Come on, I'll buy you a hot chocolate on the way.'

Helen sent Paddy a text to say that she was staying on in town and wouldn't be home till late. Paddy replied, telling her that Ciara was going to cook him dinner: a vegetable curry. Helen smiled to herself. More power to Ciara if she got him to eat some vegetarian dishes!

Clerys on O'Connell Street, one of Dublin's oldest stores, was busy as usual, but Helen saw a number of things that caught her eye, and decided to try on a few things there. She liked a navy lace suit which was exquisitely made and felt beautiful on.

'I could see myself wearing this.'

'It is lovely, but I don't think navy is your colour,' said Fran candidly.

They spent another half an hour there browsing, before heading over to Henry Street to Arnotts.

'My feet are killing me,' complained Helen, 'and I'm getting a headache. I need to sit down and get something to eat.'

'Time enough for that when the shop shuts at 9 p.m.,' declared Fran, as they went up to the huge fashion floor.

'I can't take any more,' Helen begged. 'Please, Fran, can't we call it a day? I have two really nice outfits being held for me, isn't that enough?'

A look of hesitation passed over her best friend's face and Helen had visions of the two of them finding a cosy table in one of the restaurants in Temple Bar and ordering dinner.

'Just a quick look around,' insisted Fran, leading the way.

Helen couldn't believe it! The floor was filled with a

huge array of beautiful clothes for all ages, with a great selection of Irish designers. There was no way they were going to be out of here quickly. They spent half an hour just sorting through all the different designers the shop carried.

'Look, look!' shouted Fran excitedly, passing Helen a fuchsia-pink suit. 'Try it on!'

It was stunning, but Helen couldn't see herself sitting in St Mary's in such a bright-coloured suit, and looking around the rails picked out three other things that took her interest.

Fran was right. The pink suit was a wow, but the jacket was too tight on her and they didn't have a bigger size. The black and grey top and skirt was expensive and sexy, but too young for her. As she pulled on the peacock-blue silk fitted dress with its round neck and cinched-in waist Helen immediately fell in love with it. She couldn't believe it! It was perfect.

The colour shimmered on her, and made her eyes look bluer than ever, and even though she was wrecked-looking the material gave her skin a golden glow. Holding her breath, she pulled on the short cropped bolero jacket with the mid-length sleeve that went with it. She turned around, looking at herself in the mirror, and felt excitement bubbling as she stepped out to show Fran.

Her friend's face said it all.

'Buy it, Helen! You have to buy it!'

The length, the style, the colour and – she had taken

a sneaky look – even the price were perfect. It had been designed by a young Irish designer called Celine Conroy, who had won some prestigious fashion award in New York.

Two other women who were in the fitting rooms beside her backed up Fran's advice to buy it at once.

'If I was your size and had such a figure, I'd buy it,' admitted the plump blonde in the next stall. 'It's only gorgeous on you.'

The shop was beginning to shut, and a few of the sales girls added their approval.

'I'd really like my daughters to see it first,' Helen said, looking at herself from every angle with satisfaction.

'We have a full returns policy.' The dark-haired girl who was serving her smiled reassuringly.

'Then I'll take it,' Helen decided. 'I'll pay by Visa Card if that is all right.'

Half an hour later, as she and Fran sat in Milano's sharing an antipasti starter, Helen still couldn't believe that the Mother of the Bride outfit she was going to wear to Amy's wedding was sitting in the large black-and-white bag beside her. She had a blister on her foot, was sure she had walked miles and was exhausted from trying on, but she felt triumphant that she had found the exact outfit, the perfect thing for the wedding, and it made her feel beautiful . . .

She took a sip of her wine. Thank heaven, there was no need to go traipsing the country, hunting out shops in Kildare or down in Wexford or Wicklow, as the very best rig-out had been found. It was incredible. Fran was right to have pushed her.

'Thanks so much, Fran. I couldn't have done it without you.'

'Cheers to the beautiful Mother of the Bride!' Fran smiled as they toasted the occasion.

Fran was tucking into her creamy mushroom risotto when she suddenly stopped eating. 'Helen, you need shoes! And a bag!' she said excitedly. 'And are you going to wear a hat or a headpiece?'

'I don't know,' Helen protested. 'Give me a chance, Fran! I've literally just bought my outfit.'

'Well, next week you and I are off on the hunt again,' promised Fran. 'Did you notice the lovely shoes they had in Clerys? And did you see the soft clutch bags in Harvey Nicks?'

Helen took a deep breath, excited. This was only the start of it!

Chapter Fifty-eight

Helen didn't know where the weeks went. The days of summer seemed to run together, she had so much to do, helping Amy organize the wedding. Ciara, to their great surprise, had passed her exams and taken off to Thailand with six friends.

'I'll be back five days before the wedding,' she promised, disappearing with a backpack.

Ronan had gone on a three-week holiday to Poland with Krista, who wanted to show him all the sights in her home country.

Paddy was getting back on his feet. Every day he was a little bit stronger and able to walk farther. His concentration and interest in things around him were gradually improving, too. Despite his complaints, he was sticking to a low-cholesterol diet, and was under the good care of Doctor Galligan and a physiotherapist in the hospital. Even his sense of humour was returning, which was a very good sign. Helen knew that he'd been nervous about his six-week check-up in the Blackrock

Clinic with his cardiologist Doctor Clancy and his surgeon Mr Mulligan, but when the time came Paddy passed all the medical tests with flying colours. His bypass had been a complete success, and Mr Mulligan reassured herself and Paddy that he was well on the road to recovery.

Thank heaven, she thought, trying not to let Paddy see the tears in her eyes.

To celebrate they went down to Glebe House with Amy and Dan for Sunday lunch. Eve had welcomed them warmly, fussing over Paddy, asking all about his operation, and telling him how well he looked.

The dining room was busy, and after lunch, when things had quietened down, Eve had joined them to run through some of the arrangements for the reception.

'Is there any way we can squeeze any more than seventy people into the dining room?' asked Amy hesitantly.

'Obviously when we have guests here for dinner we have a lot of couples dining, and they need slightly more space and privacy than tables of family and friends celebrating an occasion, so in the dining room we can usually only seat up to seventy. But for a wedding we would be using bigger tables, and we could top and tail each table, which would get another two people on each one. I couldn't do that in the restaurant,' explained Eve, 'but at a wedding people don't mind being a bit on top of each other.'

'How many extra do you think we might be able to fit in, then?' Amy asked.

411

'Well, I suppose we could get it up to about ninety.'

Helen knew that Amy and Dan were trying to finalize their guest numbers.

'The other thing we did at Trudy's wedding was that instead of a last-supper arrangement for the wedding table we used both sides.'

'Last supper?' quizzed Dan.

'What I mean is, at most weddings the bridal party's table faces out into the room, so that everyone can see the bride and groom and best man and bridesmaids. They have no one seated opposite them, which is actually a bit awkward. What we did for Trudy was to have people sitting opposite each other, which gave us a few more spaces. I suppose, all in all, we could stretch the seating to about ninety-five, maybe with a squeeze to ninety-eight guests in the room – but that is the very limit!'

'Oh, Eve, thank you,' said Amy and Dan, delighted.

Helen could see that Paddy was relieved that, at just under a hundred guests, the numbers being catered for were substantially less than had been originally planned, and there was no fee for hiring Glebe House. Amy's wedding budget was now far more manageable.

'What about flowers for the tables?' Helen asked.

'Well, if you want to hire a florist to do your own arrangements you are very welcome. But as you know, Helen, we usually have flowers from the garden on every table, which is just part of the service,' Eve offered. 'Trudy is a dab hand at doing them – she loves it. She did a course in floristry about four years ago.'

Helen looked at the beautiful bunch of sweet peas and lavender on the table, and the huge glass vases filled with summer roses over on the sideboard, and knew that Eve and Trudy would do a far better job than most florists.

'Oh, we'd be more than happy to go with the flowers from your garden,' exclaimed Amy, 'They're beautiful.'

Then they discussed the menu. Amy and Dan had studied it already in great detail, and had a rough choice written out.

'We'd like fish to start,' said Dan. 'We thought either the prawns or the fresh salmon with a leaf salad, followed by roast Wicklow lamb, baby potatoes, garlic potatoes and peas, and a dessert.'

'For dessert we do a lovely nougat ice cream, and serve it with macaroons and roasted peaches,' suggested Eve. 'Or there is the house special: a light chocolate and fig tart with home-made vanilla and honeycomb ice cream. And, of course, we have strawberries from the garden.'

'They all sound delicious,' said Dan, who was a total dessert man.

'Would you like to sample some while you are having your coffee?' Eve offered.

'That would be lovely,' they all agreed.

The desserts were mouth-wateringly delicious, and after much deliberation they opted for the chocolate and fig tart with ice cream. It was irresistible, and Dan and Paddy cleaned their plates.

Eva smiled as she jotted down all their choices.

'Will there be a vegetarian option?' Helen asked, thinking of Ciara.

'There is always a vegetarian option,' Eve nodded, 'and if people don't like the lamb we can offer fish as an alternative: a nice monkfish in a champagne sauce.'

'That sounds good,' agreed Amy.

'I'll email you the exact costing on your menu,' Eve said, as she ran through the arrangements with them.

There would be a welcome champagne reception when people arrived, with cheesy nibbles and iced mini cupcakes, which would be served on the terrace overlooking the gardens and lake, weather permitting, and if not, inside in the main drawing room.

Ronan's friend Paul played classical guitar, and would entertain the guests before they went into dinner, and Amy and Dan had booked a great group called Surf Club to play after the meal and for dancing.

'It all sounds perfect to me,' said Paddy. 'Absolutely perfect.'

'Yes, it's exactly what we want,' agreed Dan, excited.

'Well, you can let me know whatever you decide.' Eve smiled as they thanked her and said their goodbyes.

'Let's go for a stroll around the garden!' Helen proposed, as they stood on the front steps.

'We all need to walk off that great lunch,' said Paddy, as they headed off down towards the lake. Amy and Dan had their digital camera with them, as they wanted to get a few photographs of the gardens and house basking in the beautiful July sunshine.

On the way home Helen listened happily as Amy and Dan went through all the lovely wedding plans for their reception in a few weeks' time, poor Paddy asleep against her. The local church choir and their regular soloist, who sounded like he should be on stage, had agreed to sing at the wedding Mass in St Mary's.

'We're trying to pick out music for the ceremony,' Amy explained. 'But there are so many songs. We keep listening to religious CDs of hymns and choirs on our iPods.'

Helen laughed. It certainly made a change.

'And Bibi is back on board about making the cake; she's so good.'

'I told you she would; she loves being involved with friends' weddings.'

'Did I tell you that Carmel has offered to do all the church flowers?' said Amy, turning around to face her. 'She's always doing fabulous arrangements at home in their house, and she's done a few functions and church things before. Mum, what do you think?'

'I think it would be wonderful to have Dan's mum involved,' said Helen, genuinely meaning it. 'Having Carmel doing the flowers will make them very special.'

'She said that she'll try and do whatever I have in mind.'

'And we've finally made a decision about our honeymoon and are off to California and Hawaii,' added Dan. 'Great beaches.'

'And great surfing,' added Amy.

Helen couldn't believe it when Amy showed her the wedding invitations that had come from the printers. She and Dan had decided to use a photo that he had taken of the swans on the lake, with Glebe House and gardens behind it.

'Jilly in work helped me with my design and the print layout on it,' said Amy proudly.

Helen and Paddy were allowed to invite twenty-eight guests to the wedding, and without hesitation had gone for immediate family and their own close friends. Those who had stood by them during Paddy's illness came top of the list. Carmel, much to their surprise, had without complaint whittled the Quinn guest list down to twenty-eight, too.

On Wednesday and Thursday night they opened a few bottles of wine as they sat at the big kitchen table in Blackrock writing all the invitations to the 'end-of-summer wedding celebration' at Glebe House, and checking the list of names and addresses as they put them in their pretty gold envelopes.

Jess had wonderful calligraphy-style handwriting, and was coopted by Amy into writing the names on each invitation, while Amy and Helen packed the envelopes with a map to Glebe House and a brochure for those who wanted to stay the night.

'All the people we love and care for will be there and that's what matters,' said Amy, as with only five weeks to go before the wedding the invitations finally went off.

Chapter Fifty-nine

Jessica Kilroy took her job of arranging Amy's hen night very seriously. As Amy's chief bridesmaid and very best friend she wanted to be creative, and organize something a bit different from the usual drunken hen party spent staggering around Temple Bar or Kilkenny, or Galway or some English city, with pink Stetsons and a pair of wings on. That was certainly not Amy's style! She wanted the hen weekend to be really memorable.

Jess had considered a pampering weekend in a fancy spa or hotel, with dinner, but even though it sounded lovely it wasn't very exciting. A shopping trip to Paris or New York was too expensive, and going over the border to Newry or Belfast certainly didn't have the same cachet!

After a brilliant weekend with her family down messing around on their old boat on the Shannon the idea came to her. Sailing was one of her favourite pastimes and suddenly, like a bolt from the blue, it hit her: the Shannon and a boat!

What could be more fun? Her mam and dad's boat only slept eight at a squeeze, but for a bigger crowd you could hire a fancy cruiser that slept ten to twelve, which would be ideal for a hen party on the river . . . A gang of girls with food, wine, bunks, and a huge boat to steer and sail would be mad!

She checked it out with Aisling and Tara and Sarah, and they all thought it was a brilliant idea, too.

'Most of the girls have never been on a river cruiser. God, can you imagine the laugh we'll have!' said Tara, telling her to go ahead and book it.

She emailed everyone to check dates and warn them to keep it a secret from Amy, and had gone ahead and booked the last weekend in July with the cruiser company. She'd also worked out a route taking in pubs and restaurants and other places to stop along the way.

Seeing the cruiser *The Emerald Princess* moored down on the marina at Carrick-on-Shannon, Amy couldn't believe that they were boating instead of going to a spa. Everyone screamed with delight, and the cruiser looked amazing, sitting there at the marina waiting for them.

'Oh my God, is this our boat?' yelled Tara as nine of them assembled on Friday afternoon with their gear along the wooden jetty where the boats were moored. 'It's massive!'

The cruiser had four twin cabins and a living area which could be divided up, the couches converting into two big double beds. *The Emerald Princess* was perfect, and very different from Jess's family's ancient wooden cruiser. It had a fancy power shower, an immaculate white-painted galley kitchen, and a huge deck equipped with loungers and sun-chairs, as if they were on the Mediterranean instead of cruising the Shannon.

Jess had to sign the form declaring that she was fit to operate the cruiser, and was glad that her father had insisted that she learn to sail their boat and do her Mariner's Certificate! Everyone in her family was well used to taking their turn at the wheel and navigating locks and the waterways. However, the cruise ship company insisted that the rest of the crew of girls took a quick navigation course in a classroom, so they'd know how to manage locks and to moor up.

The next morning the other three girls would join them. Nikki hadn't been able to make it on Friday, and Sarah and Kerrie were both relying on husbands and mothers to help mind their small children as they escaped for the Saturday and Sunday away.

Jess had sent everyone an email advising them what to wear on board, but could see two pairs of sneaky high heels under jeans already. She had set a limit of one holdall per person, as storage was usually pretty limited, but this edict had been broken, too, with four of the girls toting bags more suited to a week in Marbella or Cannes than the inclement Shannon River. Jess prayed that they had at least all brought anoraks and rainproof jackets.

'Oh, Jess, it's lovely. I can't believe that you found

us such a perfect boat,' congratulated Amy, grabbing the biggest cabin for the two of them. 'It's so big and comfortable.'

'Oh, look, there's a dishwasher and a huge fridge,' remarked Mel, depositing two bottles of champagne in it.

The fridge was soon crammed, looking like an off-licence with a huge supply of alcohol, including lots of champagne, ready for tonight's pre-dinner drinks.

'There's a massive flat screen TV and DVD player in the lounge,' cheered Tara.

'And a great sound system,' informed Aisling, plugging in her iPod and giving them all a blast of Beyoncé.

Once they had thrown all the bags in their cabins and got themselves sorted out, Jess went up on deck to turn on the engine and cast off. She wanted to be out on the water and give the girls a bit of a sail up the river before they stopped to eat for the night.

'Are you sure you know how to do this?' quizzed Orla, glancing around the crowded marina and the fleet of cruisers.

'Yes, once one or two of you give me a hand up on deck, as I don't want to tip off another boat.'

Everyone was up ready to help as the engine roared into life and the boat began to move, Amy ready to cast off from where *The Emerald Princess* was moored, as Jess slowly manoeuvred the craft between the other cruisers and reversed out from the jetty and into open water to a huge cheer. Orla, armed with her mini-camcorder, recorded it all. Jess stayed calm as she steered the *Princess* upriver and let the throttle roar, giving everyone a sudden burst of speed.

'Can I have a go?' begged Tara.

'Later,' promised Jess. She intended making sure all the girls got a chance to take the wheel, but not here where the marina officer could still see them. She'd wait till they were miles away from another craft and it was safer.

As they moved upriver she could see the girls were impressed, as there was nothing like being out in the waterways, especially on a long hot summer's day! She had checked the weather forecast, and overall it was good, though there was a threat of rainfall by Sunday. Two bottles of wine were opened, and the girls stretched out on the loungers in their T-shirts and shorts, lathering themselves in sun block as the cruiser passed by fields and woods and the beautiful Shannon riverside.

'Save me some for later,' Jess joked. She wanted to show them two little islands and give them a view of Claremount House, the magnificent restored Georgian mansion which was about a mile upriver and had its own formal terraced gardens and a wooden boathouse and little jetty. She didn't believe in drinking and driving, and would save having any wine till they were safely moored for the night.

'This is bliss,' declared Mel, trailing her fingers in the water.

Jess took a break from the wheel and stopped the

cruiser as they all lapped up the sunshine. They cheered as Tara and Mel, Lisa, Amy and Orla took an impromptu dip in the water.

'It's freezing!' they roared, as they splashed around before hastily scrambling back up on deck, teeth chattering and lips, fingers and toes blue with the cold.

'You mad things! Where do you think you are?' Jess joked. 'This is not Puerto Banus or Vilamoura! The water hasn't even heated up here yet.'

'Now you tell us!' shivered Tara, wrapping herself in a towel.

Jess had it all worked out where they would moor for the night: the pretty riverside town of Tarmonbarry, which was a regular port of call for cruisers. There was a great little restaurant and bar called Donovan's just near the waterfront, and she had booked a table for them. She stood beside Lisa and Mel and Amy as each of them excitedly took a turn at the wheel.

The sun was beginning to dip from the sky as they pulled into Tarmonbarry and moored, everyone racing to change in their cabins for the night's fun. They kicked off the night with champagne toasts for the beautiful bride-to-be up on deck. Amy was certainly that, wearing a pale pink figure-hugging dress and wrap, and looking absolutely gorgeous. They took turns recounting when they had each met Amy, and how they had become friends. Jess, Tara and Aisling had been at school with her, and were her oldest friends. Orla and Mel and

Susan had been at college with her, and Lisa and Kerrie had gone on a Spanish course with her one summer in Barcelona. Amy was one of those people who just seemed to gather friends along the way.

'One more bottle of champagne and then we'll head for dinner,' promised Tara. 'We are all starving.'

Donovan's was packed when they got there, and they had to wait and have a drink before they could sit at their table. The Friday night crowd was in hearty form, and Jess recognized a few of her brother Eamon's friends at a table in the corner.

'Wow, this is a great place!' said Susan, eyeing up the local talent.

'And the menu is great, too,' added Tara, as she deliberated over the array of fresh fish on offer.

They took ages ordering, and the waitress was patient as the girls repeatedly changed their minds. There seemed to be a constant flow of wine as the meal progressed, and by the time the dessert menu came Jess had decided it was cocktail time. A spoon of ice cream or pudding nicked from someone's plate would do her, as she would prefer to treat herself to one of Donovan's renowned concoctions. Amaretto, grenadine, blue curaçao with vodka, or a rum-based cocktail. She opted for the Donovan's Delish, and almost licked the glass clean. The rest of the girls, curious, decided to try one, too.

'Wow, this place is such a find!' slurred Orla. 'I wish that there was somewhere like this in Dublin.'

Jess was arguing that she thought it was so great

424

precisely because it wasn't in Dublin, as they ordered a last round of drinks. Then the restaurant staff gradually began to clear the tables, and the bar got ready to close.

'Back to our boat,' teased Tara. 'We have a fridge full of drink there.'

Before she knew it, they were all making their way towards *The Emerald Princess*.

The night was warm, and they all sat up on deck chatting and drinking for hours before eventually sloping off to their cabins.

'I'm knackered,' said Amy, calling it a night, too, and falling on to her bunk in her bra and pants, 'but it's been so lovely.'

Jess tried not to think about how many Donovan's Delishes she had had as she grasped the ladder and climbed up on the top bunk to sleep.

'Jess, thanks,' said Amy drunkenly. 'You always believed that Dan and I would get back together, and made me believe it, too. I'm so lucky to have a friend like you! God knows what would have happened when Matt was home if I hadn't been staying with you! Matt wanted me to go away for a weekend with him, but I knew that you would kill me! Anyway, that was when poor Gran had her accident!'

'I thought you had gone away with him,' Jess confessed drunkenly. 'I phoned his house looking for you, but his mum said he'd gone to Kilkenny.'

'You what?' Amy laughed.

'I couldn't contact you or find you, and I just put two and two together and made three.' Jess giggled. 'Ciara and I drove all the way down to Kilkenny to try to find you and Matt.'

'You drove down to Kilkenny! I don't believe you.'

'Yes, and it was so embarrassing. Matt was staying in the hotel with some girl!'

'He's still such a shit!' said Amy, giggling. 'Any more confessions tonight, Jess?'

'Do you remember the night of Dan's birthday?'

'Of course I do. Why?'

'I was the girl that Liam went home with!'

'You what? You were with Liam? Oh no, Jess! He's such an absolute bastard!'

'I know,' said Jess. 'An absolute one, but I fancied him rotten then!'

Jess felt Amy suddenly reach up and take her hand. 'Jess, forget Liam and guys like him! You're too good for them.'

'Sure.' She yawned.

'Jess, you're so good, organizing this hen for me. When your turn comes to get married I'll do the same for you, I promise.'

Jess collapsed on the pillow. 'Thanks, Amy.' She giggled, trying to keep her balance in the upper bunk. 'But at the rate my love life is going I don't think I'm ever going to need a bridesmaid!'

Chapter Sixty

The river was busy as they arrived into Athlone Town, where they were due to pick up the other girls, who had travelled down by train.

They passed crowded tour boats and cruisers and dinghies as they searched for a place to moor and pick up the others.

'I told them to wait down near the quayside for us!' said Jess, craning to see if she could spot them. The Midlands market town was packed with visitors and shoppers attending the local Saturday morning farmers' market. 'I'll try and tie up here and wait for them to get on board.'

'Hey!' shouted Orla, waving madly. 'There's Sarah and Nikki! I'll tell them to run down to the quayside where we can pick them up.'

'Great,' shouted Jess, trying her best to concentrate as she carefully manoeuvred *The Emerald Princess* into position and steadied it against the bank. A few minutes later Nikki, Sarah and Kerrie stepped on to it.

'The boat is huge,' screamed Nikki, racing all around it.

'Isn't it wonderful?' Amy beamed. 'And we're having the best time ever.'

'We didn't get to bed till nearly four in the morning.' Tara laughed. 'And we had great crack in this fantastic restaurant last night.'

'I'm so looking forward to a night away from Sam and night feeds and bottles and dirty nappies,' admitted Sarah. 'If I fall asleep at the table tonight someone please wake me up, as I don't want to miss the fun!'

'Me, too,' added Kerrie. 'It's bad enough with the baby, but I'm trying to train Alice, and every night she keeps wetting her bed.'

'Yuk!' groaned the girls in unison.

'I've had it the whole way down on the train,' whispered Nikki under her breath to Amy. 'Remind me: I'm never having kids!'

As they cruised on the river through the town they had to join a queue of other boats waiting at the lock. They watched in fascination as the water level of the river changed and the lockkeeper let them pass through, and then they headed upriver.

'We are stopping for a picnic lunch on Lough Ree,' Amy announced. 'And then we'll head to Carrick-on-Shannon for the night. Jess has booked a table for twelve in Carew's, and later we can go on to the nightclub in the local hotel, Hickeys, which is very near it.'

'Wow, sounds great!' purred Kerrie, already beginning to forget about her children at home.

They sat in the sunshine with the picnic: chilled wine, sliced sugar-baked ham, rolls, salad, and baby potatoes tossed in a vinaigrette dressing, followed by two dozen pink and yellow iced cupcakes with 'Amy's Hen' iced on them – which had been provided by Sarah.

'How do you get the time to make them?' asked Orla, stunned by Sarah's baking prowess as she bit into the melt-in-your-mouth sponge.

'To be honest, I'm usually up feeding Sam during the middle of the night, and it's got way worse since he started teething, so I put on the oven and make bread or buns or cakes. It's a kind of sanity-saver.'

They took photos and reminisced about school and college and starting work.

'I'm not going to die, folks,' teased Amy. 'I'm just getting married.'

'But it's the end of a part of your life!'

'It's the end of being single!'

'The end of having fun!' added Sarah.

'Sarah!' they all chorused. 'Don't be so mean!'

'Sorry, I guess I'm so exhausted most of the time that Tom and I forget about fun.'

'You were having a lot of fun the last time you had dinner at our place,' reminded Amy.

Sarah blushed. 'Oh yeah, Tom's mum and dad had taken Sam for the night, so we went crazy. Overload of drink and sex and more drink and sex!'

429

'I think that dinner at our place came somewhere in the middle!' Amy laughed.

Jess relaxed as *The Emerald Princess* cruised along. Orla and Aisling had a good feel for the boat, so the sailing wasn't all down to her.

En route they passed a group of foreign tourists on a big cruiser similar to theirs. 'I think they must be German or Dutch,' remarked Aisling as they went by.

The group of guys looked like they were fishing, but up close you could see they were more intent on the beer cans in their hands.

'Hey! Hey, girls! You want a beer?' The guys shouted, trying to attract them to their boat.

'No, thanks!' they shouted. 'Bit too early in the day for us!'

Tara and Aisling kept up a bit of banter with the guys, discovering that they were from Frankfurt, and over on a three-day trip to Ireland. The German guys had fluent English and, like themselves, were out for a bit of a laugh on the water. Waving goodbye to them the girls headed up to the immense beauty of Lough Ree: a huge natural lake which bordered two counties.

'I can't understand why I've never come sailing on the Shannon like this before,' remarked Susan. 'It is so beautiful, far better than going and staying in crappy B & Bs in small towns. The scenery is magnificent, and it is so peaceful out here on the water. It's bliss.'

'I'll certainly do it again,' added Tara. 'It's amazing.'

It was so warm up on the middle of the lake that they all stripped off to their bikinis and lay out on the deck. The gentle rocking of the boat made a few of them doze off.

'Well, I'm having a swim again today!' Orla announced. 'Anyone care to join me?'

'You nearly froze yesterday,' Amy reminded her.

'Well, today is a lot hotter, and besides, I'm used to it!'

'I'll go,' volunteered Lisa.

'Me, too.' Susan laughed.

Before they knew it they had all agreed to jump into the lake.

'Someone has to stay on board,' warned Jess, not wanting to be a killjoy.

'I'll stay,' volunteered Nikki. 'I didn't bring a bikini with me, and besides, I have a policy of never putting foot in Irish water, as it is too bloody cold.'

Without further ado the rest of them all jumped in. The water was freezing, as predicted, so they screamed and splashed, swimming and chasing each other around, and Nikki grabbed Amy's camera and took photos of everyone.

As the icy cold water of the lake gripped them they made a mad rush to get back on deck, then wrapped themselves in their towels and downed mugs of hot chocolate and coffee to warm up.

Jess pulled on a fleece and her jeans and took over the wheel. The time was running away with them, and they had to get a move on if they wanted to make it back to Carrick-on-Shannon for the evening.

The marina was busy, but luckily Jess managed to get a mooring in one of the prettiest towns on the river. With its selection of pubs and restaurants it was always popular!

Pre-dinner they opened more champagne, and presented Amy with her friends book: a big album looking back on her life and her friendship with each of them.

Jess and Nikki had been putting it together for weeks, and seeing Amy's reaction to the photos, mementoes and individual letters from each of them they knew that all the effort – the emails and phone calls to all the girls, and the hours spent scanning photos and school and college memorabilia – had all been worth it.

'I love it,' Amy cried. 'I'll keep it for ever!'

Everyone took more photos as they each gave Amy their token hen gift, which had to come in under ten euros. There were naughty knickers, a muffin tray, a romantic cook book, a baby-doll nightie, a pink-patterned apron, a feather duster and matching slippers, a manicure set, a set of bowls and some lovely body treats.

'Thanks, girls!' said Amy, giving them all a big hug. 'You're the best.'

Then they all made a big effort to look stylish for the big night out. Jess felt a bit self-conscious, as Amy had persuaded her to wear a bright blue dress of hers instead of the black V-neck top and ruffle skirt that she had intended to wear. Amy absolutely insisted that she try on the blue dress, which she had brought along as a spare.

'I know it'll suit you, Jess. Please try it,' urged her best friend. 'It's different, but it will work, I promise.'

Jess knew that she tended to play it safe with black: a dress or a top or a skirt, anything which she considered might make her look slimmer. She was sure that the blue dress wouldn't go near her, but to her surprise it did. Amy usually wore it cinched in with a big belt, but Jess didn't need one, and instead opened two or three of the top buttons to soften the neckline. She felt good in it, and with her strappy black shoes felt she did look very different from usual. Amy looked divine in a pretty pink-and-white dress with a little rose-coloured shrug to keep her warm.

'Hey, girls, drink up! We need to get to the restaurant!' urged Jess.

Carew's was literally perched on the riverbank, an old wooden restaurant from years back that was originally a café-cum-bar for local fishermen, and over time had become one of the best restaurants in the area. Fairy lights twinkled along the wooden railings and window shutters, and honeysuckle trailed over the walls. On the small jetty, four or five circular tables were perched where you could have a pre-dinner drink, but the girls' table was ready and they were shown straight to it.

'Oh, it's lovely!' murmured Amy, delighted, as they all trooped in.

The table for twelve had flickering candles on it, and small glass vases of freesias, her favourite flower.

'Wow!' declared the girls appreciatively, as they sank into their seats near the windows overlooking the water.

'Well done, Jess!' cheered Mel and Orla. 'This is just gorgeous.'

The waiters in Carew's danced attendance on them as they ordered wine and made their choices from the extensive menu. The restaurant was totally full, and Jess thanked heaven that she had had the foresight to book it eight weeks ago. Getting a table for twelve was tough enough at any time, but on a Saturday night nigh on impossible.

Carew's deserved its reputation, as the food was superb. They ordered bottle after bottle of wine, talking away nineteen to the dozen as the restaurant gradually emptied.

'Where to next?' asked Lisa and Sarah as they all settled their bills.

'Hickey's is only a few minutes away,' said Jess, and they all gathered their bags and jackets and wraps, thanked the waiters and set off up the road.

Hickey's Hotel was caught in a time-warp with its seventies decor and style.

'But that's back in fashion again,' declared Nikki as

434

they hit the bar. The music was pounding in the night-club and they were all in the mood for dancing. Everyone cheered Amy as she took to the floor and danced to 'Venus'.

'She's got it,' yelled the girls.

Jess joined in the fun as the DJ spun a load of Motown hits followed by some Elvis Presley classics, the place jumping with a mixture of locals and tourists.

'Hey, aren't they the guys we passed on the boat today?' gestured Tara, waving madly at the group of guys standing over on one side of the room with their pints.

'Tara, stop!' warned Orla. 'You'll have the crowd of them over on top of us before you know it.'

'That's the plan.' She smirked as a tall guy in a black shirt came over to her.

The ten German guys were on a stag outing! They couldn't believe it. One of the guys, Marten Furtinger, was getting married in three weeks' time to his long-term partner Martha, with the celebrations being held in a big wedding barn in a farmhouse forty miles outside Frankfurt.

'My boyfriend Dan is going to Edinburgh for his stag next weekend.' Amy laughed, telling them all about her own wedding plans.

'Cheers for the bride! Cheers for the groom!' every-one roared, pushing on to the dance floor together. Amy lapped up the attention as Marten swung her around in his muscular arms.

Marten insisted on buying them even more drinks,

and Jess found herself being chatted up by a tall blond guy called Erik who was a pharmacist.

'I love Ireland and you Irish girls.' He smiled as he asked her up to dance.

They had such good fun, and the German guys were a laugh. They had spent most of the weekend drinking on their boat, and were out to ensure Marten remembered his last few days of freedom on the Shannon. Tomorrow afternoon they were all flying back to Frankfurt.

Jess had never been to Germany, and the only thing she really associated it with was beer, sausage, and BMWs, but Erik paid her so much attention, buying her drinks and dancing with her, that she began to enjoy his company. He was pretty nice, and she just wished he didn't live so flipping far away.

As the dancing ended and the nightclub lights went up Hickey's began to empty. Marten was footless drunk, and Jess thought it was just as well his fiancée wasn't there to see the state of him. Amy was at least standing up straight and in giggly form. Erik held Jess's hand and she hoped the night wouldn't end too soon.

'Hey, guys, thanks, we all had a great time,' slurred Nikki, who had started drinking cocktails about three hours earlier.

'Come on, Cinderella, let's get you home,' sighed Mel, grabbing her handbag.

'Can we walk you down to the jetty? We are moored there, too,' offered Dieter, who was in a serious clinch with Tara.

The girls fell into step with the guys, everyone singing as they linked arms and made their way down to the waterside.

It looked so beautiful with the lights reflected on the water, the clear sky above them speckled with stars. Jess sighed. It had been such a perfect night. She would never forget it.

Amy and Marten were involved in a big sentimental bear hug, wishing each other well with their wedding days!

Erik tilted Jess's face to his and they kissed. It was so lovely. Jess wished that they could stay on the jetty for ever.

'It was good to meet you,' he said, serious.

'Good to meet you, too.' Jess giggled.

'Come on, girls! Back on the boat!' yelled Orla.

'Hey, can't we come on board, too, for a nightcap?' pleaded Marten and a few of the guys.

'Of course they can!' beamed Amy, arm in arm with Marten as they got back on to the deck of *The Emerald Princess*.

Erik had his arm around Jess as they climbed on deck, and she was delighted to have more time with him.

Orla, Nikki and Tara were linking arms, singing Abba's 'Dancing Queen', weaving their way along the jetty and trying to balance themselves as they stepped on deck, when suddenly they all heard a huge splash and a stream of curses.

'Tara's fallen in!' Orla giggled, almost falling in herself.

Tara was soaking wet and roaring with laughter, as three of the guys bent down to help drag her out of the river. Luckily the water wasn't too deep, and she was safely on board in a jiffy, dripping all over the deck as they wrapped her in towels and blankets.

'I'm fine,' she protested. 'I hadn't planned a midnight swim but it's sure woken me up!' Giggling, she raced to her cabin with Aisling to change into some dry clothes. Emerging in tight jeans and a warm knitted sweater she demanded another drink to steady herself.

'I've had a big shock, you know!' she said, as she cuddled up to her German friend.

'You've given us all one, too,' said Amy as they raided the bar.

It was very late, and dawn was beginning to creep over the horizon when they finally got to their bunks and the last of the German guys went.

Jess had reluctantly said a final goodnight to Erik.

'I'll email you, Facebook you,' he promised, as they kissed.

'Great,' she smiled, knowing that despite seeming nice and being the kind of guy she could really fancy she was unlikely to ever hear from him again. For all she knew, he probably had a wife and two children back in Frankfurt!

She looked around the living area. Orla and Mel and Lisa were snoring in the two double beds, wrapped in the duvets, fully clothed. There were bottles and glasses and shoes everywhere. She couldn't even think about it!

'It was the best night ever, Jess.' Amy hiccupped, weaving her way to their cabin. 'The best hen night ever!'

Jess grinned. It certainly had been.

Chapter Sixty-one

Helen was out dabbling in the garden. She was trying her best to get it into some shape before Amy's wedding. With all that had happened over the past few months, the garden had been sorely neglected. Paddy would normally have kept the lawn and the hedge in good shape, but since his heart operation it had been too much for him. His recovery was slower than either of them had expected, but he was definitely making progress day by day. His energy and strength were gradually returning. Ronan had been so supportive, and to their surprise had taken a huge interest in what was going on in Paddy's firm, keeping an eye on his father's interests and making sure that the staff kept Paddy informed of the work coming in and how it was being dealt with. To see her husband and son's heads bent together discussing work and the company did Helen's heart good.

Last night when she had mowed the grass she'd noticed the weeds and moss were beginning to take a foothold. Paddy would know what to do, she hoped, to get it back in good condition. The flower beds were full of colour, but a serious bit of deadheading was needed if she wanted things to continue to bloom for the next few weeks. She fed the roses and trimmed back some of the delphiniums to encourage them to flower again, noticing that blooms were tumbling from all her pots and containers, despite infrequent feeding and watering.

The garden was Helen's retreat from the world, and as she worked in a baggy T-shirt and her old beige linen trousers she could feel her cares and worries slipping away. She was busy weeding when she heard the front door bell ring.

'I'll get it,' called Paddy, who was inside reading the paper.

She kept on, concentrating on weeding out a patch of dandelions, which were the bane of her life. She dug and attacked them with her trowel.

'Carmel's here!' announced Paddy, opening the patio door.

Helen jumped up, wondering what in heaven's name Daniel Quinn's mother was doing here on her doorstep, and why Paddy was bringing her out to the garden to see Helen literally covered in mud and dirt.

'Hello, Helen,' called Carmel, coming towards her in an immaculate pair of white trousers and a pale-blue cotton top. 'I was in the area and I thought I'd call in and see how the wedding plans were going.'

Helen scrambled to get the clay off her hands and

push the hair off her face, conscious that she was hot and sweaty and certainly not looking her best.

'I'll be with you in a minute, Carmel,' she shouted, rushing over to rinse her hands under the garden tap.

'I'll make a pot of tea and bring it out to you,' called Paddy.

Honestly, Helen thought, some days she could kill that man!

'Would you like to sit down, Carmel?' she asked, leading her over to the garden table and chair set. Thank heaven she had scraped all the bird shit off it a few days ago.

'This place is beautiful,' said Carmel admiringly. 'I didn't realize you had such a big garden. And it's south facing, which is perfect!'

'It's a sun trap.' Helen smiled as she pulled up a seat.

'I'm sorry to disturb you when you are gardening, but I wondered if there was anything that I could do to help. Do you or Amy need any extra assistance with the wedding?'

Helen sat flabbergasted. She had not expected this at all, Carmel being kind and generous!

'As you know I'm doing the flower arrangements for the church, and if I'm not treading on any toes I'd love to be able to do other things for you as well.'

Helen studied Carmel's long thin face, realizing that there was no trace of sarcasm or cynicism on it, and that Carmel genuinely wanted to help. 'It must be wonderful planning a wedding for a daughter,' Carmel said enviously. 'So different from when it's your son! Daniel is the best in the world, but he's a boy! Boys don't tell you anything, as I've discovered since having my three sons. The family dynamics are very different.'

'I suppose you're right,' said Helen.

'Eddie and I would have loved a daughter. We lost a baby girl at twenty-seven weeks,' Carmel said softly, looking at the big pink hydrangeas growing near them. 'The hospitals didn't have all the fancy equipment they have nowadays for premature babies. We baptized her Jennifer Elaine after my mother.'

'Oh, Carmel, I'm so sorry.'

'I don't know how Eddie and I got through it!' she confided. 'It was before Dan and Dylan were born so they don't remember her. They say time heals, but sometimes I'm not sure. She'd probably be married with a family by now. I'd be a grandmother, maybe. Who knows!'

Who knows? thought Helen to herself, seeing the regret still etched in the other woman's face as Paddy carried the tea tray out to them.

'Here you go, girls!'

'Paddy, you are looking so well,' Carmel complimented him. 'Are you joining us?'

'No, I'll leave you two lovely ladies in peace to have your chat about the wedding,' he excused. 'I'll take that yoke Barney out for a walk. I've to do three miles a day, and the dog makes sure I keep going.'

'Good for you!' praised Carmel. 'I wish Eddie would take a bit more exercise.'

Helen started pouring tea, unsure as to what to say.

'Paddy looks really healthy,' Carmel went on. 'He's made such a great recovery.'

'He's trying to write his Father of the Bride speech,' admitted Helen. 'Though, to tell the truth, I didn't think a few weeks ago that we'd be planning any wedding.'

'Neither did we!' agreed Carmel. 'I've never seen Dan so unhappy. It made Eddie and me both think how important the right life partner is and how awful the consequences are if you do not marry the one you love. Dan adores Amy, and he missed her so much. It's so good to see them together again. They are so happy and obviously meant for each other.'

'That's exactly how we feel, too.' Helen smiled. Feeling emotional, she changed the subject. 'I'm sure that Amy and Dan have filled you in on most of the plans, as nearly everything is well in hand. Our local church is perfect for a wedding, and Father Tom, our parish priest, is a really nice man. He's been very good to Paddy since he got sick. Amy and Dan are arranging all the readings and prayers and the music. Amy told me that you are doing the flowers for the church and making the girls' bouquets.'

'Yes, I'm delighted to do it,' Carmel said, eyes shining. 'I have to admire the way Amy and Dan have got us all more involved in their wedding.'

'I know that the celebration is much smaller than they had originally planned, and Glebe House very different from Castle Gregory, but I guarantee you that Eve

Hanlon is wonderful, and she will make certain that everything runs smoothly. I'm sure that everyone will enjoy it.'

'It has a wonderful reputation,' remarked Carmel. 'Eddie and I tried to book in there for a weekend last year, but it was full. The food is meant to be great.'

'It is,' said Helen. 'Paddy and I try to escape there whenever we can.'

'So it's quite a coup for you to get it for the wedding,' Carmel said admiringly.

'I suppose.' Helen laughed, surprised by the compliment.

'And I believe Amy's wearing a Judith Deveraux dress, after all,' Carmel said, obviously impressed.

'Yes. And the bridesmaids are wearing a fabulous shade of purple.'

'And Helen, what about you? What are you wearing?'

'Oh, I've a beautiful peacock-blue suit by Celine Conroy, and I got a lovely headpiece from the hat shop in South Anne Street to go with it.'

'Well, I'm wearing a Paul Costello silver-colour shift dress with a matching coat, so at least we're in different colours.'

'Well, as I said, the dresses are all organized and, as you know, Dan's friend Jeremy is shooting the DVD of the wedding. Then, Ronan's girlfriend Krista is taking the photographs. She studied photography in Dun Laoghaire and does a lot of fashion work. A friend of mine, Bibi Kennedy, is making the cake, and my brother Tim collects vintage cars and has offered to drive them in his old green Bentley.'

'Well done. I know how much work goes into organizing events,' said Carmel. 'Things don't just happen – people make them happen.'

'I didn't realize you did flower-arranging,' Helen admitted.

'I love flower-arranging. It's one of my hobbies.'

Helen realized how little she actually knew about the woman who was going to be Amy's mother-in-law and a part of their family.

'A woman has got to do more than just play golf.' Carmel laughed. 'I've done a few courses over the years, and decorated churches and shows, and made all kinds of arrangements for charity and raffles and gifts. Poor Eddie says the house is always full of flowers! But I'm really pleased to be involved with the flowers for the wedding.'

'Carmel, I know Amy is delighted you are doing them, as they both really want their wedding to be as personal as possible.'

'I'll call into St Mary's on my way home to see the size of the altar and the doorway, and how many pews there are, and check what kind of arrangement Amy wants running along the aisle as she walks up.'

An hour later, after swapping some wedding and mother-in-law stories, a tour of the herbaceous border and some good advice from Carmel on an enriching organic feed for the lawn, Helen cut a few flower heads for Carmel's latest arrangement. Then they said goodbye, both looking forward to the upcoming wedding on the twenty-eighth, and to the days and years ahead of a new friendship.

Chapter Sixty-two

'Hurry, or we'll be late,' called Paddy up the stairs as they raced to get ready for the wedding rehearsal to be held in St Mary's Church.

Helen applied a fresh coat of lipstick and checked that her hair and make-up were fine as she shut the bedroom door. Father Tom was going to take them all through the things they had to do during the wedding ceremony on Friday, and make sure that Amy and Dan weren't too nervous.

'Mum, have you seen my black wedges?' called Ciara, throwing all the shoes and boots in the hall cupboard out on to the floor in a heap till she found the precious pair she wanted.

Helen smiled. She had forgotten how quiet things had been for the past two months with her younger daughter away. Ciara looked well after the trip to Thailand. Her normally pale skin had turned a soft golden colour, and she seemed more relaxed and calmer. As Paddy said:

sitting on a beach contemplating the universe had done her some good!

Amy and Dan were already in the church, talking to the priest and Liam, when a few minutes later Eddie and Carmel and their two other sons, Rob and Dylan, arrived, too. Helen glanced around nervously, looking for Jess. It wasn't like Jess to be late. Ronan arrived with Krista in tow and a few minutes later Jess appeared, all out of breath.

'Sorry I'm late, but school starts on Monday and I was in checking on things and getting my classroom organized!' she apologized, slipping into a bench.

Father Tom got them to gather around him as he explained the format of the ceremony: the welcome, the readings, the lighting of the candles, the marriage ceremony itself, followed by Communion, the blessing and finally the signing of the register and the long walk back down the aisle for the happily married couple.

'Now, the first thing we will practise is the words Amy and Dan have to say to each other, as that is what everyone, including me, wants to hear.'

Amy stepped up to the altar. Her hand was shaking as she read from the booklet and, filled with emotion, her voice was barely audible.

'I know that we have a microphone, but, Amy, you need to speak up a bit,' encouraged the priest.

She tried again, but even though she was louder this time she totally forgot what she was saying. Then she took a deep breath and, concentrating totally on Dan, repeated exactly what she was meant to say.

Dan, taking his turn, missed the words, panicked, forgot everything, then turned bright red with embarrassment.

'Dan, why don't you have a go again?' urged Father Tom.

Dan was almost as bad the second time, and it took four attempts before he lost the shake in his voice and was calm enough to remember the words of the marriage ceremony properly.

'Dan, you'll have the booklet with the words of the ceremony if you get stuck,' assured the priest.

Helen thanked heaven that Father Tom had insisted on a rehearsal for everyone, as he made the young couple go through the actual marriage ceremony and exchange of rings until they had it perfectly and were both relaxed and calm.

Ronan and Rob both went up to practise the Bible readings they were doing for the wedding. Then Dylan and Ciara and Liam went through the prayers they would say for friends and family.

'Now, let's have the two mothers bringing up the gifts,' suggested Father Tom, making Helen and Carmel practise getting in and out of the bench without tripping, and carrying the gifts to the altar.

'Now I think that perhaps we will all be ready for this marriage on Friday.' He laughed as they all stood around the altar together and said a few prayers.

'Marriage is a precious gift,' he said, 'and not to be undertaken lightly. It is one of the most important sacraments in the church: the sacrament that binds a man and a woman together for the rest of their natural life and into eternity. It is the sacrament of love and joy, of honesty and truth and unselfishness, as a man and woman vow to always care for each other and to be each other's friends in good times and in bad.'

Helen could feel a lump in her throat as she listened to Father Tom.

'Paddy, do you mind me asking how long you and Helen have been married?' he asked.

'Thirty-three years. Our anniversary was in May,' said Paddy proudly.

'And what about you, Eddie? How long have you and Carmel been married?' Father Tom asked, turning to the Quinns.

'Thirty-six years,' said Eddie. 'We got married in London. I was only a lowly intern but Carmel worked night and day as a nurse to keep us going.'

'Have any of you ever thought of renewing your marriage vows?' asked the priest, glancing at them.

Helen used to think people getting married a second time was just for celebrities and Hollywood stars, but when Paddy had been lying in hospital in intensive care with machines and tubes and equipment all around him, she had wished that she could let him know just how much she still loved him and that she hadn't regretted a single day of their marriage and would do it all again if given the chance.

'Yes,' she nodded. 'I have. It's something that I would like to do some time.'

'I have, too,' said Paddy.

'Yes,' said Eddie, taking Carmel's hand.

Carmel nodded quietly in agreement.

'Well, would you each like to renew your marriage vows here this evening with me, and with your children and family as witnesses?' Father Tom asked.

'Yes,' the four of them said, without the slightest hesitation, all certain and sure that this was something they wanted to do.

Helen held Paddy's hand as Father Tom guided them through their vows, the words somehow more meaningful and beautiful with their three grown-up children standing watching.

'I do,' Helen said, eyes shining as she kissed Paddy, feeling like she was a young bride again and that the years had slipped away from them.

Carmel looked nervous as Eddie stood beside her and the priest got them also to repeat their vows. Eddie fought to compose himself as their boys looked on.

The children and their friends gave a huge hurrah, and congratulated the two couples as Father Tom finished.

'Mum, I can't believe it, you and Dad getting married again in front of us all.' Amy hugged Helen. 'It was so lovely. I'm so proud of you both.'

'You and Dad are the best,' said Ciara, wrapping her

arms around Helen fiercely. 'I love you, Mum.'

Ronan came over, his eyes shining as he congratulated them both. He kissed his girlfriend Krista, and Helen could see that her tall young son had decided that the quiet Polish girl with the long blonde hair and beautiful eyes standing beside him in the church would in time be his own bride.

They all thanked Father Tom.

'I can't wait till Friday when it's our turn.' Dan beamed at them all, wrapping his arms around Amy.

'I booked a big table for dinner for everyone to have a bite to eat over in Fitzgerald's,' said Paddy as they crossed the street to the local pub.

Helen's mind was in a spin as they sat down, Paddy ordering drinks for everyone to celebrate their own form of wedding that had just taken place. Helen could see that Carmel had been equally moved by the experience, and the two of them thanked Father Tom profusely for making them reflect on their own marriages as they renewed their vows.

'I feel wonderful,' said Helen, sipping a glass of wine. 'It was so special that I will never forget tonight.'

Glancing around the table she could see that everyone was having fun as Liam regaled them with stories about Dan's stag night in Edinburgh. Over at the far side she could see that Jess was sitting beside Rob, Dan's older brother, chatting easily. Ciara was telling Dylan and Krista and Ronan all about her travels in Thailand. Paddy looked tired and a little pale, and she was glad to see him with his pint in hand sitting down near Eddie.

She was a lucky woman: blessed with a good husband, a happy marriage and a wonderful family. Tonight, renewing her marriage vows with Paddy, the man she had always loved, had made her realize just how much their marriage meant to her.

'To the Quinns and the O'Connors!' toasted Liam, getting everyone to raise their glasses.

Chapter Sixty-three

'What a family gathering!' declared Paddy O'Connor, relishing it as everyone began to gather for the wedding. Amy had moved back home to stay with her family in Linden Crescent for the three days and Dan had decided to stay with his folks, too!

The house looked great. Helen and Ciara had the place sparkling: the couch covers and chair covers had all been cleaned, and the wooden floor re-waxed. The garden was in great shape, and Helen had huge pots of pink hydrangeas in full bloom at the front door. Amy had never seen her home look so well, and knew just how much effort everyone had put in. Even Barney had been cut and washed, and his smelly foam bed and blanket laundered. Amy couldn't believe all the neighbours and friends of the family calling to wish her well. She smiled when she saw the new mugs and cups her mum produced when she served the visitors with coffee and biscuits.

The massive table plan was spread out on their dining table and it had been all hands on deck for the past few days as they'd worked out the final seating arrangements for the reception.

People were on and off tables.

'Aunt Bonnie's deaf, so make sure to put someone beside her good ear!' warned Helen.

'Aisling went out with him, so don't put her on that table,' insisted Jess.

Dan's elderly uncle Frank needed to be near a door to get to the bathroom.

Carmel Quinn's brother, James, didn't get on with Eddie's family.

The single people didn't want to be on tables full of couples.

'For heaven's sake, put friends together and family together,' advised Helen. 'There is nothing worse than finding yourself at a wedding, sitting for a few hours at a table with a load of people you don't know, or with relations from the other side. Mixing people at a wedding table doesn't work!'

'When you put a group of friends or family together on a table everyone's happy, and well able to sort themselves out and find their own seat,' said Paddy.

Honestly, it was like doing a big puzzle, trying to work it all out. Amy checked that Carmel was happy with the tables before finally emailing the whole plan down to Eve at Glebe House.

'Thank heaven that bloody thing is gone!' Helen said, worn out with the complexities of it.

*   *   *

Amy was taking three and half weeks off from the office for her honeymoon and wedding, and was looking forward to such a long break away from work. Norah and the gang in the office had brought her for a celebration lunch in Peploes on Tuesday, and presented her with a generous gift voucher for Arnotts.

Uncle David and Aunt Anna and four wild kids had arrived from Tipperary and had taken over Sheila's for a few days. Her mother was in her element, having them around. Helen's Cousin Fiona and her husband Will had come from Amsterdam and were staying with Uncle Tim in Howth. Mary and Sinead, Paddy's two sisters, along with their husbands, had come up from Cork and were staying in the Radisson Hotel, along with a few more of his cousins. It looked like it was going to be a great family hooley!

Faye, one of Amy's oldest friends, who had grown up in the road with her, had come over from New York with her American boyfriend, Nick.

'I'm just dying to show him off to the girls at the wedding.'

The place was like a madhouse, with so many people visiting and calling, the phone constantly ringing, everyone wanting to talk to the bride!

'I think we need to chill out a bit!' Helen said, trying to ignore the mounting panic. 'So I've booked for you, me, Ciara and Jess to go to Dalkey to have a massage, manicure and pedicure, and then we'll have lunch afterwards in Harvey's.'

'But we've so much still to do,' worried Amy.

'Amy, it will all get done,' promised her mum. 'A bit of pampering and an hour or two with our feet up will do us all good. Weddings are stressful enough, God knows!'

Amy was like a lunatic, checking and rechecking the weather forecast on every station, in every newspaper and online. August had been rather unsettled, with lots of clouds and showers, and she kept telling herself that it wasn't the end of the world if it rained tomorrow – after all, they were in Ireland.

Tomorrow's weather forecast was for sunshine, with rain predicted by late afternoon on the east coast of Ireland. Helen had buried an Infant of Prague statue under a shrub in the back garden in the hope of a sunny day for Amy's wedding. Barney, however, usually prowled the garden, and in a frenzy of barking had found the statue and dug it up. Helen, running to stop him, had reburied the plaster saint in the front garden, instructing everyone not to let the dog near it.

Jess arrived at eleven and they all set out for Dalkey. Nina and the girls in Santé made a great fuss of them, asking Amy all about the wedding as the pampering began.

Amy let herself sink into the warm towels as Nina took charge of her.

'I will get all that tension and stress out of your muscles,' she promised, as she began the massage.

Jess was in ecstasy in the other room as one of the girls gave her a salt scrub plus a massage, followed by a spray tan and a manicure and pedicure.

'I think that I have died and gone to heaven,' she moaned, giving in to the transformation.

'I feel great,' declared Ciara, who had opted for the Indian head massage. She watched, fascinated, as her bitten nails were magically returned to a perfect state and her feet were scrubbed until her heels and toes looked and felt amazing.

Helen O'Connor fell asleep on the bed as all the tension and stress were kneaded from her tired, tense shoulders and back. Having her fingers and wrists massaged felt good, too, and she had a manicure afterwards.

Amy lapped it all up, the full bridal package: nails, feet, relaxing oils rubbed into her skin and finally a light golden spray tan applied.

'Lots of luck tomorrow,' wished Nina and the girls in the salon as Helen paid and they headed off for lunch.

Harvey's was busy as usual, and Amy could feel her excitement mounting as they ordered lunch. She was determined to have only a glass or two of wine, as she didn't want to be muzzy-headed or sleepy when she had so much to do. Her mum was in sentimental form and told stories about when they were kids and the silly things she and Ciara and Ronan used to do.

'Imagine! By this time tomorrow, you'll be a married woman.' Helen laughed.

Amy was nervous about the wedding, but she couldn't wait to be Daniel's wife, and for the two of them to build a life and home together.

They all tucked into the fish of the day. The plaice was served with a tangy lemon butter sauce, on a bed of greens, with Harvey's renowned sauté potatoes.

Amy and Ciara ordered the luscious-sounding chocolate dessert.

'I have to fit into that purple dress tomorrow,' bemoaned Jess, begging Amy to keep the bowl away from her. Jess was so proud of the fact that she'd had to have the dress taken in because she'd lost so much weight.

Back at home, Amy had a host of things to do, and taking out her Filofax checked that she hadn't forgotten any of them. Daniel had collected their wedding rings from the jewellers earlier on. She had packed all her clothes for the honeymoon, and printed out three copies of their flight itinerary and hotel bookings. She rattled her brain to see if there was anything else she needed to do.

Her aunts Sinead and Mary arrived at the house with their presents, dying to see how everyone was doing, just as Fran and Katie from next door called, too. Amy was embarrassed by all the wonderful gifts she was receiving, and opened a file on the computer to make sure that she remembered exactly who had given what! She thanked everyone, and Helen whooshed them all outside to the garden, to sit in the sun. Amy took Saoirse, Katie's little girl, up on her knee, wondering how long it would be till she and Dan had a baby. Tara and Sarah and Aisling called quickly to wish her well, too. Ciara and Helen made pot after pot of coffee and tea as the visitors kept coming.

Helen had made a big chicken casserole for dinner, and when all the friends and relations had left, they finally got a chance to sit down and relax. Paddy opened some wine, and Ronan had a load of Coronas on ice in the fridge, Krista slicing up limes to put in their glasses. They sat in the kitchen laughing and chatting as Ronan got out his guitar and played some of their favourite songs. Everyone sang along.

It was long after midnight when they finally got to bed. Amy fell asleep in her old room with her pink quilt, school photos, and posters of all her favourite bands and rock stars around her.

Dan had phoned her to say goodnight. He'd gone out to dinner with his parents and then down to Mackey's, their local, to have a few beers with his brothers and his dad. They laughed, comparing each other's time-warp bedrooms.

'I swear that there is a poster of Zig and Zag still on my wall,' he confessed.

'I have Riverdance!'

It seemed strange to be apart, and Amy cherished the

sound of his voice and breathing as they both finally said goodnight.

'I'll see you tomorrow,' he promised.

Amy closed her eyes, thinking of Dan as she fell asleep.

Chapter Sixty-four

Helen O'Connor woke early to the sound of soft rain pattering on the roof.

'Oh no, don't let the day be wet!' she pleaded, glancing outside as the rain fell on the flowers and shrubs. The sky was cloudy and dull, but looked like it might clear later. Paddy was still asleep, and she got up and went downstairs. She still couldn't believe it! Today was Amy's wedding day! The day their little girl would walk up the aisle to marry the man she loved. Helen put on breakfast. The full works: cereal, then rashers and sausages and pudding and tomato. Creamy scrambled eggs done the way Amy liked them, and fresh brown bread.

Fran phoned her, all bright and breezy, to check that she was up and to wish everyone luck.

'Enjoy it, Helen! Being the Mother of the Bride is great fun. You'll have a wonderful day, and remember: if you need anything I'm here.'

'I'll see you in the church,' laughed Helen.

Ronan and Paddy surfaced first, lured by the smell of the bacon cooking, then one by one the girls joined them.

'Today's the day!' sang Amy, kissing Helen as she whisked the eggs and put on some toast. 'I have a present for you and Dad.' She grinned, pulling a wrapped package from behind her. 'Open it.'

Paddy undid the paper and took the silver-framed photo out of the bubble wrap. Helen fought back the tears as soon as she saw the photo. It had been taken during a glorious summer holiday in Brittas Bay, and was of Paddy and herself lifting Amy up out of the waves when she was about five years old.

'You've been such great parents! I just wanted to say thanks,' said Amy softly. 'I hope that I'll be as good as you are when the time comes, and Dan and I have kids.'

Paddy cleared his throat, and Helen passed him a sheet of kitchen paper to blow his nose on as they all got emotional.

Better to have a bit of a cry now, she thought, rather than later on.

'Can I have my shower first?' asked Amy. 'Otherwise Ciara will mess the place and use all the hot water!' Ciara was about to object when she saw that Amy was laughing. Helen smiled, thinking of the constant battles there'd been in the house over showers and hairdryers and clothes whenever the girls were getting ready to go anywhere.

*   *   *

After breakfast Helen went upstairs to get ready, as they had booked the hairdresser's for ten thirty and didn't want to be late. Just as they were about to leave, Carmel Quinn's silver Mercedes pulled into the driveway and she arrived with the bridal bouquet and the two posies for the bridesmaids that she had made.

The flowers were beautiful, and so simple and classic. Pink baby roses for Amy, and a mixture of pink roses and purple flowers with frothy alchemilla for the girls, all tied with ribbon. They looked so professional. Helen couldn't believe how talented Carmel was, and thanked her for all her work.

'Carmel, they're so pretty. I love them,' thanked Amy.

'Put them somewhere cool,' she advised. 'I'm going to the church now, to check on the flower arrangements. I did them yesterday afternoon, and though I say it myself, they look wonderful. My sister Liz is meeting me there, and we're going to decorate the benches. The car is full of ribbons, it's all so exciting.' She laughed, hugging Amy.

'How's Dan?' Amy asked.

'He's counting down the hours, though when I left he was on the Playstation with Dylan.'

The hairdresser's was busy, but they got a huge welcome from Jonathan and all his staff. Jess had got there ahead of them, and was already having her hair washed. Jonathan assigned a stylist to each of them as he took Amy under his wing. Helen had got her highlights done a few days earlier, and just wanted Zoe to blow-dry her hair good and straight, so that it would last all day. The staff chatted about the wedding, everyone laughing and excited.

Lynn was looking after Ciara, and had pinned up part of her hair in a bouffant style at the top of her head, while the rest of her dark hair tumbled around her shoulders.

'Very sixties,' approved Jonathan as he started to dry and style Amy's light brown hair, pulling the central part back and up in a similar fashion and smoothing the ends before attaching the crystal bow with its simple veil to her head. As he pinned it into place, and checked that it was totally secure, Helen gasped, seeing Amy's face in the mirror. Her daughter looked absolutely beautiful.

Jess looked amazing, too, with her hair lifted in the centre and falling straight to her shoulders. It was a total change, with not a sign of her usual curls!

As they were finishing up Fran and Krista both arrived to get their hair done, everyone chatting about the wedding and wishing Amy well.

Helen made a dash for the car, and parked it up close to the door of the hairdresser's so the girls could avoid the sudden shower of rain.

Amy's friend Susan, a beautician, was doing the make-up for everyone, and was already at the house.

'I'll get started on you, Amy,' she said, 'as I know

Krista wants to take plenty of photos of you here at home.'

Helen retreated to the kitchen, where she had soup and salad and French bread ready for everyone. Paddy was pacing up and down the hall, nervously going over his speech. He had refused to show it to her, and she hoped that he wasn't getting too stressed and tense about it.

'Feck it!' screamed Ciara, as she ran upstairs for something. 'Mum, Barney's after puking in the hall. It's all over the place.'

A quick investigation showed the dog had also repeated the performance behind the couch in the living room, where he had been hiding.

'Paddy! Paddy, will you deal with that dog?' pleaded Helen. 'Get the shovel and clean it up before Amy or one of us walks in it. The bottle of Dettol is in the utility room.'

'Keep him away from upstairs and my dress!' yelled Amy.

Paddy O'Connor put down his newspaper to deal with the problem on hand. That was the end of his kid-glove treatment, he said to himself, as he scooped the offending mess into the bin and washed up and disinfected the areas. The house was gone mad, no wonder the poor dog had got sick. He'd probably been wolfing down leftover sausages and black pudding from breakfast this morning. He wasn't used to so many visitors and so much food, poor devil!

'Barney! Barney!' he called. 'Come on, the rain has stopped, let's go for a walk, get you out of here.'

The dog jumped up and down with excitement and Paddy put on his lead and took him down the driveway. Thank heaven they'd organized for Fran's kids to look after Barney while they were at the wedding and over-night down in Wicklow.

'You'd better behave, Barney!' he warned, heading down to the entrance to their estate.

Susan used a light make-up look for Amy, which accentuated her eyes and gave her skin a golden glow, her lips done in a peachy pink colour. Her eyelashes looked long and upswept as she grinned at herself in the mirror.

'It looks light and fresh,' explained Susan. 'But I guarantee that it has staying power.'

An hour later the girls were all made-up, and it was time to get ready. Krista, in a short black dress and a short-sleeved cream shrug, followed everyone around with her camera, as she captured the day.

Looking in the mirror Helen loved the soft grey-blue colours Susan had used on her eyes, the foundation – which evened out all her skin tones – and the brush of blush which seemed to give an extra glow to her face.

Susan had persuaded Ciara to alter her normally heavy kohl-black eye make-up, and instead had given her a sixties style on her eyes with an upswept line of black that made her look sexy and sophisticated.

Jess was thrilled with her look, as she had never got her make-up done professionally before. Susan showed her how to shape her eyes and apply shadow properly, and the right technique to make her narrow lips seem bigger and fuller.

Helen went upstairs to help Amy get dressed. Over-awed, she watched as her elder daughter stepped into the exquisite designer wedding dress. It was stunning and fitted perfectly.

'Oh, Amy love!' Helen couldn't help herself as tears filled her eyes. 'You look so beautiful.'

'Mum, don't cry or you'll get me started, and then my make-up will be ruined!' Amy said.

'I'm fine,' Helen lied, drying her eyes.

Jess and Ciara came in to see the bride, looking like two supermodels in their on-the-knee flirty purple dresses and high heels. Krista snapped away with her expensive digital camera as they all squealed and yelled with excitement when they saw each other.

'Jess, you look like you've lost stones!' congratulated Helen, noticing how pretty Jess was. Her tummy and legs and shoulders appeared slim and toned in the figure-hugging dress.

'Thanks, Helen.' Jess smiled, delighted with her new slimmed-down self and the confidence it gave her. 'It was hard, but it was worth it!'

'Mum, for heaven's sake, will you get dressed?' warned Amy. 'You'll have us all late!'

*   *   *

Paddy, back from walking the dog, was dressing in his tuxedo, adjusting his purple-coloured tie in the bedroom.

'You know, a while ago I didn't think that I would ever see this day,' he admitted, sitting down heavily on the bed. 'I didn't think that I'd ever get out of hospital, let alone walk my daughter up the aisle at her wedding.'

Helen froze. She knew just how important this day was for him, too.

'So much has changed over the past few months,' he admitted. 'It's been bloody awful, but somehow we've got through it.'

Helen came and wrapped her arms around him, kissing him.

'I knew we would,' she smiled. 'We're a tough old pair.'

'Mum!' yelled Ciara. 'Hurry up! Krista wants a photo of everyone.'

Helen took her dress off the hanger and slipped it on over her expensive new underwear. The colour was amazing, and made her feel vibrant and young. She loved the feel of the silky material on her skin and the shape of it. It was even better on than she remembered. She carefully lifted the fancy little headpiece that she had found in the hat shop in South Anne Street, and put it on her hair, making sure that it was fixed in place properly. Then, after slipping on her expensive Italian shoes, she twirled around for Paddy to see. The look in his eyes spoke a thousand words as they laughed, and he held her face and kissed her.

'You're my beautiful girl!'

'Will you two hurry on!' yelled Ciara. 'We're all waiting for you.'

Krista wanted to take more photos of the family in the house and on the stairs, and, now that the rain had finally stopped, in the garden.

Helen looked out at the bright-blue clear sky and thanked the Infant of Prague for hearing their prayers as they all trooped out to the back garden. Krista took photos of Amy and her sister and best friend with their bouquets, and Helen with her daughters in front of the roses, and Paddy and Helen with their three children, as poor Barney barked at them from the kitchen.

'Uncle Tim is outside in the car,' called Ronan.

'Helen, you'd better go down to the church,' advised Paddy. 'Everyone should be arriving by now.'

'Come on, Mum,' called Ronan. 'We all have to go. We don't want to be late.'

Krista was staying at the house to photograph Amy and Paddy as they got ready to leave in the Bentley.

'I'll meet you in the church in a few minutes,' she promised Ronan. 'I want to get Amy and Paddy arriving at the church, too.'

Taking a last glance at the house, and giving Amy a hug, Helen and the bridesmaids got in the car with Ronan for the short drive to St Mary's.

Chapter Sixty-five

As they pulled into the church car park, Helen was greeted by the sight of friends and family gathering in the sunshine and filing into the church. There wasn't a rain cloud in sight and the sky was clear and blue. She tried to quell her own nerves as she got out of the car. Ciara and Jess were all excited as they fixed their dresses, adjusted their bouquets, and stepped out to a cheer from Dan, his two brothers and Liam.

Helen said hello to a few friends, delighted with the two big bay trees decorated with white ribbons that Carmel had placed at the church entrance. As she walked across, Jeremy, who was busy with his camera filming all the arrivals, said hello to her, getting her to stop for a minute so he could film her properly. The girls moved over to the side to wait for Amy's arrival, chatting to Dylan and one of his cousins.

'The Quinns and Gran and loads of others are inside,' said Ronan, after walking into the church to see what was happening. 'Dad sent me a text to say he and Amy are leaving home in a few minutes. I'll get Rob and Liam to ask everyone to move into the church.'

Helen could hear the music inside the church, and waited while the last few slipped into their seats. Then she took a deep breath to gather herself, linked arms with Ronan, and began the walk up the aisle to her seat. Carmel had tied lacy hydrangeas, pink roses, pretty purple daisies and lavender and white ribbon to every second bench. Fran and Tom and Maeve and Andy gave Helen a huge smile as she walked up the long aisle on her son's arm. She felt like she was walking on air, she was so happy and so proud of her family.

She went over to Dan to say hello. He looked so handsome in his tuxedo, standing tall and nervous beside Rob and Liam. She couldn't ask for a better son-in-law, and she hugged him before saying hello to Carmel and Eddie.

Carmel, slim and elegant in her silver shift dress and coat, had a sweeping cream and silver hat complementing her outfit.

Sheila was in her element, sitting up in the front pew, wearing her peach suit, a stylish hat trimmed with peach and pink and cream chiffon roses perched jauntily on her head.

'Mum, you look gorgeous,' Helen said to her, giving her a hug and a kiss as she sat in beside her.

The altar looked magnificent, with two huge arrangements of giant cream hydrangeas and blowsy end-of-summer pink and cream roses mixed with tall purple and cream delphiniums and green leaves. Carmel had done a wonderful job creating such a display.

Helen could hear a ripple of excitement go through the congregation and guessed that Paddy and Amy must have arrived outside. The musicians started the music as Ciara and Jess walked slowly up the aisle in their sassy purple dresses, their pink and purple posies in their hands, both looking fantastic and smiling at friends and family. As they reached the top the bridesmaids slipped into the seats in front of Helen.

Helen held her breath as Paddy and Amy now began to walk up. She turned to watch father and daughter, arm in arm, walk past all those who loved them. Amy was bright-eyed and smiling with happiness as Paddy proudly led her up to the altar towards Daniel, the man she loved.

Paddy stopped at the top, where Daniel was waiting, and formally placed Amy's hand in that of her beloved. Daniel's eyes shone with love as he took Amy's hand.

Helen tried not to cry as the young couple stepped forward together and stood at the altar, Jess taking Amy's roses.

Helen smiled as Paddy, relieved, sat in beside her.

The ceremony was beautiful: the hymns, readings and prayers, and especially Father Tom's wonderful sermon, which made everyone laugh but also reflected on the importance of the marriage they were witnessing.

Helen had to fight to control her emotions when Amy and Dan made their vows to each other in front of the whole congregation. They were relaxed and word-perfect and there was a huge cheer when Father Tom declared them formally husband and wife. Helen reached for Paddy's hand as the young couple lit the marriage candle.

Every piece of music was special – Schubert's 'Ave Maria', the Gaelic 'Ag Criost an Siol', Fauré's 'Pie Jesu', Leonard Bernstein's 'One Hand, One Heart'.

Everyone in the small congregation had played their part, and before she knew it, the ceremony had ended and Father Tom had invited Amy and Dan and their families into the sacristy to sign the marriage register.

As she looked at the wedding ring on Amy's finger Helen said a silent prayer for a lifetime of happiness for her daughter and her husband. As she did so, Krista took more photographs.

'Are we ready to go?' smiled Dan, eyes shining as he clasped Amy's hand.

The music of Mendelssohn's 'Wedding March' swelled and filled the church as Amy and Dan stepped back out from the altar again and began to walk down the aisle hand in hand, their friends cheering and clapping for the happy couple. The air was electric with excitement as Jess linked arms with Rob and Ciara with Liam and they walked behind the bride and groom. Eddie, laughing, took Helen's arm, with Paddy and Carmel following behind. And finally, Ronan held his gran's arm and slowly walked the old lady in her finery down the church, to huge applause.

Amy and Dan stood together in the warm sunshine near the church porch, greeting all their wedding guests as they came out of the church. Jeremy set up the camera to record everyone as Krista mingled among the crowd taking photos.

'Mr and Mrs Quinn!' screamed Sarah and Tara in unison, giving them both hugs and kisses. Sarah's husband Tom wished them luck.

Amy was all smiles as everyone complimented her and Dan, told her how beautiful she looked and wished them both all good things.

'Amy, what a beautiful wedding!' Fran hugged her, squeezing her tight. 'You look absolutely gorgeous. Helen and Paddy are so proud of you!'

'And I'm proud of them, too,' Amy said, glancing over at her parents, who were busy chatting to Uncle Brendan and Claire and Auntie Mary and her husband Jimmy.

'What a Mother of the Bride!' said Fran, coming over to her. 'You look amazing, Helen, and Paddy looks so fit and handsome.'

'He was determined to be well for today,' admitted Helen, who at times had wondered if the wedding was going to be too much for Paddy.

'Well, it's great to see you both looking so proud and happy,' Fran added. 'That's what it's all about.'

'You look lovely, too.' Helen admired Fran's fancy turquoise dress and wrap.

'I'm poured into it!' confessed Fran. 'I was half an hour trying to get myself into my new pair of Spanx, and I don't know how I'm going to last the day in them. God knows what will happen when I need to go to the bathroom!'

Helen laughed. Leaving Fran and Tom chatting to her sister-in-law she went over to check that her mother was OK. Sheila Hennessy was in top form, entertaining everyone around her with memories of her own wedding during 'The Emergency'.

Amy and Dan, along with Dylan and Rob and Liam, who were all wearing dark shades, were standing surrounded by their friends, laughing and enjoying themselves.

'I think we should be making a move to Wicklow,' suggested Paddy. 'Eve will be expecting us.'

Ronan and Rob and Liam were instructed to get everyone moving as the bus they had booked for travelling to Glebe House pulled into the car park. Amy and Dan drove off to cheers and much honking of horns in the Bentley as everyone set off for Wicklow.

Chapter Sixty-six

Helen and Paddy O'Connor couldn't believe how well Glebe House looked as they turned up the avenue and approached the old house. The place was magical, bathed in sunshine, the lake sparkling in the distance, the borders and flower beds in full summer bloom. They checked in with Trudy and made their way to their room, then quickly freshened up before joining their guests downstairs. Eve had set tables and chairs and parasols out on the terrace surrounded by beautiful herbaceous borders and the first guests to arrive were laughing and chatting, sipping mojitos and Pimms and champagne. Ronan's friend Paul was playing his guitar, and music filled the air as people introduced each other.

Krista called the family and the bride and groom down to the lake for a few photos.

'Oh, Helen, this place is stunning,' declared Carmel as they posed for photos, 'far nicer than any castle! Do you see the swans on the water? It's so romantic here.'

Helen looked around. Having a summer family

wedding here in Glebe House couldn't be more perfect!

She watched as Krista, serious and in complete control, photographed Amy and Dan, and then the brides-maids and Liam and Rob, before turning her attention to the family groups: the O'Connors and the Quinns. Sheila insisted on a big group photo of her family, her children and grandchildren. 'Might as well, as they are all here, before I kick the bucket,' she said.

'I need the bride and groom for a few more shots,' demanded Krista, as the rest of them returned to the garden to top up their drinks.

'What a great place for a wedding, sis,' said Helen's brother, Tim, coming up to give her a hug.

'Thanks for the car.' She smiled at him.

'It's the least an uncle with an old Bentley can do!' he joked.

He and his wife were tanned after ten days in the South of France, at their apartment near Cannes.

'You and Paddy should go down for a break there after the wedding,' he offered. 'The place is sitting there empty, and the pool is lovely. After all you have been through in the past few months you deserve to put your feet up and laze. You'll be near everything and can walk most places!'

Helen was tempted by her older brother's offer. A wealthy publican, he was extremely generous to all the family.

'Tim, I'll talk to Paddy, try to persuade him,' she promised. 'A break in France would be lovely.'

Carmel Quinn took her by the arm and insisted on introducing her to her brother, James, and to Eddie's older brother Donal and his wife. They were lovely people and were full of praise for the wonderful wedding setting!

Eve came over to Helen to check that she was satisfied with everything, and to tell her that they would be ready to get people into the dining room in about ten minutes.

Helen and Paddy had eaten in the dining room at Glebe House many times over the years, but seeing it dressed up for a wedding Helen couldn't believe how beautiful it looked with its long white linen tablecloths, and magnificent arrangements of flowers in matching glass vases on the mantel over the big fireplace and on the giant mahogany sideboard. Every table was bedecked with three or four antique glass vases filled with pretty garden flowers with a white or pink ribbon tied in a neat bow around them. There were candles everywhere, and each place held a place card tied with ribbon to a bunch of lavender and rosemary from the garden.

'Eve, it's beautiful,' murmured Helen, 'absolutely beautiful.'

'We aim to please,' smiled Eve as she helped people to find their tables.

Everyone rose and cheered as Amy and Dan, arm in arm and eyes shining, entered the dining room and made their way to the top table to sit down. They had decided to have the speeches first, conscious that Paddy might get overtired, and that Eddie Quinn hated speaking in public and only did it under duress.

Helen noticed Ciara talking disdainfully to Liam; and that Dan's brother, Rob, seated beside Jess, seemed totally smitten by the glamorous bridesmaid and was lavishing attention on her. Jess's face glowed as the two of them talked. They have hours together, thought Helen as she and Eddie chatted.

Liam Flynn stood up to introduce the proceedings, as the waiters went round the tables filling everyone's glasses.

Helen could sense Paddy's nervousness as he fiddled with his linen napkin and glanced at the paper he had his speech written out on.

'You'll be fine,' she whispered as Paddy stood up to do his Father of the Bride speech. The room went quiet as everyone turned to listen to him.

'On behalf of my wife Helen and myself I would like to warmly welcome you all today to our daughter Amy's wedding to Daniel. I would like to thank Eve Hanlon of Glebe House for her magnificent hospitality and to thank head chef Sean Delaney, his beautiful wife Trudy, and the staff here for the wonderful meal we will all enjoy in a short while. Glebe House is renowned for its food! I would also like to thank Father Tom Doorly, a family friend, for marrying Amy and Dan on this very special day. I should also mention and thank Carmel, Dan's mother, for making the wonderful flower arrangements in the church today and the beautiful bouquets for Amy and the girls. Ciara and Jess looked so stunning walking up the aisle today ahead of us. I'd also like to thank Tim Hennessy for driving Amy and Dan today, and Bibi Kennedy for making the most beautiful wedding cake. Amy and Dan wanted this day to be special, and by joining us here you have all helped to make their wedding day one they will always remember.

'Helen and I and Ronan and Ciara are delighted to see both families united and to welcome Daniel to the O'Connor fold. The first time I met Daniel he'd fallen asleep on our living-room couch after walking Amy home from some charity ball. I went to read the Sunday papers and found this stranger asleep in a tuxedo. We became friends, and I soon discovered that he is a perfect gentleman, and is now considered so much like another son in our house that I even heard Helen asking him the other night to put out the bins!

'Now, to Amy! Amy, as most of you know, is a wonderful girl, a very special daughter, and it would always take a very special man to win her heart. From the minute Amy was born she has brought joy and happiness into our lives; from her first word, first step, first day in school, and first day in college she has brought sunshine to everything she has done. She is kind and thoughtful, and has a bright clever mind that is always interested in the world around her and the people she meets. She is as beautiful on the inside as she is on the outside.

'When she was six years old she told me that she would marry a prince and live in a castle and eat honey on toast every day. I'm not sure that she still wants to live in a castle or eat honey on toast every day, but I do know that today Amy married her prince . . . Daniel. I could see it in the shine of my daughter's eyes when she walked up the aisle and Daniel took her hand. Amy has been a wonderful daughter, a wonderful sister, a wonderful granddaughter, a wonderful friend to all those who know her, and now will be a wonderful wife and life partner for Daniel.'

Paddy stopped for a minute and took a few sips of water from the glass on the table. Helen held her breath, hoping that he was OK.

'A good marriage is very special,' he said, beginning again. 'Sometimes we take it for granted, but when life gets rocky or we get ill, like I did a few months back, then we realize the importance of having the person we love by our side. I want to thank my own lovely bride, Helen, for still being at my side, and I wish Amy and Daniel a lifetime of happiness and joy together, always being at each other's side. Would you please all be up-standing as we toast Amy and Daniel!' asked Paddy. 'To the bride and groom!'

The whole room rose, and Helen could see tears in Amy's eyes as she came over and gave her dad a big hug and whispered 'thanks'. Everyone loudly toasted 'the bride and groom' before sitting back down again.

Paddy, relieved that his duty was over, sat down as

Liam took the microphone and began to introduce Eddie.

Poor Eddie was almost shaking as he stood up, keeping his speech very short and simple as he warmly welcomed his new daughter-in-law Amy to the Quinn household, and mentioning that he and Carmel had two more single sons who needed wives if there were any takers. Helen noticed Jess, who was sitting beside Rob, turn bright red as Rob laughed heartily at his father's remark. Eddie thanked Paddy and Helen for the reception and wished Amy and Dan long life and good fortune in their marriage.

Daniel was up next. Standing tall and proud beside his bride, he spoke from the heart: 'I love Amy and always will. I knew practically from the minute I first spoke to her that she was the girl I wanted to marry. There may have been a few ups and downs getting here . . .'

Everyone yelled and stomped and laughed and Dan had the good grace to look embarrassed.

'But I promise, Amy, my beautiful wife, that I will love her till the end of time.'

Helen smiled, listening as he thanked everyone.

'There is another lovely lady in Amy's family who has also stolen my heart,' he continued. 'And that is Sheila Hennessy, Amy's wonderful grandmother.'

Eighty-four-year-old Sheila stood up to take a little bow as everyone cheered her, and then she sat back down beside Ciara.

'I want to say a big thanks to my gorgeous sister-in-law Ciara and Amy's best friend Jess, the two beautiful bridesmaids who helped with organizing the wedding and look like a pair of supermodels in their purple dresses,' said Dan, finishing up with the traditional toast to the bridesmaids.

Amy, taking her courage in hand, stood up, holding the microphone firmly.

'I want to thank you all for giving us the most beautiful day in our lives, a day that Dan and I will always remember. Thanks, Mum and Dad, Ciara and Ronan and Gran, for just being you, the best family ever. Thanks to Carmel and Eddie and Rob and Dylan, my new family, for the great welcome. Thanks to Jess for being the very best friend a girl could ever have. From holding my hand on our first day at school to organizing my hen weekend, Jess, you have always been there for me!

'I want to say to Dan that I love him and always will. I'm so lucky that I went to that charity ball that Jess and Tara helped to organize and was put sitting beside him at the table. My dinner date got drunk, and so did his, and we ended up talking for most of the night. There was a taxi strike and so we walked home together. My dad didn't know what had happened when he found Dan on our couch the next day. But the rest, as they say, is history. Dan, you make me laugh and you're obsessed with teaching me to surf, and almost from the night we first met I realized that I wanted to spend the rest of my life with you.'

Amy couldn't believe the huge applause she got and could see Jess and Ciara and the two mums had been very moved by her words. Dan, all emotional, hugged her close as Liam, the best man, got up to speak.

Liam's dark eyes flashed as he began by telling a load of stories about various mishaps and fun times shared at school and college with his best friend Daniel Quinn. Helen cringed, not really wanting to know so much about Daniel's drunken exploits as a teenager and a student.

'I knew when Amy arrived on the scene that Dan's single days were numbered. At great expense Dan and I had worked and scrimped and scraped and saved to get tickets to see Liverpool play against Barcelona. It was going to be the weekend of a lifetime, drinking and watching our favourite team play in Spain. However, it was also the weekend of Amy's birthday, and Dan suddenly refused to go, saying that he had to take his girlfriend out for her birthday. I couldn't believe it, and we actually had a punch-up! I was so annoyed with him for choosing Amy over Liverpool! Despite me giving him a bloody lip two years ago, Dan still asked me when the time came to be his best man. My friend has picked a beautiful girl to be his bride, and I know that Daniel will be a wonderful husband. I wish them both luck and happiness, and on behalf of all the guests thank the O'Connors for the wonderful wedding reception. I'd now like to call on Father Tom to say the Grace before the meal.'

'Well done, Liam!' said Paddy, shaking his hand and passing him a pint. 'We can all relax now and enjoy the food and the wine.'

Helen looked around the table, glad that the formalities were out of the way and that she didn't have to worry about Paddy making a speech later. Amy and Dan only had eyes for each other. She smiled to herself when she saw Paddy, animated, telling Carmel all about his operation. Her husband looked handsome and well again. His colour was good and he had finally lost that worried expression he'd had since the surgery. His grey hair was a little longer than usual, and he had trimmed down, losing his bit of a paunch. All those walks with Barney, along with the healthy heart diet regime, were paying off.

Eddie was beside her, and was great company. He and Father Tom enjoyed Sheila's stories as the waitresses began to serve the seafood starter. At the other side of the table she caught Carmel watching approvingly at Rob and Jess laughing together. Carmel had been telling Helen earlier about Rob's job in UCD, where he lectured in the science department.

Outside, the sun was beginning to set over the lake, and a flock of birds took to the sky as the evening slipped away.

The candles were lit, and they flickered on tables all around the room as everyone finished their meal. They drank coffee as Amy and Dan got up to cut the beautiful

487

wedding cake. Everyone gave a cheer when they saw the two marzipan surfers with their boards that Bibi had made to go on top of the cake, with its iced waves and breakers.

As the staff cleared away some of the tables to set up the dance floor, Helen and Paddy slipped away out to the terrace to get some fresh air. The night was still warm, with a slight breeze coming in off the water. Amy was outside, laughing away with all her girl friends, and Sarah, Nikki and Aisling were all begging Tara to keep away from womanizer Liam, who'd been eyeing her up all day. Helen, smiling, searched for Ciara, and saw her engrossed in conversation with Paul, the young guitarist, who was telling her about some concert he was playing in. She looked so pretty and young as she and the young man laughed and he tried to show her some chords on his guitar.

Helen and Paddy turned to go back to the bar, where their friends were, and Maeve's husband Andy insisted on buying them drinks.

The music started and Rob and Jess came to find Helen and Paddy and tell them that the first dance was about to begin.

As the band began to play Amy and Dan stepped out on the wooden floor, taking each other's hands as they began to dance to 'You're Just Too Good To Be True', the Burt Bacharach classic, as everyone watched and cheered and Jeremy filmed them.

'Come on, Mother of the Bride, let's show the lovebirds what we can do,' teased Eddie, leading Helen on to the floor as Paddy and Carmel began to dance, too. Ciara was dancing with Liam, and Jess and Rob were laughing away together on the far side of the floor as the rest of the wedding party joined in. Ronan was up dancing with Krista, who was finally able to relax and enjoy herself.

'Great day and a great night!' said Eddie, twirling Helen around the floor as the band went into another Bacharach song followed by a little Sinatra. 'What a wonderful wedding!'

It had been a perfect wedding, Helen thought, far better than they had ever imagined or planned it to be.

Amy and Dan's eyes said it all as they danced together in the centre of the floor.

Helen changed partners, moving from Eddie back into Paddy's waiting arms. Carmel and Eddie danced together near them.

'Love you,' said Paddy, nuzzling her hair.

'Love you, too,' she said, resting her head against his shoulder as they danced and moved to the music.

'You do realize we got married again!' he said, tilting her face to his.

'Yes.' She smiled, kissing him, taking in the candles and the flowers and the music and the friends and family gathered around them.

'That Father Tom is a wise man!'

'Yes,' she agreed. 'Definitely.'

'Amy and Dan are having a fantastic time. They're a great young couple with their lives ahead of them.'

'This old couple aren't doing too badly either,' she teased.

'The night is young . . .'

Helen laughed, Paddy's heart beating close to hers, their children and their children's friends and their family and close friends all dancing around them on this perfect moonlit night as the music echoed across the lake.

Acknowledgements

For my family, James, Mandy, Laura, Fiona and James, son-in-law Michael Hearty and little granddaughter Holly.

Special thanks to Mandy and Michael – a wonderful bride and groom! Also thanks to Tom and Breda for being such great in-laws. What a perfect summer wedding we all enjoyed.

To my agent, Caroline Sheldon, for all her support and belief over the years. Also thanks to Rosemarie and Jessica Buckman.

Thank you to my editor Linda Evans. What a delight to find that we are on the same page! It's been great working together.

To all the team at Transworld UK, especially my copy-editor, Lucy Pinney, for her sensitive work on the text, and to Vivien Garrett and Sarah Whittaker. Aislinn Casey for spreading the word! Also thanks to Eoin McHugh at Transworld Ireland. Thanks for all your work on my book, it is much appreciated.

To Gill and Simon Hess, Declan Heeney and Helen Gleed O'Connor and all in Gill Hess Dublin. What a great team!

Special thanks to Francesca Liversidge for all her support and encouragement and friendship over the years.

Thanks to Grace Murphy for the medical advice. (Any errors are my own.)

Thanks to Barbara MacKenzie, cake-maker extraordinaire, for all her wedding wisdom.

For all the wonderful friends who enrich my life. You are the best!

A TASTE FOR LOVE
By Marita Conlon-McKenna

Alice loves to cook. She believes the secret of
good food is to cook with passion.

Her love affair with cookery has taken her from her
parents' seaside hotel, to Paris and then one of Dublin's
finest restaurants. Then she marries **Liam,** and is
happy to hang up her chef's hat and cook
for her family and friends instead.

But now she's cooking for one!

Her marriage to Liam over, it's high time she
learns to stand on her own two feet and begin
again . . . urged on by her friends Alice
decides to open a cookery school.

The Martello School of Cookery opens its doors
and Alice begins to teach a group of total strangers
to create food that is tasty and delicious. And in the
comfort of the kitchen these strangers find that
there is much to learn, not just about baking and
sautéing – but about recipes for life . . .

Available Spring 2011
9781848270398

THE MATCHMAKER
By Marita Conlon-McKenna

Maggie Ryan can't help it! She constantly finds herself trying to match things and people together and with three bright, beautiful, *single* daughters she decides that a little romantic matching is needed.

However, Maggie's quest to find the perfect partner for each of her reluctant daughters is proving difficult. Grace has had enough of heartbreak and given up on men, deciding instead to concentrate on her career, and Anna believes that no man can ever live up to her romantic ideals. While single-parent Sarah devotes so much time to her little girl Evie that romance constantly passes her by.

Determined to get *'rings on those fingers'* Maggie Ryan believes that the arrival of new neighbour, bachelor Mark McGuinness, is an opportunity far too good to be missed!

9781848270138

THE HAT SHOP ON THE CORNER
By Marita Conlon-McKenna

Hats! Hats! Hats! Upbrims, sidesweeps, silks, ribbons and trims all become part of Ellie's life when she inherits the little hat shop on Dublin's South Anne Street. But the city is changing and Ellie must decide if she wants to follow the hat-making tradition of her mother or accept a generous offer to sell the shop.

Encouraged by her friends, Ellie takes on the hat shop and her quirky designs and tempting millinery confections soon attract a rich assortment of customers all in search of the perfect hat.

Creating hats for weddings, shows, fashion and fun, and falling for the charms of Rory Doyle along the way, Ellie is happier than she has ever been before. But as her fingers work their magic she discovers a lot can happen in the heart of a city like Dublin . . .

'Warm and uplifting – an absolute joy to read'
PATRICIA SCANLAN

9780553817898

THE STONE HOUSE
By Marita Conlon-McKenna

Everything changes for Kate, Moya and Romy when
Maeve, their mother, falls critically ill. They return
from Dublin, London and New York to Rossmore
and the old stone house overlooking the Irish Sea
where they grew up – but ancient jealousies
surface as each sister confronts the past and
the decisions they have made.

For Kate it is time to re-examine her role as a
high-flying lawyer and single parent. Moya must
take a good look at her marriage to the charming but
unfaithful Patrick. Romy, who hasn't set foot on
Irish soil for years, has to find the courage to face
her family. Over the years Maeve labelled her
daughters; Kate the brains, Moya the beautiful,
and Romy the bold one. Now it is time for
all three to break out of the box.

A gripping story of love, loss and the power of
sisterhood and family relationships to survive
the deepest hurts and secrets from one
of Ireland's best-loved writers.

9780553813685